# The Sister's Secret

**By Jennie Felton**

# JENNIE FELTON

## The Sister's Secret

HEADLINE

First published in Great Britain in 2018
by HEADLINE PUBLISHING GROUP

1

Cataloguing in Publication Data is available from the British Library

ISBN 978 1 4722 4092 7

Typeset in Calisto by Avon DataSet Ltd, Bidford-on-Avon, Warwickshire

Printed and bound in Great Britain by CPI Group (UK) Ltd, Croydon CR0 4YY

HEADLINE PUBLISHING GROUP
An Hachette UK Company
Carmelite House
50 Victoria Embankment
London EC4Y 0DZ

www.headline.co.uk
www.hachette.co.uk

For my grandson, Barnaby Sam Lazenbury.

With much love and best wishes for your A-level exams and hoping you get a place on the university course of your choice.

Go, Barney!

# *Acknowledgements*

A huge thank-you to everyone who has come with me on my journey through the Families of Fairley Terrace! This is the fifth and final book in the series, but rest assured, some of the people we have met will be making cameo appearances in my future books with a similar background – I've come to love them too much to abandon them completely, and I hope you, my dear readers, have too.

I'd never have made it this far without the support of my wonderful editor Kate Byrne and my lovely agent Rebecca Ritchie. I can never thank you two enough. And heartfelt thank-yous are also due to the team at Headline – in particular Emily Gowers, my copy editor Jane Selley, publicists Phoebe Swinburn and Jennifer Harlow, Martin Kerans in Production and the Sales team, especially Becky Bader, Helen Arnold and Olivia Allen.

Last but not least, thank you so much to all my readers – I hope you enjoy reading my books as much as I enjoy writing them. I love to hear from you, either by email or on my Facebook page or Twitter account, and I'm really grateful for all the good reviews you have given me. They help so much in spreading the word! Also, I promise to try to make the blogs on my websites appear more regularly – often I have been too engrossed in writing the next novel to keep them up to date!

# Chapter One

## April 1901

Rowan Sykes didn't know whether it was the loud knocking at the back door immediately below her bedroom window that woke her, or the raised voices. Or even if she'd been asleep at all. She'd lain awake feeling sorry for herself for so long after she'd said her prayers, and Mammy had tucked her in, drawn the curtains to shut out what remained of the daylight, and left the room, pulling the door almost closed behind her, that she really couldn't be sure. Everything seemed to have merged into one, sleeping, waking, a sort of muddled dream.

What she did know was that the day she'd been looking forward to for weeks was over, and nothing had gone the way she'd hoped. In fact, everything that could have gone wrong had done so. And it would be another whole year before it was time for High Compton fair again.

The fair was very special, her teacher, Miss Yard, had told the class. Centuries ago, in 1249, King Henry III had granted the town a special charter to allow it to be held in the street. In those days it had been a livestock fair, when cows, sheep and even horses had been bought and sold, and a bit of that still went on early in the day. But in recent years, much to the delight of the local children, the afternoon and evening had been given over to things that were much more fun. There were sideshows and rides – shooting galleries, roundabouts and swings, and stalls selling toffee apples, sugary sweets and cockles in twists of greaseproof paper. Rowan didn't care much for the cockles. Daddy always had a plate of them for tea on a Saturday when he came home from watching the football match, if High Compton had been playing at home, and they tasted mainly of the vinegar he sprinkled liberally on them. But she loved toffee apples – they were the best thing in the whole world.

Besides the smaller rides, there was also a switchback called the Noah's Ark that was set up in the town square. Rowan had never ridden on it – Mammy said she wasn't big enough. But she'd been hoping that this year she'd be allowed. After all, she was five now, and would be six in November. At the thought, she had thrilled with anticipation and excitement.

This morning, however, to her utter dismay, she had woken to rain falling from a leaden sky.

'Not much like Fair weather,' Daddy had said, brushing the moisture from his shoulders when he came in from a trip to the privy on the opposite side of the track that ran along the back of Fairley Terrace.

'No, you can't go in this.' Mammy's lips were pinched into the tight line that was her usual expression. Mammy was not a smiley person, but Rowan thought nothing of it as she had never known her any different. 'Nobody with any sense would even think of it.'

'Oh, but . . .' Rowan wailed.

'It's early yet. It might brighten up later on.' Daddy winked at her, a conspiratorial wink. 'You know what they say – rain before seven, clear before eleven.'

'Old wives' tale,' Mammy muttered under her breath.

'Well, let's hope not. I want to get my runner beans in today. The trench is all dug and ready.' Daddy always planted the runner beans on High Compton fair day.

'A couple of days won't make much difference. Come and eat your breakfast, Rowan, before it gets cold.'

When she'd finished her bacon, egg and fried potato, Rowan returned to the window. It had misted up in the heat from the kitchen fire. She rubbed it clear with her sleeve. Nothing had changed; it was still raining, running in rivulets down the pane and making puddles on the track. She drew patterns with her finger in what remained of the steam and pretended she was casting a magic spell.

'Rain, rain, go away. Come again another day.'

By mid morning, she was hopeful the spell was working. The sky had lightened and the rain no longer pattered against the window.

'Mammy! It's stopping!'

'For goodness' sake, Rowan, come away from that window and find something to do!' Mammy snapped. 'You're not going to the fair if there's any chance it's going to start again. I've got enough washing to dry without adding your clothes to it.'

Mammy took in washing to help make ends meet, and when the weather was bad it had to hang on a line strung across the kitchen until there was room on the airer in front of the fire. A wet Monday was the worst. But Dr Blackmore's wife had had visitors and had sent a pile of bedlinen and towels when they had left yesterday.

Tears of disappointment pricked Rowan's eyes, but obedient as usual, she went up to her room and fetched a drawing book and pencils.

3

It wasn't fair! she thought as she spread everything out on the kitchen table. Unless the rain stopped completely, Mammy would never let her go. Daddy might say it would be all right, that they could dodge the showers, but in the end Mammy would have her way. She always did. Just to rub salt into the wound, she knew that Earl, her brother, would go this evening with his mates – Earl was seventeen and did as he pleased.

If Laurel was here, she'd find a way to take Rowan, whatever the weather. Laurel was her older sister, older even than Earl, and she had a way of twisting Mammy round her little finger. Rowan could never understand how she managed it, but was glad of it all the same. Laurel was her ally, standing up for her, telling her she was beautiful, even though the children in her class at school called her fat and ugly and laughed at the white ribbons Mammy tied in her hair. Laurel could make everything – well, almost everything – right, or at least a hundred times better. She would know how much Rowan wanted to go to the fair, and would have defied Mammy and taken her.

But Laurel wasn't here. She worked in Bath and had lodgings there, only coming home on her days off. Rowan missed her dreadfully.

Sometimes, just sometimes, she wondered about her other brother, Samuel, who was older than Earl but younger than Laurel. What would it be like if he lived nearby? Would he take her part as Laurel did? But really she scarcely knew Samuel. When the family had moved to Somerset, into number 5 Fairley Terrace, recently vacated by people who had gone off to South Wales, Rowan had been just a baby, while Samuel, at thirteen, was already working in the pits back in Yorkshire. He'd come with them initially, but he hadn't stayed long. The only job open to him was as a carting boy – on his hands and knees for pretty much the whole of his working day, dragging a putt of coal by a

4

rope that ran around his waist and between his legs from the coal face to the passageways where the roof was high enough for ponies to take over the job. His skin had chafed until it bled, the dialect of the other boys and the colliers was unintelligible to him – as was his to them – and he missed his pals and the good times they had shared. Just a month he'd lasted. Then he'd gone back to Yorkshire, lodging with the family of one of his old friends. He didn't often visit, but when he did, Rowan swelled with pride at how handsome he was, and how big and strong, with eyes that twinkled just like Daddy's.

Miraculously, by dinner time the rain had stopped completely and there was enough blue in the sky to make a pair of sailor's trousers, as the saying went. Enough for Mammy to agree that Daddy and Rowan could go to the fair, though she herself would be staying at home trying to get Mrs Blackmore's sheets dried and ironed. The sun even showed itself as they headed along the road to town, Rowan holding Daddy's hand and skipping along beside him.

The fair spread out over all the roads leading to the square. They stopped at a roll-the-penny stall, where Rowan first won tuppence, then lost it along with the other threepence Daddy gave her. Daddy hustled her past a tent proclaiming 'Fivepence to see the Bearded Lady', but stopped to buy her a toffee apple and a twist of cockles for himself.

She was loving every moment, but still it was the switchback ride in the town square that attracted her most of all.

'Please, Daddy, can we go on it?' she begged.

They were on the opposite side of the street, heading for the children's roundabout, but Rowan was hanging back, tugging on Daddy's arm.

'Please! I really, really want to ride on that one.'

'The switchback? I don't know about that . . .'

But smiling at her enthusiasm, he let her lead him back to the edge of the small crowd gathered around the ride.

Cars shaped like animals with bars across the front of the seats and attached to a central spindle were whirling round an undulating track; music blared from a hurdy-gurdy but it couldn't quite muffle the screams of the laughing passengers. Quite a lot of the cars were empty; tonight, when the youth of the town – Earl included – came to the fair, there would be a scramble for places, perhaps even a fight when the pushing and shoving began.

Rowan tugged on her father's arm.

'Please! I could sit on your lap . . .'

'We'll see. Just let me eat these cockles. And you'd better finish your toffee apple. If you drop it down yourself your mam will have something to say about it.'

The ride was slowing. A swarthy young man with a mop of dark curls emerged from what she supposed was the control hub at the centre of the switchback, stepping on to the still-moving platform and swinging himself with easy grace between the occupied cars ready to release the bars and let the occupants out. Rowan stared, fascinated. He looked like a character from a storybook. The hero, of course . . . She only wished she could be so daring! She was even afraid to turn somersaults over the bar of the big iron roller that was used to flatten the football pitch. She wanted to do it – oh, how she wanted to! – but when she reached the head of the queue of children she absolutely couldn't. Launching herself off the metal drum was quite beyond her, and she'd be forced to give up, climb down again and slink away with the jeers and jibes of the others echoing in her ears.

'Scaredy cat!'

'Don't want us to see her bloomers.'

'Nor her fat arse.'

'Fatso scaredy cat!'

But she wouldn't be afraid to ride on the switchback. Not if she was on Daddy's lap, with his arms round her waist, holding her tight. Or tucked in beside him, her head against his chest. It would be so exciting.

'It's stopping, Daddy! Come on!'

But his hand was on her shoulder, thrusting her urgently away from the ride.

'Not today, my love.'

Someone jostled her; she dropped her toffee apple, bent to pick it up and was almost bowled over by a woman with a toddler in a pushchair.

Her father grabbed her arm, just managing to save her before she fell.

'Leave it. It'll be dirty.' He sounded impatient, cross even. More like Mammy. Daddy didn't usually let things like that bother him.

'But my toffee apple . . .'

'We'll get you another one. Come on. And it's going to rain again. We'd best get home before it starts or your mam will have my guts for garters.'

It was true: the sky had darkened again, the sun vanished in a bank of threatening cloud.

'Come on. D'you want another toffee apple or not?'

She nodded, but tears of disappointment were pricking her eyes and she dragged her feet as they made their way back up the street to the toffee apple stall.

'Cheer up now,' he said, sounding much more like himself, as he paid the vendor. 'We got to the fair, didn't we?'

'Yes, but—'

'Worse things happen at sea.'

It was one of his favourite sayings. Rowan couldn't see what that had to do with anything. She bit into the toffee apple, but it wasn't as satisfyingly good as the first one. All she could taste was bitter disappointment. She hadn't got to ride on the switchback, they'd hardly done anything, and now it was going to rain again and there was nothing ahead of her but the long trudge home.

As if reading her thoughts, Daddy said, 'Want a ride? Then we might make it in the dry.'

He hoisted her up onto his back. She clung on with one arm around his neck, clutching the toffee apple in her other hand. It was some consolation. She liked piggybacks and Daddy didn't give them to her as often as he used to when she was little. 'You're getting too heavy,' he'd say, and she supposed that was true. She remembered a time when she hadn't been tall enough to see over the windowsill in her bedroom. Now she could kneel up on it with no trouble at all.

Because Daddy walked fast, they were almost home before the rain began in earnest. He broke into a jog down the lane and along the track, jolting Rowan so she had to hang on with both hands.

'So you managed to get caught then,' Mammy grumbled as he set her down in the kitchen.

''Twasn't much.'

'Enough to get you wet.' Mammy put down the knife with which she'd been slicing bread and grabbed a towel from a hook beside the sink. 'Here, Rowan. Dry your hair before you catch your death.'

'It's not cold,' Daddy protested mildly.

'Wet hair won't do her any good. You can't be too careful.' She began to rub Rowan's head. 'It's all sticky, too.'

She fetched a comb, tugging it through Rowan's hair, where it caught on a knot, making Rowan squeal.

'What in the world have you been up to?'

Rowan investigated the knot. It *was* sticky. She'd got toffee in it, she supposed, when she'd been juggling the toffee apple and hanging on to Daddy at the same time.

'We'll have to wash it out when you have your bath,' Mammy said, and Rowan's spirits sank still lower.

Saturday night was bath night – Daddy and Earl would be out and Mammy would bring in the tin tub and set it in front of the fire. Rowan hated it. The water was always either too hot or too cold, and there was only ever a couple of inches in the bottom of the tub, the metal rim of which cut into her back. And having her hair washed was the worst of all. Mammy cut up slivers of soap and melted them in a mug of boiling water to use as shampoo; Rowan hated the smell of it and it always got into her eyes, no matter how tightly she squeezed them shut. And the rough towel would make her neck sore, and her fine straight brown hair would have become so tangled up that getting the comb through it was really painful.

'Go and get out of those wet clothes,' Mammy said. 'Then bring them down for me to dry.'

Earl was in the sitting room, sprawled on the sofa sorting his collection of cigarette cards.

'All right, Tiddler?' he greeted her.

Rowan didn't answer. She was feeling too resentful towards Earl. He'd go to the fair later and do just as he pleased. He always did. If he wanted to ride on the switchback he would, and nobody would stop him. She wished she was grown up like him and Laurel. Life just wasn't fair.

Rowan wasn't really a moody child, but just now she felt quite wretched, as if everything was conspiring against her. And the day she'd so looked forward to, but which had gone all wrong, wasn't getting any better. Her favourite blouse was wet,

9

and the one she'd changed into was stiff and scratchy. The toffee apple had taken the edge off her appetite, but Mammy made her eat all her bread and butter, even the crusts, which stuck in her throat. Earl had used her best pencil to scribble down the numbers of the cigarette cards he still needed to complete the set and broken the lead. And then there was the hated bath to endure. By the time she went to bed, depression had settled over her like a dark cloud.

Nothing would seem so bad if she had some friends her own age, she thought wretchedly. But she didn't. There were no children her age in Fairley Terrace, and even if there had been, she thought they would probably be horrid to her like the children in her class at school, leaving her out of their games and calling her names. Nobody seemed to like her. Because she was fat and plain, and Mammy and Daddy didn't talk the same way they and their parents did. Their Yorkshire accents sounded funny even to Rowan, since she had lived here in Somerset all her life.

Tears pricked at her eyes as she lay in her narrow bed, squinting into the twilight.

Some day, she promised herself. Some day I'll be pretty, and I won't be fat any more. I'll be grown up, like Laurel, and I'll have lots of friends. Maybe even a special one . . .

But that day seemed a very long way off.

If only I lived in a fairy tale . . .

She was drifting now, drifting . . . trying to think happy thoughts . . .

As she became muzzily aware of the loud banging and the raised voices, it seemed they were part of a dream. Mammy. Then Daddy. Shouting. But that was strange, because Daddy hardly ever raised his voice. She'd only ever heard him really angry once or twice that she could remember, both times with

Earl: once when he'd come home drunk on rough cider, and once when he'd got into a fight with some lads from Hillsbridge, High Compton's twin town just down the road. Mammy didn't often shout either. She just became silent and cold, banging things and going about with a face like thunder. No, it was a dream. It had to be . . .

But she felt sure she wasn't asleep. Confused and a bit frightened, she pushed back the coverlet and slipped out of bed, padding across the rag rugs and the bare boards to the window, and parting the curtains just enough to be able to see out.

It was properly dark now, not twilight as it had been when she went to bed. The moon and stars were hidden by a thick blanket of cloud. Rowan could just about make out the shape of the outhouses on the far side of the track and the figure of a man, dark against a shaft of light spilling out of the scullery door. She could still hear raised voices, but she couldn't make out what they were saying.

Then the man – whoever he was – suddenly staggered backwards, crashing against the wall of the outhouses and going down so she could no longer see him in the deep shadow. Now it was Mammy who was silhouetted in the shaft of light – she knew it was Mammy, short, plump, almost as wide as she was high. Her arm was raised and she was slashing it up and down as she did when she beat the rugs – thwack, thwack, thwack – except that the carpet beater was black, and this, whatever it was, gleamed in the reflected light just as the poker and fire irons did when the flames in the fire were high . . .

Startled and frightened, though she didn't know why, Rowan took a quick step backwards, caught her foot in the rag rug and fell. She caught her shoulder on the edge of the iron bedstead, gasped, curled herself into a ball. Her heart was thudding and her shoulder throbbed painfully. She inched further under the bed so that the bedspread formed a curtain around her, little sobs escaping her tight throat in quick, almost silent gasps.

How long she remained there she didn't know. But when the trembling in her limbs turned to shivers of cold, she pushed herself out, listening. Everything was quiet and there was nothing but blackness in the gap between the curtains – the back door must be closed now, so no glimmer of lamplight spilled out and reflected on the outhouses.

She climbed back into bed and huddled beneath the covers trying to get warm. After a while she stopped shivering and everything began to get a bit muzzy.

She slept.

The next thing she knew, it was morning. She could hear the familiar sounds of everyday life in the kitchen below. The rattle of crockery. The tinkle of cutlery. The smell of bacon frying wafted up the stairs.

She got out of bed, pulled on her dressing gown and thrust her feet into her slippers. The shadow of the night terror still hung over her like an invisible shroud, heavy and threatening. She crossed to the window and pulled back the curtains nervously, but everything looked as it always did, rain-washed but normal, the tiled roofs glinting in the light of the morning sun. The sky above the outhouses was mostly blue, pale periwinkle, and the clouds were white and fluffy. It looked as if it was going to be a fine day.

Her feeling of apprehension lifted a little, and she went downstairs. Mammy was cooking bacon, sliding it onto a plate to keep warm in the oven; through the back door, which was ajar, she could see Daddy leaning against the wall, smoking a cigarette. The bench was still too wet to sit on, she supposed. Of Earl there was no sign. There rarely was on a Sunday morning. He and his mates were always out late on a Saturday. Today he would be having his usual lie-in, and Mammy would let him. After all, he had to be up by five on weekdays.

'All right, my love? Sleep well?' Mammy asked Rowan over her shoulder.

Rowan sat down on the edge of a chair. She had to ask.

'Who was that man?'

Mammy stopped what she was doing, a forkful of bacon dangling between pan and plate.

'What man?' Her tone was sharp.

'Last night. There was a man. At our back door.'

'Whatever are you talking about?'

'There was. I saw him. And you and Daddy were shouting. And you . . .' Her eyes went to the fireplace: the irons were all in their usual place, gleaming in the glow of the fire as if they'd been freshly polished. But that was nothing new. Mammy was very house-proud: she got through goodness only knew how many tins of Brasso on the fire irons, the fender, and the door-knob and knocker. '. . . you were outside in the rain,' she finished lamely. 'I saw you from my window.'

'And what were you doing out of bed, I might ask?'

'I woke up. It was the noise . . .'

'Huh!' Mammy snorted. 'That was our Earl coming home, I expect. Late, as usual. And he'd had a drink – again. Your dad wasn't best pleased, I can tell you.'

Rowan frowned.

'It wasn't Earl.'

'Course it was.'

'It wasn't.' Rowan didn't know how she knew; she just did.

'You were half asleep, I expect. Either that or you were having a bad dream.'

Rowan picked at the hem of her dressing gown. Perhaps that was it. It did seem that way now, in the light of day. She used to have awful nightmares, wake screaming, and have to get into bed with Mammy and Daddy before she could go back to sleep. They hadn't happened so much lately – 'Now you're too big to come in with us,' Mammy said sceptically. But all the same . . .

'I was so frightened I got under the bed,' Rowan said.

'You did *what*?'

'I got really cold.'

'Whatever next, you silly girl! You could catch your death. And with your bad ear, too. If you were in a draught . . . It's not aching, is it?'

Rowan had suffered an ear infection when she was little; they'd feared she was getting a mastoid. She remembered terrible pain, and a succession of linen cloths heated in front of the fire and then pressed against her ear. It was still weak, Mammy said, and made her wear a bonnet to go outside in winter – something else the other children teased her about. And it was true, she did still get a lot of earaches, which were horrible.

'There wasn't a draught,' she said doubtfully, the spectre of the burning, throbbing pain suddenly more real than her confused memories.

'Morning, my little princess!'

Daddy had come back inside. He ruffled her hair, and she breathed in the familiar and oddly comforting smell of fresh tobacco smoke.

'Hello, Daddy.'

'She thinks she heard something going on last night,' Mammy said. 'I've told her it was either our Earl coming home late, or she was dreaming.'

'That's what it'll have been,' Daddy said, and winked at her. 'You and your dreams, Rowan.'

Rowan looked up trustingly into his very blue eyes. She loved those eyes – why couldn't hers be that colour? Laurel's were. And Earl's too. While hers were a sort of muddy green, the colour of the water in the goldfish bowl when it needed changing . . .

She pushed the thought aside, determined not to fall back into her bad mood of the previous day.

'Well, it seems like we've seen the last of that rain,' Daddy said. 'Reckon I'll be able to get my beans planted today.'

'You'd better do that. They'll be late coming up otherwise.'

'Soon as I've had my breakfast I'll go out and see to them,' Daddy said, not mentioning the fact that yesterday Mammy had said a few days wouldn't make any difference. 'Lucky I got the trench all ready before the rain came, so it won't take me long.'

'Sit up, then, and I'll fry your egg.'

The fat sizzled as Mammy broke two eggs into it – one for Daddy, and one she'd share with Rowan. The kettle sang on the hob. The smell of the bacon tickled Rowan's nose and made her hungry.

'Can I help plant the beans?' she asked.

'No you can't!' Mammy snapped. 'The ground will be sopping wet. You'll stay in here, madam, until it dries up a bit.'

Rowan caught Daddy's eye across the table. He grinned at her, tipping his head in that conspiratorial way that made her feel warm inside. She smiled back at him, the feeling of oppression quite gone now.

A bad dream. That was all it had been. This morning the sun was shining, and all was right with the world.

# *Chapter Two*

## June 1905

'Morning, Mrs Sykes.'

At the sound of Cathy Donovan's cheerful voice calling across the picket fence that separated their two gardens, Minty Sykes shifted the basket of laundry from her hip so that it rested on the not inconsiderable shelf of her stomach and sighed inwardly.

Whatever had made her choose this very minute to hang out the washing? Unlike most of the folk who lived in Fairley Terrace, Minty was not a sociable sort, and couldn't abide idle gossip. It seemed to her that everybody around here wanted to know everybody else's business, while she was not the least bit interested, and certainly didn't want folk knowing hers. She couldn't understand them popping in and out of one another's houses, sharing cups of tea and borrowing anything from a jug of milk to a cup of sugar or flour. May Cooper at number 1 and Dolly Oglethorpe at number 3 were forever at it, and leaving their doors on the latch, too, or even wide open in summer – anybody could just walk in and help themselves if they had a mind to.

You didn't often see Queenie Rogers at number 2, but she was a queer one anyway. Suffered with her nerves, they said, and had done ever since Frank, her only son, had been killed in a terrible accident in the pit. But that was a long time ago – before the Sykes family had moved from Yorkshire to Somerset, into number 5, when the Buttons who had lived there had vacated it and gone off to South Wales. Thirteen years ago, the accident was. Surely it was time the woman pulled herself together? Minty had little patience for that sort of carry-on. Bad things happened to everybody. That was just life. You had to square your shoulders and make the best of it.

The families further down the rank weren't too bad, apart from that terrible woman Hester Dallimore at number 9, who delighted in being the one in the know about everything and spreading it far and wide. Lottie Weeks at number 7 had called with a basket of eggs when they'd first moved in, but Minty had made it clear she wanted her privacy, and there'd been no more eggs. Then there was the old man with the bad chest at number 8 who never went further than the bench outside his door, and the daughter who looked after him, and the Withers family right at the end in number 10, who sometimes called in on Cathy Donovan next door – Cathy who she'd managed to run right into this morning. The two families were related by marriage, Minty understood, though she wasn't sure how, and had never bothered to find out.

Cathy was all right, as far as it went, even if she had married one of the Donovans, who were a right shower from what she could make out, though to be fair, Ewart, Cathy's husband, seemed respectable enough. She was a pretty little thing, though Minty could make a fair guess that she'd been on the flighty side before a husband and children had clipped her wings. Three of them there were, two boys who were both at school now – right rascals, the pair of them! – and a girl, Freda, just three. She was always dressed up like a dolly in Minty's opinion, in petticoats and pinafores, and judging by the washing Cathy was hanging out, she got through a fair few in a week.

'Lovely day!' Cathy called, pegging hair ribbons onto the line.

'Not too bad.' Minty could never bring herself to agree wholeheartedly with anyone, though it was true, the sun was already hot though it was not long after ten in the morning.

She set down the laundry basket and took out a tablecloth. Once she had it on the line, it would form something of a barrier between her and Cathy. A sheet would have been better, but it would hang down in the mud if she didn't fix the prop quick sharp, and then the line would be out of reach for the smaller items she had to hang out.

Cathy, however, was not to be deterred.

'I was talking to your Laurel yesterday,' she said, coming over to the fence.

'Oh yes?' Minty said non-committally as she reached into the basket for a pillowcase.

Laurel was a sight too friendly with the next-door neighbour for her liking, though given that they were much of an age, she supposed it was inevitable.

'She's got a job at the cottage hospital starting next week, she tells me, and she's got this week off before she starts,' Cathy said. 'Lucky to get in there, so close to home.'

Minty was affronted. She was very proud of Laurel, who had begun her working life as a machinist at a shoe factory. She had learned typing and bookkeeping at evening classes and secured a job for herself running the office for a private investigator in Bath, and was now going to work in the office of the cottage hospital, just up the road. A much more suitable position for a young woman. Minty hadn't cared for the thought of her daughter working for a private investigator.

'I don't think luck had much to do with it,' she said stiffly. 'She's good at what she does. Mr Sawyer is very sorry to lose her.'

'You'll be glad to have her back home, though.'

Minty said nothing. Truth to tell, two women in one kitchen was one too many in her opinion. Laurel had only been home for a couple of days, and already she was poking her nose in, wanting to do fancy bits of cooking and baking,

'And she'll be glad to be back, I know that,' Cathy went on, unabashed. 'She missed you all something terrible. Especially your Rowan. Laurel thinks the world of her, doesn't she?'

'They're close, yes.'

'It's natural, I suppose, what with Rowan being her only sister, and the gap between them. She was quite a help to you, I expect, with you being an older mother.'

Minty bristled, but Cathy seemed not to notice.

'And she's growing up so fast! It seems like only yesterday she was the age my Freda is now. She'll be going up to the board school soon, I suppose?'

'Next year. She'll be ten in November.'

'And before you know it, she'll be leaving and looking for a job. Perhaps she'll go into secretarial work, like Laurel.'

'I doubt it,' Minty sniffed. 'We haven't got money to waste on evening classes. Laurel saved up and paid out of her wages.'

'Well, Rowan will do well in whatever she decides to do,' Cathy said. 'She's a bright girl.'

Minty nodded, gratified by her neighbour's praise for her daughter, but unwilling to show it.

'I'd better be getting on, I suppose.' At last, to Minty's relief, Cathy picked up her laundry basket.

Even now she hadn't finished, though.

'We've had some good news, too. Ewart's sister and her husband are coming back from America. I used to work with her in the draper's shop – Maggie Donovan she was then. I was her apprentice, and she trained me up, until . . .' She paused. *'Until she had to leave in a hurry,'* she had been about to say, but that would be disloyal to Maggie, of whom she was very fond.

'Anyway, she and Josh Withers – that's Mr and Mrs Withers's son . . .' she jerked her head towards the end of the rank, 'they went off to New York and got married, and they've been there ever since. But now they're coming back. No place like home in the end, I suppose.'

'No, you're right there,' Minty said.

At last she was able to hang the sheet, pegging it up between her and Cathy.

And at last Cathy took the hint and headed back across the track to her own house.

Well, well, Minty thought to herself as she finished hanging out the washing and went back indoors for the next load. So that little hussy has had enough of America and they're coming back here. I don't know how she has the nerve to show her face.

Little as she liked gossip, the story she'd heard from Hester Dallimore soon after they'd moved here had been lurid enough to pique her interest – and arouse her righteous outrage.

Maggie Donovan, who had once lived in the house next door with her less than respectable family, had been engaged to Jack, one of the Withers boys. Like Frank Rogers from number 2, he'd been killed in the accident at the pit when the rope bearing the hudge was severed and twelve men and boys, just starting their day's work, had plunged to their deaths. Maggie's father, Paddy, had also been one of them. Not that he was much loss to anyone, from what Minty had heard – an Irish good-for-nothing, and Minty knew all about them, more was the pity. And just to make matters worse, there was some story that it was his own son who had been responsible, and that he had drowned himself in a local lake to escape hanging for it.

Anyway, then, almost before her fiancé was cold in his grave, this Maggie had taken up with his brother and got herself in the family way. Minty had noticed how Cathy had very nearly let it out before she stopped herself, but she knew what she had been about to say all right. Then, if you please, she'd married some man old enough to be her father – for his money, Minty supposed. It wouldn't have been out of shame for being an unwed mother. A girl from a family like that wouldn't know the meaning of the word.

To cap it all, they hadn't been married any time at all when the old man had died of a chill – a bit funny that, Minty thought. Maggie had helped him on his way like as not; she certainly hadn't taken care of him as she should. And the next thing, very conveniently, Josh Withers, the baby's father, had suddenly appeared back on the scene and the pair of them had gone off to America together. The story was put about that she'd gone to finish some stained-glass window in a cathedral in New York that her husband had made. A likely tale! Minty thought. What would a girl like that know about stained-glass windows? Well, whatever they'd been up to it must have all gone haywire and now they were beating a hasty retreat back to England.

Well, she only hoped they had somewhere to go when they got back. She hoped they weren't thinking of moving in with Ewart and Cathy until they could find a place of their own. She didn't want their sort next door. Or even down the rank with the Withers family. That was more likely, she supposed; they'd have more room there. Always assuming the two of them were still together. Maggie could have got through any number of men by this time . . .

Minty shook her head, her mouth a tight, disapproving line. Some folk! Disgraceful, the way they carried on.

Well, at least she could hold her head up high. They might not have much. She might have to take in washing to help make ends meet. She might wish Laurel would meet a nice man and get married, that Samuel and his wife and family were nearer, instead of being so far away in Yorkshire, and that Earl would settle down instead of trying her patience by wanting to be a Jack-the-lad.

But at least she had her respectability, and she had Rowan.

Really, nothing else mattered.

In the narrow seams far below the green fields, Earl was sitting with his father and some of the other miners, leaning against the jagged tunnel wall as they ate their cognockers of bread and cheese and drank cold tea from their stone water bottles. Occasionally one or other of them would break off a bit of bread and toss it to the mice who came creeping out when they got a sniff of food, and as they ate they talked – 'chewing the fat', they called it.

Earl, however, was deep in thought, turning over an idea that had been nagging at him for some days now. He was fed up with being a carting boy. Six years, doing the same back-breaking job day after day was enough for anybody. He liked working alongside his father, it was true, and the weals on his back caused by the rope attached to the putt of coal had long since healed, though the scars remained, white and livid against the skin that was already beginning to be mottled black from the coal dust.

But he was twenty-one years old now; it was insulting to be called a 'boy', and he was ready to graduate to being a collier. Two or three of his mates had left to go to South Wales, where the seams were deeper and less faulted than they were here in Somerset, and Earl had decided he'd like to join them. He hadn't mentioned it yet to his mother or father; Dad would understand, he thought, but Mam was a different matter, She'd kick up hell's delight, as like as not. Best, he thought, not to say anything until it was settled.

'Back to work then, lads.' Ezra Sykes folded the kerchief his cognocker had been wrapped in and stoppered his tea bottle. 'Come on, our Earl. Get that putt of coal out of the way so we can start filling another.'

'You're a slave-driver, Dad.' But he said it without rancour. If he had to cart, he'd rather do it for his father than anyone else. He just wished he didn't have to cart at all . . .

As he dragged his putt of coal away from the coal face towards the topple, the steep incline that led down to the road below, he was still thinking about it, not really concentrating on what he was doing. He didn't notice the nail jutting out from one of the wooden pit props until he felt the sharp pain in his arm, just above the elbow. He swore, gritted his teeth and crawled on, but he could feel hot blood coursing down, and when he touched it, his fingers sank into a deep gash several inches long. By the time he reached the topple, his shirt was soaked with blood and he realised he'd have to do something about it. He tipped the putt of coal into the waiting half-full tub but didn't trust himself to take it down to the roadway. He scrambled down and made his way to the shaft, where he signalled for the hudge to take him to the surface. It came clanking down – no outdated and dangerous rope nowadays, but a strong iron chain – and he climbed into it.

23

The noonday sun was hot as he emerged into the pit yard and crossed to the office block, where he knew there would be bandages in the somewhat basic first-aid store.

'What's up, boyo?'

Taffy Jones, the manager, was at his desk, shirtsleeves rolled up to the elbows, collar unbuttoned, face – squashed like a bulldog's, Earl always thought – shiny with perspiration.

'Hurt my arm, sir. I'm bleeding like a pig.'

'Bloody careless! You want to watch yourself. Well, you know where the bandages are. In that cupboard. You don't expect me to nursemaid you, do you?'

'No, sir.'

Earl, dripping blood on to the oilcloth-covered floor, opened the cupboard door, found a bandage and managed to wrap it around the wound, tying the ends with the help of his teeth. All the while Taffy glowered at him, eyes narrowed to slits in his fleshy face.

'Go on then. Get going. You're wasting good working time. But clean up that mess first.' He indicated the blood spots on the oilcloth floor with a jerk of his head.

Quite suddenly, Earl had had enough. He swung round to face the manager.

'While I'm here, sir, I might as well tell you. I'm going to be leaving. I'm going to Wales.'

'Wales? You think the valleys are paved with gold, eh?' Taffy, as his name suggested, was Welsh himself; he'd come to Somerset to take a promotion that he'd known would never come his way in the rich pits of the Rhondda. 'Take it from me, boyo, they're not.'

'I'll take my chance on that, sir.'

Taffy sat back in his chair, fished a handkerchief out of his pocket to mop his damp brow and regarded Earl squarely.

24

'If that's the way you want it. But if you go, you can take your father with you.'

For a moment, Earl couldn't take in what the manager had said.

'What?'

'You heard me. Your father's not getting any younger, and he's sounding a bit chesty, if I'm not much mistaken. Shouldn't think they'd want him in Wales. But I've got plenty of good men all too ready to take his place. It's carting boys I'm short of. So like I say. If you go . . .'

'You'd get rid of Dad?'

Taffy shook a cigarette out of a packet and lit it.

'That's about the size of it. So think on now, before you do anything in a hurry.' Deliberately and contemptuously, he blew a stream of smoke directly at Earl. 'Now get underground again and shift some coal before I decide to get rid of the pair of you here and now. Go on, get out of my sight.'

Lost for words, Earl went. It was only when he was heading back to the hudge that the anger began, boiling inside him. 'You bugger!' he muttered. 'You bloody bugger!'

He wished he could storm back into the office and land a punch squarely on the manager's jowly jaw. But what good would that do? He'd be dismissed, and it would be the end of Dad too.

And what would he and Mam do then? Taffy was right: it was unlikely he'd find another job at his age, and it was true he was a bit wheezy sometimes, especially in the mornings. Perhaps his chest would improve if he was no longer breathing in coal dust, but then again, without a job to go to it wouldn't only be the family's income that would suffer, Dad would be wretched. He'd think he'd been thrown on the scrap heap, and he wouldn't be far wrong. God alone knew what it would do to him. And worst of all, their house went with the job.

No, angry as he was, Earl knew he couldn't precipitate what he knew would be a slow decline in the father he loved and respected. Much as he wished he could put two fingers up to Taffy Jones and walk away to a brighter future, he just couldn't do it. He was trapped. And he could see no way that he could ever be free.

The mixed class was busy writing. 'My Pet' was the subject for composition today. Pens dipped in and out of inkwells, girls flicked ribbon-tied bunches and plaits back over their shoulders, boys ran inky fingers between their necks and their tight, scratchy shirt collars. It was hot and stuffy in the classroom, though the big sash windows had been opened as far as they would go, and many glances were thrown at the hands of the wooden cased clock on the wall behind the teacher's desk, willing them to move more quickly towards three, when the bell would jangle and signal release. That wouldn't be for almost another hour, though, and most of the pupils were chafing against being incarcerated on such a lovely day.

Not so Rowan. Head bent over her desk, she was writing furiously.

'My Pet'. When Mr Sims, who taught the top class, had set the subject, she had been dismayed. She didn't have any pets. Mammy said they only made work and were dirty. You never knew what you might catch from them. She couldn't openly admit it, though. It would have just been something else for the other children to make fun of.

She'd thought for a few minutes and decided she'd write about an imaginary pet, one she'd like to have. Mr Sims wouldn't know any different and it would be fun to make up a story for a change.

*My pet is a rabbit called Snowy*, she wrote. *She lives in a hutch at the end of the garden. Her fur is white as snow and silky soft and the inside of her ears is pink, like a seashell. When I get her out for a run on the grass she skips and hops so it's quite hard to catch her. And if I don't stop her she eats the lettuce, which makes Mammy cross. One day . . .* she paused, trying to work out an adventure, *a fox came into the garden . . .*

All heads turned as the classroom door opened and Mr Shearn, the headmaster, came in. He was a stocky man, with spectacles perched on a beaked nose, and he stood for a moment inspecting the class over the top of them.

'As you were. Carry on with what you're doing.'

He made his way between the rows of desks and forms to where Mr Sims was perched on the corner of his desk, and spoke to him in a voice too low for the pupils to be able to hear what he was saying. Then he swung round, looking straight at Rowan and beckoning to her.

'Rowan Sykes. Would you come with me, please?'

Startled, Rowan put down her pen and slid out of the form. Twenty pairs of curious eyes followed her and colour flamed in her cheeks.

All manner of thoughts chased one another round inside her head as Mr Shearn led the way through the adjoining classroom, where more pairs of curious eyes followed their progress.

What could it be? Had something happened to Mammy or Daddy? She remembered once when Tommy Barnett had been pulled out of class, and that was because his father had been killed in a roof fall in the pit. She began to tremble. If anything had happened to Daddy, she couldn't bear it . . .

'Don't look so worried,' Mr Shearn said as he opened the door to his office. 'You're not in any trouble.'

He pulled out a chair and motioned to her to sit, then went around to his own side of the desk and pushed a sheet of paper across to her.

'Read this through – take your time – and then I'm going to ask you some questions.'

Puzzled, Rowan looked down at the printed sheet. The piece seemed to be a description of life in India. There were a lot of words she'd never come across before, but when she concentrated on the context they seemed to make sense.

After ten minutes or so, Mr Shearn leaned across and turned the paper over.

'Are you ready?' She nodded, realising this was a test of some kind. 'Now, what did you make of what you read?'

'It's geography, sir. How people in India live. What they eat. Their houses. The churches . . .' she searched her memory, 'temples.'

Mr Shearn began firing questions at her and Rowan answered as best she could. At last he sat back, satisfied.

'Very good, Rowan. Mr Sims was right. You are a bright girl. I think with extra tuition you would be a good candidate for a scholarship to grammar school.'

Rowan stared at him, not knowing what to say.

'I'd like you to ask your mother to come in and see me – to-morrow, perhaps? – so that we can discuss it. Will you do that?'

Rowan nodded, still too bemused for words.

'Good. You can go back to your class now. And don't forget to thank Mr Sims for excusing you.'

Rowan went. Mr Sims had collected the composition books, and was piling them on the corner of his desk. Rowan handed him hers, with its incomplete story.

'I'm sorry I didn't finish it, sir. And thank you for letting me go.'

'That's all right, Rowan. I hope Mr Shearn was pleased with you.'

'I think so, sir.'

Blushing again, she went back to her desk. Twenty pairs of curious eyes followed her once more.

The clock on the wall now said five minutes to three. Rowan had the sinking feeling that when the class was released, she was going to be the target for a lot of unwelcome attention.

She was right. As they filed out of the classroom, through the cloakroom and into the yard, Beatie Emery came up close behind her and tugged sharply on her hair. Rowan tried to ignore it, but Beatie came alongside her, jostling her against the wall.

'Hey, you, fatso!'

'Leave me alone.'

Beatie was not only a bully, she was also tall for her age, and athletic, always winning races on sports day and making run after run for her team when they played rounders, while Rowan usually missed the ball altogether. As a consequence she was popular with girls and boys alike, though perhaps the fact that nobody wanted to be her enemy had something to do with it. Admired and feared, she ran a gang of girls who were always ready to do her bidding or risk expulsion from the magic circle – 'the Club', as they called it. Now two or three of them joined her, laughing and jeering at Rowan's distress while remaining at a respectful distance. Beatie was the general, they were the foot soldiers.

'What did Sir want you for?' Beatie demanded.

'Nothing.'

'Liar! You were gone for ages.'

Rowan could feel tears pricking behind her eyes; she fought

them back. If she cried, they'd taunt her for being a baby, too. Somehow she gathered her courage.

'Mind your business, Beatie Emery.'

Beatie's face contorted with fury.

'What did you say?' One hand shot out, pinning Rowan against the wall. With the other she snatched the ribbon from Rowan's hair, scrunching it up and tossing it to the ground.

'I said mind your business,' Rowan repeated, shaking but defiant. Somehow it came out even louder than before.

'Have some respect!' Beatie grabbed a handful of the hair that was now falling across Rowan's face and jerked it sharply so that her head banged back against the rough stone. 'Don't you talk to me like that, fatso!'

Rowan squeezed her eyes tight shut to stop the threatening tears, so she didn't see her sister push through the circle of jeering girls and grab Beatie by the arms. But suddenly she was free, and when she opened her eyes it was her attacker who was backed up against the wall.

'Laurel!' Rowan tried to say, but no sound came.

'Don't you ever, ever try that again.' Laurel's fingers were biting into Beatie's shoulders; Rowan thought she was going to shake her, but she didn't, just glared into the girl's face, her blue eyes flashing fire. 'You hurt her and I'll hurt you, my lady. Do you hear?'

Beatie was nodding. Never before had Rowan seen her look so frightened – or even frightened at all.

'You'd better not. All right?' Laurel released her, then bent to pick up Rowan's ribbon and caught her by the hand. 'Come on, my love.'

She marched Rowan away across the playground, an arm around her shoulders. And now the tears did begin to flow, trickling down Rowan's flushed cheeks. She was grateful to

Laurel, glad that Beatie had had a taste of her own medicine, but she was afraid it would only make things worse. Laurel wouldn't be there tomorrow, or the next day, and Beatie would want revenge for her humiliation. There was no way Rowan could win and it would just go on and on.

'Are you all right?' Laurel asked as they emerged onto the road.

Rowan nodded, wiping away her tears with her sleeve.

'So what was that all about?'

'Mr Shearn had me in his office today.'

'You've been in trouble?'

'No. He wanted me to take a test . . .'

As she said it, hope flared in Rowan's heart. Perhaps what the headmaster had suggested could be the answer to all her problems. If she was at a different school she wouldn't have to see Beatie and the others day after day, year after year. If you had to pass an exam to get there, then surely the other pupils would be like her, eager to learn. She wouldn't stand out like a sore thumb. Perhaps she would even lose some of her puppy fat before she started there, and no one would treat her as a joke. It would be a fresh start . . .

Excited and eager suddenly, she told Laurel what Mr Shearn had said.

'A scholarship? A posh school?' Minty banged a bowl of stewed rhubarb, still warm from the oven, onto the tea table. 'I've never heard anything so ridiculous in my life! Does Mr Shearn think we're made of money?'

'A scholarship would mean it's paid for, Mam,' Laurel said.

'That's as maybe. But how's she going to get there? On the train. They wouldn't pay for that, I don't suppose. Nor dinners, nor trips gallivanting here, there and everywhere. There'd be all sorts of extras, I shouldn't wonder. Not to mention a uniform.

She wouldn't get that for nothing, would she?'

'I don't know, Mam. If you go and see Mr Shearn, you can ask him.'

'I shan't be doing anything of the sort. I haven't got time to waste chewing the fat over such a daft idea.'

'It's not a daft idea, Mam. Just think what it could do for Rowan. A good education like that . . .'

'All it would do would be to give her ideas above her station.'

'Is that such a bad thing? She's clever, Mam. She doesn't fit in with a lot of the children in her class. They bully her because she's different. Thank goodness I went to meet her out of school today is all I can say. If I hadn't . . .'

'Yes, well, I agree with you there. I'd just like to get my hands on them. If I go to see Mr Shearn at all, it will be to tell him he needs to keep an eye on that Beatie Emery. But not to talk about scholarships and posh schools we can't afford.'

Laurel was silent for a moment, pushing a square of bread and butter round her plate.

'What if I was to pay for her uniform and her train fares?'

Minty snorted. 'And how are you going to manage that on what you bring home? Unless the hospital are going to pay you a lot more than you've let on. All I can say is, if you've got money to throw around, you can give me a bit more for your keep. Goodness knows I could do with it. Now eat up, do, our Rowan. That's rhubarb pulled fresh this morning. I did it specially for you. I know how you like it.'

Obedient as ever, Rowan spooned up a few chunks of rhubarb. But she didn't really feel like eating. She was still upset by Beatie's attack on her, and she was disappointed, though not surprised, at Mammy's reaction to Mr Shearn's suggestion, though she'd allowed herself a glimmer of hope with Laurel being so enthusiastic about it.

'Hello! We're home!' Her father's voice. The back door slammed shut.

'You get on and eat up,' Mammy said. 'I've got to go and see about the bath for your dad and Earl. And let's hear no more nonsense about posh schools. We don't want to worry your dad with that.'

'I'll talk to her again,' Laurel said as Mammy bustled off into the scullery.

Rowan nodded, but said nothing. She couldn't see what good it would do. If Mammy's mind was made up, all the arguing in the world wouldn't get her to change it.

And yet, unbelievably, somehow Laurel managed it.

'What's the best time for me to see Mr Shearn then?' Minty asked next morning. She sounded impatient and her lips were set in a tight line, but at least it seemed she wasn't dismissing the whole thing out of hand.

What had Laurel said to bring about this change of heart? Rowan wondered. But she couldn't ask her; she'd gone up to the farm for a jug of milk and some eggs to make a toad-in-the-hole for dinner.

Dear, darling Laurel! Rowan thought she loved her sister more than anyone in the world. Except perhaps for Daddy.

# Chapter Three

Standing at the rail of the great ocean liner, Maggie Donovan –
or Maggie Withers, as she had been for the past six years – found
herself thinking of the last time she had done this. Not just the
last time – the first and only time . . .

Today it was New York the ship was preparing to leave; then
it had been Liverpool. Maggie vividly remembered the way she
had felt as she stood there with Patrick, just a baby, in her arms.
Her apprehension at what lay ahead of her. Her determination
to do a good job restoring the stained-glass window made by her
late husband, Lawrence, which had been damaged in transit to
the New York cathedral for which it had been commissioned. It
had been one section of a glorious triptych that he'd designed,
cut and put together in his workroom in the garden of the house
on the outskirts of Hillsbridge, and his dying wish had been that
she should complete the work. She'd felt such a task was way
beyond her as a novice in the art of stained glass, but he'd taught
her well. To her enormous relief, she had managed to restore his
work to almost the standard she felt it deserved.

But most of all she remembered the gaping hole in her heart
that had ached unbearably that day, to be leaving not just
England, but Josh Withers, love of her life, father of her little
boy. And then the burst of disbelieving joy when she had seen

him running along the dockside, a carpet bag slung over his shoulder, yelling to the sailors who were making ready to raise the gangway.

Now she glanced at him, standing alongside her at the rail – at his strong profile, his windswept dark hair, his broad shoulders and the muscles that rippled in his arms beneath the rolled-up sleeves of his shirt – and felt her stomach twist with love. The same love she had been unable to deny, hard as she had tried, in the aftermath of the terrible accident that had claimed the life of her fiancé, Josh's brother Jack – and her own father too. The same love that had resulted in the birth of Patrick. Deeper, stronger by far than the almost sisterly affection she had felt for Jack. She'd known then that it was special, a once-in-a-lifetime meeting of two bodies, souls, hearts and minds that went far beyond mere physical attraction, potent though that was. And she knew it now. There would never be anyone for her but Josh, and she felt safe and happy in the sure knowledge there would never be anyone for him but her.

I am so lucky! she thought. How many people lived their whole lives and never found a love like this? And she had been lucky in so many other ways too. Lucky to have had a happy childhood and a loving family, even if they had been looked down on by the other residents of Fairley Terrace. Lucky – and this thought always made her feel a little guilty – not to have married the wrong brother. Lucky to have been rescued by Lawrence when she was pregnant, alone and facing the shame and hardship of being an unwed mother. Lucky to have discovered a talent for drawing and painting that would have lain fallow had it not been for Lawrence's encouragement. And lucky to have two wonderful children, and another on the way.

Maggie's gaze dropped to Patrick, standing between her and Josh at the rail and listening intently to what Josh was telling him as he pointed out the sailors loosening the moorings of the great ship. He would turn nine soon after they reached England, and with his curly hair and dark eyes he was already the image of the father he idolised.

Nora, at five, took after Maggie, with the fair skin and copper-coloured curls that came with her Irish heritage. She adored Josh too, and was now clutching her father's trouser leg as she stood on tiptoe to peer through the narrow gap beneath the rail.

The children were one of the reasons Maggie and Josh had decided to return to England – them and the new baby she was carrying. Life in America had been good to them – Josh had found work as a carpenter, and Maggie had been able to boost their income by selling some of her artwork. But recently she had been hit by a delayed bout of homesickness.

She missed her brothers – Ewart, who had married her apprentice Cathy, and Walter and his wife and children. Though Walter and Connie lived in Yorkshire, a good way from Somerset, it was still a great deal nearer than the other side of the Atlantic Ocean. In England they would be able to visit a couple of times a year, if not more, and Maggie was anxious that her own children should get to know their cousins. For all the opportunities here in America, she still felt that family was more important.

She and Josh had thought about it long and hard. Accommodation was not a problem: Lawrence's house, where she had lived with him after their marriage, lay empty. For a while it had been rented out, but no new tenants had been found since the last ones had moved out a year ago. Lawrence's workshop was completely untouched; that it should remain locked up and out of bounds had been the one stipulation she had insisted upon. Maggie was hopeful she would be able to use it to draw and paint, and perhaps make small items of stained glass that she could sell to supplement their income.

There was a shed, too, which could be converted into a workshop for Josh. He was a skilled carpenter, and though for the time being at least he would have to find full-time employment, he had hopes of building a reputation on his own account – custom-made furniture, doors and window frames, and perhaps smaller items such as toys and ornaments.

The more they'd talked things over, the more enthusiastic they'd become, and Josh had added the argument that he would like to be closer to his parents. Neither of them was getting any younger, he'd said, and since Jack had been killed, he was their only son. He'd like to be around to keep an eye on them in their last years, to help them out with the everyday demands of life as they became less able to cope, care for them when they were sick, even be on hand at the end.

'If anything happened to one of them while we're over here, I'd never be able to get back in time,' he'd said, and whilst he hadn't elaborated, Maggie had known what he was thinking. He didn't like the idea of his mother or father being laid to rest and him not there to pay his last respects or to comfort the surviving parent.

And so the decision had been made. They'd booked a passage on the *Caronia*, one of the newest liners of the Cunard fleet, which had only made her maiden voyage in February, disposed of most of the things they'd accumulated during the time they'd been here, and packed the rest into trunks and suitcases.

And now here they were, boarded and ready to sail. Watching the activity on the dock. Knowing as they sailed past the Statue of Liberty that it was probably the last time they would see her.

The realisation sent a little pang through Maggie. She'd been happier in America than perhaps at any other time in her life. But the people who had made her happy were going with her. It was a country she was leaving, not her precious family.

Blinking back a tear that she knew was nothing but sentimental nonsense, she glanced away from Josh and the children, taking in the full sweep of the deck.

A young man was standing at the rail a little further along to her left. Unusually, he was entirely alone, rather than with travelling companions, and Maggie wondered why. He appeared to be in his early twenties, and was tall and, she thought, good-looking. Longish fair hair, the colour of summer wheat, was being blown about by the gusting wind, and the arm that he raised to brush it off his face was muscular despite his slender frame and tanned to the golden brown that the fair-skinned could sometimes turn if they didn't burn red, as she did. To all intents and purposes, a golden boy. And yet . . .

As Maggie looked at him, she was suddenly overcome with a feeling of unease. It was almost as if a cloud surrounded him, an aura of darkness. Something bad had happened to him. Or was going to happen. Or perhaps it was that he was carrying some dark secret . . .

A shiver whispered over her skin with the alarming certainty of it.

In the old days, when she was young, she'd often had such insights, even occasional moments of clairvoyance. Sometimes they had come as a dream, such as the one she'd had the night before the disaster at the pit. Walking with Dad and Frank Rogers . . . the ground suddenly giving way beneath her feet . . . falling, falling . . . And next day both Dad and Frank had died that way, hurtling to their deaths when the rope bearing the hudge had given way.

Her ability to see things had been both a gift and a curse,

inherited along with her red-gold hair, she supposed, from the Irish in her.

But it was a long time now since she'd had any such experience. Her subconscious seemed to have been subdued by her busy life; there had been no room for flights of fancy. And that was all this could be, she told herself. Relieved of the everyday tasks that kept her too busy for such things, she was letting her imagination run away with her.

The fact that the young man was alone meant nothing. His travelling companions were probably below decks, inspecting their cabin. Or he was on his way to be reunited with a sweetheart. Maybe he was a businessman travelling to set up a new contract, or perhaps he had been visiting relatives in America. There was nothing whatsoever to back up the notion that there was something very wrong in his life. If she told Josh the thought that had occurred to her, he would laugh at her, tell her she was being silly. And he would probably be right.

The men on the dock seemed to have finished their work: ropes that had been wound round hawsers were now coiled on deck, and the gangway was raised.

A loud honk, and then another, from the ship's twin funnels made her jump.

'I think we're off,' Josh said unnecessarily.

A narrow gap had opened up between the dock and the ship's hull; looking down, Maggie could see a ribbon of dark and murky water growing wider.

She bent to pick up Nora so that she could see better.

'I'll have her,' Josh said, hoisting the little girl into his arms. 'Say goodbye to America, Patrick.'

'Goodbye, America!' Patrick shouted, his voice reedy against the thrum of the ship's engines and the gusting wind.

They stood there together at the rail, a tight family knot, as the distance between them and the shore increased.

'Home!' Maggie said. 'We're going home!'

And she thought no more about the young man, still alone, who was, like them, watching the shores of America recede into the distance.

Two days into the voyage, the novelty of being at sea had well and truly worn off. Nora had been seasick almost from the moment they reached open water, and Maggie, too, felt queasy most of the time. She hadn't suffered this way on the voyage out, so she assumed her condition was to blame; the morning sickness that afflicted her seemed to have got worse with each new baby. Patrick wasn't seasick, but he was bored and restless. Heavy rain and gusting winds had kept them below decks for much of the time, and even when he and Josh did venture out, there was nothing to look at but rolling grey waves as far as the eye could see.

Their cabin was fairly spacious, and Maggie was glad she'd persuaded Josh to book them into first class, something he'd thought was an unnecessary extravagance. But it was just a cabin, not a suite with interconnecting rooms, such as some of their fellow passengers enjoyed, and it had no bathroom – they had to use the public facilities.

Yesterday Maggie had decided it was time the children had a bath. She'd made the necessary reservation through their cabin steward, who in turn notified the bath steward, and this morning at the appointed time the hot water was delivered. But Nora was too poorly to be moved, and it was Josh who hopped into the tub with Patrick, while Maggie stayed with her little daughter.

That distraction over, Josh had taken Patrick to one of the communal lounges, where they played cards for a bit. But it wasn't long before he'd tired of that. The Fullerton boys – the two sons of a wealthy industrialist with a suite on the same deck as Josh and Maggie – had come into the saloon, and before long some of the older passengers who were trying to read quietly were complaining about the noise and disruption.

'Come on, Patrick. Time to go.'

The Fullertons might be prepared to let their sons run wild, disturbing their fellow travellers, but Josh was not.

He hustled a resentful Patrick back to their cabin. Maggie, crouched on the floor beside Nora's bunk, was holding a basin as the little girl vomited into it. She glanced up as Josh and Patrick came in. Her green eyes were anguished, and the dark circles were sooty smudges in a face as white as alabaster.

'Oh, Josh, she just can't stop being sick. I'm really worried about her.'

'It's only a few more days. Then she'll be fine,' he tried to reassure her.

Nora raised her head. Tears were running down her pale cheeks and she resorted to the baby language she'd grown out of long ago.

'Don't like it, Mommy! Nora want to go home!'

Maggie wiped her daughter's face, consumed by anxiety and guilt.

'We should have waited until she was older before we attempted this. She's so weak. Just look at her . . .'

'She'll be fine,' Josh said again. 'It's you I'm worried about, Maggie. In your condition . . .'

'I'm all right,' Maggie said impatiently.

'You're not. You're exhausted. You were up half the night with Nora. Why don't you lie down for a bit? Have a sleep. I'll watch her.'

'Well, if you're sure . . .'

'Course I am.'

'And you won't leave her?'

'What do you think?'

'Oh, Dad!' Patrick moaned, realising that he too was going to be cooped up in the cabin.

'Read a book or something,' Josh said. 'Can't you see your mother is tired out and your sister is ill? Just be grateful you're not the one who's seasick.'

Patrick cast a baleful glance at Nora. Once upon a time he had been the centre of his parents' world; since she had come along he'd been pushed out. And it would be even worse when the new baby arrived.

No sooner had the thought crossed his mind than he felt guilty. Nora was all right really, and he was sorry she was sick; the trouble was, she was a girl. He didn't have much time for girls, frightened as they were of their own shadows – or pretending to be – crying or acting all coy to get their own way. He hoped the new baby would turn out to be a boy.

Still feeling a little resentful, he rummaged under his pillow and found the book he had been reading last night – *Kim* by Rudyard Kipling. Yesterday he'd been quite interested in it, the story of a boy living in a fascinating world of which he knew nothing; today he found it impossible to immerse himself in the tale. He didn't want to be stuck here in a stuffy cabin reading; he wanted to be having adventures himself. Having fun with boys his own age, like the Fullertons. They were probably still in the saloon, or exploring the ship. They hadn't been dragged back to their cabin because some frowsty old folk had complained about the noise they were making.

Curled up in a corner between the fitted wardrobe and the door, he wondered if he dared creep out to look for them. His mother was fast asleep, and had been almost from the moment she climbed into her bunk. And his father was preoccupied with

Nora, who was being sick again. He'd probably not even notice Patrick had gone, and by the time he did, he wouldn't leave Nora to search the ship. He'd be for it when he came back, of course, but it would be worth it for an hour's fun.

He closed his book and put it down, then inched forward until he was able to reach the door handle. Holding his breath, he carefully pulled it down. It made a slight click and he froze, but his father, his back towards Patrick, was still attending to Nora. Patrick guessed the sound had been rendered inaudible across the cabin by the thrum of the ship's engines. Hardly daring to breathe, he pulled the door open just wide enough to squeeze through, then scuttled out on his hands and knees and pulled it closed after him.

A big grin lit up his face. He was free! He ran along the companionway to the saloon where he'd last seen the Fullertons. But the two boys weren't there, only the old men, a couple of whom were now playing a game of draughts.

Disappointed, Patrick went back out into the companionway, wondering where he might find them. He passed the dining room, which was empty but for a steward laying up the tables for lunch, and a bar where children were not allowed. He climbed a flight of stairs and found himself in another companionway, with doors on either side that he guessed led to more cabins. At the far end, facing him, was another door, made not of wood, but metal.

Where did it lead? Patrick wondered. Oh well, if he couldn't find the Fullerton boys, he might as well have an adventure of his own.

He grasped the handle, which was quite stiff but eventually gave, and pushed the door open. And then, without any warning, he was suddenly flying through the air, propelled in a crazy arc, his feet dragging behind him. He let go the door handle and plopped down onto the rain-sodden boards of an open deck. For a moment he simply lay there, stunned. What had happened? He didn't know, only that he was being drenched by rain and sea spray, his shoulder hurt, and so did one knee. Then, as the wide-open door, buffeted by a gale-force wind, banged against his head, he realised. The wind had taken it, catapulting him after it.

He tried to scramble up, but slipped and fell back again. No matter how he tried, the wind was too strong for him. Never in all his life had he known anything like it. Rain, each drop a shard of ice, was stinging his face, hands and bare legs; his short trousers, already soaked through, clung wetly to his thighs.

He was shivering now in violent spasms. A sob of panic caught in his throat as he battled the elements, trying to crawl back to safety only to be met by a solid wall of wind. What could he do? Nobody knew he was here, and it might be ages before Josh even began to look for him. In the meantime . . .

'Hey – what are you doing out there?'

An enormous rush of relief flooded through Patrick's veins. He looked up to see a man standing in the doorway, bracing himself against the frame. Patrick didn't know him, didn't remember ever having seen him before, but never had he been so pleased to see someone.

'I can't . . .'

'Give me your hand.' The man's voice was distorted by the roar of the wind, but as he reached out, his meaning was clear enough.

Patrick managed to inch forward a little across the streaming deck and grasp the outstretched hand.

'Come on now.'

The man grabbed him by the shoulders and yanked him inside. Then he reached out for the door; it took all his strength to pull it closed, fighting gust after gust of that unbelievable wind.

'This is hardly the weather for a stroll around the deck,' he said with a smile.

Patrick wrapped his arms around himself. His teeth were chattering and to his shame he could feel hot tears trickling down his wet cheeks.

'I wasn't going for a stroll . . . I just wanted to see . . .'

'And you found out, didn't you? You'd better get back to your cabin. Do you know which one it is?'

Patrick nodded. 'Yes. But I'm really going to be for it . . .' He broke off. A figure he instantly recognised had appeared at the far end of the companionway.

'My mom!' he blurted, and began to run towards her.

When Maggie had woken and realised Patrick was no longer in the cabin, she had been horrified.

'Where is he?' she had demanded.

'Gone off exploring, I suppose.' Josh didn't sound unduly perturbed.

'And you didn't go after him?'

'I couldn't leave Nora and I didn't want to wake you. He'll be back when he's good and ready. He can't come to much harm, can he?'

'Not much harm? We're in the middle of the Atlantic Ocean! Goodness knows what he's up to!'

'You worry too much, Maggie. He's a big boy now, and sensible for his age.'

'Well if you're not going to go and look for him, I am!' Maggie flared.

Josh got up. 'All right, all right. I'll go if that's what you want.'

But Maggie was already at the door of the cabin, anxiety

fuelling her anger. She wasn't aware that she was remembering her brother Billy drowning in Newby Pond, but subconsciously perhaps what had happened all those years ago had left its mark on her, and now, surrounded by a wild sea, she was gripped by terror that something terrible might happen to her son. Besides, if Josh was so unconcerned, she wasn't convinced he'd search thoroughly.

'No. I'll go. You stay with Nora.'

As she checked the saloon and the dining room, her anxiety grew. Surely he wouldn't have gone up on deck in this weather? Oh, Patrick, Patrick . . . where are you?

She climbed a flight of stairs, her heart thudding in her throat. And then, as she emerged into another companionway, there he was, running towards her. She almost sobbed with relief, but as he reached her, throwing his arms around her, she was overcome with puzzled consternation.

'Patrick! You're wet through! What on earth . . .'

'I'm sorry, Mom.' He sounded close to tears.

'Hopefully he's none the worse for his adventure, though.'

She looked up. The young man she had noticed at the rail on the day they had sailed was standing there, his tall frame seeming to block out what little light there was in the companionway. The young man who it had seemed to her had been surrounded by a dark aura.

The unease she had felt then came flooding back, driven to near frenzy at seeing the state Patrick was in.

'What have you done to my son?' she flared.

The young man smiled, not rising to her accusation.

'He was looking for adventure and got himself into a bit of a pickle.' He spoke with a combination of accents Maggie couldn't place: part American, part something else.

'What are you talking about?' she demanded.

46

'He saved me, Mommy!' Patrick's dark eyes were bright with tears. 'I fell out the door and I couldn't get back in . . .'

'You what?'

'I think he opened the door and the wind took it,' the young man said. 'It's blowing a gale out there. Luckily I saw it was open, and I was able to give him a hand.'

'Is that right, Patrick?' Maggie was still suspicious.

He nodded, the tears welling. 'I'm sorry, Mommy. I just wanted to see what was through the door, and then—'

'Oh, you silly, silly boy!'

She turned to the young man, ashamed now that she had let her quite unfounded suspicion of him make her jump to the wrong conclusion.

'If that's the case, then thank you.'

'No problem.'

'Come on, Patrick. Let's get you out of those wet clothes.'

With a brief nod to the young man, she took her son by the shoulder and led him back along the companionway.

By the next day, Nora seemed to be recovering. Though still pale and frail, she was well enough to be taken to the dining room for breakfast, and Maggie managed to persuade her to eat some porridge.

She didn't recognise any of the other passengers in the dining room – hardly surprising, since she had barely left the cabin – and to her relief, since she was still feeling ashamed at the way she had flown at him yesterday, the young man was not amongst them.

Later, however, when they went to the lounge, there he was, still alone, and sitting in one of the easy chairs with a book open on his lap. They'd have to pass right by him to get to a free table where they could play a game of cards.

Maggie hoped to skedaddle by without him seeing them, but as they approached, he looked up, smiling at Patrick.

'Not looking for adventure today, then?'

Patrick shook his head, a bit shamefaced.

'Certainly not,' Maggie said. 'He had quite enough of that yesterday.'

Josh, who had been leading the way, carrying Nora, turned, looking at Maggie and the young man enquiringly.

'It's thanks to this gentleman that we got Patrick back safe and sound,' she said, anxious now to make amends. 'And I am sorry if I . . .' She broke off, not wanting to draw attention to her unfounded accusation. 'I was too worried to think straight. And I never stopped to thank you properly either.'

He shrugged slightly. 'That's all right. There's no need to thank me.'

'There's every need! I dread to think what might have happened if you hadn't found him. I'd never have thought to look outside in the weather we were having.'

'I saw that the door was open. I'm sure you'd have seen it too.'

'If the gale was too strong for Patrick, it might well have been too strong for me. Really, we're most grateful. Aren't we, Josh?'

'He should never have gone out there.' Josh sounded a little defensive; he was still feeling guilty that Patrick had crept off on his watch. 'But thanks anyway. We owe you.'

They moved on, settled at the vacant table and got out the pack of cards. To begin with they played Snap, Nora's favourite game, but before long her head was drooping against Maggie's shoulder and Patrick was clearly bored with what was a game for little ones.

'I'll take her back to the cabin and you two can play whist, or sevens,' Maggie said.

She got up. The young man, she saw, was still sitting alone with his book.

'Why don't you ask if he'd like to join you for a game?' she suggested.

'What?' Josh was shuffling the cards. 'We don't know him.'

'He didn't know Patrick, but he saved his life. He's all on his own, Josh. He'd probably like some company.'

'He is nice,' Patrick offered.

'All right, you go and ask him, Patrick.'

Maggie smiled to herself. At the lounge door she looked back: the young man was following Patrick back to their table. If, as she suspected, he was lonely, it would go some way to repaying him – and make her feel less guilty about what she had suspected him of, and about the way she had spoken to him yesterday.

As she sat in the cabin beside a sleeping Nora, Maggie found herself wondering again about the young man: who he was and why she had had such negative feelings about him. When Josh and Patrick returned some time later, she was ready with a battery of questions.

'So – how did you get on with him?'

'Very well. He seems a nice chap.'

'What's his name?'

'David.'

'David what?'

'He didn't say. Or if he did, I can't remember.'

'Is he English or American?'

'English, I think.'

'He doesn't sound English.'

'Well, he said he was on his way home, so he must be.'

'So what's he been doing in America?'

'Oh, Maggie, I don't know. We were playing cards, not twenty questions.'

'You're hopeless, Josh!'

'And you're too nosy by half.'

'I'm just curious, that's all.'

'Same thing.' She pulled a face at him, and he grinned. 'You can ask him yourself. We've agreed to have dinner together tonight. But for goodness' sake don't pry if he isn't forthcoming. Really, it's none of our business.'

'Don't worry, I won't. I'm not another Hester Dallimore.'

'I should hope not.'

Like most folk who had lived in Fairley Terrace, both of them had suffered from their neighbour's nosiness. Nevertheless, Maggie was determined to find out what she could about the young man who had captured her imagination.

In the event, when he joined them at their table, he made it surprisingly easy for her.

'I thought Patrick and Nora might like these,' he said, producing an envelope and drawing out several sheets of paper printed with small, brightly coloured pictures that Maggie instantly recognised as scraps. She'd bought them sometimes for the children to stick in their scrapbooks or on to cards, but not often, as they were quite expensive.

'I'm sure they'd love them!' she said, feeling ashamed once more of the suspicions she'd harboured about him.

'These are all sailors.' He passed a sheet to Patrick. 'You see? One is climbing the rigging, one is sitting on a cannon, and so on. And this . . .' he pushed another across the table towards Nora, 'I thought you might like funny cats.'

'Thank you!' Patrick cried. 'That's fantastic!'

'Their scrapbooks and glue are all packed, of course, but

when we get home I'm sure this will be one of the first things they'll want to do,' Maggie said, looking at the cat pictures he had given Nora. 'I've never seen any more beautiful than these. Where did you find them?'

Faint colour rose in David's cheeks.

'I made them.'

'You made them! Maggie exclaimed, astonished. 'But . . .'

'I'm a chromolithographer by trade,' he explained. 'Most of the scraps you see in the shops come from Germany – they're very advanced in the technique over there. But I like to draw and I'm quite good at transferring my images onto the printing plates, so the firm I was working for in Boston encouraged me to experiment. These are the result.'

'I suppose that's not unlike what I do,' Maggie said. 'I work in stained glass, using my own designs. And Josh is an artist of sorts as well – he's a carpenter, but he makes toys and ornaments too.'

For a few minutes they talked about the similarities and differences in their work, then Josh spotted a waiter gliding between the tables and they broke off to peruse the menu and make their choices. They'd skip the soup course – consommé was not ideal for the children. Thin as it was, Maggie had visions of it going everywhere if the ship rolled unexpectedly, and she couldn't imagine there was much goodness in it. But the baked haddock would be perfect for Nora, whose stomach was still behaving uncertainly, and so would a small portion of roast turkey. The others all decided on roast lamb with green peas and boiled potatoes. To David's amusement, Patrick was already looking ahead to the puddings.

'Coconut sandwich! And can I have ice cream as well?'

'We'll see.' Maggie was thinking that a return to two courses, with no choice at all, was going to be something of an anticlimax for him when they got home and the cooking was all down to her.

'So if you had such a good job in Boston, why are you going home to England?' she asked David while they waited for their fish.

'Oh . . . things to do,' he said, evasive for the first time.

Josh shot her a warning look, but she continued all the same. 'Where do you call home in England?'

'I have friends in London.'

'And your family? Where are they?'

Josh had had enough. 'We're headed home for Somerset,' he said, kicking Maggie under the table. 'It's a small mining town, and I don't suppose you would ever have heard of it, but it's near Bath.'

'Really! I was thinking I might come down that way myself,' David said.

'Well, if you do, you must look us up. Maggie would love to show you her workshop and compare notes, wouldn't you, Maggie?'

Although she was dying to ask why David had thought of coming to Somerset, Maggie knew better than to ask. If she did, Josh would be angry with her, and besides, she had the feeling she would not get a satisfactory answer. He might be happy to talk about his work, but when it came to more personal things, that was a different story entirely.

'Of course, you'd be very welcome,' she said, pushing aside the doubts about him that still lingered despite all the evidence to the contrary.

The fish had arrived, tiny portions settled in the centre of bone-china plates. Maggie turned her attention to helping Nora eat hers without scattering bits all over the table, and the conversation returned to printing, stained glass and carpentry.

By the time they'd finished the meat course, Nora was tired and fidgety and Maggie took her back to the cabin, leaving Patrick eagerly awaiting his ice cream.

She was feeling very tired herself, and when she'd tucked Nora in, she lay down too and was asleep the moment her head touched the pillow. She didn't hear Josh and Patrick return; the cabin was in darkness, and when she came to some time later, there was no sound but the throb of the ship's engines. For a few minutes she lay cocooned in warmth and a feeling of contentment, all curiosity about David forgotten.

We're going home, she thought. Then the gentle rolling motion of the waves lulled her back towards sleep, and she knew no more.

Nora was sick again. Maggie could scarcely believe it. She'd thought her daughter's stomach had become used to the constant motion. Confined once again to the cabin, emerging only for meals after Josh and Patrick returned from theirs, she saw nothing of David, though her husband and son, it seemed, were spending a good deal of time with him.

'Have you found out any more about him?' she asked Josh.

'For goodness' sake, Maggie, give it a rest! Haven't you got anything else to think about?'

'Actually, no,' Maggie retorted, stung. 'Sitting with a sick child all day isn't what you might call stimulating.'

'Well, another day and we should be docking,' Josh said, regretting his sharp response. 'It's been rough for you, I know, but it will soon be over.'

And thankfully it was. As they stood on the deck watching land take shape on the horizon, Maggie thought she had never seen a more welcome sight. The skyline might be less romantic than the approach to New York – there was nothing beautiful about the port of Liverpool as seen from an incoming ship – but it was dry land. And it was home! Maggie felt herself welling up with emotion. Until this moment she hadn't truly realised just how much she had missed it.

As they headed for the gangway, laden down with as many of their belongings as they could carry, Maggie saw David ahead of them in the queue. He dropped back, and they exchanged a few words as they shuffled forward.

'That's it then,' he said unnecessarily as they stepped onto the dock. 'Thanks for your company. It made the voyage pass much more quickly.'

'Ditto,' Josh said. 'And don't forget – if you are in our part of the world, do look us up. You've got the address.'

'Will do.' His fair head bobbed above the heads of some of the crowd as he walked away.

'You gave him our address?' Maggie asked.

'Why not? I don't suppose he'll come, but you never know.'

'No.'

As he disappeared from sight, Maggie didn't expect she would ever see him again.

# Chapter Four

The minute she heard the back door open, signalling Minty's return from her meeting with Mr Shearn, Laurel hurried into the scullery, still clutching a cleaning rag and a tin of beeswax she'd been using to polish the living room table. Ever since her mother had left for the school an hour and more ago she'd been like a cat on hot bricks, wondering what was being said, and what the outcome would be. She'd wanted to go along too, but her mother would have none of it. 'Mr Shearn won't be best pleased if the whole family go traipsing into his office,' she'd said, and that had been an end of it.

'So how did it go?' she asked anxiously.

'At least let me get my coat off!' Minty snapped.

'Sorry, it's just that—'

'What I could do with is a nice cup of tea.'

Laurel wasn't sure whether this boded well or not, but she'd made a fresh pot only a few minutes ago knowing it would be the first thing her mother would want.

She scuttled back into the living room, retrieved the pot from the hob and poured tea into two cups she'd set out ready. Minty came in and sat down opposite her, blowing on her tea to cool it before taking a few sips and smacking her lips.

'That's better.'

'So?' Laurel prompted her impatiently.

Minty sighed, and drank some more tea before answering.

'Well, I've agreed to Rowan taking the exam. That's what you wanted, isn't it?'

Laurel felt the tension drain out of her neck and shoulders.

'And he thinks she stands a good chance?'

'He wants to give her extra lessons to get her ready for it. She'll sit it in February and we'll know by May or June whether she's got in.'

'Does he want paying?' Laurel asked.

'No, for a wonder. He'll do it in school time, though he might keep her later some days. I suppose it's a feather in his cap to get one of his children into a posh school in Bath. But we shall have to find the money for her uniform and any extras, just as I expected.'

'Well, as you know, I promised to help out with that. Anything that's left over after you've had your housekeeping can go towards whatever she needs.'

Minty huffed, holding her cup between both hands.

'Oh, Laurel, I don't know about that. You can't run yourself short.'

'I can and I will, Mam. I want her to have the best chance in life. She deserves it. And hopefully my wages will be going up a bit soon.'

'Where d'you get that from? You don't even start until next week.'

'I know. But I won't only be working for the hospital. I'll be doing the accounts and paperwork for some of the local doctors too. There's just a couple of them at the moment that bring their books in, but with my qualifications the hospital board hope they can persuade a few more to make use of me. They'll pay the hospital, and the hospital will put my money up accordingly.'

'You never said.' Minty's tone was accusatory. Though she was totally uninterested in other folk's business, she hated being kept in the dark where her own family was concerned.

'No, because there's nothing definite yet. I shall just have to see how I get on.'

'Hmm. Well. Let's hope something comes of it.' Minty finished her tea and put down the cup. 'Another thing: while I was there, I had a word about that girl that's been bullying our Rowan, and he's promised to keep an eye out.'

'Oh, good.' But Laurel didn't hold out much hope of it making a difference. No teacher could be watching constantly, and in any case, though Beatie Emery might be wary of physically attacking Rowan again after her intervention yesterday, it wouldn't stop the name-calling, or her making Rowan's life a misery by cold-shouldering her and making sure all her cronies did too. What was more, things were only likely to get worse with Rowan being pulled out of class or kept behind after school for extra tuition. It would just give the bullies further ammunition.

If she was successful in winning a scholarship, of course, it would get her away from them when the time came for leaving the church school, but that was a whole year away – a whole year for her to be subjected to unpleasantness. And it had probably been going on for some time already. She'd kept it to herself, ashamed most likely.

I should have realised something was wrong, Laurel thought, guilty as well as anxious. But then, she was so rarely at home. She'd missed so much of Rowan's growing up and it was a constant regret to her. But she had to work, and that work had taken her to Bath. There was no way she could travel each day; lodgings there had been the only answer. Then there had been the evening classes in typewriting and bookkeeping because she hated her job in the shoe factory and wanted to better herself, and finally the position she'd obtained working for Edgar Sawyer, a private investigator. She'd really enjoyed that, fascinated by the cases he took on and all the diverse clients who sought his help. But it had meant she often had to work on a Saturday, so that Sunday was the only day she could go home to High Compton, taking the early train back to Bath on Monday morning.

She should have noticed, though, that Rowan went very quiet on Sunday evenings. She *had* noticed, but surmised it was because Rowan was sad she had to leave next day. She knew her sister looked forward to her coming home, and for her part she loved spending time with her. On fine days they would go for long walks, when Laurel would point out and name the flowers in the banks, fields and woods, and some-times they would pick some and take them home to put in a jam jar – primroses and bluebells in spring, cowslips, corn-flowers and marigolds later on. In late summer they would collect blackberries in a paper bag to make pies, though they ate half of what they picked, their lips and fingers stained purple from the juice.

Wet days were more problematic. When Rowan had been little, Laurel would read to her, or write down the stories she invented, or stick pictures and cards into her scrapbook with thick paste made from flour and water. Nowadays of course Rowan could read without help and write her stories down for herself, but when she'd finished she would read them to Laurel, who never ceased to be amazed by her vivid imagination.

Laurel had always got a sinking feeling when the day came to an end, and assumed that the reason Rowan went quiet was because she was feeling the same way. Now she realised it was much more than that – Rowan was dreading going to school and having to face the bullies again. And even though Laurel would be on the spot now instead of miles away, she really didn't know what she could do to make things better.

'I just don't understand why all this started,' she said, shaking her head. 'She's such a lovely girl.'

'That's the root of the trouble, if you ask me. She knows how to behave herself properly and they don't.' Minty got up, crossing to the hob and lifting the teapot. 'Do you want another cup? I think there's enough left for both of us.'

'No, I'm fine, thanks. You have it. I'll get on with the dusting.'

Laurel retrieved the rag – the tailpiece torn from one of Ezra's old shirts – and began cleaning the mantelpiece over the fire-place, removing the ornaments one by one and dusting them carefully before replacing them. The green bone-china shepherd and shepherdess, the wooden candlesticks made from the timbers of HMS *Neptune*, which had seen service at Trafalgar, a vase that could never be used for flowers because it had a deep crack in it. But as she worked, she was thinking: Mam had probably hit the nail on the head.

Rowan was a child who was eager to please, to do as she was told, and all the rules and regulations Mam laid down would mean she was excluded from much of the mischief children liked to get up to. If she was offered a gobstopper, she'd be more likely to say 'I'm not allowed' rather than take it and suck it on the quiet. When she first started school, she was probably trying so hard to be good she'd come over as a spoilsport and a goody-goody.

Even the way Mam dressed her would have added to the other children's negative perception of her. The white ribbons in her hair rather than the usual brown or navy blue, the bonnets to protect her bad ear, the insistence on a wad of pink Thermogene under her vest if the weather was especially cold and wet to keep her chest warm and ward off bronchitis or even pneumonia – Laurel could see the problems this might cause amongst children who came from families that never bothered about such things and who were allowed to run wild. Mam did it with the best of intentions, of course: she only had Rowan's welfare at heart, and it wasn't Laurel's place to interfere, much as she would like to.

And her puppy fat didn't help matters either. Laurel had once suggested it might be a good idea if she ate fewer steamed jam roly-polies and batter puddings, but Minty had huffed and puffed at the very idea. Rowan was big-boned, like her, she said. And a growing child needed plenty of good food if she was to stay healthy. Laurel had thought privately that Mam and Rowan were no more big-boned than she herself was, but she'd known better than to say so.

Laurel, at twenty-five, was in fact a very attractive young woman. She'd never been overweight; the suet puddings and dumplings had had no effect on her, but then, she supposed, she'd run it all off playing with her two brothers and their friends. She'd been something of a tomboy, out from dawn till dusk in the countryside that surrounded their Yorkshire pit village, swinging across the river on a rope tied to a sturdy branch of an overhanging tree – and sometimes falling in! – racing up hill and down dale, barely stopping to catch her breath. She'd been a rebel too, finding ways to get around Mammy's rules – which had been far less rigorous than those she imposed on Rowan, if memory served her right – and sometimes simply breaking them with no heed for the consequences. She hadn't been afraid to stand up for herself with her peers, though she hadn't often had to. She'd been popular with the other girls when she was Rowan's age, and later on, when they started taking an interest in a pretty face and a developing figure, with the boys too. But despite the fact that she had never walked in Rowan's shoes, she could still empathise, and her heart bled for the lonely little girl.

It wouldn't always be this way, though, Laurel comforted herself. One day Rowan would lose the puppy fat and blossom. When her cheeks were less chubby her neat features would come into their own and she would be really pretty. The makings of it were already there in the small straight nose, heart-shaped jawline and thick dark lashes that fringed her aquamarine eyes. She'd grow in confidence, too, if she could win a scholarship to a good school.

Yes, hard though the present might be, Rowan had a bright future ahead of her. And no one would be more proud and delighted than Laurel herself.

Laurel was in the sitting room helping Rowan with some home-work Mr Shearn had set her – he hadn't wasted much time, she thought wryly – so she didn't hear the sound of a motor engine in the track outside the back door, though it attracted the curious attention of a number of the neighbours. The first she knew of it was when Earl, who had been sitting outside with Ezra smoking a cigarette, called through to her: 'Someone to see you, Laurel.'

'To see me?' Surprised and puzzled, Laurel pushed back her chair and got up. 'Just carry on, Rowan. You're doing fine.'

Wondering who on earth it could be, she went out to the scullery. The back door was wide open, and framed in the door-way was a man wearing a leather jacket in spite of the warmth of the evening. Goggles were pushed up onto his forehead to reveal a good-looking face adorned with a neatly clipped moustache. He was perhaps in his late twenties or early thirties.

Laurel's heart did a disconcerting flip.

'Ralph! What are you doing here?'

'Come to see you, of course.'

Ezra and Earl had both forgotten all about their cigarettes and were staring with undisguised interest at both the man and the motorcycle, parked on its stand in the middle of the track, and Laurel was aware of Minty peering over her shoulder. 'You had no business!' she said, embarrassed and flustered.

'It seems like the only way I'll get to see you now. Can't we talk?'

'There's nothing to talk about.' The words hovered on her lips, but he was unbuttoning his jacket, a sure sign that he had no intention of departing any time soon, and Laurel realised she was not going to get rid of him so easily.

But neither had she any intention of having a conversation here, with her family – and probably the neighbours too – for an audience.

'We'll go down the garden.'

She flounced across the track towards the gap in the out-houses, past Minty's rose bushes and the small patch of lawn, yellowed now from the lack of rain in recent weeks, stopping only when she reached Ezra's vegetable garden, where his prized runner beans were already climbing up their sticks.

'How did you know where to find me?' she demanded, turning to face him.

'I got your address from Edgar Sawyer.'

'How dare you? How dare *he*!'

'I had to see you, Laurel.' He reached for her hand, pulling her close, and for a moment the familiar scent of his leather jacket was in her nostrils, and the equally familiar chemistry that had sparked between them from the very first time they had met threatened to weaken her resolve. Then the anger flared again.

'Ralph, you know it's over. Why couldn't you just leave it?'

'I'm crazy about you, Laurel. You know that.'

'And you're also married. You have a wife, Ralph. Does she know you're here?'

Momentary guilt flickered across the handsome features.

'No, I didn't think so. I suppose you told her you were just going for a spin on a nice summer evening. The same way you lied to her every time you crept out to meet me. Well, I'm not having it. I'm not prepared to be "the other woman". And I'm not prepared to be responsible for breaking up your marriage either.'

'It's been over for years. I'd never have married Amy if Bertie hadn't been on the way . . .'

'But you did, Ralph. And you didn't even tell me you had a wife. I had to find that out for myself.'

Pain, sharp as razors, made her heart contract as she remembered. When she'd first met Ralph, a homeopathic doctor whose consulting rooms were situated on the ground floor of the building where Edgar Sawyer had his office, the attraction had been instant. She'd thought that at last she had found someone who could resurrect feelings she'd thought would lie dormant for ever. For months she'd been on a roller coaster of joy and excitement, hope, disappointment and frustration. And then one day she'd discovered the reason for the times he'd turned up late for a meeting, or not turned up at all. 'You do know, don't you, that he's married?' Edgar Sawyer had said, almost casually, and her world had come crashing down around her.

'I should have told you. I'm sorry,' he said now, reaching for her hand again.

Angrily she jerked it away.

'Yes, you should. How could you deceive me like that?'

'I was afraid of losing you.'

Another flash of something close to hope. Gathering all her resolve, she snuffed it out.

'I can't do this, Ralph. Why do you think I gave up my job and moved away?'

'But don't you see? Really, it's the ideal solution. I could easily come out on my motorbike to see you. I wouldn't be likely to bump into anyone who knows me out here . . .'

'That's exactly what I mean! The deceit! Just go, Ralph, please just go!' She was shouting now.

'Is everything all right?' A face appeared over the garden fence. Ewart Donovan! He must have been working on his own garden and she hadn't known he was there. Laurel's face flamed.

'Yes, fine thank you, Ewart,' she called, and turned back to Ralph, hissing through gritted teeth: 'Go on, leave! And don't come back!'

He raised his hands in mock surrender.

'You know where to find me if you change your mind. We had something special, Laurel. Don't throw it all away.'

With that, he walked away down the path. Laurel remained where she was until she heard the motorcycle engine putter into life and chug away. She was shaking from head to foot, mortified that Ewart Donovan had overheard at least part of the conversation as well as upset by the confrontation. Should she have a word with him? He'd obviously been concerned enough to intervene. But she couldn't bring herself to. At least he wasn't a gossip who'd spread her business to all and sundry, but he was sure to tell Cathy. She'd have to offer some kind of explanation when she next saw her.

And what on earth was she going to say to Mam? She couldn't tell the truth: that the main reason she had changed her job and moved away from Bath was not to be nearer to the family – although of course that was a bonus – but to escape from an illicit love affair. Mam would be outraged. She'd have to pretend he was just a man she wasn't interested in who was pursuing her. And all the while she'd feel as if her heart was breaking . . .

Why did it have to be like this? It seemed that falling in love with the wrong man was her speciality. This wasn't the first time she'd followed her heart, only to have it broken.

She stood for a few minutes, hands pressed to her mouth, composing herself, then headed back down the path.

Ezra and Earl were still outside, Earl smoking yet another cigarette.

'Who were that then?' Ezra asked.

'Oh, someone I knew in Bath.' Laurel tried to keep her voice steady. 'You won't be seeing him again, I hope.'

'I did rather get that impression,' Ezra said equably.

Good old Dad, Laurel thought. Taking everything as it comes, as usual. And Earl was more interested in the visitor's mode of transport than in the man himself.

'Fancy him having a motorbike! And a Triumph too! He must have a bit of money to have one of those.'

'Funny-looking contraption if you do ask me,' Ezra said. 'Just like a pushbike really, except for all the works attached under the crossbar.'

'That's what saves your legs, Dad . . .'

Laurel left them arguing the merits of a motorised bicycle and went inside.

Minty was in the scullery, ostensibly tidying the cupboard beside the sink, though Laurel guessed she was lingering there to ask a few questions out of Rowan's earshot. She looked up, her eyes beady in her doughy face, as Laurel came in.

'So what was all that about?'

Laurel repeated what she had said in answer to Ezra's question, adding, 'I'd really rather not talk about it, Mam.'

Minty sighed deeply, and nodded.

'I suppose you'll tell me when you're good and ready. At least I hope you will. Right now you look as if you could do with a cup of tea.'

'I certainly could. And I've got to get on with helping Rowan with her homework, too.'

She went back into the living room, where Rowan was still poring over her books, only grateful that she had got off so lightly. For now. Minty wouldn't let it go for ever. Laurel only hoped Cathy didn't mention to her anything that Ewart might have overheard. And that Ralph Riley had realised that pursuing her was a waste of both time and petrol.

# Chapter Five

To Laurel's relief, when she ran into Cathy the next day, her friend made no mention of the altercation in the garden. But, determined as she was that the affair was over, it had upset her, bringing all her old feelings for Ralph to the surface, reminding her of the good times they had shared before she had discovered he was married. And for some reason the bubbling cauldron of emotion had resurrected other memories, much older – and even more poignant – of another lost love.

Oh Callum . . . Strange the way her heart still twisted when she whispered his name softly to herself. How clearly she could still see his face – more handsome than anyone had a right to be – with his thick, coal-black curly hair and eyes the colour of deep rock pools when the sun shone on them, still feel the excitement his devil-may-care attitude had generated in the pit of her stomach. Everything about him had been exciting – his rogueish smile, his Irish accent and the words he used that were unfamiliar to her, his romantic and equally unfamiliar way of life – it had all thrummed in her blood like the jangling music of the fairground hurdy-gurdy.

She'd tried to forget him, but somehow he was always there, and always would be, casting a long shadow she could never quite escape.

And now her heart was aching all over again. This time for a man she still had feelings for even though she despised him for deceiving both her and his wife.

Just to make matters worse, Laurel had realised she had left her fountain pen behind when she vacated her office in Bath for the last time. How that had happened she couldn't understand: the pen was her pride and joy, saved up for and bought when she had first got the job. She could only imagine it had rolled to the back of her desk drawer. She'd written to Edgar Sawyer, hoping he had found it and recognised it as hers before her replacement clerk took possession of the desk and possibly her precious pen too! She hadn't heard back from him yet, but when she did, providing her pen was safe, she would have to make a trip back to the office to collect it, and the possibility that she would run into Ralph was a very real one, given that his surgery was in the same building.

Well, she'd cross that bridge when she came to it. She was due to start her new job next week, and if she wanted to make a good impression on her employers, she needed a clear head, not one that was filled with turmoil, confusion and regrets. The post at the hospital offered new beginnings. Laurel was determined to make the most of them.

At about midday every Saturday, the men who worked the dark seams beneath the green countryside gathered in their local public houses to share out their teams' earnings. Some went straight home, giving their wives their entire pay to be spent as they thought fit, some stayed for a few drinks with their mates first, some parted with more than they could afford, along with a scrap of paper that served as a betting slip, passing it surreptitiously to the bookie's runners, young lads who hung about in the street outside.

Earl wasn't much of a one for gambling, though he did have the odd flutter on a horse or a football result. Really it was a mug's game, he thought. His father maintained the bookie always won in the end, and having once lost an entire week's wages on a much-fancied runner in the Grand National, Earl had decided his father was probably right. But a couple of his pals lived in hopes of a big win, and that Saturday, after the pot had been shared out, there was a heated discussion over a few pints as to the likeliest victors in the afternoon's races.

'What d'you fancy then, Earl?' Ted Young brushed beer foam from his top lip with the back of his hand.

'None of 'em really.' Earl was glancing down the list of runners.

'Come on, you've got to pick one at least.' Tommy Blanning had already written his selection on a page torn from an almanac. 'Where's your get up and go?'

'It got up and went if you ask me,' Ted chortled.

'Oh, all right. Give us a piece of paper then.'

Tommy tore another page from the almanac and pushed it across the table, together with a stub of pencil, and Earl ran his eye down the list of runners again.

'Okay. Pretty Polly in the three o'clock, and that's it.'

'Doesn't stand a chance,' Tommy scoffed. Though he generally lost more than he won, he considered himself something of an expert.

'It's good odds.'

'Not if it comes in last.'

'An' we all know why you picked that one,' Ted said grinning.

'So what?' Earl had been after Polly Brimble, a pretty girl from Hillsbridge, for some time, though he hadn't yet managed to persuade her to go out for a walk with him. 'Maybe she'll bring me luck.'

'You hope.'

Earl scribbled the details on the slip of paper, then the three lads sorted out some money, finished their pints and left the pub.

As they'd expected, Reggie Yarlett, a skinny lad in short trousers and hobnail boots, was hanging about just outside the door. He took their slips and cash, pushing it all into the pocket of a jacket that was a size too big for him – a hand-me-down he hadn't yet grown into, by the look of it.

'Don't you lose it,' Tommy warned.

The lad made a rude gesture in his direction and set off at a clumsy trot.

'Hey – look!' Ted had spotted a Humberette cyclecar drawn up at the kerb where the road leading to the Catholic church forked off from the main street. Motors were as rare a sight in High Compton as they were in most places, always worthy of attention. 'Isn't that Taffy's?'

'Looks like it.'

Taffy Jones, manager at Marston Colliery where they all worked, had rolled up in the vehicle for the first time a couple of days previously, causing quite a stir, and parked it outside his office window so that he could keep an eye on it.

'Let's have a gander.'

They strolled down the street to the Humberette, circling it, and giving the tyres a surreptitious kick.

'Don't look very substantial,' Ted commented.

'More than you or I could afford.'

Substantial or not, they couldn't help but be impressed by the contraption, with its red bench seat and matching wheel hubs. A lady's hat lay on the seat, wide-brimmed straw with long chiffon streamers that could be tied beneath its owner's chin to keep it from blowing away. It must belong to Mrs Jones, the lads supposed – Taffy must have driven her into town on some errand and she had taken it off rather than wear it into a shop.

'Hey, you'd look good in that, Earl!' Tommy reached into the cyclecar and picked up the hat. 'Go on – try it on.'

'Try it on yourself!'

'No, you got the looks for it.' He plonked the hat on Earl's head, and entering into the spirit of the thing, Earl tied the streamers in a flouncy bow around his neck.

'What d'you think then, lads?'

'Hey, miss! Give us a kiss!'

'Bugger off!'

Like the others, Earl was in high spirits, money in his pocket and a couple of beers in his belly. He minced away from Tommy, dancing round the car and tossing his head jauntily. Ted and Tommy were doubled up with mirth and Earl's vision was severely restricted by the billowing chiffon, so none of them noticed Taffy Jones and his wife emerge from the hardware shop a little further down the street. The first they knew of it was a bellow like an angry bull.

'What the devil do you think you're doing?' Earl stopped mid caper. 'That's my wife's new hat!'

Enraged, Taffy made a grab for it just as Earl struggled to untie the bow, and there was an ominous rending sound as the chiffon ripped.

'Oh!' Mrs Jones had reached them now, a little out of breath, her plump cheeks puffed and scarlet with outrage. 'Idris! Do something! My hat . . .'

Steam was practically coming out of Taffy's ears.

'Bloody hooligans! I've a good mind to have the law on you!'

''Twas only a bit of fun, Mr Jones . . .'

'Fun my arse! You've been drinking!'

'There's no law against us having a drink.' Tommy had put a safe distance between himself and the furious pit manager.

'But there is against helping yourself to property that doesn't belong to you. And I'll have less of your cheek, boyo!'

'Leave it, Tommy,' Ted warned.

Taffy waved the torn chiffon ribbon beneath Earl's nose.

'You'll pay for this. Your wages will be docked next week. And if any damage has been done to my motor . . .'

He walked around the cyclecar, brushing off a speck of dirt here and there and making a thorough inspection. Earl thought he seemed almost disappointed that he could find nothing else to blame the lads for.

'Make yourselves scarce, the three of you.'

The lads knew better than to argue. Leaving Taffy to attempt to console his distraught wife, they headed off down the street, doing their best to appear unfazed. But Earl was only too aware that Taffy would be ready now to haul him over the coals for the slightest misdemeanour. He wished he could go somewhere conditions were better, well away from Taffy Jones, but he couldn't. It had been made all too clear to him that his father's job depended on him remaining as his carting boy. There was no option left to him but to grin and bear it.

One thing, though, had him smiling again before the day was out. Pretty Polly romped home at fourteen-to-one in the three o'clock race.

'Lucky bloody sod!' Tommy commented as he kissed goodbye to his own stake money.

'See? I told you!'

Earl was jubilant. The winnings would more than make up for Taffy Jones docking his next week's pay. He only hoped that he would be as fortunate where the real pretty Polly was concerned.

* * *

As the pony and trap came to a halt outside the wicket gate set amid high laurel hedges, Maggie Withers swallowed hard at a lump that had risen in her throat, the memories flooding back.

For a fleeting moment she was once again the desperate and frightened young woman who had first come here hoping for a job as a housekeeper that would enable her to keep and raise the child she was carrying. But instead she had become Lawrence's wife. He had offered her security and asked nothing in return. He had nurtured her artistic talent. He had accepted Patrick as his own child. She had come to love him – not in the way she loved Josh, but more as a father figure – and also to love the creeper-covered cottage that sat in a triangle of land where three lanes converged.

A faint smile twitched on her lips as she remembered the chaos that had met her that first time she stepped inside: not an inch of clear space anywhere for the piles of newspapers, books and used crockery; the dark-stained wood floor and worn rugs soiled with mud and leaves trodden in from the garden. She hadn't even fancied the cup of tea or hot chocolate he had offered her – she'd thought the crockery would need a good wash before she could bring herself to drink from it. But she'd soon changed all that. What had so clearly been a bachelor's abode had become a warm and welcoming home and her memories of the time she had spent there were mostly happy ones.

When Lawrence had died so tragically the cottage had passed to her, and though she had scarcely lived in it since, having gone to New York to fulfil his dying wish that she should restore the stained-glass window he had been working on, seeing it now, nestling amongst the shrubs and hawthorns, felt like coming home. But at the same time it was a fresh start for her and her little family, a place where she and Josh could raise their children and perhaps make their dreams of building a profitable business a reality.

'Come on, Maggie, are you going to sit there all day?'

Josh was helping Fred Carson unload their baggage and stacking it beside the wicket gate.

'Yes, come on, Mom!' Patrick jiggled impatiently as he tried to peer between the bars.

Maggie climbed out of the trap and lifted Nora down. The little girl ran to join her brother, and the moment Josh lifted the latch and pushed the gate open they disappeared inside, eager to see their new home.

Maggie picked up one of the holdalls and followed more slowly. There must have been a storm this morning – the old familiar scent of rain on grass and leaves mingled with the perfume of the roses, which were in full bloom. They needed pruning, Maggie noticed; indeed, the whole garden was looking uncared for, but she'd have plenty of time to attend to it in the weeks ahead. Her gaze moved to the outbuilding that had been Lawrence's studio: ivy had grown up, almost obscuring the windows and door, but at least it indicated that her instructions had been adhered to and the tenants hadn't been making use of it. All the tools of her late husband's trade would be there untouched, just as he had left them, ready for her to take up where she had left off.

Patrick was darting in and out of the bushes, his face a picture of excitement. Nora, trotting after him, caught her foot in a tree root, tumbled to her knees and began to cry. Maggie rescued her, brushing her down.

'It's just a bit of dirt, my love. You're not hurt. Don't you want to see inside?'

The door key was exactly where it always had been, hidden under a flowerpot beside the water butt. Maggie fitted it into the lock, and turned to wait for Josh, who had paid Fred Carson and was now carrying their bags down the crazy-paved path towards her.

He'd only been here the once, when he'd heard she was going to America and might not come back, and the visit had been torture for both of them. When he was unable to change her mind, Josh had believed she was just making yet another excuse to prevent them being together, when quite the opposite was true. She had wanted nothing more than to be with him, but she had also been determined to keep her promise to Lawrence. She hadn't known then that Josh would follow her to Liverpool and board the *Campania* just in time before she sailed; he hadn't even known it himself. He'd brought a toy railway engine he'd made for Patrick – she still had it, packed carefully in one of the holdalls – and she knew that both their hearts had been breaking as he gave it to his son, knowing that this might be the last time he would ever see him.

Now, very aware that this was the house where she had lived with Lawrence, she wanted to ensure that Josh felt it was his home as much as hers.

'You go in first,' she said.

Josh set down the bags he was carrying and his eyes met hers, dark and full of love, and she knew he understood.

Then, almost before she realised what was happening, he bent, one arm beneath her knees, the other around her shoulders, and lifted her into his arms.

'I reckon this is what's called for,' he said with a smile.

And with their children following excitedly, he carried her over the threshold.

On Monday morning, Laurel made sure she set off for the hospital in good time, riding her bicycle for the first mile or so, then getting off to push it up the steepest part of the hill. The rubber handle grips felt sticky and she realised her hands must be moist with perspiration – not from exertion but from the nerves that were fluttering in her stomach. Everything was going to be so different to what she was used to. Edgar Sawyer had been an easy man to work for, and for the most part he'd left her to her own devices; in fact, quite often it had been her who had chided him about the need for keeping proper records and not confusing the filing system. The hospital, she felt sure, would be run on much more efficient lines, and any mistakes could have serious consequences. As for the doctors she would be working for, already she felt in awe of them.

Ralph is a doctor, she reminded herself. But somehow that was different. A homeopathic practice wasn't the same as having patients' lives in your hands, doling out proper medication, doing operations, even. And they would be relying on her not to make stupid mistakes . . .

Laurel wiped her moist hands on her skirt, remounted her bicycle and rode the last few yards to the hospital, which was set on the brow of the hill, overlooking green fields and the outskirts of High Compton. Only the slag heap – the batch, as they called it – was higher, rising like a black carbuncle from the surrounding countryside.

When Mr Seabrook, chairman of the committee that had interviewed her, had offered her the job, he'd said she should report to Matron, but as she went in through the main doors it was a small, neat woman wearing not a uniform but a brown and yellow checked blouse and brown skirt who stepped forward to greet her. She was, perhaps, in her late forties or early fifties. Wire-rimmed spectacles made her brown eyes look enormous, and her hair, now greying and swept back into a tight knot, had also once been brown, judging by the streaks that remained, dark amidst the grey.

'You must be Miss Sykes.' She held out her hand. 'I'm Miss Perrett. I've been asked to come in this morning to familiarise you with the office where you'll be working.'

'Oh!' Laurel was a little taken aback. 'Is it your job I'll be taking over then?'

'It is indeed. One I've done for more than twenty years.' Her tone was prim, yet touched with pride. 'I'm taking retirement in order to care for Mother. She can no longer be left alone, even though I reduced my hours to part-time working. So it is with great sadness that I am forced to relinquish my duties. But the least I can do is ensure that the handover is as smooth as possible. Matron is rightly very particular about the way business is done. As is Mr Seabrook, of course.'

'Of course.'

Laurel had been quite intimidated by Mr Seabrook, who, although he was now quite old and not a little doddery, still retained all the authoritative presence of the founding partner of a well-respected legal practice in High Compton. Yes, she could well imagine he would expect a high level of competence in the running of the hospital's records, accounts and day-to-day administration.

Miss Perrett led the way through double swing doors and along a corridor. A nurse pushing a trolley flattened herself against the wall to let them pass, nodding a respectful good morning. The retiring secretary clearly commanded respect amongst the staff. But the office she led Laurel into was far less impressive – little larger than a cupboard, the walls lined with filing cabinets. A desk and chair occupied the remaining space, but at least it faced the window, with a view out over fields and hedgerows, and the typewriter that sat in the middle of the desk was a magnificent specimen – an almost new Remington, its shiny black casing adorned with small posies of pink and white flowers. It was a far cry from the one Edgar Sawyer had provided her with – that hadn't had a proper casing at all and looked as if it had come out of the ark.

For the next hour or so, Miss Perrett ran through Laurel's duties, explained the filing system and showed her the accounts books. Soon after ten o'clock a knock at the door announced the arrival of a junior nurse with a trolley bearing a small tea urn, milk, sugar and biscuits.

'Ah – most welcome, Heal,' Miss Perrett said, making a neat pile of the paperwork laid out on the desk so that it would be safely out of the way of any spillage. 'You'd like a cup of tea, I expect, Miss Sykes?'

'Thank you, I would,' Laurel said, grateful for a break in which to gather her thoughts.

'So – you have been working for a private investigator?' Miss Perrett said when the tea had been dispensed and the nurse left with her rattling trolley.

'Yes.' For some reason Laurel felt a little embarrassed about her previous employment. Somehow the description 'private investigator' sounded less than respectable. Her friends had often asked salacious questions about the nature of the investigations, but Laurel couldn't imagine that the prim Miss Perrett would be interested in the gory details. 'Though it's not nearly as exciting as it sounds,' she added.

'No murders or scandalous affairs?'

Perhaps Miss Perrett was not quite as prim as she appeared.

'No murders. He wasn't exactly Sherlock Holmes. And only a few scandalous affairs.' Laurel wasn't going to go into detail about those cases, nor mention the fact that she had sometimes suspected Edgar might be mixed up in shady dealings, though none had ever crossed her desk. 'Mostly though it was tracing the beneficiaries of wills, or lost relatives.'

'I hope you won't find your work here too boring by comparison. Although we do have our moments of excitement . . .' An unexpected twinkle appeared in the brown eyes behind the owlish spectacles. 'Now, I haven't yet mentioned the private work you will do for some of our local medical practices. The larger ones employ a full-time secretary, of course, but where there is only one doctor working alone it hardly merits that. Dr Blackmore – you'll know him, no doubt – is very old school, always reluctant to send out the bills. If I hadn't nagged him into it he'd have gone bankrupt long ago. I've always gone to him on a Friday morning, though you have to set aside most of the day to get things shipshape. Then there's Dr Hicks, who's just down the road in Stanton Magna, quite a stickler and, between you and me, the exact opposite of Dr Blackmore. If bills are not paid promptly, you'll have to be sure to send out reminders.'

Laurel nodded. 'Yes, of course.'

'You'll find Dr Mackay over in Hillsbridge much easier to deal with,' Miss Perrett went on. 'He's young and likes to keep things up together. He brings his books and paperwork here to be dealt with. My days of walking so far are long since over, I'm afraid.'

She crossed to a shelf and took down a ledger, which, unlike most of the others with their scuffed binding and well-thumbed pages, looked quite clean and new, and a similarly pristine cardboard folder.

'These are his. The bills are sent out once a month, though quite a lot of his patients like to pay in cash as they go. I've made up the books to date, but he'll pop in at odd times with his receipt book and a note of ongoing charges, so be prepared for that.'

'And the doctors pay the hospital for my time?' Laurel said.

'Yes. And there is the incentive that if you bring in more work it will be reflected in your salary. I wasn't interested in taking on more, but you may well feel differently. Although of course I should point out that if you upset any of the doctors and they decide to take their books elsewhere, then I would expect that your salary would be reduced accordingly.'

'Yes, of course . . .' Laurel was beginning to feel apprehensive again.

Another knock at the door, and then it was opened before Miss Perrett could utter a response. A tall, lanky man with a mop of reddish-brown hair who looked to be in his middle thirties came breezing in. He was wearing a tweed jacket that looked as if it had seen better days and carrying a medical bag.

'Dr Mackay!' Miss Perrett greeted him. 'We were just talking about you.'

'All good, I hope.' He spoke with a soft burr that Laurel recognised as Scottish.

'Of course!' But a faint colour had risen in Miss Perrett's cheeks. Dried-up old spinster she might appear, but she had a soft spot for the doctor if Laurel was not much mistaken.

'I'd a patient to visit on the women's ward, so I thought I'd look in and introduce myself to our new clerk while I was here.' He turned to Laurel with a friendly smile. 'You must be Miss Sykes. You'll be looking after my accounts, I understand.'

'I hope so,' Laurel said.

'If you do as good a job as Miss Perrett here, we shall get along just fine. But we're certainly going to miss her.' He turned his smile on the older woman, and her flush deepened, though Laurel knew it was one of pleasure.

A shadow darkened the doorway and another man came into the room. Stockily built, with bushy jet-black sideburns, and formally dressed in a black coat, waistcoat and striped trousers, he could scarcely have been more different to the cheery, casual young doctor, though he was probably not that much older.

Laurel recognised him as one of the board who had interviewed her for the job, sitting on the right-hand side of Mr Seabrook. She hadn't cared for the look of him then, and she didn't care for the look of him now, but she told herself she shouldn't make snap judgements about people.

'Mr Sinclair. This is an unexpected pleasure!' Miss Perrett's colour was still high, but not now from pleasure, Laurel judged.

'Aubrey.' Dr Mackay nodded briefly in the newcomer's direction. 'I must get on with my rounds,' he said to Miss Perrett, 'but just let me wish you all the best for your retirement,' and to Laurel: 'I'll be back with some more work for you before long, no doubt.'

Then he was gone, obviously anxious to escape the stuffed shirt, who seemed to have the knack of making everyone uncomfortable.

'I promised Mr Seabrook I would look in and ensure our new appointment is settling in.' Mr Sinclair addressed Miss Perrett almost as if Laurel wasn't there, then turned to her, looking her up and down. 'I hope Miss Perrett is setting you on the right track. She will be sorely missed.'

'I'm sure Miss Sykes will be more than able to keep up standards.' The older woman saved Laurel from replying.

'Good. Very good.' Without another word, he turned and marched out of the room as if he were a general inspecting a military parade.

'Don't be put off. His bark is worse than his bite,' Miss Perrett said, closing the door, which he had left open.

'He was on the panel that interviewed me,' Laurel said. 'Who is he?'

'You don't know? Mr Sinclair is a partner in Mr Seabrook's firm of solicitors. If and when Mr Seabrook retires, he will take over his responsibilities – which will include the chairmanship of the hospital board.'

Laurel felt a twinge of misgiving. Intimidating as Mr Seabrook had been, she thought she would far rather he was her employer than the unpleasant Mr Sinclair. She hoped it would be a long while before that happened.

# Chapter Six

It was well after four on Friday afternoon before Mr Shearn eventually brought Rowan's session of extra tuition to a close, but she didn't mind that. She enjoyed sitting at the desk in the headmaster's room, working through the sheets of arithmetic problems or pieces of comprehension, then standing beside his chair as he marked her answers and explained the things she had got wrong or not understood properly. Not that she made many mistakes, and she glowed with pride when he praised her efforts. She enjoyed being stretched. Too often in normal lessons she was frustrated at the inability of some of her classmates to grasp the things that came so easily to her, and the length of time the teacher had to spend explaining the same thing over and over again when she was eager to learn something new.

Another advantage to being kept late was that the other children had long since left by the time Mr Shearn released her. Not that they'd bothered her too much since Laurel had caught them bullying her and made an example of Beatie Emery. Beatie and her gang still ostracised her, turning their backs and whispering in a tight little huddle, but there had been no more physical attacks and less name-calling. And Dorcas Deacon, who sat next to her, had actually been quite friendly towards her, lending her a rubber when her own made a dirty splodge on the paper when they were drawing a map of England, and offering to do a swap with her for some of her cigarette cards – she saved the ones that Earl had discarded as surplus to his own collection.

Dorcas wasn't one of Beatie's closed circle; she and a couple of others usually played by themselves, and they lacked the magic that seemed to touch Beatie. Florrie Ball had an iron splint on one leg and a built-up shoe, Maisie Ford was none too bright, and Trixie Peek, small and thin with a permanent drip on the end of her snub nose, had only just stopped wetting her knickers, which had been a source of great amusement to the others when they were hung over the guard round the coke stove to dry. But Rowan was grateful that Dorcas was now inviting her to join in their games, even if it was only holding one end of the long skipping rope while Florrie held the other.

When Rowan emerged from Mr Shearn's office and went out into the playground that Friday afternoon, the block of privies on the far side of the yard was casting long shadows on the sunlit concrete and a cloud of dust was rising from a trench that ran along the edge of the yard beside the gate. Mr Thomas, the caretaker, and his wife and daughter lived in a cottage that backed onto the school, and the slope of the road meant that while their front door was at street level, the back was several feet beneath the playground. As she neared it, Rowan could see the top half of Mrs Thomas, beating a rug hung over a washing line, and hear the regular thwack-thwack as the beater struck the brightly coloured knotted rags on the hessian base.

Suddenly, unexpectedly, she was remembering the night, so long ago now, when she'd been woken by a commotion beneath her bedroom window and seen Mammy doing something similar to what Mrs Thomas was doing now. Though it was years since she'd thought about it, the memory was crystal clear. Because she had been so frightened, she supposed.

A shiver ran through her as she remembered huddling beneath the bed, too afraid to move although she was shivering with the cold. Mammy had said she'd just been having a bad dream, and Rowan supposed that must have been it. Certainly next day everything had seemed to be quite normal: Mammy grumbling, Daddy putting in the beans he'd been unable to plant the previous day because of the bad weather, Earl sleeping late after a night out at the fair. And it had never been mentioned since. Even if it hadn't been a nightmare, she must have been half asleep and imagined it, she thought. But all the same, and in spite of the warmth of the afternoon, the memory sent a shiver down her spine.

Trying not to think about it any more, she hoisted her satchel up onto her shoulder and set out on the long walk home. The hot sun was warming the leather and Rowan smiled as she smelled it. Laurel had bought the satchel for her – 'Something for when you go to school in Bath,' she'd said, as if it was already a dead certainty. It wasn't brand new; Laurel had got it in a second-hand shop, and there were a few signs of wear – a scratch here, a scrape there, and an ink splodge or two on the inside of the flap where someone else had marked their name and then erased it. But now 'Rowan Sykes' was written there in thick black ink, and with the satchel on her shoulder Rowan could almost believe she really had got the longed-for scholarship and was a pupil at a school where nobody would scoff at her for wanting to learn.

As she turned off the main road into the lane that led to Fairley Terrace, she could hear the shrill shouts of children playing. The Donovan boys from next door, she guessed.

Mammy was forever complaining about the noise they made, as well as the hopscotch grid they drew on the path with a bit of chalky stone.

'Nippers will always be nippers,' Daddy would say, equable as he invariably was, and Mammy would argue:

'You're at work and you don't have to listen to them, Ezra. I don't know why they have to scream like that. Why can't they play quietly? There's no need for screaming.'

Rowan guessed her mother would be fuming now at the disturbance. She wouldn't want to close the door and windows to shut out the racket on such a warm afternoon.

She turned the corner into the track that ran along the rank of houses, and sure enough, there they were, two tousle-headed lads – Ollie and Percy Donovan – tearing about like madmen as they chased each other and fought over a pig's bladder they used for a football. But they weren't the only ones. Besides their sister Freda, who was fussing over a doll in an orange box on wheels, there was another little girl and a boy she guessed was about her own age, neither of whom she had ever seen before. The girl was bending over Freda's makeshift pram; the older boy appeared to be refereeing the younger ones' kickabout.

As she approached, Ollie, the older of the Donovan boys, booted the pig's bladder hard and high. It flew straight at her, catching her full in the chest so that it almost knocked the wind out of her. She staggered, caught off balance, and her satchel slid down her arm, scuffing on the ground before she could stop it. An apple that she'd taken for her lunch but not eaten shot out of the front pocket and rolled across the track.

The two young culprits stopped short, freezing as if they had been turned into pillars of salt; the girls looked up for a moment from their perambulator, then went back to their make-believe world. But the older boy, the one Rowan had never seen before, came running up the track towards her.

'Hey – are you all right?'

He was taller than her by several inches, with a mop of dark curly hair and dark eyes, but it was his voice that caught Rowan's attention. He spoke with a drawl unlike anything she'd ever heard before.

'I think so,' she said, bending to pick up her satchel.

The boy was retrieving her apple.

'Here.' He held it out to her. 'Are you sure they didn't hurt you?'

Rowan shook her head, overcome by sudden shyness.

'They're mad, the pair of them,' he said. 'Hey – come here, you two, and say sorry.'

The Donovan boys had no intention of going anywhere near Rowan. Not that they had any quarrel with her, but her mother was always lambasting them, and they had her down as tarred with the same brush.

'Sorry!' they called, keeping their distance. Ollie retrieved the pig's bladder from where it had rolled into the gutter and they began kicking it about again, albeit less boisterously than before.

'D'you live along here?' the boy asked Rowan.

'Yes. Next door to those two.' She began to walk towards her back door, and he fell into step beside her.

'What's your name then?'

'Rowan.' She was avoiding looking at him.

'I'm Patrick Withers, and that's my sister, Nora.' He nodded in the direction of the little girl who was playing with Freda Donovan. 'My granny and grampy live down the end of the rank, at number ten. And these troublemakers are my cousins. Their father is my mom's brother.'

'Oh . . .' It was all too much for Rowan to take in, even if she wasn't feeling flustered by the attention of this strange boy. 'But . . . ?' *Why do you have that funny accent?* she wanted to ask, but of course she did not.

'We've just got here from America,' Patrick said, as if he had read her mind.

'America!' Rowan was startled out of her shyness. 'What – you're here on holiday?'

'No, we've come back here to live. On the biggest ship you ever saw.'

Rowan had never seen a ship bigger than a paddle steamer, but it wasn't that that caught her attention.

'You're going to live *here*?' she asked, surprised. There were no empty properties in the rank, and she couldn't imagine how another family could fit into the Donovans' house.

'No, not here. In a house – well, a cottage – near here. It's really nice. It's got a big yard . . . Mom calls it a garden.'

'We've got a garden.' Rowan pointed in the direction of the long strips behind the privies and outhouses.

'Ours goes all round the house.' Patrick was fascinated by it – he'd never seen a house with a garden before last week. 'We've got trees and everything. I'm going to get Dad to put up a rope on a branch so I can swing on it.'

Rowan was impressed. There was a tree down by the river with a rope attached to a branch. The boys, and even some of the girls, hung on to it and took a running jump to get from one side of the river to the other, but she had never dared to try it.

The Donovan boys were beginning to be boisterous again, shrieking at the top of their lungs as they ran up and down the track. Suddenly Rowan's mother appeared in the doorway, her face as red as the geraniums in a pot beneath the window.

'Can't you play quietly?'

'We're not doing no harm, missus!' Ollie yelled back, and then, perhaps emboldened by the presence of his older cousin, kicked the pig's bladder in her direction.

'You little . . . !' Moving very fast for a woman her size, Minty stooped and picked it up. 'I'm having this. I'm not putting up with the racket you're making any more.'

'You can't do that, missus!' Ollie cried, dismayed. 'That's ourn!'

'I think you'll find I can.'

'Whatever's going on?' Cathy emerged from her doorway.

'I'll thank you to keep your boys under control,' Minty snapped. 'I don't want to fall out, but they really are the limit.' She jabbed the pig's bladder with her thumb. 'Kicked this right at me, your Ollie did, and I'm keeping hold of it till they can learn to behave.'

'Oh, I'm sorry, Mrs Sykes. They're just letting off steam, but they should know better than to . . . Let me have the ball. I'll take it in . . . I'm ashamed of you two,' she added, with a stern look at the young culprits.

Reluctantly Minty handed over the pig's bladder, and wiped her hands on her apron.

'Well, I hope they'll behave themselves in future.' She turned towards Rowan, seeming to notice the boy with her for the first time. 'Who's this then?'

'That's my nephew, Patrick.' Cathy spoke for him. 'Josh and Maggie's son. I told you they were coming home from America, didn't I?'

'Oh, well . . .' Minty huffed. 'Come on, Rowan – in!'

Rowan hesitated, looking at the boy and then at her mother. She'd been enjoying talking to him, enjoying the fact that he wasn't sneering at her but treating her as an equal, and fascinated by the fact that he had lived on the other side of the Atlantic.

'In, I said!' Her mother moved to one side, gesturing to Rowan like a policeman directing traffic and glowering at Patrick.

Rowan gave him a faint apologetic smile and did as she was told. But as her mother slammed the door shut after them, she turned to her, hurt and bewildered.

'Mam, why—'

'I don't want you talking to the likes of him.' Minty's lips were set in a hard line.

'But he was really nice! He—'

'His mother is no better than she should be. Nor his father, from what I hear of it. Not the sort we want anything to do with. Let's just hope they don't come visiting next door too often.'

She crossed to the sink, washing her hands with a bar of carbolic soap, and Rowan went into the living room, where she dusted off her precious satchel with her handkerchief.

She was embarrassed at the way Minty had spoken to her in front of the boy, and puzzled too as to what she had meant about his mother being 'no better than she should be'. He'd seemed perfectly respectable as well as kind and friendly, and she was upset that she had been forbidden to speak to him again. But it wasn't in Rowan's nature to disobey, or even to question her mother. Mam knew best. She was all-wise. All-powerful.

Or so it seemed to Rowan.


'What was all that about?' Maggie asked when Cathy came back in carrying the pig's bladder.

'Oh, nothing really. Just my neighbour being her usual miserable self. I don't know what's the matter with her. I know my boys can be a bit noisy, but they're just kids being kids. It's her daughter I feel sorry for. Poor Rowan. She's a nice little girl, but my goodness, does Mrs Sykes keep her on a tight rein!'

'That's a recipe for trouble if ever I heard one.'

'Yes, I wouldn't be surprised if she kicks over the traces when she's older. I certainly wouldn't blame her. But it's none of my business.'

Maggie shook her head. 'Some people!'

'She's an old cow and no mistake. But who knows what's made her like she is? Now, you were telling me how you're going to make one of the outhouses into a workshop for Josh when we were interrupted . . .'

Maggie and Cathy resumed their earlier conversation, and Minty Sykes and her funny ways were forgotten.


'I'm going to Bath tomorrow,' Laurel said as they were having tea.

'What – to see that chap with the motorbike?' Minty's eyes were beady and suspicious in her puffy face.

'No. To get my fountain pen.'

A letter had arrived a couple of days ago from Edgar Sawyer, saying that yes, Laurel's replacement had found the pen in the back of the desk drawer, and Laurel was anxious to have it safely back in her possession as soon as possible. She loved that pen, and really missed it. The one she'd borrowed to make entries in the hospital account books was horrid and scratchy by comparison.

She only hoped she didn't run into Ralph Riley. Sometimes he saw patients on a Saturday, and she had to pass right by his consulting room door to get to her old office. And yet at the same time, a small treacherous part of her was hoping she might see him. For all her good intentions, all the determination she'd summoned up to end what she now knew had been nothing more than a sordid affair, Laurel acknowledged she still had feelings for him.

'Can I come with you?' Rowan begged.

'No, missy, you can't,' Minty said sharply – she was still smarting at the thought of Rowan talking to that Donovan boy, as she thought of him, even though she knew his name was Withers. 'You've got homework to do that Mr Shearn set, haven't you?'

'She's got the whole weekend yet,' Laurel argued. But Minty was adamant. If Rowan was to stand any chance of the scholarship she and Laurel were so keen on, she was going to have to keep her nose to the grindstone.

Next morning as she walked to the station to catch an early train to Bath, the conflicting emotions concerning Ralph still bubbled inside Laurel, unsettling her, and by the time she reached her old office – and Ralph's consulting rooms – her heart was thudding and her stomach felt as if it had tied itself in knots.

The door that opened onto the street was, as usual, unlocked, but as she went into the entrance lobby she saw that Ralph's door, with its gleaming brass plate, was firmly closed. Either he was with a patient or he wasn't in today. She hurried past and up the flight of stairs.

Edgar Sawyer's offices were on the first floor. The plate on his door – 'E. Sawyer, Private Investigator' – was no less impressive than Ralph's, but Laurel knew that once inside, there was no comparison. Whereas Ralph's consulting rooms were freshly decorated and furnished with no expense spared, Edgar's offices were badly in need of some loving care and attention. The heavy old desks were scratched and pockmarked, the chairs had wonky backs, the wallpaper was faded and peeling in places and the paintwork yellowing. A private detective made far less than a homeopathic consultant, and Laurel had sometimes wondered how her employer managed to pay her wages.

She opened the door without bothering to knock. The room it opened into was the one that had been her office. From it, another door, the paintwork scuffed, led to Edgar's sanctum. It was closed – Edgar was with a client, she guessed.

She crossed to the desk that used to be hers, sat down in the typist's chair and opened the top drawer. The tray of pencils, erasers and other oddments that she had always kept so neat was overflowing beneath an untidy stack of envelopes. Laurel frowned. Her successor clearly wasn't as keen on keeping things shipshape as she had been. She slid her hand beneath the envelopes, but the pen wasn't there. Edgar must have taken it for safe keeping when he'd received her letter. But at least the new secretary hadn't purloined it for herself.

Well, nothing for it, she'd have to wait until he finished with his client. She could hear the soft hum of voices coming from behind the closed door to his office and she knew better than to interrupt.

For want of something better to do, she pulled the old typewriter towards her. How many times had she broken her fingernails on those metal-ringed keys! Yet touching them again made her feel strangely nostalgic. She'd been happy here, and the work had been so interesting. Much more so than she'd found it so far at the hospital. But hopefully she'd get used to it in time, and she was looking forward to visiting the surgeries of the doctors whose accounts she was going to be keeping.

The door to Edgar's office opened and Edgar and a tall young man with fair hair flopping over his forehead emerged.

For a brief moment Edgar looked startled to see her there, but he quickly recovered himself, merely nodding an acknowledgment for all the world as if she still worked here.

'I'll be in touch.' He was ushering the young man out.

'I'll wait to hear from you.'

The young man had an accent that wasn't local – certainly not a Somerset burr, nor the classless ring of some of Edgar's gentlemen and lady clients, the ones whose business was always treated in the strictest confidence. As for his appearance, he looked too young to be checking up on a straying wife, one of the most common reasons for clients to seek Edgar's help. Laurel's curiosity was piqued. She only hoped he *was* a client, and not a prospective partner in some shady business. Edgar was not above pushing the boundaries of the law – on more than one occasion she'd got the impression that there had been close calls and had worried that he would end up in serious trouble. But it wasn't her problem now.

After exchanging a few more words with the young man in tones too quiet for her to hear what they were saying, Edgar breezed back into the office.

'Well, this is quite like old times! For a minute there I thought I was seeing a ghost!'

Laurel smiled. 'I'm very much alive, I'm glad to say.'

'You've come for your pen, I'm thinking.'

'And you'd be right. It's good to know your detection skills are as sharp as ever.'

This was something else she was missing – the cheery banter between her and her employer.

'How is my replacement getting on?' she asked. 'By the state of the desk drawer, she's not very tidy.'

'I wouldn't know about that. But she's not a patch on you, Miss Sykes, and she's not keen on working Saturdays, as I expect you've noticed. You can have your old job back any time you like.'

'I wish . . . But I'm afraid I won't be coming back so long

as . . .' She broke off, signalling the consulting rooms beneath the office with a flick of her eyes.

'I know, I know.' He pulled a packet of cigarettes out of his pocket, extracted one and placed it between his lips. 'And what about your new job? I suppose you've got all them young doctors chasing after you now.'

Laurel laughed. 'The only ones I've met so far are old and crusty.'

That wasn't quite true, she thought, remembering the red-haired young Dr Mackay. But she'd only met him the once, very briefly at that, and though he had seemed friendly, he certainly hadn't shown the slightest interest in her on a personal level.

And just as well! Like Ralph, he probably had a wife at home. There was no way Laurel was going to make the same mistake twice.

'I've got to be going if I'm going to catch my train home,' she said. 'If I could just have my pen, I'll leave you to get on with your detecting.'

Edgar went into his office, returning with the pen and also his coat.

'Here you go.' He handed her the pen, and shrugged into the coat, his eyes narrowed against the smoke from the cigarette clamped between his lips. 'I've just got a bit of business to attend to, then I'm taking the rest of the day off myself.'

He ushered her out of the office, and locked the door behind them.

As she made her way back to Green Park station, Laurel found herself wondering again just what business it was Edgar had to attend to, and whether it had anything to do with the young man who had seemed such an unlikely client. Just don't do anything silly and get yourself into trouble, Mr Sawyer, she thought.

Really, it was nothing to do with her, but after working with him for so long, it was impossible for her not to be concerned.

David Mason – the name he went by nowadays – walked briskly down the street in the direction of the railway station, deep in thought and hoping that the meeting he'd just had with Edgar Sawyer would pay off. Giving up a good job in Boston and coming back to England had been a huge gamble – not the first he'd taken in his life. Ironic, he thought, that the same reason he had gone to America in the first place was why he was now back in the land of his birth. And it meant he had to start all over again. He'd been gone so long it was almost as if he was in a foreign country. He had no job, no means of supporting himself apart from what was left of his savings, and nowhere to live. At present he was staying with an old friend in London, dossing down on a sofa in a cramped terraced house in Whitechapel, but he couldn't stay there for ever, and in any case he was anxious to get away from the city. It held too many memories for him, and none of them good ones.

This part of the world, though, would suit him very well. Green fields and fresh air, and perhaps . . .

He stamped on the thought before it could take shape. Better not to get his hopes up. Just wait and see how things developed. But all the same . . .

If he believed in fate, the omens were good. What a strange coincidence that the family he'd met on the voyage back to England should live so close to where he hoped to be. It seemed like serendipity that he should have happened to be in exactly the right place to find the little boy, Patrick, in trouble – if it hadn't been for that, he would never have got to know them. He was pretty sure they'd meant it when they'd invited him to visit them if he was in this part of the world, but it was much too soon yet for that. They'd scarcely have unpacked their bags, let alone settled in. Time enough to call on them when he came back.

And if things worked out, he *would* be back.

But for the present all he could do was wait, and trust that Edgar Sawyer would do what David had asked of him.

# Chapter Seven

As summer dreamed towards autumn, neither Rowan nor
Laurel gave much thought to anything but work.

Getting used to the hospital's ways of working – so different
to what she was used to – was a challenge for Laurel, and she
was anxious too to make a good impression on the doctors
whose clerical work she had taken on. Another practice in one
of the outlying villages – a Dr Clarkson – had also approached
the hospital board to ask if he could take advantage of a similar
arrangement. Laurel was gratified to think that he must have
heard good reports of her work, and was grateful for the extra
income, but it meant yet another pressure on her time, and she
often found herself staying at her desk well beyond her specified
hours to get everything done.

As she got used to the new regimes, she would speed up, she
was sure, but for the moment it was all proving a bit stressful. At
least, though, it meant her every waking moment was occupied,
leaving her little time to dwell on her disastrous affair with
Ralph. She was in no doubt but that she had made the right
decision in ending it, but that didn't do away with the undertow
of sadness for her shattered hopes and dreams, nor the treacherous longing she still felt for him. It was good that she had so
many new responsibilities to occupy her. If she was still working

for Edgar Sawyer in the office above Ralph's she wasn't sure she would have been able to remain strong.

As for Rowan, she was completely absorbed in her studies. Mr Shearn had set work for her to do during the summer break, and she had a session with him every Saturday morning in the front room of the schoolhouse. In the second week of August, however, he and his family were taking a holiday in Weymouth, and instead of the usual arithmetic and comprehension exercises, he had given her two books to read.

The first, *Treasure Island*, she had zipped through, enjoying the adventures and even the shiver induced by the sinister Black Spot. The second, however, was more of a challenge. *A Tale of Two Cities* was page after closely printed page of prose she struggled to understand in a language that was often unfamiliar to her. It was slow going, and she was more concerned with how far she could get each day than with enjoying the story.

'Aren't you ever going to take your nose out of that?' her mother complained. 'You ought to be out in the fresh air, making the most of this good weather.'

Rowan uncurled her legs and got up, keeping her place in the book with her finger. It was hot and stuffy in the kitchen, and the sunshine outside was certainly inviting. She could sit on the bench outside the back door so long as the Donovan boys didn't come out making a racket and disturbing her, or . . .

'I'll go across the fields for a bit,' she said.

'All right. But make sure you listen out for the hooter so you're home in time for dinner.' The hooter at the railway wagon works across the valley always sounded at twelve midday to tell the workers it was time for their break, and many of the locals found it convenient too for telling the time. 'And mind you don't get that book dirty, or you'll have Mr Shearn after you,' Minty added.

'I won't.'

She set off up the lane, sliding on hands and knees under the barbed-wire fence, and into the field beyond, until she found a spot where the ground shelved slightly. She sat down in the hollow, resting her back against the grassy bank, and opened her book again, but the sun glared on the page, blurring the words and hurting her eyes. For a while she persevered, but she was beginning to feel drowsy – she had read last night until well past her usual bedtime, trying to finish a chapter.

She slid down into the hollow, rolling onto her stomach and resting her head on her arm. The grass smelled hot and sweet, and the silence was broken only by the distant gurgle of the river as it trickled over the stones, and the occasional hum of a bumblebee.

Never mind Charles Darnay, Sydney Carton and Lucie Manette for now. She'd come back to them later. Mr Shearn was only trying to broaden her education by getting her to read this boring book. She wouldn't have to answer questions on it in the exam . . . Her mind was drifting. Perhaps she dozed . . .

'Are you all right?'

She came to with a start, jerking her head up so abruptly a sharp pain shot up her neck.

The boy who was related to Cathy-next-door was standing on the bank, looking down at her with a concerned expression furrowing his face.

'Ouch!' She sat up, rubbing her neck. 'You made me jump.'

'Sorry. I thought . . . I was worried that . . .' He didn't elaborate, just thrust his hands into the pockets of his shorts, looking vaguely awkward now.

'I think I must have gone to sleep,' Rowan said, taking pity on him. 'I'm supposed to be reading this book, but it's . . . well, actually, I think it's too old for me.'

'Why are you reading it then?'

'Mr Shearn – that's the headmaster – thinks I should.'

'Why?' Patrick seemed genuinely puzzled.

Rowan didn't want to explain. She thought it would sound as if she was showing off if she told him about the scholarship. And besides, Mammy had forbidden her to talk to him.

'I suppose your mam is visiting next door to us,' she said, thinking that Minty would not be best pleased. She was always tight-lipped and disapproving when she saw Maggie Donovan pass the window, and would shut the back door as if she might catch some horrible disease.

'Yes, but I didn't want to have to play with my cousins again. They're . . .'

'Just little.'

'Yeah. So I've been exploring. It's nice round here, isn't it? With the river and everything.'

'I suppose. I never think about it really.'

'Anyway,' he said with a sigh, 'I'd better be going.'

He turned, scrambling up the steep rise and heading back across the field.

Rowan watched him go with some relief. She felt oddly flustered, but at the same time regretful. Whatever Mammy thought of his mother, he did seem nice, and it was good to be able to talk to someone more or less her own age. But he was a boy. Even if she hadn't been forbidden to have anything to do with him, it wouldn't be any good. Boys played with boys. Rough games. Mostly they thought girls were pathetic – except for Beatie Emery, of course.

The stillness was suddenly broken by the mournful wail of the wagon works hooter echoing across the valley.

Time to go home. But she didn't want to go for a minute or two – she didn't want to catch up with Patrick Withers.

He might think she was following him. She hoped he'd be indoors before she turned the corner into the track behind the rank.

A flush began to creep up Rowan's neck and into her cheeks and she felt awkward and flustered all over again, though for the life of her she didn't know why. Nor could she understand the funny little flutter inside, as if a butterfly had been trapped in her stomach. All she knew was that, reluctant as she was to come face to face with Patrick again, a tiny unrecognisable part of her wanted it very much.

Rowan wasn't the only one experiencing emotions she didn't understand. Earl, too, was puzzled by certain changes in his feelings, and even his behaviour. And it all stemmed from the company he was keeping these days. Until recently he'd always been something of a Jack-the-lad, with an eye for the girls. Always up for a lark with his mates even if it did frequently land him in trouble – with his father, with Taffy Jones, sometimes with the law in the shape of Sergeant Love. But since he had begun walking out with Vicky Weaver, all that was changing, and no one was more surprised than Earl himself.

It hadn't begun well. In fact the first time they'd met he'd very nearly walked away from her in disgust – he'd been under the impression he had a date with Polly Brimble, the girl from Hillsbridge he'd fancied for some time.

The previous Friday evening he, Ted Young and Tommy Blanning had been hanging around in High Compton high street, lounging against the railings that followed the course of the river, smoking, joshing and watching the girls go by, when he'd spotted Polly and a couple of her friends parading arm-in-arm along the pavement.

'Hey, pretty Polly!' he'd called out as they passed. 'You're a long way from home! Come over to Compton to see me, have you?'

Polly tossed her head, but she gave him a come-hither look that he took to be encouragement.

'Come over here!' he called.

She giggled and gave one of her friends a little nudge.

'Who d'you think you're ordering about, Earl Sykes?'

'Come on, Polly, don't be like that.'

She let go of her friends' arms and came over to him while they walked slowly on.

'Like what?' she asked, flicking her eyelashes – eyelashes that looked as if she'd rubbed boot black on them – and pursing her mouth into an expression of feigned innocence.

'You know very well.'

'I do not!'

'Come out with me one night then, and I'll tell you.'

This was usually the point where he expected her to laugh, make some rude remark and walk away. That was usually how their exchanges went. She'd flirt, lead him on a bit, then leave him cold. This evening, however, she held his gaze challengingly.

'If I do, will you stop bothering me?'

'Can't promise. That's for me to know and you to find out.'

'All right. Next Friday? You'll have to come to Hillsbridge, though. I'll be outside the town hall – seven o'clock?'

Earl couldn't believe his luck.

'I'll see you then,' he said, trying to sound nonchalant.

'Don't stand me up,' she warned. Then, with another flick of her eyelashes and a toss of her head, she walked on to where her friends had stopped to wait for her. The three linked arms again and set off down the street, heads close together – presumably Polly was telling them about the date she'd agreed to.

'Well I'll be damned!' Tommy Blanning exclaimed. 'She's seen you off more times than I've had hot dinners!'

'I knew she couldn't resist my charm for ever.' Exultant, Earl tossed his cigarette butt into the river. 'Come on, lads, let's go up the pub. First round's on me!'

The following Friday, once he'd had his bath and his tea, Earl got spruced up, as he called it, in a freshly ironed shirt, Sunday-best trousers, and boots he'd polished till he could practically see his face in them and set out for the two-mile walk to Hillsbridge. He whistled as he walked, feeling chirpy and full of expectancy. He was in for a good evening, he thought. Polly Brimble had quite a reputation, and Earl was in hopes he would strike lucky. The clock in the tower over the market hall was just striking seven as he turned into the street that led to the town hall, and he quickened his pace. It wouldn't do to keep her waiting.

But when the town hall and the square that fronted it came into view, he couldn't see any sign of her. A few lads were sitting on the steps that led into the billiards room, and a couple of women who had stopped to talk on the corner looked as if they were about to go their separate ways, but of Polly there was no sign.

Oh well, it was a woman's prerogative to be late, he thought. He lit a cigarette and leaned against the wall, quite prepared to wait.

'Earl?'

He hadn't taken any notice of the girl who'd rounded the corner; probably wouldn't have noticed her at all except that she was addressing him directly. She was small and slender, wearing a high-necked white blouse with a cameo pinned at her throat, and a brown skirt. Light brown hair was drawn away from her face, which would have been very pale had it not been for the flush of colour staining her cheeks.

'She's not coming,' she said.

Earl's heart sank. 'What d'you mean, she's not coming?'

'She's not coming to meet you.' Her voice trembled with nervousness, and Earl recognised her now as one of the girls who had been with Polly the previous week.

'Charming!' he grated. 'And she's sent you to do her dirty work. What'd she drag me all the way over here for then? She was just having a laugh, I suppose.'

'No . . . she's not like that.'

'Doesn't sound like it. The little bitch!' He was seething with disappointment and rage at being played for a fool.

'No – you don't understand. It wasn't for a joke on you. She . . .' She broke off, twisting a fold of her skirt between her fingers.

'She what?'

'She was trying to fix me up with you. She meant well really. She knows I like you.'

Earl could scarcely believe his ears.

'And she thought tricking me would work, did she? That I'd just go for a walk with you instead? What does she take me for?'

The girl's lip trembled.

'I told her she shouldn't have done it. It was really stupid. But look . . . I'm not expecting you to . . . I only came because I didn't think it was fair to leave you waiting, and not knowing. So . . . well, I came to explain. And now I'm going home.'

She turned and started to walk away, but not before he had seen the tears glistening in her eyes.

He didn't know what made him call after her, but he did anyway.

'Hey – wait!'

She kept on walking. Earl hesitated, torn between his annoyance and a sudden burst of sympathy for the girl. He didn't suppose it had been her idea; it was just the sort of silly trick Polly Brimble would think clever. And it had been brave of her to come and tell him the truth instead of just leaving him standing.

He made up his mind and started after her.

She was just passing the police station when he caught up with her.

'Hey, look, it's not your fault,' he said.

She half turned towards him, her chin coming up.

'No, it's not. I didn't know what she was going to do.'

'She knows I fancy her, I suppose.'

'Everybody fancies Polly.'

'Yes, well, not any more. I'm one she can cross off her list.'

'I don't suppose she'll be that bothered.'

She sounded rueful. It couldn't be much fun going about with a girl who had only to flutter her eyelashes to have every boy in sight chasing after her, Earl thought.

They'd reached the high pavement at the entrance to the churchyard; rooks cawed in the overhanging trees.

'Where are you going now?' he asked. Stupid question.

'Home, of course.'

'We could go for that walk if you like.' He didn't know where that came from. He'd surprised himself as much as he'd surprised her.

She threw him a quick, startled glance.

'You don't have to.' But there was an eagerness in her tone that somehow made her even more vulnerable than before.

'I asked you, didn't I? We could go along the river.'

She caught her lip between her teeth. She really was quite pretty, he thought. Not striking like Polly – but who cared about Polly? Not him. Not any more.

'Come on then,' he said.

That had been back in July. Now it was September, and Earl was still seeing her. He couldn't work out what had got into him, and his mates didn't help, joshing him, telling him he'd better watch out or he'd be tied down before he knew it.

'Don't be daft,' he always replied. Getting tied down was not in his plans, never had been. Or not for years, anyway. Not until he'd lived a bit, seen the world. But somehow, getting away from High Compton didn't quite have the attraction it used to.

Even his mother had remarked on the change in him.

'Well, I don't know who this girl you're seeing is, but it's a treat, I can tell you, not having you coming home the worse for drink every Saturday night. Just so long as you don't go bringing another sort of trouble to the door . . . You know what I'm talking about, don't you?'

'Oh, Mam, for goodness' sake!'

But he wasn't going to tell her – and certainly not his mates – that there was no chance of that. Vicky never let him do more than kiss her. As soon as his hands started to wander, she'd put him in his place. It drove him crazy, especially when he thought of some of the other girls he'd walked out with, who were only too ready for a bit of a tumble. But at the same time he felt oddly protective of her. He couldn't ever remember feeling that way about a girl before.

No, Vicky Weaver had got under his skin and no mistake. And Earl didn't know what to make of it.

From his bedroom window in the house where he had taken lodgings, David Mason had seen the postman making his way down the street. He buttoned his shirt as he watched the man's slow progress, turning into entrances where the gates either hung crookedly on their hinges or had been removed altogether, walking down cracked paths between unkempt bushes and scrubby lawns. A few gardens were brightened with patches of colour – bright orange marigolds, pink and yellow snapdragons, a rose bush or two – but for the most part the outlook was depressing and uniformly grey.

David couldn't wait to get away from it. This certainly wasn't what he'd come to England for. But for the moment there was little he could do but wait. Each morning he watched out for the postman, hoping for word from Edgar Sawyer; each morning, so far, he'd been disappointed.

The postman had now reached the path leading to David's new temporary home, just a few streets away from where he'd bedded down on a friend's sofa when he'd first arrived back in London. The man had a couple of letters in his hand, and a moment later David heard the clunk of the letter box as he pushed them through, immediately followed by the fierce yapping of his landlady's little mongrel dog, Buster, as he raced into the narrow hallway to attack them.

David reached for his hairbrush and ran it quickly over his head, not bothering to check the result in the flyblown mirror above the dressing table. Not that there was much point: the reflective coating was so badly worn it was nigh impossible to see himself properly in it. Then he grabbed his coat from the upright chair beside the bed and hurried down the rickety staircase.

Mrs Moss, his landlady, was just disappearing back into the kitchen, Buster jumping up at her in a vain attempt to grab the letters.

'Anything for me?' he asked, trying to make it sound casual.

She was flicking through them – a manila envelope that was probably a bill, a pale blue one addressed in a thick, crabbed hand, and a picture postcard.

'Doesn't look like it.'

His heart sank.

'What is it you're expecting, anyway?' she asked, looking up at him narrowly.

'Oh – nothing.'

She snorted. 'Well, you're mighty anxious for "nothing", is all I can say.'

David didn't reply. He had no intention of telling her his business. Six pounds, ten shillings for a bed and three meals a day was the deal, and he reckoned that was more than fair. It didn't entitle her to ask him personal questions, and Mrs Moss took the hint.

'Hmm. Well. I suppose it's all right for some. I wouldn't mind a week at Clacton,' she said, propping the postcard on the mantelpiece between the clock and a china figurine. Then she rammed a slice of bread onto a toasting fork. 'If you'd like to do this, I'll poach you an egg to go on it.'

David took the toasting fork from her and sat down on the leather-topped box beside the fire, holding the bread to the glowing coals.

So – still nothing from Edgar Sawyer. If he didn't hear from him soon, there'd be nothing for it but to go down to Somerset himself.

The thought was not unappealing.

# Chapter Eight

It was Cathy Donovan who gave Laurel the news, catching her one morning in early October as Laurel was getting her bicycle out of the shed ready to ride over to the hospital.

'Awful about that man you used to work for, isn't it?'

Laurel stopped, resting the bicycle against her hip.

'What's that?'

'You didn't see yesterday's paper then? *The Bath Chronicle*?'

'We don't have it, no.'

'It was front-page news! I'd show you, but I used it to light the fire.'

'What did it say? What's happened to Mr Sawyer?'

'He's only been murdered, that's what. In his office – well, near as. A policeman on night patrol noticed the door was open, went to see if everything was all right – he thought there were burglars in there, I expect – and there was Mr Sawyer, slumped down just inside. Stone-cold dead. And blood everywhere . . .'

'Oh!' Laurel hung on tight to her bicycle; for a horrible moment she thought she was going to faint. 'He'd been *murdered*?' she managed.

'Stabbed. That's what they're saying.'

'That's terrible!' She could scarcely believe it.

'Just think, Laurel, it could have been you! I always thought it was a bit risky, working for a private detective. He made a lot of enemies, I expect. And had to mix with all sorts . . .'

Laurel pulled herself together with an effort.

'I've got to go, or I'll be late for work. But thanks for telling me, Cathy.'

'I thought you'd want to know.'

Laurel mounted her bicycle and set off along the track, her senses reeling from the shock of it. Mr Sawyer – murdered! Oh, she'd always known there were dangers associated with being a private investigator – on more than one occasion Edgar had come to the office sporting a black eye or a cut lip inflicted by some furious lover whom he had caught in a compromising situation with a client's wife. But to be stabbed to death in the hallway of the office building . . . Who would do such a thing?

She thought again about the murky dealings she had long suspected that Edgar was involved in. He was a chancer as well as an investigator and the company he kept was not always savoury. Perhaps somehow, somewhere, something had gone very wrong, and he had paid the price.

Laurel's lip wobbled and tears filled her eyes. She'd always got on with him very well; he'd been good to her. Something of a rogue he might be, but he didn't deserve to die like that.

She pushed down hard on the pedals, and the wind blew the tears off her cheeks.

In the smallest bedroom of the house that had used to belong to Lawrence, her first husband, Maggie Withers was curled up on the floor beside her little daughter's bed, singing softly.

Just a song at twilight, when the lights are low
And the evening shadows softly come and go . . .

She let her voice tail away. Nora's breathing was even now, and by the soft light of the lamp she had set on top of the chest of drawers Maggie could see her eyes were closed.

For a moment she remained motionless, watching and listening, then she got up and tiptoed to the window, pulling the curtains closed.

It was a ritual that had become established over the last months since they had returned to Somerset. Until then there had never been a problem with getting Nora to sleep. But ever since they'd been here, the little girl had become restless at bedtime. She didn't want the curtains drawn while she was still awake; she didn't want Maggie to leave her. When Maggie tried it, more often than not she'd hear Nora's footsteps on the stairs, and she'd appear in the doorway, flushed, tearful, sucking on a thumb and clutching Sally, her rag doll, under one arm.

The change had unsettled her, Maggie realised, and she needed lots of reassurance until she was confident in her new surroundings. Hardly surprising, really. Coming back from America had taken a lot of adjustment for all of them. She herself had found being back in England strange at first, and she had been born and brought up here. Even the house had seemed different, the ceilings lower, the rooms much smaller – or at least it had done when she'd first walked in after an absence of almost six years.

She'd got used to it now, rearranging furniture that the tenants had moved to their liking, and making it homely with little personal touches. The shelves that had once held Lawrence's books were now home to the children's toys and games; new copper pans gleamed on a hanging rack Josh had put up in the kitchen. Once again it felt like a home – the place where she'd found a safe haven, where she'd given birth to Patrick, nursed Lawrence through his last illness.

Oh, Lawrence. Here, in the house they had shared, he still seemed to be everywhere; she felt his presence so strongly she half expected to see him when a door blew open or a shadow moved. It was almost as if he was still here, watching over them.

She'd spent a whole day cleaning his workshop of the dust and cobwebs that had accumulated. Now, everything was as it had been, the workbench brushed down, tools and brushes cleaned and returned to their racks, the long, thin strips of lead tidied on their brackets, the kiln raked out and ready to light. The table where she had worked on her own designs was set out too with paper, pencils and watercolours, though she didn't know when she'd have time to use them. For the moment, cooking, washing and generally looking after her family was keeping her fully occupied, and soon there would be a new baby to care for. At the thought, Maggie laid both hands across the swell of her belly, feeling for the little lumps that materialised from time to time – a tiny hand or foot. This baby was an active one; sometimes it kicked so hard it made her jump, and it often kept her awake at night.

'Reckon he's going to be a footballer,' Josh had said, and Maggie knew he was hoping for another boy, one whose early years he wouldn't miss out on as he had missed out on Patrick's. He'd been there throughout with Nora, of course, but that was different. He idolised her, but Maggie knew there was always a special bond between a man and his son, and the sooner the relationship was established the better. Patrick was a sensitive boy who felt things deeply in a way Josh found difficult to understand. He could be impatient when Patrick's eyes filled with tears over something he didn't think warranted it, and she sometimes wondered if perhaps he thought that Lawrence's influence at the most formative time of Patrick's life had something to do with it.

113

Not that it seemed to worry him, however, that they were living in the house that had belonged to her first husband. But that was Josh all over. Things were what they were, and he simply accepted them. And he was pleased, she knew, with the workshop he'd set up in another of the outbuildings.

He'd been taken on again as a carpenter at Marston, the colliery where he'd learned his trade, and an outsider might have thought that he would have had quite enough of working with wood by the time he got home. But making pit props and the like was one thing, whittling a bookend or a small toy quite another, and he and Maggie still dreamed of setting up a profitable business together. The shed wouldn't be big enough to make doors and window frames or pieces of furniture, but when the time came they'd sort something out, and for now Josh was perfectly happy with his little lair.

The sound of voices floating up the stairs cut into her reverie. Josh, yes, and Patrick . . .

And another voice, not one she instantly recognised although something about it sounded vaguely familiar. Then Patrick was tearing up the stairs.

'Mommy! Mom!'

Maggie quickly left the room, pulling the door closed behind her.

'Patrick! Shh! You'll wake Nora!'

He skidded to a halt, grabbing hold of the banister.

'But Mom!' he said in an exaggerated whisper. 'You'll never guess who's here!'

It came to Maggie in a flash who it was that the half-recognised voice belonged to.

The young man they'd met on the voyage home.

David. Whatever his name was.

* * *

'Well,' she said, 'this is a surprise!'

'We did say he should look us up if he were in this part of the world,' Josh said. 'And here he is.'

'So I see.'

'I hope it's not inconvenient,' David said.

'Of course not. It's good to see you. Hasn't Josh asked you to sit down?'

'Give me a chance!' Josh gestured in the general direction of the sofa and easy chairs, which were drawn up in a crescent around the fireplace. 'Make yourself at home, David.'

'And I expect you could do with a cup of tea,' Maggie added.

'Or something stronger?' Josh suggested.

'Tea would be fine. I'm staying in a pub in Hillsbridge, so there'll be plenty of opportunity for me to have a drink later if I want one.'

'The Miners' Arms?' Maggie asked, busying herself with the kettle and teapot.

'The one beside the market hall.'

'Oh no, that's the George. My! You were lucky to get in there.'

And I bet it's costing you a pretty penny! she thought. The George catered for the well-to-do – businessmen and bosses, the professional classes, even some of the local gentry. They drank in the saloon bar, held their meetings in an upstairs room. She wouldn't call it a pub so much as a hotel.

'I'm only staying there the one night,' David said, as if he'd read her thoughts. 'I had an interview this afternoon at the printing works in High Compton. When I come back, though, I shall have to look for something cheaper. I don't like being in digs, but—'

'You're coming back? You got the job then?'

'For my sins,' he said with a smile.

'I'm not surprised.' Maggie set a small occasional table between the end of the sofa where David had sat down and Josh's chair. 'If those scraps you gave the children are anything to go by, they're lucky to have you. You and Nora loved them, didn't you, Patrick?'

'They were good.' Patrick scuttled across to the bookshelf to fetch his scrap album; he opened it and showed it to David. 'See?'

'Glad you liked them.'

'Oh, I did! And so did Nora. Though she spoiled some of hers . . .'

'So when do you start at the print works?' Josh asked.

'Next week. I'm just going back to London to collect my belongings, and then I'll be back, looking for lodgings. That's one of the reasons I looked you up, to tell the truth,' David admitted. 'I thought, being local, you might know of someone with a room to let.'

Josh shook his head.

'Sorry, mate, but we've only been back five minutes ourselves.'

'We could put a card in some of the shop windows for you,' Maggie suggested, pouring tea. 'You'd want to be in High Compton, I expect. Then you wouldn't have so far to go to work.'

'I wouldn't mind a bit of a walk. I just need a roof over my head.' David stirred sugar into his tea. 'And I can't afford to put up at the George for too long.'

'Well, you could always stay here with us until you get yourself sorted out, couldn't he, Maggie?' Josh suggested.

Maggie was taken aback. They had only the three bedrooms – hers and Josh's and one each for Patrick and Nora. But what else could she say?

'Well . . . yes.'

116

'That's kind, but I wouldn't want to put on you . . .'

'It would have to be the sofa,' Josh said to her relief. She'd half expected him to suggest Nora should go in with Patrick so that David could have her room!

David chuckled. 'Wouldn't be the first time.'

'Not what you'd choose, though,' Maggie said. 'We'll do our best to find you lodgings before next week, David. And Patrick – it's your bedtime.'

'Oh-h!'

'You've got school tomorrow.'

He'd started at the church school in Hillsbridge at the beginning of the autumn term.

'Off you go, now. You'll see David again. And don't wake Nora!' she called after him.

'So – what have you been up to since we saw you last?' Josh asked, reaching for his mug of tea and settling back for a chat with the man who, in spite of their short acquaintance, seemed to have become a friend.

'What in the world made you say he could stay here?' Maggie demanded when David had finally left. It was almost ten o'clock; they'd been talking for the best part of two hours.

David had told them his plans for the future – he hoped to be able to put enough by from his wages to eventually buy the equipment needed to set up in business himself, specialising in the printing of the scraps that had so impressed Maggie and Josh.

'A pipe dream, I suppose,' he'd said, 'but they really are in demand, and as I said before, mostly they're imported from Germany.'

As to why he had chosen to come to this part of the world, they were really still not much the wiser.

'I came down here once on holiday and fell in love with it,' was the only explanation he gave. 'And when I made enquiries about print firms round and about, I found out there were vacancies at Bensons in High Compton.'

'A lot of local people work there,' Josh had said.

'It's a big enterprise,' David agreed. 'And they seem very open to progress. So – here I am!'

Yes, and going to be sleeping on our sofa by the sound of it, Maggie had thought, not best pleased.

Now, however, when she mentioned it to Josh, he was unrepentant.

'He saved Patrick's life, didn't he? It's the least we can do. And he seems a nice chap.'

'I suppose,' Maggie said.

But she was still wondering just why David had chosen Somerset of all places, and why he had put up in the George in Hillsbridge rather than a much cheaper hostelry in High Compton.

And wishing she could rid herself of the unease she felt that there was more to David than met the eye.

Edgar Sawyer's funeral took place three weeks after his body was discovered in the hallway of the office in Queen Square. An inquest had recorded a verdict of unlawful killing, but though the police investigation had so far yielded no answers as to the identity of the assailant, the post-mortem had established that he had died from knife wounds to the chest and abdomen and the coroner was satisfied there was little to be gained from delaying the burial.

Determined to attend, Laurel had asked Louisa Cook, the young lady who had replaced her as Edgar's secretary, if she would let her know when arrangements were made, and Louisa had done so, telephoning her at the hospital.

It was a grey day in early November, with storm clouds threatening rain, when Laurel, dressed in her best black coat and a hat borrowed from her mother, left home to catch the train to Bath. Normally on a Wednesday she went to Dr Hicks's surgery once she'd dealt with the mail and any urgent correspondence at the hospital, but she'd asked if she could take the morning off, promising to come in later, and arranged with Dr Hicks to work during his evening surgery instead of in the afternoon.

It would make for a very long day, and Laurel was dreading every aspect of it. But she felt compelled to attend the funeral. She had, after all, worked for Edgar for a long time, and as far as she knew he had no close family or even many friends. It would be awful, she thought, if the chapel pews were empty and there was no one to stand by the graveside as he was lowered to his final resting place.

The rain had begun in earnest by the time the train pulled into Green Park station, and Laurel was glad she'd brought her umbrella. The chapel and cemetery were in Bathwick, on quite the other side of Bath – she wasn't even sure of the best way to get there – and she would have arrived looking like a drowned rat without it.

Though she'd thought she'd allowed herself plenty of time, a church clock somewhere nearby was striking eleven as she finally turned into the cemetery. It housed an Anglican mortuary chapel as well as the Nonconformist one where Edgar's funeral service was to be held, but she recognised it from the description Louisa had given her – a tiny stone building shaped a little like a honeycomb, with a slate roof rising to a point and a porch topped with a bell arch. The service had already begun, she realised, as she stepped inside and heard the minister's voice echoing round the circular walls. She gave her umbrella a shake, propped it in a corner of the porch and crept into the back of the chapel.

As she had thought, it was almost empty. The undertaker and the four black-suited bearers were occupying the front pew, so Maggie guessed there were no close family mourners. A couple of men who might have been friends or drinking companions sat in the row behind them. Apart from them, there was only a woman in a battered hat – the chapel cleaner, Laurel guessed – and two men in damp overcoats who had also chosen to sit in a pew towards the back.

Policemen, Laurel thought, as she recognised one of them as the inspector who had come out from Bath to interview her a few days after the murder. Seeing him there made her uncomfortable; she'd been less than helpful, she knew.

He'd asked if she knew of anyone with a grudge against Edgar, or if there had been any fallout from any of the cases he had been handling during the time she was working for him. She'd pointed out that Mr Sawyer's line of work inevitably made him enemies, but she couldn't think of anyone in particular, and in any case it was now four months since she had left his employ – his present secretary would be best placed to provide up-to-date information. The inspector had returned rather tartly that naturally they had already spoken to her, and would also be questioning all the clients who appeared in his files. She didn't envy him that, Laurel had thought. She'd always done her best to keep Edgar's records up to date, but they went back years – he didn't like anything to be thrown away. She couldn't imagine that the motive for murder lay in the past – such a violent attack seemed far more likely to have been the result of something much more recent, but she didn't think it was her place to say so.

Neither had she mentioned any of the shady dealings she

suspected Edgar had been mixed up in. After all, they were only suspicions, no more than that, and much as she would like to see his killer brought to justice, she was reluctant to speak ill of the dead. She didn't want to stir up anything that might show Edgar in a bad light.

Now, she shifted uncomfortably on the hard pew, hoping the policeman wouldn't buttonhole her and ask her more questions. Hoping perhaps he wouldn't even notice her. But she thought that was unlikely. Wasn't it the reason policemen attended the funerals of murder victims – in the hope that someone connected to the crime might be there? Even the perpetrator, come to gloat. But she couldn't imagine that anyone in this little gathering might be a violent killer.

Most of the words of the funeral service passed her by as she stared at the plain, simple coffin resting on a trestle in front of the altar, thinking of the Mr Sawyer she'd known – bluff, at times bordering on the crude, but always kind, to her at least – and wondering how and why he'd met such a terrible end.

Then the bearers were hoisting it, shouldering it and shuffling down the narrow aisle towards the door. As they passed her, not one of them gave her a second glance.

She hadn't noticed the freshly dug grave on her way in; she'd been in too much of a hurry. Now, as she followed the little procession out into the rain-soaked cemetery, she wondered how she'd come to miss it: a cavern surrounded by green baize and planks of wood, with what looked like another fresh grave to one side of it.

She hung back. It wasn't her place, she felt, to follow too closely. The two policemen, too, had stopped on the path, watching the interment from a distance.

And then she saw him. Crossing the grass to join the burial party beside the grave. Her heart missed a beat.

121

Ralph. Tall. Handsome. Expensively dressed. Every inch the professional gentleman. Strangely, it hadn't occurred to her that he might be here. He and Mr Sawyer had had very little to do with one another, beyond a greeting if they happened to pass in the hallway. But she should have thought. Should have guessed that it was at least a possibility.

He was late, of course. Perhaps he'd had an appointment with a patient. But now he was here, and panic closed her throat. She couldn't give him the chance to speak to her. A funeral was quite the wrong place for a confrontation. She had to get away, but to reach the gate she would have to walk almost directly past the grave . . .

Thank goodness for her umbrella! She lowered it in front of her face and crept as far along the path as she dared, waiting for the committal to end. She was aware of the policeman – Inspector Turner – watching her, and wondered if she was arousing his suspicions and he would come after her. But she couldn't worry about that now.

The moment she saw the minister turn from the grave, she scuttled for the gate, not stopping until she reached the end of the road. She looked round once – no one was following her.

She crossed the main road at a more sedate pace and walked down a street lined with tall, elegant buildings. But her pulses still raced and a nerve jumped in her throat.

How was it he could still do this to her? It was wrong, so wrong, and yet just that fleeting glimpse of him had resurrected all the old feelings. After Callum she had told herself that never again would she allow herself to be so besotted by a man. Yet here she was, just as churned up inside as she had been then, no matter that now she was old enough to know better.

*Love makes fools of us all* . . .

Laurel didn't know where she'd heard that, but she could only think how true it was.

She couldn't regret attending Mr Sawyer's funeral, but she wished with all her heart that Ralph had not been there. Stirring up all her old emotions, just when she was trying to make a new life for herself.

# Chapter Nine

So often throughout her life Maggie's psyche had given her warnings of things to come, sometimes in a dream or a sudden random thought, sometimes simply a sense that something was wrong, an inexplicable feeling of sadness or a rush of anxiety. But that day towards the end of November she had no warning at all.

As usual she had been up before dawn, making breakfast for Josh before he left for the colliery, getting the children ready for school and walking part of the way with them. She didn't go all the way to the school gates, just as far as the main road. Patrick was quite old enough now to look after Nora, and would probably have felt uncomfortable if his classmates had seen him walking with his mother. Besides, the hill was a long drag on the way back, and at a little over seven months pregnant she found it very tiring.

She walked with them as far as the long straight where hedgerows and open fields gave way to terraces of cottages on either side of the road. There she kissed Nora, patted Patrick's shoulder and stood to watch them until they were out of sight. Then she walked back the way they had come, calling in for a jug of milk at a farm she passed, as she so often did, and stopping to exchange a few words with the farmer's wife before heading home.

Far from feeling depressed or anxious, she was actually brimming with a sense of purpose that bordered on excitement. Today she might at last be able to find the time to settle down in the workroom and make a start on some sketches for the first of the projects she had planned. The idea had been taking shape in her head for some time now – a shade for an old brass candle lamp she'd found at the back of the cupboard beneath the stairs. In her mind's eye she could see it, six or eight panels made up of fragments of stained glass. But she needed to get something down on paper to be sure it was viable, and the past few weeks she'd scarcely had a moment to call her own. David had taken Josh up on his offer and had been staying with them, sleeping on the sofa in the living room and taking his meals with them.

She couldn't really say he'd been any trouble – he'd gone out of his way to fit in – but it had made extra work for her all the same, and she hadn't really liked the feeling that her home was not quite her own.

He'd gone now, thank goodness. They'd managed to find him lodgings with a widow woman who lived in a terrace of cottages midway between Hillsbridge and High Compton, and he'd moved out, bag and baggage, at the weekend. At last she had been able to get everything straight again. Josh, she knew, had been sorry to see him go, but she felt nothing but relief. If Josh wanted to go out and meet him for a drink a couple of times a week, that was fine with her. She was just glad she could stop having to be a good hostess and get back to normal.

Back at home, she finished clearing away the breakfast things, did the washing-up and dusted the living room – a job that needed to be done every day with the fire burning from early morning till bedtime. Then she made herself a cup of tea and carried it over to the workshop.

Immersed in her plans, sketching, measuring, sorting out bits of glass that had already been painted in jewel colours but not used for Lawrence's triptych, she realised the morning had sped by, and it was only when she returned to the kitchen to make another cup of tea and a cheese sandwich that it occurred to her – she'd forgotten to make the beds.

Leaving the kettle on the hob, she went upstairs. She'd turned back the covers on the big double bed when she'd got dressed; it only took a few moments to remake it. But Nora's sheets were tangled and Patrick's room was horribly untidy, drawers left open, their contents tumbled, his nightshirt inside out and lying where he'd dropped it, books and toys scattered about the floor.

'Oh, Patrick!' she sighed.

In the middle of clearing up the muddle, she suddenly remembered she'd left the kettle on the hob. It would be boiling by now, spitting all over the freshly polished tiled surround and fizzing in the fire. If enough water evaporated it might even boil dry. She made a dash for the stairs.

Just what happened next she was never quite sure. Perhaps she caught her toe on a loose board, or tripped over an unnoticed discarded toy, or simply lost her footing. Whatever, she was suddenly catapulted forward, then she was tumbling, the shock of hitting each tread as she fell reverberating through every bit of her body. She landed in a heap at the foot of the stairs, and lay for a moment dazed from the shock of it, and hurting all over. Then, as she tried to pick herself up, the world spun around her. Her vision blurred, darkness creeping over her like a sudden nightfall, her legs gave way beneath her and she collapsed again, limp as a rag doll, onto the stained board floor.

'Maggie? Maggie!'

The voice seemed to come from a long way off. Puzzled, she opened her eyes; it was David, bending over her.

'What . . . ?'

'Lie still for a minute, Maggie.'

Dazed, confused, she obeyed, then struggled to sit up again.

'But . . . what happened?'

'You must have fallen down the stairs. Take it easy now.'

'I'm all right,' she started to say when a searing pain in her stomach stopped her words. She caught her breath as it tightened like a steel band around the deepest part of her and she felt a rush of something hot and wet between her legs.

'Oh no!' she gasped.

Again she tried to get up; this time David helped her, his hands beneath her arms, and supported her to the sofa.

She was trembling now with terror.

'The baby! I think it's coming!'

Even as she said it, another pain gripped her and she doubled over, hugging herself with her arms.

If David was feeling the same panic as she was, he did not show it. As the pain eased, he carefully lifted her legs onto the sofa and plumped a pillow beneath her head.

'Just stay there. I'm going for help.' He was heading for the door.

'But I can't have the baby! It's too soon!' she sobbed. And then, ludicrous as it might seem at such a time, she remembered the cause of all this. 'The kettle!' she called after him. 'Can you take the kettle off?'

He stopped, turned.

'What?'

'The kettle. It's going to boil dry.'

He doubled back and went to the hob, where the kettle spat and hissed.

'A pot holder. Use a pot holder, or you'll burn yourself . . .'

'Don't worry about me.' But he used the pot holder anyway, two squares of fabric stitched together and stuffed with rags, to remove the kettle and set it down on the tiled surround. Then he headed back for the door.

'I'll be as quick as I can.'

Then he was gone, and Maggie was alone, striving to remain calm, riding out the waves of pain, trying to tell herself that it would be all right, even though in her heart she already knew it would not be all right at all.

Josh was eating his snap – bread, cheese and pickles – when the message reached him, relayed by Walt Bridges, the colliery undermanager, who had taken the telephone call.

'You'd best be going home. It seems your wife's had an accident.'

Josh started, alarm chilling his blood, though as yet the undermanager's words made no sense to him.

'What d'you mean – my wife's had an accident?'

'I couldn't say, lad, more than it's something about a fall. But the chap who rang sounded pretty shaken up. Said you needed to get there quick sharp.'

Josh didn't wait for more. He dumped his half-eaten snap on the bench beside him, grabbed his coat and ran out, stuffing his arms into it as he went. His bicycle was propped up against the wall of the carpenter's shed; he mounted it and raced out of the colliery yard, his legs working like pistons, his thoughts churning.

What the hell had happened? Was Maggie all right? And the baby? And who was it who had telephoned for him? Isolated as their cottage was, there were no near neighbours. Could it have been the postman? Most days he was the only caller. They were too far out of the way for the baker or the milkman to deliver. Maggie made her own bread and collected milk direct from the farm along the road. Had she gone into Hillsbridge or Dunderwick for some reason? Been knocked down by a horse and cart, or even a motor vehicle? Although they were few and far between, accidents involving them weren't unknown – darned new-fangled contraptions that they were, and folks driving them who didn't really know what they were doing.

But a fall, Walt Bridges had said. That didn't sound so bad. She'd broken a leg, perhaps, or her arm. If that was it, it would make things difficult, but at least it would slow her down a bit. Always on the go, Maggie was. He'd told her she ought to take things easier in her condition . . .

Sweat was running down his face and neck by the time he reached the top of the long winding hill and the roof of their house appeared over the top of the hedges, brown and bare for winter. Then, as he rounded a bend in the road, he saw a pony and trap drawn up alongside the triangle of grass in the centre of which the house and garden were situated, and his heart began thudding in his throat.

Dr Blackmore drove a pony and trap. If the doctor had been sent for, it must be something bad.

Josh pressed down hard on the pedals, the muscles in his legs burning as he raced along the lane. Yes, it was Dr Blackmore's pony and trap all right. He skidded to a stop in front of the pony, which, fortunately, was too old and placid to be startled by him, dropped his bicycle into the hedge and sprinted through the gate and up the path.

When he burst into the living room, it was empty but for a man sitting in the chair beside the fire, elbows resting on his knees, head in hands.

'David?' he said, startled.

David straightened. 'Christ, Josh, I'm glad you're here.'

'What's happened? Where's Maggie?'

'The doctor got her upstairs. She's having the baby.'

A wail from the bedroom was all the confirmation that was

needed. Josh turned without another word and sprinted up the stairs. The door to his and Maggie's room was closed; another series of moans came from behind it.

Without a second thought he threw the door open. Maggie was lying on the bed, gripping a pillowcase tied to the rungs of the headboard, her face contorted with pain. As he stood there, momentarily transfixed, the doctor rose from his chair beside the bed and came towards him, waving his hands in the sort of gesture one would use to shoo geese.

Josh backed away; the doctor followed, closing the door behind him.

'That's no place for you, Mr Withers.'

'But Maggie . . .'

'There's nothing you can do at the present but wait. Just make sure there's water on the boil, and more clean towels wouldn't come amiss.'

'She's having the baby?'

'I'm afraid so.'

'But it's too soon!'

'Unfortunately nature doesn't always follow the rules. It seems your wife had a fall, and this is the result.'

Another anguished moan from behind the closed door.

'Please – downstairs now, and let me get back to my patient.'

Elderly Dr Blackmore might be, but he could still exhibit an authority that was not to be argued with. Men, unless they happened to be medical practitioners, had no place in the birthing chamber. At best they were useless, at worst a hindrance. And as likely as not to pass clean out at what they were witnessing. One patient was quite enough, in Dr Blackmore's opinion.

'You'll let me know . . .' Josh began, but the doctor had already gone back into the bedroom, closing the door behind him.

Helpless, desperately anxious, Josh turned and descended the stairs.

'What the hell happened?' he demanded of David.

David shook his head. He looked very white and shaken.

'And what are *you* doing here?'

David rose from the chair, pacing the room.

'I cycled over in my dinner time to bring Maggie a small gift to thank her for putting me up. And it's lucky I did. I found her at the bottom of the stairs. She must have fallen and knocked herself out – or fainted.'

'She fell down the stairs?'

'I suppose so. She wasn't making much sense. Then she started having pains. I rode my bike over to Hillsbridge and luckily the doctor was still in his surgery, not out on his rounds. While I was there, I rang the pit to let you know what had happened, then came back with the doctor in his pony and trap.'

'You left her here on her own?' Josh could only imagine how frightened Maggie must have been.

'What else could I do?'

'Yeah . . . of course. You did the right thing. But she shouldn't be having the baby yet. It's not due for another couple of months. How the hell did she come to fall down the stairs?'

'Your guess is as good as mine.'

'I need a drink!' Josh went to the chiffonier and got out the half-bottle of brandy they kept for medicinal purposes. 'Do you want one?'

'Better not. I ought to be getting back to work now that you're here.'

'You say you left your bike in Hillsbridge?'

'I'll just have to walk.'

'It's a hell of a way. You'll have missed half a day's work by the time you get to High Compton.'

David shrugged. 'Can't be helped.'

'Take mine,' Josh offered. 'It's in the hedge by the gate. I shan't be wanting it today.'

'Are you sure?'

'Yes – go on. Leave it in Hillsbridge where you left yours, and I'll pick it up when I can.'

'Thanks. You're a good friend, Josh.'

'No, it's me that should be thanking you. God knows what would have become of Maggie if you hadn't found her when you did.'

And God knows what's going to happen to her anyway, he thought, worried out of his mind, as David left.

He found a tumbler and poured a generous measure of brandy into it. He only wished there was a good deal more in the bottle. It was going to be a long afternoon.

'What's going on?' Patrick came bursting in, Nora trotting behind him.

They'd been surprised to get all the way home alone; Maggie usually walked partway to meet them. Their faces were rosy, both from the cold and the blustery wind that had sprung up, and from running from the moment they'd spotted the pony and trap outside their house.

'Who does that horse belong to?'

Josh got up from the chair where he had slumped when he could pace the floor no more.

'Now look – you're not to be worried, but—'

Patrick had noticed the glass and the empty brandy bottle on the table, and even across the room could smell the fumes on his father's breath.

'You've been drinking!' he accused.

Josh ignored this. 'Your mam's having the baby,' he said.

'But not yet!' Patrick objected. 'After Christmas, you said.'

'Well, it's coming early.'

'Wow! I'm going to have a little brother – today!'

'Sister!' Nora put in belligerently. 'Can I see her?'

'The baby hasn't arrived yet,' Josh said, adding a silent prayer that it wouldn't be much longer. 'And children . . . you must prepare yourselves. He – or she – might not . . . well, he might not be very well. He's not really ready to be born.'

'You mean he might die?' Patrick said bluntly. 'Like Mrs O'Leary's kittens?'

Mrs O'Leary had been a neighbour in New York; when her cat had had a litter of kittens, the two smallest ones had not survived. Josh had suspected this owed more to a bucket of water than to difficulties with the birth, but he'd been sure not to mention this to the children.

'He might,' he said, as evenly as he could.

'Oh.' Patrick looked crestfallen.

'Mommy's not going to die though, is she?' Nora was regarding him pleadingly, her eyes – so like Maggie's – huge in her small flushed face.

Josh wished he could be sure of that. The groans and cries coming from upstairs had grown weaker as the hours ticked by, and truth to tell he was terrified for Maggie. But he didn't even want to think about that, and he didn't want to frighten the children unnecessarily either.

'I'm sure Mommy will be fine,' he said, trying to sound reassuring.

'That's all right then,' Nora said trustingly. And a moment later: 'Daddy, can I give the horse an apple? He must be really hungry.'

Josh shook his head wonderingly. He couldn't think beyond his desperate anxiety for Maggie and the baby, and it was beyond his comprehension that anyone, even a child, could be interested in feeding a horse at a time like this.

But it would keep her out of mischief – and out of earshot of the sounds coming from upstairs.

He took an apple from the fruit bowl.

'Go on then. Patrick will cut it up for you. And Patrick – go with your sister and make sure she keeps well away from the horse's back end. We don't want him kicking her.'

'All right, Dad. You can count on me.'

The boy's face was serious now. At least he understands the situation, Josh thought. He's growing up fast.

And he prayed to a God he was not sure he believed in that he would not have to finish his growing up without a mother.


'I'm sorry, Maggie,' Dr Blackmore said. 'There was nothing I could do.'

Maggie didn't reply. She lay back against the pillows, exhausted. Her face was paper white, her breathing shallow.

It was over. She'd delivered her baby – a little boy, the doctor had told her – but she'd failed him. All these months he'd been inside her, nurtured, protected, and now . . . a moment's carelessness and it had come to this.

Her baby. Wrapped up in a towel, for all the world like a parcel for posting, or a bundle of rubbish.

'I'll send for Mrs Harvey,' the doctor was saying as he washed his hands in the china basin on the washstand. 'She'll come and make you comfortable.'

'Oh . . . not her, please!' Maggie moaned weakly.

She'd never forgotten the horrible woman who had tended her for the long hours through which she'd laboured with Patrick, if 'tended' could ever be the right word for the treatment she'd meted out. A big-boned woman with rough hands and an even rougher manner, who had seemed to take pleasure in her pain and discomfort. A cruel, cold-hearted woman, who had looked like a great crow in her black nurse's cape when she'd entered the house. A crow – or an avenging angel.

But for all that, Patrick had been born alive. The hours of suffering had been worthwhile. They had gone from her mind completely as she cradled him in her arms, put him to her breast. This time, though . . .

'Can I see him, please?' Maggie asked.

Dr Blackmore raised an eyebrow. It wasn't wise, in his opinion. As soon as he'd seen there was nothing to be done for the child, as soon as he'd cut the cord, he'd whisked him away, out of sight.

'Please!' With an enormous effort, Maggie raised herself a fraction.

'All right. But don't move! You must conserve your strength, and we don't want you bleeding again.' The doctor was afraid that if he didn't do as she asked, she might try to get to the baby herself the moment his back was turned.

He picked up the small bundle and carried it to the bed. Drawing back a corner of the towel to reveal a head, pointed from the effort of being born, sticky with blood and mucus, he placed the child in her arms. Maggie gazed down at the small wizened face, her lip trembling but her expression transformed to one of pure unadulterated love. Then she carefully drew the towel back further, stroking a tiny wrinkled hand, each finger tipped with perfectly formed fingernails.

For long moments she remained motionless and silent. Then:

'Matthew,' she whispered. 'Your name is Matthew. Did you know that?'

A tear rolled down her cheek, splashing onto the small, defenceless head. Then she rewrapped the baby so that only his face was showing, and looked up at Dr Blackmore.

'Thank you.'

He took the child from her. 'You can leave all this to me.'

Her heart contracted.

He gathered his things together, repacking his medical bag.

'Mrs Harvey will be with you soon,' he said.

And then he, and her precious dead son, was gone.

'Oh, Maggie, I thought I'd lost you.'

The redoubtable Mrs Harvey had been and gone and she had been less rough with Maggie than she had been before; perhaps she felt some sympathy at the baby's loss, though if she did, she mentioned not a word of it. The children had been fed. Now they were in bed, and, Josh hoped, asleep. They'd been upset, naturally, about what had happened, Patrick in particular. He was old enough to understand, and he was a sensitive boy, softer in many ways than his little sister.

Now Josh lay beside Maggie on the bed, holding her hand, her head resting against his shoulder.

'We've lost our baby,' she said, her voice flat and devoid of emotion.

'But we might so easily have lost you too. Oh, Maggie . . . you should have been more careful . . .'

'I didn't fall down the stairs on purpose.'

'I know. Of course you didn't. But when I think of it . . . Thank God David found you, is all I can say.'

'Why was he here?'

'He came to bring you a gift to say thank you for letting him stay here until he got his lodgings. I don't suppose he got around to giving you whatever it was, though.'

'No.' She laughed softly, mirthlessly. 'You'll probably find it downstairs, whatever it is.'

'I expect so.' He hadn't noticed anything likely lying about, but then he hadn't really been looking. 'I'm just grateful he happened to call today. If he hadn't . . .'

He broke off, choked by emotion. Yes, he was of course dreadfully sad at the loss of their baby, the little boy he had thought would allow him to recapture the lost years of Patrick's infancy. But at the same time he was immensely grateful that . . .

'I don't know what I'd do if anything happened to you, Maggie,' he said.

And he had never uttered a more heartfelt word.

# Chapter Ten

Christmas and New Year came and went, the dark and bitterly cold days of January turned wet and wild in February, and often Laurel was soaked to the skin by the time she had cycled to the hospital or over to the doctors' surgeries and home again.

Rowan took her scholarship exam, and was nervous but hopeful that she'd done enough – she'd written from the moment she was told to turn over her paper until she was instructed to put down her pen.

Maggie was slowly recovering from her miscarriage, physically at least, although emotionally she was still on a roller coaster. She came of stoic stock; she tried to tell herself she was lucky to have two fit and healthy children when so many people lost theirs to some sickness or other in infancy, but she couldn't shake off the sadness that lay heavy on her heart, or stop the tears that flowed when she was alone.

David visited often – he'd spent Christmas with them as Maggie had not liked to think of him alone in his lodgings but for the landlady. Since he'd been so good to her when she had fallen down the stairs and lost her baby, she'd realised she'd been wrong about him. Something of a mystery he might be, but he was kind and caring and she dreaded to think of what might have happened if he hadn't been there for her that day.

And in all that time there was no real progress in the investigation into Edgar Sawyer's murder.

It wasn't for the want of trying on Inspector Turner's part. He'd worked his way through Edgar's records, beginning with the most recent, setting on one side any that might possibly have provoked a violent reaction from one of the parties involved, and either spoken to them himself or had his sergeant interview them. For the most part they had been less than pleased to have their private business brought to light, especially by the police, and in one case he'd been hopeful he might be on to something. An errant husband whose wife had left him as a result of the evidence Edgar had provided her with had been receiving financial assistance from her father to prop up his ailing business; now that his affair with a lady of ill repute had been confirmed, the father had refused to continue bailing him out, and he was facing ruin. But it soon became clear that on the night in question the man had been in Bristol, losing what little money he had left in a gambling club, and like all the others this most promising lead had led to yet another dead end.

After ploughing through five years' worth of files, Inspector Turner had decided there was no point in going any further back in the records. This wasn't a case of revenge being served cold, he felt sure. The frenzy of the attack seemed to indicate that the motive – if there was one – was much more immediate than that.

Neither had his enquiries amongst Edgar Sawyer's friends and acquaintances proved any more fruitful. A bunch of rogues they might be, and he suspected one of them at least might be withholding evidence. But if they were, he was not going to get it out of them without making an arrest, and he had no grounds for that. The homeopathic doctor whose consulting rooms were on the ground floor of the building had been charming, but clearly knew nothing, and pleas to the public for anyone who might have been in the area that night and seen something suspicious to come forward proved similarly unhelpful.

There were the usual cranks and crackpots, eager to be at the centre of attention, who variously claimed to have seen a gang of thugs, a man with a wooden leg (all that was missing was the parrot on his shoulder, the inspector thought bitterly), and the blind beggar who spent his days sitting on the pavement outside the Roman baths with a placard and an upturned cloth cap beside him. He discarded them all.

The only witness he found in the least credible was a gentleman who had been on his way to dine at the Francis Hotel on the side of Queen Square that was at right angles to the row of buildings where Edgar Sawyer had his office. When he had passed Edgar's office he had noticed a girl lurking nearby, and later, when he had been seated at a table overlooking the square, he could see she was still there, walking up and down the pavement. It had struck him as unusual. Young ladies were not normally out alone on dark evenings, and this one was little more than a child. But he was unable to provide much in the way of a description, and in any case the inspector thought it was highly unlikely that the murder had been committed by a woman, and certainly not a young girl.

But it was interesting all the same. Had the witness been mistaken about the girl's age? Was she older than she looked – a prostitute soliciting for business? But ladies of the night rarely frequented genteel Queen Square; they were more likely to be found in the main streets – until they were moved on – or hanging about near the city's less salubrious hostelries. So who was she, and what had she been doing there? Could it possibly have been the young lady who worked for Edgar? Or her predecessor? Might she have come back to the office to see him for some reason? Certainly she'd been at the funeral, the only woman present. He thought he might have another word with her . . .

But before he could do so, new and pressing cases landed in his lap. On successive nights two prostitutes had been found beaten and strangled, and a third had thrown herself – or been thrown – over the balustrade and into the river just below the weir. Inspector Turner was worried there might be a modern-day Jack the Ripper at work in the city, and that was a far more serious affair than a stabbing, now five months old, that had more than likely been the result of a burglary gone wrong – the conclusion he had more or less come to.

The new cases, he decided, were in need of his full attention, and the files on the Edgar Sawyer murder were left to gather dust on a shelf in his office.

Earl was worried. That in itself was unusual. It wasn't in his happy-go-lucky nature to let anything bother him for long. And the reason he was worried was even more unusual. It was Vicky.

Until now, girls had never caused him sleepless nights. He'd walked out with more than he cared to count, fancied some of them rotten, tired of them, left them. There were plenty more fish in the sea. But this time was different.

Vicky wasn't at all herself and he was beginning to wonder if perhaps she was going off him. What other explanation could there be? If they went for a walk, she'd say she was tired and wanted to go home, even though they'd only been out for perhaps half an hour or so. When he was relating some amusing incident or near-disaster at work, she often didn't really seem to be listening, and though she had never been a chatterbox, now she was quieter than ever. Besides all this, she no longer seemed to want to kiss and cuddle. Perhaps she was fed up with having to rebuff his advances, he thought, but wasn't it only natural he should try to take things further? And hadn't she always seemed to enjoy the tussle?

Earl couldn't understand what was going on and found he was fretting about it. He'd been seeing her for seven or eight months now, about ten times as long as any of his previous romances had lasted – if they could be called that. In that time he'd changed almost beyond recognition from the tearaway he'd once been, and it was Vicky who was responsible. Even Mam had commented that she was glad to see he was growing up at last. Now he was sure only of one thing.

He didn't want to lose Vicky.

It was a Saturday evening in April when things came to a head. He'd walked over to Hillsbridge and knocked on the door of the semi-detached house a few hundred yards beyond the church and in the shadow of one of the high rises that surrounded the valley in which the town was set. Vicky was the only one of her siblings still living at home; both her brothers and one sister had married, and the other was away in service.

The door was opened by Vicky's mother, dressed and ready to go out from the look of her, in a black straw hat trimmed with silk flowers, a silk corsage pinned to the lapel of her coat.

'Come in, Earl.'

'Thanks, Mrs Weaver.'

He liked Vicky's mother, and she seemed to like him. He was always made welcome in her house, and he couldn't help but compare her with his own mother. Unlike Minty, she always had a smile on her face, and she liked to see the best in everyone rather than the worst.

'We're just off out,' she said as he came into the hall. 'There's a concert party on at the town hall, and we do enjoy Stanley Bristow's concerts, don't we, Fred?'

'Oh ah, he d'a put on a good show,' Vicky's father agreed, emerging from the kitchen.

'I should tell you, though, our Vicky's not well,' Mrs Weaver went on, lowering her voice. 'She's up in her room, has been ever since her tea, which she didn't eat, I might add. If I could have stopped you coming over tonight, I would.'

'What's wrong with her?' Earl asked, a sinking feeling beginning in the pit of his stomach.

'She seems tired out and down in the dumps and she says she feels cold all the time. I wonder if she's picked up one of those bugs that's been going around, and you don't want to be catching that. So if you want to go on home, she'd understand.'

'I'm not worried about that, Mrs Weaver.'

It was no more than the truth: he had the constitution of an ox. What he *was* worried about was whether Vicky was fabricating an excuse to get out of seeing him.

'It's up to you. I'll give her a shout. But if you do decide to go out, you don't want to be going too far.' She went to the bottom of the stairs. 'Vicky?' she called. 'Earl's here.'

'Come on then, m'dear, we ought to be making tracks, or all the best seats will be gone.' Fred Weaver headed for the front door.

'We'll leave you to it then, Earl.' Mrs Weaver followed him. 'Cheerio for now. We won't be late.'

'Bye, Mam. Bye, Dad.' Vicky was halfway down the stairs.

As the front door closed after them, Earl glanced at her apprehensively. She did look a bit peaky, it was true, but then she never did have a lot of colour in her face – except when she blushed.

'What's up with you, then?' he asked. 'Your mam says you're not well.'

'Oh . . . it's nothing. I just don't feel myself, that's all. Shall we go in the kitchen?'

143

'If you like.'

But that wasn't promising. They usually went into the front room, though admittedly that was when her parents were at home, so that they could have a bit of privacy. But there was a sofa in the front room – good for a cuddle – and nothing but hard dining chairs and a couple of small easy chairs in the kitchen. Nothing they could snuggle up on together. Was she just making excuses?

'It's nice and warm in there,' Vicky said by way of explanation, and sure enough, she went straight to one of the easy chairs that flanked the fireplace.

I could have warmed you up, Earl wanted to say, but instead he sat down in the other easy chair, facing her, and asked: 'Is there something else wrong, Vicky?'

'I'm just cold, that's all,' she said, a bit impatiently.

You're cold all right, Earl thought despairingly, and suddenly could bear the uncertainty no longer. Better to get to the bottom of this even if she did end up telling him to get lost. Anything would be better than this feeling he had of a noose around his neck and a trapdoor beneath his feet, just waiting to open.

'Have you gone off me?' he asked bluntly.

Her eyes came up to meet his, puzzled but, to him, evasive.

'What?'

'You've been really off lately. As if you don't fancy me any more. Do you want to finish? Is that it?'

'Oh, Earl, no! What makes you think that?'

'I just said. The way you've been acting. Like you're not interested any more.'

'I'm sorry. It's just that I don't feel very well.'

'Are you telling me you haven't felt well for weeks?'

'I haven't.'

'You never said.'

'It's nothing to make a fuss about. I haven't been sleeping properly – I expect that's it.'

'And it's not just an excuse because you don't want to go out with me?'

'Course not.'

There were tears in her eyes, and dark circles beneath, he noticed now. Perhaps it was true, she really wasn't well, and she'd been trying to hide it. And had managed it so well that even her mother hadn't noticed anything until today. He felt an inexplicable twist of alarm.

'Vicky . . .' He couldn't find the words to express this sudden concern, and in any case she was going on.

'I haven't said anything because I thought you'd think I was a proper wet blanket. I was afraid you'd get tired of me and go off with someone else.' Her lip trembled. 'I've always been afraid of that. After all, you never wanted to go out with me in the first place, did you?'

'I didn't plan it, no. But—'

'It was Polly Brimble you fancied. If she hadn't tricked you into it, you'd never . . . I've always thought you're only going out with me to spite her, if you want to know the truth.'

'Oh, Vicky . . . I wouldn't have kept it up all this time unless I wanted to, would I?'

She shrugged helplessly. 'I don't know. You never say.'

'Well, I thought you knew. I didn't think there was any need.'

It was true, he wasn't one for sweet talk. Not even now, with Vicky more or less begging for reassurance.

'How am I supposed to know if you never say anything? And besides, I know I'm not as much fun as some other girls would be. They'd let you do what you want and I won't, and that's bad enough without me being a wet blanket as well . . .'

'Will you stop going on about being a wet blanket?' Earl snapped, exasperated. 'Yes, I would like to do more than have a kiss and a cuddle, but that's just natural. It doesn't mean I'd look elsewhere for it. It's you I want, and I can wait.'

'Wait for what?'

'Well – until we're married, I suppose.'

Her eyes widened. He'd shocked her almost as much as he'd shocked himself.

'Earl! Are you . . . ?'

'Asking you to marry me? Yes, I suppose I am. So what do you say?'

Her lip trembled again, and the tears that had been threatening filled her eyes, though they were now tears of happy disbelief.

'I'd say yes, of course.'

'That's all right, then.' He got up, went to her chair and took her hand. 'Let's go in the front room. It's not very comfortable out here.'

He saw the doubt flicker across her face; she was thinking that he'd only said what he'd said to get his wicked way at last.

'Oh, all right then. We'll stay here.'

He sat down on the arm of her chair and pulled her towards him, noticing as he did so that there were places on the crown of her head where he could see her scalp, pink and a little flaky, shining through her baby-fine hair.

'Vicky?' he said, alarmed. 'Is your hair falling out?'

She raised a hand to her head.

'There has been a lot in my comb lately.'

Earl felt alarm stirring again. He should be feeling elated: Vicky wasn't going to dump him, it was just that she wasn't well. But 'just not well' didn't really seem to describe it. The tiredness, the feeling cold all the time, and now on top of all that her hair falling out.

'Does your mother know about this?' he asked.

'I haven't told her, no. I don't want to worry her.'

'Well, I think you should. And if you're still the same after the weekend, you ought to see a doctor.'

'There's no need for that.'

'I think there is. You want to be fit if we're going to get married.'

She smiled up at him. 'All right. I will. Just one thing, though . . . You haven't told me yet that you love me.'

He shook his head. They weren't words that came easily to him. In fact, he'd never really thought them, let alone said them, and never expected to. But it was the truth, he realised now. He did love her. And if it would persuade her to go to the doctor and get to the bottom of all this . . .

He pulled her close again, buried his face in her soft hair.

'Love you.'

'And I love you.'

For the moment Earl forgot all his anxiety. Whatever it was that was wrong with Vicky, it couldn't be anything serious. She was only nineteen, with her whole life ahead of her. A life together.

The glow that spread through him at the thought was enough to warm them both.

'I've asked Vicky to marry me.'

Sunday morning: the Sykes family were having breakfast, all seated around the table. It was as good a time as any to make the announcement, Earl thought.

He'd lain awake for a long time after he got home last night, going over and over it in his head. It still didn't seem quite real to him, but there was no going back now.

'Well done, my lad! She's a cracking girl,' Ezra said.

'Oh, Earl, that's wonderful news!' A forkful of egg and bacon was poised halfway between Laurel's plate and her mouth.

'You're going to get married!' Rowan exclaimed. 'Oh, can I be a bridesmaid?'

Earl looked at Minty, the only one who had not spoken. 'Mam?'

'And what's her father got to say about it?' she asked, tight-lipped as usual.

'I haven't spoken to him yet.' Vicky's parents hadn't arrived home from the concert by the time he'd left, earlier than usual, as Vicky was still feeling unwell and he thought she should get to bed.

'Well, you'd better then, hadn't you?' Minty said, banging her cup down into its saucer. 'Before he hears it from somebody else.'

'Can't you ever be happy about anything, Mam?' Earl asked, exasperated.

'I'm happy as long as everything's above board and as it should be,' she returned tightly.

Laurel and Earl exchanged glances; Rowan wriggled uncomfortably.

'And I'm sure it is, m'dear,' Ezra said mildly.

'Just as long as it is, and not a cover-up.'

The others were left in no doubt as to her meaning. As always, respectability seemed to matter more than anything else to Minty.

Rowan was in bed and asleep when a commotion woke her. She pushed back the covers and got up, frightened. Every step she took towards the window was like trying to walk in soft sand, shifting with the pull of the tide. But she had to find out what was going on. Perhaps if she tried to swim instead of walking . . .

She spread her arms and managed to lift her legs. They came out of the sludge with a slurp and she kicked out in a semblance of the breaststroke Daddy had tried to teach her once when they'd gone to Weston-super-Mare for the day.

It worked, but the fear inside her was growing until she could scarcely breathe. She reached the window and pulled back the curtains, but everything was shrouded in foggy darkness. She could see nothing.

Then a figure materialised out of the fog. A man. Go away! she shouted, but he didn't seem to hear her. Go away!

And then he was staggering backwards. And someone – she couldn't see who – was raining blows on his head. Thwack! Thwack! Thwack!

She was too late.

She started to scream . . .

Rowan woke with a start. Her hands were clenched to fists, her heart thudding, and she was shaking from head to toe.

For a long moment she lay motionless, afraid to move a muscle. Then her conscious mind, numbed by fright, began to work again.

A dream. It was only a dream. But so real! A replay of the scene she had witnessed – or thought she witnessed – as a little girl.

Terrified to go back to sleep in case it began again, she forced herself to work her way to the edge of the bed and get up. She crossed to the window, not wanting to draw back the curtains but knowing she had to satisfy herself that nothing and nobody was there.

And of course nobody was. The moon, bright and clear, illuminated a deserted track and outhouses with their doors closed, all shut up for the night. Nothing stirred.

The dream was fading a little now, though the aura of it

remained. She felt just as she had felt all those years ago. It was a long while before she could bring herself to go back to bed, and even longer before she fell asleep again. Thankfully the dream did not return.

Next morning she told Minty about it, because the bad feeling still clung to her like a shroud.

'You're worried about your exam, I expect,' Minty said. 'Try and forget about it. You've done your best. You can do no more.'

Rowan nodded slowly. She supposed her mother was right.

She longed to ask her whether something really had happened that long-ago night, or whether it had been just a dream then too. But she knew what Minty would say. There was no point going over it again. And no point either worrying whether she'd done enough to win the scholarship she so desperately wanted, especially if it was upsetting her like this.

But the memory of the dream was clouding her day, and it refused to go away.

# Chapter Eleven

As spring became summer, Maggie felt her spirits reviving. The sadness was still there, a dull ache around her heart that refused to go away, but she was making a determined effort to get back to her old self. The longer days in themselves were cheering, the blossom on the trees had given way to full green leaf, the meadows were long and lush and dotted with wild flowers, and she awoke every morning to birdsong from the blackbirds and thrushes that lived in her admittedly rather wild garden.

Most days, as soon as her morning chores were finished, she took herself over to what had been Lawrence's stained-glass workshop. She had plans for a circular plate that could either hang in a window or be part of it, and had already made a start on it. In the centre, on a ground of clear glass, would be a cluster of reddish-brown oak leaves – she'd found some that were perfect for copying last autumn and set them aside – and the border would be narrow panels in shades of green. She'd had to ask Josh to help her with stretching the lead that provided the framework – what Lawrence had done so easily was quite beyond her; she simply didn't have the strength to do it – but all the other stages of the process came naturally to her: tracing the design onto a piece of glass, painting the leaves, using first the camel-hair brush and then the badger, carefully cutting them with a diamond and teasing them out ready to be fitted into place.

The weather was warm, so at times the heat from the kiln, fired with wood and charcoal, was almost unbearable, but Maggie didn't care. She wanted to get this piece done if she possibly could before the long school holidays began. Once the children were at home all day, she'd have little time to herself, and nor did she want it. Since losing baby Matthew, Patrick and Nora had become all the more precious to her.

She worked sometimes during the long evenings too, when the children were in bed, and it was there one evening when it was approaching ten o'clock that Josh found her, attempting to complete one more section before darkness fell.

'Come on, Maggie. You've done enough for today.'

She didn't look up. 'I won't be much longer.'

'I think you should stop now.' He came up behind her, took the brush from her hand and laid it down on a piece of rag. 'Don't think I don't know why you're doing this, but you'll wear yourself out.'

'I'm fine,' she countered. 'And yes, you might be right that I don't think so much about . . . our loss when I'm occupied with this, but that's not the only reason. I want to get better at it. I'll never be as good as Lawrence was, I know, but I want to be as good as I can be. So that we can work together. Build up a little business as we planned.'

Josh shook his head. 'I don't know that that is ever going to happen,' he said. 'It was a nice dream, but we can't rely on selling trinkets to put food on the table. And I just don't have the room in the shed to make things like doors and window frames that might be more profitable. We'd be hard pressed to manage if I wasn't bringing in a regular wage.'

Maggie turned to face him directly.

'We'll never know unless we try. And I have money put by from what Lawrence left me.'

Josh's mouth set in a hard line.

'That's not for spending on everyday living.'

'What is it for, then?'

'It's yours. Something to fall back on if ever you should need it.' Maggie opened her mouth to argue, but he silenced her with a look. 'I won't have my family supported by another man's money. It's my job to provide for you and the children, and myself as well.'

'Oh, Josh – you and your pride . . .'

But of course it was one of the things she loved about him. And she knew too the unspoken thought that was in his mind when he said that the money Lawrence had left her might one day be needed to provide the wherewithal to keep her and the children. Though he rarely spoke of it, he had never really got over the cruel and untimely end to the life of his own brother. She had been engaged to Jack when he had been killed in the terrible tragedy at the pit. Had they already been married, she would have been left a widow, and destitute. As had her mother, Rose. Josh's job as a colliery carpenter didn't carry with it the dangers a miner faced every day, but the loss of his brother had made him realise just how fragile and uncertain life was, and he wanted to be sure that she would not be reduced to poverty should the unthinkable happen.

'Of course, there may be no need to touch that money,' she said, retrieving the brush and beginning to clean it. 'Or at least not to begin with. If you were to make some small toys in your spare time, and I do more panels like this one, and perhaps paint some pictures . . .'

'And where would we sell them?' Josh interjected.

'I could take a stall in the market.'

'I can't see that bringing in much of an income,' Josh said, always the realist.

'But it would be a start. And I could take some samples round to the shops.' Maggie was warming to her theme.

'In High Compton and Hillsbridge? Nobody sells that sort of thing.'

'Exactly! But I wasn't thinking of the little local shops. I was thinking more of Bath.'

'Certainly there'd be more of a market there,' Josh conceded.

'You see? I'm ready to do whatever it takes. It could work, Josh! I'm sure it could!' Her eyes were shining now with excitement. 'It's my dream. And I'm going to make it a reality. Oh, say you'll help me!'

'Ah, Maggie.' It was so long since he'd seen her this excited. At last she looked like the old Maggie, bursting with energy, determined to overcome any difficulties, however insurmountable they seemed. The Maggie he had fallen in love with. 'Of course I'll help you.'

He put his hands round her waist, pulling her towards him. All too often in the last months her response to intimacy between them had been lacklustre, a submission rather than a sharing of love. Even a kiss or a caress seemed to trigger a withdrawal in her. Now, however, all the old warmth and closeness was there once more.

'Thank you, Josh.' Her arms went round him too, her body moulding to his, the perfect fit, just as it always had been. He kissed her, gently at first and then deeper, and felt her desire rising to match his.

'Oh, Josh . . .' she whispered against his cheek. 'I want you so . . .'

He needed no more telling. He rucked up her skirt, unbuttoned his trousers, and took her there against the workbench.

When it was over, she laid her head against his chest and he buried his face in her hair, mussed up now, and escaping its combs. It smelled a little smoky from the fumes of the furnace, with a hint of turpentine where she had tucked a strand behind her ear with oily fingers, but also sweet and clean.

'I love you, Maggie Withers,' he said softly.

'I love you too,' she murmured into his shirt.

Standing there in one another's arms it was as if the years had rolled away. All they had shared, the joys and the sorrows, the adventures and the life-changing experiences, was just extra layers binding them together. At the heart of it all they were still the same two people who had fallen in love under what had seemed like impossible circumstances. Two people who had been drawn together both physically and emotionally by a magnetic attraction too strong to resist. In that moment they were as one. Just as they always had been. And, God willing, always would be.

'Laurel . . . ?'

Laurel looked up from the book she was reading, sitting on the small patch of lawn between the flower beds and the vegetable plot. It was a warm Sunday afternoon in July; she'd helped her mother wash the dishes, and scoured the tiles where the potato saucepan had boiled over and left a salty splodge, and was now relaxing, making the most of a well-earned break before her week's work began again tomorrow.

Besides which she could scarcely bear to put the book down. Sherlock Holmes was back – alive! He hadn't died at the Reichenbach Falls after all – somehow he'd escaped! And there were thirteen new stories to devour. So far she'd read only three of them.

Laurel had always loved the Sherlock Holmes stories, and

now they reminded her of her days working for Edgar Sawyer, though he'd had nothing whatsoever in common with the great detective, and his end had been far less romantic and far more final.

Now she put her finger in the page to keep her place in *The Adventure of the Solitary Cyclist*, feeling a bit annoyed at the interruption.

'What's the matter, Earl?'

He dropped to the grass beside her, leaning back on his elbows.

'That doctor you used to know when you worked in Bath . . .'

'Ralph?' she said, startled.

She'd never talked to Earl, or any of the family, about him. They'd never even have known he existed if he hadn't come to see her that evening just after she'd left her job with Edgar Sawyer, and even then Earl had been more interested in his motorbike than he was in the man.

'Yes. Is he any good?'

'I really couldn't say. He's got plenty of patients, so I suppose he must be. Why?'

'I'm wondering if he could do something for Vicky.'

'Oh, Earl . . . I don't know . . .' She *did* know Vicky was poorly, and that Earl was worried about her. She hadn't been well when they'd got engaged back in the spring, and she still wasn't well now. 'What does her own doctor say?'

Earl snorted. 'Not a lot. He said he thought she was anaemic – whatever that might mean – and he's got her mam cooking liver for her two or three times a week. She's sick to death of it, but it doesn't seem to be doing any good. I reckon she ought to see somebody else – he's getting on a bit, is Dr Blackmore – and I thought of your friend.'

'He's not my friend,' Laurel said quickly.

'I thought seeing how he came all the way out from Bath to see you . . .'

'He shouldn't have. There's nothing between us.'

'But you must know him quite well . . .'

Better than I should, Laurel thought, and not as well as I wanted to . . .

'What are you suggesting?' she asked.

'I wondered if you could have a word with him. Ask if he could see her.'

Laurel's heart sank. She'd guessed from the very start of this conversation that this was where it was leading and hoped she could avoid it. Apart from glimpsing him at Edgar's funeral, it was almost a year now since she'd seen Ralph, and she'd begun to put their disastrous affair behind her. The last thing she wanted was for her feelings for him to be reignited.

'I don't know what he charges, but I should think he's a lot more expensive than Dr Blackmore,' she said, making one last stab at putting Earl off the idea. But her hopes were soon dashed.

'I don't care what it costs.'

Laurel sighed inwardly. But what could she say?

'All right,' she said. 'Just let me have a word with one of the doctors I work for first. Dr Mackay is a lot younger than Dr Blackmore and more in touch with the latest research. We'll see what he comes up with, and if he thinks it's a good idea, I'll get in touch with Ralph.'

'Thanks, Laurel! I wouldn't bother you, but I'm worried to death about her.' Earl got to his feet. 'I'll leave you to it, then.'

He walked away, back towards the house, and Laurel opened her book again. But she couldn't concentrate on a single word. All she could think of was Ralph, how she would feel and what might happen when she saw him again.

* * *

In the event, she decided it might be wisest not to take her family's personal problems to Dr Mackay. At Christmas he had asked her if she would like to accompany him to a drinks party, which it seemed was an annual get-together for the local doctors. Laurel had politely refused, making an excuse that she'd promised to help her mother make the Christmas cake. She'd imagined she would feel totally out of place at such a gathering, and besides, though she liked Dr Mackay, she didn't think it was a good idea to get involved with him socially and perhaps give him the wrong idea – that she was interested in him, which she certainly was not. After Ralph, she didn't want a man – any man – in her life. She might be totally wrong about Dr Mackay's intentions, but she didn't want to take the chance. Far better and safer to keep their relationship on a purely professional footing or things could get awkward.

He'd taken the hint – and goodness knows he should have, since her excuse was so clearly just that – but to her relief he hadn't taken umbrage either. Since then he'd been his usual pleasant, easy-going self, so she'd wondered if perhaps she'd misinterpreted his intention in asking her to the party. But she didn't want to risk doing anything to give him the impression that she looked on him as anything other than her employer, and talking to him about her brother's fiancée's health problems might just cross a line she didn't want to cross. Far better to seek advice from Dr Hicks, whom she always visited at his surgery in Stanton Magna on Wednesday. Crusty he might be, but he was also a committed family man who wouldn't see fifty again.

When the day came, she managed to make her work on his books last until the door had closed after his final patient, then broached the subject.

'Dr Hicks – I wonder if you could give me some advice . . .'

She went on to tell him about Vicky's symptoms, but even as

she spoke, she saw his eyes narrowing, and before she could finish, he lifted a hand, stopping her in her tracks.

'And who is the young lady's physician?'

'Dr Blackmore.'

'I'm sorry, Miss Sykes.' His lips were thin beneath his waxed moustache. 'It would be quite improper for me to comment on a patient of Dr Blackmore's, or on his diagnosis or treatment.'

Laurel flushed. 'I'm only asking your opinion, Doctor.'

'And I'm telling you it is not for me to express one. Unless, of course, the young lady wishes to change her allegiance and register with my practice. Might that be the case?'

Laurel shook her head. 'I don't think so. She lives in Hillsbridge.'

'Then I'm afraid . . .'

Laurel's flush deepened. 'I'm sorry, Doctor. I shouldn't have asked.'

'No, my dear, you shouldn't.'

Humiliated, Laurel got her things together. She was only glad she hadn't taken the problem to Dr Mackay. She would have placed him in just the same awkward position, and being the pleasant, friendly man he was, he might have found it far more difficult to say what Dr Hicks had just said.

Really, there was no other avenue open to her but to approach Ralph. Little as she wanted to, she couldn't let Earl down.

She telephoned him from the hospital when she was alone in the office the following Monday. As she had anticipated, Edith Yarrow, his receptionist, answered.

Though they had worked in the same building for some years, Laurel knew her only slightly and had never exchanged more than a few words with her; Edith was not the sort of girl to be either approachable or friendly. She came from a well-to-do family and, Laurel had always thought, considered herself a cut above the secretary of a private investigator. Really there was no necessity for her to work at all, but she was also a very modern young woman who had no intention of sitting at home painting watercolours or stitching tapestries while waiting for a suitable husband, and Ralph had once told Laurel that Edith was involved in the suffragette movement.

'It's Laurel Sykes,' Laurel said now. 'I used to work—'

'Yes, Miss Sykes,' Edith interrupted her. 'How can we help you?'

Her tone was cut-glass – and icy. Perhaps she spoke the same way to all Ralph's patients, but somehow Laurel doubted it. She'd known, without explanation, who Laurel was, and Laurel suspected that she also knew she and Ralph had been having an affair.

'I was wondering if I could speak to Mr Riley,' she said.

'I'm afraid not. Mr Riley is with a patient. Did you want to make an appointment?' Still stiff, and rather arch.

'Not without speaking to Mr Riley first.'

Laurel had thought long and hard about this. If Vicky was as poorly as Earl said she was, getting to Bath and back again would tire her out. What she was hoping was that she could persuade Ralph to come out to Hillsbridge to see her.

'As I just said, I'm afraid that's not possible at the moment. Mr Riley can't be interrupted when he is consulting.'

'Of course not.' Laurel threw caution to the winds. 'Perhaps you could ask him to call me when he's free.'

'I'll certainly pass on the message. What number should he call you on?'

Laurel gave her the number, hoping that she would be alone when – if! – Ralph called her back. If Matron knew she was using the hospital telephone for her own private purposes, she wouldn't be best pleased, and Matron was not someone Laurel wanted to upset. In the year she'd been working here, she'd discovered that not only was Matron a redoubtable character in her own right, she was also quite likely to report any misdemeanour back to the hospital board.

Luck was with her. It was almost one o'clock when the telephone shrilled, and she had just decided she would eat her sandwiches at her desk so as not to miss Ralph if he rang instead of on a bench in the hospital grounds as she had been doing during this spell of good weather. Not that she was in the least hungry: she'd been tense and jumpy all morning, and the butterflies fluttering in her stomach would, she thought, make eating impossible.

As she took the receiver from its hook, a nerve jumped in her throat, and it was all she could do to keep her voice steady as she answered.

'High Compton Hospital.'

'Miss Sykes?' Not Ralph, but Edith Yarrow.

'Yes, this is Miss Sykes.'

'I have a message from Mr Riley. He'd like to speak to you face to face rather than on the telephone. He could either see you one evening, when he's finished consulting, or on Saturday morning at, say, midday.'

Frustration flooded through Laurel in a hot tide. She'd hoped Ralph would have realised by now that whatever had been between them was over, and moved on. Now she could see he had not. What did he think he had to gain by asking – no, commanding! – her to come to Bath to meet him? Did he think she'd changed her mind, or that he could still change it for her? How could he be so arrogant? But the fact of the matter was he held all the cards. If she wanted to talk to him about Vicky, she was going to have to face him.

She thought quickly. A Saturday morning would probably be the safest option. But it was more than a week since she'd promised Earl she'd try to arrange for Ralph to see Vicky, and he'd already asked her several times if she'd yet managed to do anything about it and looked frustrated about the delay. Besides which, she didn't know that she wanted the prospect of meeting Ralph again hanging over her all week.

'Would tomorrow evening be suitable?' she asked.

'Tomorrow. At six.'

She sensed the disapproval in Edith Yarrow's voice. Or was it jealousy?

Laurel did a quick calculation. If she left work promptly and missed her tea, she was fairly sure she could catch a train that would get her to Bath in good time.

'Please tell Mr Riley I'll be there,' she said.

As she replaced the telephone, her hand was shaking.

School had broken up now for the long summer holiday, and still there had been no news about Rowan's scholarship exam. Mr Shearn had promised that he would send her the result as soon as it came in, and the waiting was making Rowan horribly nervous. When she'd left the headmaster's study immediately after sitting the papers, she had felt quite confident, but that confidence had faded as time went on. Now she'd reached a stage where she had almost accepted that she had failed, and each morning she watched for the postman with a feeling of dread and held her breath as Minty sorted through any letters, then gave a little shake of her head.

'No, nothing, Rowan.'

'There's no point getting yourself in a state about it,' Laurel had said when she saw Rowan nibbling the skin around her fingers – a sure sign she was getting worked up about something.

'You've done your best. You can't do more than that. And I'm sure everything will be fine.'

And Ezra would chuck her under the chin, and say in that patient, resigned way of his: 'Cheer up, princess. It's not the end of the world.'

But to Rowan it felt exactly like that. The end of her hopes and dreams, anyway. And having to go to the secondary school with the same children who had tormented her all these years . . . She cringed inwardly as she imagined what they'd say if she failed after all the extra tuition she'd been pulled out of class for.

'Thought you were better than us, didn't you?'

'That took you down a peg or two, Miss Clever Dick.'

But though the thought of failure made her feel physically sick, there was nothing she could do now but wait, hope and pray.

# Chapter Twelve

Outside the house in Queen Square Laurel hesitated for just a moment and took a deep, steadying breath. She'd caught the train to Bath by the skin of her teeth, then spent the entire half-hour journey rehearsing what she would say to Ralph, but still she wasn't at all sure where she'd begin. So much depended on what he had to say to her. Perhaps he wouldn't try to rekindle what they had once shared, but her instincts told her otherwise.

Why else would he have insisted on seeing her face to face, here at his consulting rooms? What other possible reason could there be? She hadn't been given the chance to explain that her reason for wanting to speak to him was a purely professional one. He most likely thought she'd had a change of heart. Well, she'd soon put him right on that.

Making up her mind, she rang the bell. For long moments there was nothing but silence, and she wondered if perhaps he'd brought her here on a fool's errand as some kind of punishment. Then she heard the click of an inner door opening and footsteps on the tiled floor. The door opened, and there he was. Handsome as ever. Well groomed as ever.

'Well – Laurel,' he said.

'Ralph.' Her voice was tight.

'Do come in.'

She stepped past him into the hallway, remembering suddenly that this was where Edgar Sawyer had been found dead. Had he answered the door to someone that night in October, just as Ralph had done now? Though it was a warm evening, and her face felt hot, she shivered and turned into the outer office of his consulting rooms.

Following her, Ralph said, as if he'd read her thoughts: 'Dreadful about poor Edgar, wasn't it?'

It wasn't how she'd expected the conversation to begin, but she was grateful for it.

'Terrible. They're no nearer to finding out who was responsible, I suppose?'

'I think not. Some crazed vagrant from the streets, in my opinion. The police inspector checked everyone connected to his recent cases, as I understand it, and could find no one who had both motive and opportunity. They questioned you about his clients, I imagine?'

Laurel nodded. 'They did, but I couldn't think of anything useful to them.'

Ralph indicated to her to go through into his inner sanctum – a spacious room with high arched windows overlooking the square. Two upright but well-upholstered chairs were drawn up in front of an oak desk and behind it was a captain's chair with a green leather seat, while a low chaise against one wall served as an examination couch. But for a narrow border the stained-board floor was covered with an enormous Chinese rug in vibrant shades, and watercolours of certain Bath landmarks – the Abbey, Sally Lunn's shop, the Parade Gardens – hung on the walls. It was a room designed to impress – and to make Ralph's patients, most of whom were well heeled, feel at home. Remembering their assignations, Laurel avoided looking at the chaise.

'Do sit down, Laurel.' Ralph gestured towards one of the pair of chairs. 'Would you like something to drink?'

'No, thank you.' She didn't want this to become a social event.

'Then I hope you don't mind if I do.'

From a cabinet he produced a bottle of whisky – single malt – and a crystal tumbler, and poured himself a generous measure. Then he set it on the desk, and, instead of going around to his captain's chair, took the other of the pair beside Laurel, moving it round so he was facing her.

'Yes, poor Edgar. A bad business,' he said, returning to the subject. 'I have to say, I've thought more than once that it could just as easily have been me. As you know, I'm often here alone, working late. I could well have been the one who opened the door to some knife-wielding lunatic. Since that night I've been careful to take certain precautions. There's a loaded revolver in my desk drawer . . . Oh, don't look so shocked. I do have a licence, though of course by rights the gun should be kept under lock and key.'

'Well I'm glad you didn't have it levelled at me when you answered the door tonight,' Laurel said, trying to make light of this startling revelation.

'Hardly. I was expecting you. And angry as you were when I came to High Compton to see you, I really didn't anticipate your intention in coming here tonight was to do me harm.' He rolled the whisky around the tumbler, took a sniff and then a judicious sip. 'So tell me, Laurel, why are you here? Is it because you've had a change of heart? Because that's what I'm hoping.'

His eyes met hers and in spite of herself she felt the old attraction spark between them, and with it a pull of longing.

'No, Ralph,' she said. 'Nothing's changed. You're still married, I assume, and I'm done with creeping about behind your wife's back. Not that I knew that was what we were doing at the time. If I had, I'd never have—'

'And if I hadn't been married?' His eyes were still holding hers.

'But you were. You are.' She wasn't going to give him the satisfaction of hearing her say that if he wasn't married things would be quite different. That she missed him dreadfully. Still had feelings for him. That she had only ever felt this way about two men, and he was one of them. That the memory of how her other love had ended was always with her, and she had no intention of putting herself in the position where history could repeat itself.

'Please, Ralph, let's not talk about it. That's not why I'm here. I've come for your professional advice. My brother's young lady – well, fiancée really – is ill, and her doctor seems to be at a loss to get to the bottom of it. I wondered if you'd see her, perhaps treat her.'

He sipped his whisky. 'Tell me about her.'

She did, and he listened, putting in the odd question here and there.

'So what do you think could be wrong with her?' she asked eventually.

His eyes were narrowed now, thoughtful.

'It's difficult to say. The symptoms you describe could be caused by any number of things. I'd need to see her, examine her, and even then maybe . . .'

'But you might be able to give her something that would help?'

'I can make no promises.'

'Would you come out to see her? I don't think she's fit to travel all the way to Bath.'

'It's unusual. But I could.'

There was one other thing she should mention.

'Can you give me some idea of your fee?'

He smiled faintly. 'My usual patients, Laurel, range from the well-off to the wealthy, and my fees are set accordingly. But seeing as we are *friends* . . .' he laid emphasis on the word, 'I'd be prepared to waive them entirely in this case.'

'Oh no, I'm not looking for favours,' Laurel said quickly. 'Earl is quite ready to pay your fee, whatever it is.'

'I suspect he could ill afford my usual charges,' he said smoothly, 'but perhaps we could agree on a compromise. If I am able to help his fiancée, I'll take the cost of the medication.'

Laurel bit her lip. She really didn't want to agree to anything that would put her in debt to Ralph. But neither did she want to go back to Earl empty-handed.

'And your expenses,' she said. 'And at least something for your time.'

'My expenses won't amount to much. A gallon of petrol for my motorcycle, perhaps. So if it would make you more comfortable, I'll agree to that. As to my time . . .'

His eyes met hers again directly; again the imp of longing twisted in her gut.

'Being with you, even if it is only for half an hour, and in the company of your future sister-in-law and her family, will be payment enough.'

The colour rose in her cheeks.

'I'm sorry – I know I made a mess of things when I came out to High Compton to see you,' he went on. 'And I'm sorry, too, that I didn't tell you myself about my wife and son, but as I said, I was too afraid of losing you. It was wrong of me, and stupid. I should have known you'd hear it from someone else and make up your mind without giving me the chance to explain.'

'No explanation would have made a difference, Ralph,' she

said tightly. 'You're a married man, and that's an end of it.'

'But I won't always be, Laurel. I married Amy when we were both far too young because it was the only decent thing to do when Bertie was on the way. But he's fifteen now. He'll be a grown man before we know it, and making his own way in the world. And I shall be free to live my life the way I choose.'

Laurel frowned, scarcely able to believe what she was hearing.

'You can't mean you'd divorce her? That would cause the most terrible scandal. Not to mention the expense . . .'

He moved his chair a little closer to hers, reached across and took her hand.

'I love you, Laurel. It's you I want to be with. Whatever the scandal, whatever the cost, it would be worth it to me. People would forget in time, and as you know, I am not without means. If only you'll be patient for a while longer, we will be together, I promise you.'

'Oh, Ralph . . .'

She should snatch her hand away, she knew. Tell him in no uncertain terms that her mind was made up. That she absolutely would not resume their affair or be the cause of the break-up of his marriage. That coming to see him today had been a terrible mistake.

But oh, she'd missed him so! Every day since she'd left her job with Edgar Sawyer. There had been no one to take his place, and she didn't want there to be, just as, until she'd met Ralph, there had been no one but Callum. She didn't give her heart lightly, but when she did, it seemed, the love consumed her, even when it was hopeless. Callum had left her broken, and still she'd wanted no one but him. Ralph was a married man, but she couldn't forget him, couldn't cut him out of her heart no matter how she tried. And it seemed he loved her too, so much that he was prepared to sacrifice his reputation for her, not to mention it costing him dear. He was offering her hope for a future together, and the prospect of it was dizzyingly tempting. The pot of gold at the end of a far-off rainbow.

'Oh, Ralph,' she said again, softly. 'I don't know . . .'

But in her heart, she already did.

She had given up so much in her life; this was a chance for real happiness.

If she hadn't come to see him today, perhaps she could have remained strong. But fate in the shape of Earl's Vicky had given her a push in Ralph's direction. Perhaps that was an indication that it was meant to be.

'When would be a good time for me to see my newest patient?' Ralph asked, businesslike again. But his hand still covered hers.

'The sooner the better really.' She strove to sound businesslike too, but she was aware of the double meaning of her words and felt a little shiver of anticipation run through her.

'Tomorrow, then?'

'Yes.'

'So – give me the address.' At last he released her hand, but the prickle of warmth on her skin where his fingers had touched remained.

In the hallway he smoothed back her hair, a tender gesture she remembered well, and kissed her lightly on the cheek. He wasn't rushing her, and though all her senses were crying out for him, she liked that.

'I love you, Laurel.'

She met his eyes and smiled, not ready yet to repeat the words back to him, but glowing inwardly all the same.

'Are you leaving now too?' she asked.

'I've got a few things to finish up. I'll see you tomorrow.'

He opened the door. The evening air felt cool on her hot cheeks. And then the door had closed behind her and she was walking across the square in the direction of Green Park station, her feet seeming to float over the paving stones.

For the first time in more than a year, Laurel felt truly alive.

The exhilaration lasted until she reached the station, where she sat on a bench on the platform, waiting for her train.

You stupid, stupid girl! she chided herself. What are you getting yourself into?

But still she could feel no regret, just a tingle of apprehension alongside the wellspring of hope for the future.

Green Park was the end of the line, and when the train pulled in and the passengers had disembarked, Laurel boarded and found a seat in a third-class carriage.

She thought of Ralph, still in his consulting rooms in Queen Square. Was an unhappy marriage the reason why he worked such long hours? She hoped he would leave before it got dark, and realised the deep-seated effect Edgar's murder had had on her. It could just as easily have been Ralph as Edgar who had opened the door to the killer that night. Suppose they returned? All alone in the building Ralph would stand no more chance than Edgar had done. A loaded gun in his desk drawer wouldn't save him unless he had some warning. If anything should happen to him now, just as she'd found him again, she couldn't bear it.

A thought came to her unbidden, and a chill ran through her. What if it hadn't been a random killing? Really there was no reason to suppose some vagrant had suddenly gone mad and killed indiscriminately, and as far as she knew there was no reason to believe it had been a robbery gone wrong. Nothing had been stolen, and the viciousness of the attack pointed to it having been carried out with the full intention of causing harm. The police had believed the assailant was a disgruntled client of Edgar's, or someone whose misdemeanours he had uncovered, bent on revenge.

But supposing Edgar hadn't been the intended victim at all? Supposing it had been Ralph? There must, surely, be some failures amongst the patients he had treated. Had there ever been a case when something had gone badly wrong, and he had done harm instead of good? Could it be that a grieving relative had blamed him, and come to his consulting rooms to mete out retribution? Or had he had a dalliance with another woman when Laurel had walked out on him? A married woman, perhaps, with a furious cuckolded husband? The very thought of him with someone else sent a knife through her own heart.

But the fact remained: Ralph and Edgar were of similar height and build. In the dimly lit hallway it wasn't impossible that the attacker had mistaken one for the other, especially since Ralph's surgery was on the ground floor, and the attacker might reasonably expect it to be him. If the door had been left on the latch as it so often was, someone could have walked straight in, perhaps just as Edgar was leaving . . .

With a tremendous effort, Laurel stopped the horrible train of thought. Speculation like this would drive her insane. Instead she concentrated on the green fields slipping past the windows of the carriage, and imagined herself and Ralph walking through them, hand in hand.

In between worrying about her exam results, Rowan sometimes found herself thinking about Patrick, the nephew of Cathy-next-door and grandson of the Withers family at the end of the rank.

She'd seen him only a few times since the day he'd found her dozing over *A Tale of Two Cities* last summer, and never to speak to, though she only had herself to blame for that. When he came to visit his grandparents or his aunt next door, she kept well out of sight, while surreptitiously watching for him from her bedroom window. Once, he'd looked up and seen her, and waved, and she'd ducked back, her face flaming. And it wasn't just because Minty had forbidden her to speak to him, though that gave her the perfect excuse to herself. It was also because of the way he made her feel – the flutters in her stomach, the edge of nervous excitement like nothing she'd ever experienced before, as if she was on the brink of something momentous, though she didn't know what.

This summer he'd come to Fairley Terrace less often. His mother still visited regularly, but she only brought the little girl, Nora, with her. Spending a day with relatives must be pretty boring for Patrick, she imagined, since his cousins were so much younger than him, and he was opting to stay at home or go out to play with friends now that he was old enough to be left alone. But whenever she heard Maggie at the door of number 6, calling out to Cathy: 'Anyone home?' her heart leapt, only to sink again when she saw Patrick was not with her.

How stupid was that? She wouldn't speak to him even if he was there. But for some reason she just wanted to see him, even if it was only from her bedroom window. She liked those tingly feelings; she liked *him*. Perhaps one day, when she was older, and not so shy . . . and her mother less strict . . . But there her daydreams stopped short, and even when she was alone she could feel her cheeks growing hot, though she really didn't know why.

That Wednesday afternoon in July was hot and sultry, the sun obscured by dark, threatening clouds, and rather than walk across the fields as she so often did and risk getting caught in a thunderstorm, Rowan had taken her book to the little patch of lawn between the flower beds and the vegetable patch. She spread out an old blanket and settled herself on it, lying on her stomach – without the blanket, the dry, coarse grass prickled at her bare arms and legs.

Mr Shearn had loaned her yet more books, and amongst them was one she was particularly enjoying – *Little Women* by Louisa May Alcott. Of the four sisters the story centred around, Jo was her favourite; she even wrote stories, as Rowan herself liked to do, and she found herself identifying with Jo. And in her mind's eye, Patrick was Laurie. Rowan was hoping very much that Jo and Laurie would end up together.

Voices floated up from the track. Mrs Oglethorpe and Mrs Weeks, by the sound of it. She'd seen Mrs Weeks pass by with a shopping bag over her arm earlier; presumably Mrs Oglethorpe had been outside and caught her on the way back.

Everything went quiet for a bit, and then suddenly the silence was broken by shouts and screams from the next-door garden – the Donovan boys, Ollie and Percy, chasing one another up and down the path, shrieking as usual. Rowan tried to ignore them, but she had to admit, her mother had a point when she complained about them.

Propped up on her elbows, she covered her ears with her hands. But she couldn't shut out the squeals, nor, a few minutes later, the voice calling her name.

'Hey – Rowan!'

She went very still, a little thrill, half alarm, half pleasure, running through her. She knew who it was instantly, though she must have missed Mrs Withers and her children arriving. Perhaps they'd come much earlier, had dinner with Granny Withers up at the end of the rank and only just come down to see Cathy Donovan.

She looked up. Patrick Withers was standing on the other

side of the fence, peering over. Already she could feel the colour rising in her cheeks.

'Oh, hello,' she said.

'Do you ever do anything but read?' he said.

Her flush deepened. 'I like reading,' she said defensively. 'Don't you?'

He shrugged. 'Not much. I'd rather be out exploring. I think I might be an explorer when I grow up. Like Dr Livingstone. Or a sailor. We came all the way from New York on a ship. It was really exciting. My sister Nora was seasick, but I wasn't. Not at all. Though I did nearly get swept overboard.'

'Oh, golly!' Rowan didn't really know what to say. By comparison her own life seemed dreadfully dull.

'What do you want to do when you grow up?' he asked.

'I'm not sure.' Then, from *Little Women*, inspiration struck. 'I think I might be a writer.'

'What – books and stuff?'

'Yes.'

'That's why you read so much.'

'I suppose.'

An awkward silence. But he was still there, looking at her. She shifted uncomfortably, part of her wishing he would go away, part wanting him to stay and talk. If only she could think of something interesting to say . . .

'Rowan!' Her mother appeared on the path. 'Rowan! Can you come and help me put the sheets through the mangle?'

Rowan got to her feet, not sure whether to be relieved or not.

'Sorry, I've got to go.'

Minty stood unmoving until Rowan reached her, her face as black as the threatening thunderclouds overhead. Then she put her hand in the small of Rowan's back, giving her a little shove in the direction of the house.

The mangle was pushed back against the wall of the outhouse as it always was when it wasn't in use, and Rowan was in no doubt at all: her mother didn't really want her help. She'd seen her talking to Patrick Withers and was determined to get her away from him. She hurried across the track, fearful that Minty would begin haranguing her here, within his earshot. But at least this time she didn't do that.

'What have I told you about talking to that boy?' she demanded as soon as the door closed after them.

'I couldn't help it,' Rowan said. '*He* was talking to *me*.'

'You could have got up and walked away.'

'That would be rude – and mean.' Rowan knew all about what it felt like to have someone walk away when you spoke to them. 'And he's really nice.'

Minty snorted, a sound of disgust that was more eloquent than any words.

'Why can't I talk to him anyway?' Rowan asked.

'Because.'

'But Laurel's friendly with Cathy. And she's his auntie.'

'Don't answer back.'

'But—'

'That family are not the sort I want you mixing with. Besides, you're far too young to be having anything to do with boys.'

Rowan had heard it before, Minty tutting when she saw some very young couple holding hands, or, on one occasion, actually kissing.

'We weren't doing anything wrong!' she protested.

'That's how these things start,' Minty said darkly. 'Just you stay indoors until they've gone. And in future, keep well away from him.'

Rowan plopped herself down in a chair and opened her book.

There was no arguing with her mother. But for perhaps the first time in her life, she felt resentful.

The seeds of rebellion had been sown.

'I meant what I said, Laurel.'

Ralph had ridden his motorcycle from Bath to Vicky's home in Hillsbridge, where Laurel was waiting for him. Earl had wanted to be there too, but by the time he'd got home from work and had his bath, there was no way he could make it, even if he missed his tea, so Laurel had cycled over alone. Earl had arrived since, though, as Ralph was finishing his consultation with Vicky in the front room, and now he was with her and her parents, talking over what the doctor had said.

The consultation seemed to have gone well. Vicky's mother had, like Earl, been willing to try anything, though her father had been more sceptical. But when Ralph, Vicky and Mrs Weaver had finally emerged from the front room, even he had been impressed by Ralph's confident and professional manner.

He hadn't been able to make a definite diagnosis. 'There's an imbalance in her system that needs correcting, but there could be a number of reasons for that,' had been his verdict. But he had prescribed a couple of medications, and left her some starter doses to be going on with – 'Just one or two drops in water, daily' – which he believed would help, though 'If there is no improvement, there are other things we can try,' he'd said. 'Once we establish which medication is the right one, we'll have won the battle.'

Laurel hadn't cared for his use of the word 'battle', but of course she said nothing, and when she accompanied Ralph out to thank him and see him off, there were other things on their minds.

'I meant what I said. I love you, Laurel, and I think you love me. Let's not throw away what we have. It's precious.'

'You'd really leave Amy?' she asked, torn between longing and her conscience, which troubled her still. 'Whatever it might entail?'

'In a heartbeat. As soon as Bertie is grown.'

'Oh, Ralph . . .'

'You're coming to Bath to collect more of the tinctures I've prescribed for Vicky, aren't you?' he said. He had given her just enough to be going on with, and Laurel had offered to pick up further supplies as it was much easier for her than it would have been for Earl. 'We can talk some more then. And it will give you time to think things over. I don't want to pressure you into doing something against your will. But I think you feel as I do. At least I hope you do.'

He was fastening his motorcycling jacket as he spoke; the smell of the leather once again revived her old fond memories and made her ache with longing. All she wanted was to be in his arms, with her face buried in that leather jacket and his chin resting in her hair. Wanted it so much it was all she could do not to go to him here and now. But of course she couldn't do that, here on the main road between Hillsbridge and Dunderwick.

'I think you ought to be going,' she said instead. 'It looks as if that storm that's been threatening all day is heading this way, and it's going to be pouring with rain before long.'

He reached out and touched her lips, parting them slightly with his finger.

'I'll see you soon, then?'

She nodded. She was lost, and she knew it.

He started the motorcycle, winked at her and smiled, and then he was gone. She watched until he had disappeared round the corner out of sight, then went back into the house.

* * *

The letter from Mr Shearn dropped through the letter box a couple of days later. The postman had been early; it was already lying on the breakfast table when Rowan came downstairs.

When she saw it there, her hands flew to her mouth.

'Oh, Mam . . .'

'I haven't opened it yet,' Minty said. 'I was waiting for you.'

'I should hope so!' Laurel was finishing her breakfast before leaving for work. 'It is addressed to Rowan after all!'

'I don't think I can . . .' Rowan was shaking from head to foot.

'All right. I will.' Laurel picked up the envelope before Minty could. 'Are you ready?'

'No – no . . .' Rowan said from behind her hands.

Laurel slit the envelope open with the bread knife anyway, slid the sheet of paper out.

'It's all right, Rowan – you can look at it,' she said, her face wreathed in smiles.

Rowan took the letter from her. The words seemed to leap from the page.

'I did it!' she whispered, still scarcely able to believe this wasn't a dream. And then, louder, so that she was almost screaming: 'I did it! I did it!'

Laurel was out of her chair now, grabbing her sister, whirling her round and round, every bit as excited and pleased as Rowan herself. Only Minty seemed unmoved.

'Well done,' she said. But her lips were tight. She'd gone along with this, but that didn't mean she had to like it. 'You've got a lot of hard work ahead of you, you know.'

Rowan was far too happy to care.

# Chapter Thirteen

By the time of her eleventh birthday, which fell in November, Rowan was beginning to get used to her new school, and she loved everything about it. She loved the elegant building in Portland Place, she loved the ordered atmosphere, and she loved the lessons, which stretched her as she had never been stretched before. Her classmates were all girls who were eager to learn, so there were no unwelcome disruptions. Rowan was in awe of some of them – they spoke in cultured tones and clearly came from well-to-do families – but they were far too polite to make unpleasant comments about her as the bullies at her old school had done. And she'd already made a friend – Mary Wilmott, who was a scholarship girl like her and lived in Oldfield Park.

The only thing she didn't care for was the long walk from the railway station to the school, but Mary had an even longer walk, which took her close to the station, and before long the two of them were meeting up and making the trek together.

One very wet morning, a motor pulled up beside them and Alexandra Stephenson, one of the grandest girls in the form, called to them to get in. It was being driven by her father, an eminent specialist at the eye hospital, and he had taken pity on the two girls who were looking, as Minty would have put it, like drowned rats. Rowan had never ridden in a motorcar before, and was dumbstruck in the presence of the great man, but after that he always stopped to give them a lift if he passed them, for which they were immensely grateful.

It was always teatime before Rowan got home in the afternoon, and then there was homework to do before she fell, tired out, into bed. But she was happier than she could ever remember, apart from when she was very small.

She had always looked forward to her birthday. Each year Minty made a special tea, with a big iced fruit cake and candles, and the whole family would be there to see her blow them out. Even when she had been working in Bath, Laurel had made a special effort to get home for the celebration. Then there were presents to be opened – she always left them until teatime, though she was bursting to know what was inside the exciting packages.

This year, however, everything was put into the shade by preparations for another important event. Earl and Vicky were going to be married on the first Saturday in December.

Though she still tired easily, Vicky was much better. Opinions varied as to whether it was as a result of Ralph's potions, or whether she'd simply shaken off some infection and would have got better without them. Minty tended to think it was all a put-up job, as she called it, a ruse to get Earl to marry her, but she had the good sense not to say so in front of either of them, though she became very tight-lipped when they sang Ralph's praises.

Whatever, there seemed no need to delay the wedding any longer, and the date had been set. To her delight, Vicky had asked Rowan to be a bridesmaid, along with her unmarried sister, Ethel, and her little niece Gwendoline. Laurel was making Rowan's dress, something that was causing her a great deal of worry, for she was no seamstress, and she wasn't very adept at using the sewing machine Vicky's mother had loaned her. Each evening she would sit at the kitchen table, her determination fired up. Tonight she would get the thing working perfectly. Tonight would not end with her packing everything away close to tears of frustration. She could do it, she could! And the dress would be everything Rowan wanted it to be.

There would be no sewing tonight, however. Not on Rowan's birthday. After tea, and the present-opening, they'd play some games, and perhaps have a sing-song. Rowan was growing up fast and Laurel wanted to be sure this birthday would be another happy occasion to tuck away in her treasure box of memories when family parties were a thing of the past.

As soon as she'd finished work for the day, she collected her bicycle, loaded her things into the basket and set out for home. It was a much easier ride in this direction, downhill most of the way, and then along the flat straight that led to Fairley Terrace. As she bowled down the hill, the chill wind whipped at the shawl she had tied over her hair, stung her cheeks and turned the tips of her fingers numb inside her gloves, but she scarcely noticed.

Ralph had telephoned her this afternoon as he sometimes did, and though she was always worried that she was going to be caught out by Matron coming into the office, or the lady who manned the telephone exchange from the front room of her cottage listening in to their conversation – as Laurel felt sure she did if she wasn't busy with other calls – it was worth the risk just to hear his voice. Besides – the sneaky thought crept into her mind – if word should get out about their affair and his wife got to hear of it, perhaps it would mean they could be together sooner rather than later. Prickles that were part apprehension, part excitement ran down her spine when she thought of it. Whilst the guilt still niggled at her deep down, and appre-hension as to what Mammy would have to say about it, she was also floating on a cloud of sheer joy. He loved her. She loved him. They made each other happy. How could that possibly be wrong?

She glowed now as she re-ran in her mind the things he'd said to her earlier, relishing each one.

She was bubbling with excitement too over the birthday present she'd bought for Rowan – and again, she had Ralph to thank for that. A couple of weeks earlier she'd seen the very thing in the window of the jeweller's in High Compton high street – a tiny silver locket on a velvet ribbon. She'd fallen in love with it instantly and knew that Rowan would love it too, but when she'd gone inside to enquire the price – the little white tags attached to the items for sale by a thread of cotton were always written in code or turned over so as not to deter potential customers – she'd realised the locket was way beyond what she could afford. Her savings had been exhausted buying Rowan the uniform, books and equipment she'd needed to start her new school, and as she was paying her sister's train fares to Bath each day and helping out with any other expenses, there had been no chance to replenish them.

She'd mentioned the locket to Ralph for no other reason than because he always wanted to know every detail of what she'd been doing since they'd last seen one another.

Since winter had set in, making it uncomfortable for him to come to High Compton on his motorcycle, she'd begun taking the train to Bath one evening a week, making the excuse at home that she was meeting an old friend, and implying that the friend was a young lady. Sometimes, if Edith Yarrow had packed up and left for the day, they got no further than his consulting rooms, but usually they went for something to eat at

183

a restaurant where Ralph was reasonably sure he wouldn't run into anyone he knew, or be recognised.

That night it had been a small, dimly lit private dining room, where the food was excellent and the serving staff discreet.

'I honestly don't know what to get her now,' she'd said. 'It was so perfect, I can't think of anything else. But I couldn't possibly afford it.'

'You think a great deal of your sister, don't you?'

Ralph's eyes had been on her face, thoughtful, musing, and Laurel shifted a little in her scat, uncomfortable under his piercing gaze.

'She's everything to me.'

He smiled slightly, his eyes challenging now.

'And where do I fit in?'

'Oh, don't be silly!' Laurel said quickly. 'You know how I feel about you. That's quite different.'

'I should hope so!' He was silent for a moment, dabbing at the corners of his mouth with a linen napkin. Then his eyes returned to hers. 'Would you let me help out? With this locket for Rowan?'

'Oh, Ralph – no!'

'I'd like to. It clearly means a lot to you. And if you think it would mean a lot to her . . . well, why not?'

'Because . . . I just couldn't. It wouldn't be right. I'd never have mentioned it if I'd thought . . .'

He reached across the table to take her hand, which was curled around the stem of her wine glass.

'I know you wouldn't. Unlike my wife, who thinks I'm a gold seam to be mined. Amy is a taker. If I hadn't had the prospects of a career that would reap rich rewards, I don't believe she would have even looked at me twice, let alone trapped me into marrying her. She'd have found someone else to keep her in the manner to which she wished to become accustomed. But you . . .' He squeezed her fingers. 'You haven't a mercenary thought in your head. Which is why it pleases me to help you out if I can.'

Though his words warmed her, just as the wine was doing, still Laurel shook her head.

'You've done more than enough already, treating Vicky for free. Besides, the present must come from me, otherwise it wouldn't mean anything.'

'Then suppose we call it a loan? You can pay me back when you're able.'

'But unless I get a pay rise or take on more work, I don't know when that would be. I've promised to support Rowan through school, and that will be another four years at the very least . . .'

'And maybe by then you'll be my wife.' Ralph lifted her hand to his mouth and kissed it. 'My dearest, you have all the time in the world to repay me. And in ways far more important than money.'

Perhaps it was that that had made her weaken, perhaps it was the wine, or perhaps it was because she did so want to be able to give Rowan the locket. But when they parted that night, the banknotes to pay for it were tucked in her bag.

Next day, on her way to Dr Blackmore's surgery, she made a detour to the jeweller's shop because she was so afraid the locket might be sold by the weekend. That evening, at home, she tied a pink ribbon round the box and wrote a card: *With all my love, Laurel.*

Now, cycling home on the afternoon of Rowan's birthday, she glowed as she imagined her sister's face when she opened it

The warmth from the well-stoked fire enveloped her the moment she opened the kitchen door, and she took off her gloves and unbuttoned her coat. Minty was already laying the table for tea, and the cake, resplendent with eleven candles and one in the centre for luck, stood in pride of place, together with a bowl of jelly and another of stewed plums, bottled last autumn.

'Where is everybody?' Laurel asked, sliding the shawl off her head and folding it over her arm.

'Rowan's up in her room, doing her homework, and your dad and Earl aren't home yet, though I hope they won't be too much longer. As it is, they'll have to have their baths in the outhouse tonight.'

'But it's bitter out there,' Laurel objected.

Minty huffed. 'Well, they can't have their tea mired in coal dust, can they? And I'm getting everything nice in here.'

'For goodness' sake, Mam, put the bath in front of the fire like you always do. Me and Rowan will stay out of the way till they've finished. They'll catch their deaths outside.'

'They'd get on with it quick sharp, though, wouldn't they?' She banged down a plate, then straightened it. 'Perhaps you're right, though. I've got to say I don't like the sound of your dad's chest lately, and he does seem to get out of breath a lot quicker than he used to.'

'Yes, I'd noticed that too.'

Really it would have been impossible not to notice the wheeze and rattle, which had got much worse since the bad weather had set in, and it worried Laurel. Ezra had been down the pit ever since he was twelve – only a year older than Rowan was now – and the chances were high that he was developing silicosis, the miner's disease. It was an awful prospect: that he would end up like poor old Mark Lapham at number 8, unable to walk further than the bench outside his door before his breath gave out and constantly coughing up coal-black phlegm into a stained rag. But she wasn't going to think about that today. She didn't want anything spoiling her enjoyment of Rowan's birthday.

She ran up the steep flight of stairs and onto the narrow landing, where she pushed open the door to Rowan's room.

'Happy birthday, my love!'

Rowan was curled up on her bed surrounded by books and exercise books. A fire burned in the little grate – one of the few benefits of being a miner was cheap coal, and Minty had taken to lighting it in the afternoons before Rowan got home so that the room would be warm for her to do her homework undisturbed.

She looked up now, her face wreathed in smiles. 'Thanks, Laurel!'

'Have you had a nice day?'

'Yes, I have. I got some cards from the other girls and Mary gave me a present . . . look!' She rummaged in her satchel and pulled out her home reader – chosen from a list of works of fiction the girls were expected to work their way through during the school year. Something jutted from between the pages; Rowan opened the book and carefully took out a bookmark, pressed flowers mounted on a strip of white card. 'Isn't it lovely? She made it herself. I started using it straight away so she'd know I was pleased, but really it's too nice for that and I'm afraid of damaging the flowers.'

'It would look nice under the glass on top of your dressing table,' Laurel suggested.

'It would, wouldn't it? I'll get Earl to lift it off for me.'

Laurel nodded. 'Right. I'll see you later.'

She crossed the landing to her own room, which was bitterly cold by comparison with Rowan's, took off her coat and laid it across the bed. She'd been glad of the extra warmth it provided last night, and would probably need it again tonight. She hung her shawl over the back of the chair beside the bed and folded her scarf on top of it. Then she went to the top drawer of her tallboy and got out the little jeweller's box tied with ribbon and the card she'd written for Rowan.

She should wait, she knew, till after tea, following the time-honoured custom. But she didn't want to wait. She wanted to give her gift to Rowan when they were alone. Now. Making up her mind, she went back across the landing to her sister's room.

Rowan looked up, surprised to see her again so soon.

'We've got to stay up here until Dad and Earl have had their baths, and my room feels like an eskimo's igloo,' Laurel said. 'Besides, I wanted you to have this.' She held out the box and the card. 'Happy birthday, darling.'

'Oh, thank you!' Her eyes sparkling, Rowan took them. 'Whatever is it?'

'Open it and see.'

'But . . . won't Mammy be cross that I didn't wait to open it with my other presents?' Rowan asked, ever the dutiful child.

'Who cares?' Laurel said recklessly.

'Really?' Rowan was fingering the box eagerly.

'Go on, open it. I'll set things right with Mammy.'

Laurel needed no second bidding. Although she was bursting with impatience, she untied the ribbon carefully and laid it on top of the pile of books beside her. Then she lifted the lid of the little box.

'Oh! Oh, Laurel – it's beautiful!' Her voice made no secret of her delight.

'And so are you.'

'I've never seen anything so beautiful! Is it really mine?'

'Of course it is!' Laurel laughed, though her throat was suddenly tight with emotion and tears pricked her eyes. 'Do you like it?'

'I love it! Can I put it on?'

'With your school uniform?'

'Why not? I won't be able to wear it tomorrow, of course. We're not allowed to wear jewellery in school.'

'Go on then.'

As Rowan struggled to fasten the ribbon at the nape of her neck, Laurel went to help her.

She'd been right, the locket was perfect. Somehow it seemed to complement Rowan's neat features, and the ribbon lent colour to her pale skin. She was beginning to lose her puppy fat, Laurel thought, and when she did, she was going to be really pretty.

A rush of love rendered her speechless for a moment. Then: 'I can't believe you're eleven years old already,' she said, her voice a little shaky. 'Eleven years!'

Voices from downstairs announced that the menfolk were home.

'There's Dad and Earl by the sound of it,' she said, and the moment passed. 'Hurry up and finish your homework, and when they've had their baths, we'll be able to go down and tuck into your birthday tea.'

'I've more or less finished. Will you test me on my Latin vocabulary?'

'Well, I'll try.'

Rowan handed her an exercise book into which she had carefully copied the verbal declensions.

'*Amo, amas, amat,*' she recited.

'What does it mean?' Laurel asked.

'I love, you love, he loves . . .'

Laurel smiled. It seemed to sum up perfectly the way she was feeling.

# Chapter Fourteen

Maggie set down her end of the wooden workbench she was helping Josh to move from the centre of her workshop so that instead it was up against the wall and out of the way, and looked down at her hands where the edge of the bench had cut into her palms and fingers, leaving deep red dents.

'I'd never have guessed it would be this heavy.' She sounded out of breath, and the blood was pounding in her temples.

'It is solid wood.' Josh had set his end down too. Now he repositioned his hands and was flexing his muscles in preparation to take the strain again. 'Come on, we're nearly there.'

'I wish I hadn't suggested moving it now. Can't it wait until we can get Patrick to help?' Maggie brushed away an imagined sheen of perspiration from her forehead with the back of her hand, leaving a dirty smear.

'Let's finish it now we've started. You can do it.'

Maggie sighed theatrically. 'Slave driver.'

She took her end once more and between them they shuffled the bench to its new position, leaving the centre of the workshop clear for Josh's much lighter carpenter's bench, which was to be moved in from the outhouse he had been using as his own workshop.

The roof there had sprung a leak, and in the heavy rain that had fallen in the last few days, water had begun pouring in. Josh had already moved his tools, as he was concerned they might rust in the damp atmosphere, and he didn't want his workbench rotting either. But there was another reason too for bringing it into Maggie's domain: he'd need the extra room to allow him to carry out their latest project, while Maggie could just about manage to do her part in a smaller space.

It had come about as a result of an order she'd been given whilst manning the stall she'd been running at Hillsbridge's Saturday market for the last month or so.

She'd been lucky to get the pitch, she knew. It wasn't in the most ideal of positions, tucked into a corner that had previously been used by other stallholders for storing empty crates and pallets, and some of them had complained about having to take their rubbish away with them. But she'd managed to sweet-talk the supervisor into letting her use it, and he'd even helped her set up a trestle to serve as a counter. He'd also promised that as soon as one of the regular pitches became vacant, he'd give her first refusal – he'd been impressed, she thought, by the quality of the wooden toys Josh had spent all his free time making, and her own contribution of trinkets and stained-glass panels. There was nothing else remotely like them amongst the other stalls – the greengrocer's, the dairy, the knick-knacks and jewellery, and the flower stall, which at this time of year had nothing more exciting than rather weather-battered chrysanthemums to offer.

Business had been slow to begin with, but with Christmas just around the corner, things were looking up. Though she knew the items she was selling were worth far more, Maggie was canny enough to keep her prices low, and now customers were snapping up the little wooden ducks on wheels, the dolls' furniture and the stained glass. Maggie thanked her lucky stars they'd built up a good stock before she'd taken the stall.

One thing she'd tried out was a small panel similar in design to the leaf plate she'd made, and which now hung against their sitting room window. The new panel was oblong instead of round, and Josh had made a stand for it, like a three-sided picture frame with graduated sides, so that it could be displayed on a windowsill where the light could shine through it. She'd set it up on the trestle with a candle behind it to show what the effect would be, and it had generated enormous interest, though it hadn't yet sold when Maggie was ready to begin packing up – despite the market remaining open into the evening, she made sure she left in time to get home and make the children's tea. There was always a hiatus anyway at this time of day, and the crowds were thinning as a portly gentleman came puffing down the aisle between the stalls.

'Ah – good – you're still here,' he said, coming to a halt beside the trestle.

'You've just caught me.' Maggie was boxing up what was left of the doll's-house furniture. 'What can I help you with?'

The man didn't reply for a moment, gazing closely at her stained-glass panel in its stand.

'Beautiful,' he said. 'My wife noticed it when she was here earlier, and insisted I come and have a look at it myself.'

'You'd like to buy it?' Maggie asked, trying to conceal her eagerness. Transporting the piece to and from home without damaging it was something that worried her.

'Possibly. But that wasn't what we had in mind. My wife has always wanted a front door with a stained-glass panel. If I was to find a carpenter, would you be able to make something similar to this that could be fitted into it?'

Maggie's heart leapt. This could be a way into getting the business they'd planned.

'I can do better than that,' she said. 'My husband is a

carpenter, as it happens. He made the stand – and all those wooden toys. But he can also do bigger jobs and I'm sure he'd be happy to make a door for you. I could fit the glass panel and we could deliver it to you complete.'

'Capital! Capital! I can see this is my lucky day.'

Mine too, Maggie thought. Aloud she said, 'You can tell me if you have any preferences as to colour and so on, and I'll prepare some designs for you. Then, if you still want to go ahead, my husband can visit you to talk about the wood, and take measurements.'

'Capital!' the man said again. 'You'll want my name and address. Do you have pencil and paper?'

Maggie did – a small pad on which she kept a tally of the items she had sold – but she'd already packed it away. She rummaged in her bag and found it, and a pencil.

'The name is Jordan, Denzil Jordan. Number twenty-two, Waterloo Road.'

The name meant nothing to Maggie, but she knew Waterloo Road as one of the main roads out of Hillsbridge, and she guessed that number 22 would be one of the pairs of lias-stone villas at the top of the steep rise. It was an area for professional people, and in any case she couldn't imagine an ordinary working man being able to afford such luxury as a new door with a stained-glass panel.

Patrick had come to meet her and help her transport any unsold items home. She told him excitedly about the new development.

'It's what we've been working towards ever since we got back from America,' she said. 'Your dad making doors and window frames as well as toys and things.'

Patrick, who had inherited his father's practical streak, frowned.

'Where's he going to do that? There wouldn't be room in his workshop.'

'We'll sort something out,' Maggie said. Already she knew the answer – she'd have to sacrifice space to allow Josh to move into her much larger workroom. If the business took off as they hoped, they would, in time, have to look for alternative accommodation – something Josh and David were already talking about, as David was anxious to find premises for the printing business he was planning to set up. But for the moment they had to make do with what they had. She could just about manage, she thought. And although it was far from ideal, it would be worth it if she and Josh could begin to realise their dream.

Which was why, on that cold, dank Sunday morning they were struggling to set up the new arrangement. She'd come up with some designs – sprays of flowers, tulips and roses, and leaf arrangements similar to the one she'd done before and was so pleased with – and Josh had discussed the door with Mr and Mrs Jordan. It wouldn't be anything fancy – the stained-glass panel would be the main feature – and Josh thought he could make it quite quickly once he had the space to work in.

Maggie brushed her face with her hand, leaving yet another dirty smudge.

'We're making it happen, Josh!' she said triumphantly. 'Didn't I tell you we could do it?'

'We're not there yet.'

'No, but we will be. We'll have built a reputation before you know it.'

'Oh, Maggie.' Josh shook his head, smiling at her enthusiasm. 'You are the most determined woman I ever met.'

'Perhaps I've had to be.'

'You're also one of the muckiest.' He pulled out a handkerchief. 'Here – wipe your face.'

She took it and scrubbed at her cheeks.

'Better?'

'No, you've still missed it. Come here.' He took back the handkerchief and scrubbed at the dirty patches himself. 'If you're going to be a businesswoman, Mrs Withers, you'd better start looking the part.'

'Cheek!'

This was the way they were now, an old married couple, comfortable enough with one another to tease and josh. But a couple whose love was as passionate as it had ever been, and enriched by the heartaches and happiness they had shared. She was, Maggie thought, the luckiest woman in the world.

David's landlady, a Mrs Perkins, was talking non-stop as usual. Perhaps it was because she spent most of the time on her own, he thought, and hid a smile as he wondered if she talked to herself when she was alone, this stream of inconsequential rambling. If she'd always been like this, he pitied her poor dear departed husband. It couldn't have been much fun, having his ear bent ceaselessly when in all likelihood all he had wanted was some peace and quiet after a hard day's work. But then again, he had probably been immune to it and done what David was doing now – shutting himself off from the constant repetition of stories he'd heard a dozen times before.

Back in the summer, when he'd realised there was no escaping the interminable chatter, David had taken to going upstairs to his room, making the excuse that he had letters to write or a book to read. But it was too cold now to spend long up there, away from the warmth of the fire. He might well have an early night, though, he decided. There were only so many times you could say 'Fancy that!' or 'Well, I never did!' and Mrs Perkins wasn't someone you could have a proper conversation with. The simplest remark would only set her off again on a story or opinion of her own. Which was just as well. It gave him time to think. And goodness knows, he had plenty to think about.

Though he would have much preferred to be alone, with no interruptions, David was managing to give the impression of listening to Mrs Perkins whilst actually mulling over the surprising turn of events of the last few days – at last the main reason that had brought him here to Somerset was bearing fruit.

Now he was trying to decide what his next move should be. And whether the time was right to make a move at all.

'Goodness me, I thought it was a bride!'

Rowan looked round, blushing but nevertheless pleased, to see Cathy Donovan emerging from the house next door.

'No, it's just me,' she said with a giggle.

It was the day of Earl and Vicky's wedding, the first Saturday in December, and Rowan had gone outside to watch for Fred Carson's pony and trap, which had been booked to take the family to Hillsbridge, where they would meet Vicky and her family.

'We can't walk all that way in our finery,' Minty had said. 'And what if it should be raining? We can't have our Rowan spoiling that dress before she even gets to the church.'

Thankfully it wasn't raining. It was a brittle, bright day, the sun shining in a sky the colour of early bluebells, but it was bitterly cold. Minty had inherited a third-hand fox-fur cape from an aunt who had been a lady's maid, and had dug it out of the back of the wardrobe for Rowan to wear, but she was already shivering in her thin georgette dress. When she was ready, however, she had been too excited to sit still; besides, she had wanted to show herself off to the neighbours, not just hurry out and be squashed into the trap with the others.

When she'd looked at herself in the long mirror in Laurel's

room, she'd been thrilled with the reflection that looked back at her. Yes, she was still undeniably a bit overweight, though not as overweight as she had been, but the layers of filmy fabric floated nicely over her rounded stomach and hid the plump knees she hated. Laurel had taken her hair up into a bouffant style, leaving delicate curls to hang loose and frame her face, and tucked a tiny sparkling coronet into it. Then she'd arranged the fox fur round Rowan's shoulders and fastened it with a loop and button beneath her chin.

Rowan hadn't seen the fur for years, though she remembered dressing up in it when she was little, and it smelled strongly of mothballs. But: 'That'll go when you're out in the fresh air,' Laurel had said, and Rowan hoped she was right; the smell was tickling her nose, and she didn't want to have a sneezing fit just as Earl and Vicky were making their vows.

Now she basked in Cathy's admiration – and Cathy wasn't alone, either. Maggie Withers, who her mother said was no better than she should be, emerged from the doorway too, followed by Freda Donovan and Maggie's little girl Nora. Was Patrick there too? she wondered, and though she still squirmed with embarrassment whenever she met him, she rather hoped he might be watching from the window. He wouldn't want to admit he was interested in a bridesmaid on her way to a wedding. That would be a sissy sort of thing.

Freda Donovan, however, was doing nothing to hide her curiosity.

'Oh, pretty!'

She advanced towards Rowan, clearly bent on feeling the delicate fabric, and Cathy grabbed her by the arm and yanked her away.

'Don't touch!' she warned. 'Rowan doesn't want your sticky fingers messing up her dress.'

Jennie Felton

At that moment Fred Carson's pony and trap turned the corner, and other doors opened up and down the rank.

'He's here!' Rowan shouted, the excitement prickling again and bubbling up so she could scarcely contain it.

'Right.' Minty came out, straightening the silk flower in the lapel of her best coat, and pointedly ignoring Cathy and Maggie. 'Are you going to help me up, Mr Carson?'

'It's all right, Mam, I'm here.' Earl handed her into the trap, then lifted Rowan in before going round to sit up front with Fred.

'You all look lovely!' Cathy called as Laurel and Ezra emerged from the house. 'I hope everything goes off all right.'

'Thanks, Cathy.'

Ezra closed the back door after them, wheezing a bit, and they both climbed up into the trap.

'Reckon you'll have to sit on my lap, my love,' he said, and Rowan climbed onto his knee, proud and happy to have his arm round her waist, the father she adored.

Fred turned the pony and trap and they were off, all the neighbours watching them go. As they turned the corner, Rowan glanced over her father's shoulder and was gratified to see Patrick standing beside Maggie. So he had come out to have a look after all! If he had but known it, he had just made Rowan's day.

As the organ began to play the Bridal March, all heads turned to watch the small procession making its way up the aisle. Vicky, her pallor making her look fragile and almost ethereally beautiful, leaned on the arm of her father, who was puffed up with pride and stuffed into a suit shiny with age, a tight collar cutting into his neck. Vicky's niece clutched a small posy of silk flowers as if her life depended on it, while Vicky's sister Ethel and

Rowan brought up the rear, in dresses as identical as was possible given that they had been made by different people.

Tears gathered in Laurel's throat and filled her eyes as they approached. Weddings were always emotional occasions, that moment when a smiling bride walked towards her love waiting for her at the altar steps, and this one was especially poignant. They'd been so worried about Vicky, and now here she was looking like a princess, and so happy, and it was Laurel's brother who waited at the altar. Earl and Vicky were going to live with Vicky's parents once they were man and wife, and Laurel was going to miss him. Then there was Rowan, looking so grown up and beautiful in the dress Laurel had sweated blood over; she couldn't have been more proud of her. And added to all that was the thought that maybe one day soon she herself would be the bride, on her way to becoming Ralph's wife. If he divorced Amy they probably wouldn't be able to be married in church, and that was a sadness to her, but the important thing would be that they would be together.

Laurel swallowed the tears of happiness and turned to glance at her mother.

'Oh, Mam,' she whispered.

Minty was watching the procession too, her eyes fixed on Rowan and her mouth set in a hard line – perhaps even harder than usual.

'She's growing up. She's not a little girl any more,' she muttered, and though her words were almost lost in the swell of the organ, Laurel heard, and knew what her mother was thinking.

'She'll be fine, Mam,' she whispered back.

'I certainly hope so.' Her voice was low and bitter.

Vicky was at Earl's side now; he turned to smile at her, and Laurel thought he was hardly recognisable as the young tearaway he had once been. That was what love could do for you.

The music ceased, and in the hush that followed, the rector's voice rang out.

'Dearly beloved, we are gathered together here in the sight of God and in the presence of this congregation to join together this man and this woman in holy matrimony . . .'

The service had begun.

# Chapter Fifteen

## February 1910

'Well, what do you think?'

Josh waved an arm expansively to take in the farmyard, outbuildings and stables, all derelict now, the paintwork peeling on the doors and window frames. But the stonework was still solid, walls that had been built to last for generations, and the tiled roofs still more or less watertight as far as he could tell. There was a problem with parts of the guttering, but nothing that couldn't be fixed relatively quickly, and with the incessant rain of the last few days it would be nothing short of a miracle if there wasn't the odd puddle here and there.

It was still raining now. The torrents had eased to a thick, cold drizzle, but the heavy blanket of cloud threatened more to come. It might even snow. Maggie thought she had felt something more solid than mere rain on her face since they'd emerged from the farmhouse and before she had put up her umbrella.

'Let's go home and talk about it,' she said.

'Don't you want to have another look around inside?' Josh asked.

'No, I've seen all I need to. And we can always come back another day when the weather's more cheerful.'

'As long as someone else doesn't snap it up from under our noses.'

'Josh – does it look like the sort of place that's going to be snapped up?'

She saw Josh's face fall and immediately regretted the sharpness of her retort. She hated to dampen his enthusiasm, and she knew how much it would mean to him to buy this place, with all its potential for expanding their growing business. It was, after all, what they'd been working towards ever since they'd come back to England.

'Honestly, Josh, I don't think anyone else is going to be looking at it any time soon,' she said more gently. 'It's been empty for several years, hasn't it, and it's not as though it's a working farm any more. The land was sold off when Farmer Crook died.' *To pay off his debts*, she could have added, but didn't.

'I suppose you're right. And we shouldn't do anything in a hurry,' Josh conceded. 'But you've got to agree, it's perfect. I'd have my own workshop with plenty of room, and so would you. And we could offer David the stable block for the printing equipment he wants to get, and he could live in the room above. The rent would help pay for whatever we want to do with the house – and come in handy when the new baby arrives and you don't have as much time for your work.'

Instinctively Maggie's hands went to her stomach, pressing against the slight swell that was a new life beginning inside her, as if to protect it. The terrible sadness for the loss of baby Matthew had never left her, nor the guilt that came from knowing it was her own carelessness that had caused the miscarriage. Though days and sometimes weeks could go by without her consciously thinking about it, still Matthew was an ache around her heart, a cold, hard nugget of regret deep inside. The grief could catch her unawares and bring her up short as she saw Patrick turning from child to young man, heard Nora's infectious giggle, watched them play together. Patrick was very good with Nora, rarely pushing her away as many boys of his age would. At those times tears would ache in her throat to know that Matthew would never grow up as they were growing up, never laugh or play as they did. There was a vacant space in all their lives: the loved and longed-for child who had never so much as drawn breath.

For some time after the tragedy Maggie had not wanted another baby. To even consider it had seemed like a betrayal of her lost son. But as time passed she had begun to yearn to hold a newborn – *her* newborn – in her arms. To feel the tug of an eager mouth at her nipples. To have that sweet baby scent in her nostrils, the smell of soap and milk and innocence.

Three years and more had passed and she had not fallen pregnant. Each month she'd hoped, with increasing intensity; each month she'd wept inwardly at the first smear of menstrual blood. Once she'd been almost two weeks late, and with each passing day her hopes had risen. She'd said nothing to Josh, hugging her secret to herself. But it had come to nothing, and Maggie had despaired. This was her punishment. She'd been entrusted with a precious new life and she had failed her baby. Now she would never again be a mother.

And then, miraculously, it had happened. At first she was afraid to believe she wasn't just imagining the familiar signs, then breathlessly optimistic. Now, three months pregnant, she was racked with anxiety. If something befell this baby she couldn't bear it, would never forgive herself. And as Josh mentioned it so casually, here in the farmyard, the terror rose in her throat, almost choking her.

Take nothing for granted . . .

It wasn't the ideal time, of course. Just when they were thinking of moving into accommodation that would allow them to grow the business, which had taken off more spectacularly than either of them had dared to hope. But it wasn't just the business that was in need of more space. As the children had grown, the little house that had once been quite adequate seemed to be shrinking, and with another addition to their family, living conditions would become even more cramped. Neither Patrick nor Nora would want to share their bedroom with a small brother or sister, and the baby couldn't remain in a crib in Maggie and Josh's room for ever. Though the thought of all the upheaval when she was heavily pregnant was not an inviting one, it was the answer, and the impending arrival was what had prompted Josh to start looking in earnest for something that would suit their needs.

The old Crook place, to his mind, fitted the bill perfectly.

Only half a mile from their home, on the Hillsbridge road, it had been the farm where Maggie used to go for a jug of milk when they first returned to England. But when Farmer Crook had died, there was no way his widow could keep the place going – for years he'd struggled himself, and had probably worked himself into an early grave. Mrs Crook had gone to live with one of her daughters – also a farmer's wife – in the depths of the Somerset countryside, on the Mendips. The meadows where their cows had once grazed and the fields where they'd grown crops for winter feed had been sold to a neighbouring farmer, but the farmhouse and outbuildings remained empty and unloved.

When Josh had unlocked the heavy old kitchen door with the key the Crooks' solicitor had loaned him, however, Maggie's heart had sunk.

The kitchen was vast compared to her own, with an old range fireplace, a row of stone sinks below the window and a flagged floor. But it was depressingly dim, and Maggie wrinkled her nose at the pervasive smell of damp and mould.

'Good size,' Josh said approvingly.

'It's very dark,' Maggie ventured.

'What d'you expect on a day like this?' He crossed to a big kitchen table, obviously left behind when Mrs Crook had moved out, rapping it with his knuckles and rubbing his thumb over the grain. 'This is a good bit of wood. I could do something with this.'

Josh, ever the carpenter.

'We're here to look at the house, not the furniture,' Maggie said.

'Just saying. We shall need a bigger table . . .'

Maggie didn't think she would ever fancy a meal off it, no matter what Josh did to it. She didn't think she'd fancy food in this kitchen at all, if she was honest. But she knew this wasn't the moment to say so.

She moved around the kitchen opening cupboards, discovering a walk-in larder and trying to muster some enthusiasm.

'There's a sitting room here.' Josh had gone into a room leading off. 'Looks quite cosy.'

Maggie thought it anything but. Though marginally an improvement on the kitchen, it had the same dark and depressing feel, and the wallpaper was coming away in one corner, drooping down to reveal the bare wall beneath that might be a damp patch.

There was also a sofa and two armchairs, their covers faded and marked with age.

'Don't even think about it,' she warned.

'I'm not! I'm a carpenter, not an upholsterer,' Josh retorted. 'Besides, I like our sofa. Come on, let's have a look upstairs.'

Maggie followed him up a steep flight of uneven stairs to a landing where the floorboards creaked and shifted underfoot and the ceiling was uncomfortably low, so that Josh had to duck his head.

'That's because it's along the side of the house,' he explained, undeterred. 'It'll be higher in the bedrooms.'

'But you'd forget and bang your head on the door frames,' Maggie said.

'I'd get used to it.'

'If you say so.'

He was right about the bedrooms, though. There were five in all, leading off the landing, one as big as their three put together, Maggie thought, the others descending in size to one not much more than a box room because, presumably, it was under the eaves. Thankfully they had been emptied of almost all the furniture, and the three largest had small fireplaces with grates.

'We could soon get the place warmed up and dried out,' Josh said. 'And just look at that view!'

Maggie followed him to the window. It was true, even on a murky day like today, the view was stupendous, looking right out across the Hillsbridge valley.

'When it's clear, I bet you can see for miles,' Josh said, and Maggie had to agree. She was used to being surrounded by a wall of trees; this open aspect gave her her first positive feeling about the place.

When they explored the outbuildings and stables, she was forced to concede they would be ideal, too. Still, as they stood in the farmyard in the rain, having locked up for the final time, her overwhelming feeling was that all she wanted was to turn her back on this depressing place and go home.

'Come on, Josh,' she said, taking his arm. 'Patrick and Nora have been on their own quite long enough. Goodness only knows what mischief they're getting up to.'

'Yeah, all right.'

He started across the rain-soaked farmyard. But as they reached the road, he turned back for one last look, and Maggie could see the enthusiasm writ large across his face.

She had a horrible feeling that in the end she would have to go along with it. His dream. Hers too, except that she hadn't imagined it anything quite like this.

She was right. Even as she pointed out problems and negative aspects, she knew she was fighting a losing battle. Josh was dead set on having Hillview Farm, as it was properly called, and she knew it would be wrong to flatly refuse to consider it simply because the place made her feel claustrophobic, almost panicky.

They'd been back several times, taking the children. Patrick was almost as enthusiastic as Josh, except for being sad at the prospect of leaving his tree swing behind, but Nora was less sure.

'It smells funny,' she proclaimed.

'Once we've got fires going and given the place a good clean, it will be fine,' Josh had assured her, and Maggie had thought: yes, but how many buckets of soapy water will it take? And who's going to be the one doing the scrubbing?

They'd also taken David along, and he had immediately accepted Josh's offer of the stable block for a workshop and accommodation. That, Maggie knew, was the final piece clicking into place.

Over the past years the two men had formed a firm friendship, and Josh's dream of setting up in business together had stretched to include David. Rather than just Maggie and Josh, now it would be almost a commercial commune. Like Josh, David would do bread-and-butter work – calling cards and wedding invitations, black-edged bereavement cards and official notices – but with the specialist equipment he intended to get, he would also venture into producing fancy goods, like the scraps that had so impressed them when they'd met him on the voyage home. He'd need his own premises for that, and he was anxious too to move out of his lodgings and into a place of his own.

Maggie had mixed feelings about him living and working in such close proximity. She'd grown to like him, and she could see no valid reason why the arrangement should not be perfectly successful. He was pleasant and easy-going. He was good with the children, who were very fond of him. He had no bad habits as far as she was aware that would make him a disagreeable neighbour or a bad tenant – he didn't partake excessively of hard liquor, he wasn't a womaniser. Though he was still single and had no serious relationships – again, as far as she knew – he didn't indulge in liaisons with women of ill repute. 'He's happy with his own company,' Josh had said when she'd asked him about it. But beyond that, he couldn't say.

'Perhaps he's had his heart broken,' Maggie had suggested, but Josh had simply replied that that wasn't the sort of question he was going to ask.

And of course, he wouldn't. It wasn't in his nature. Josh accepted folk at face value, listened if they cared to talk, but would never push the limits into what he called prying, and chided Maggie for her curiosity.

The trouble was that she *was* curious. She'd never forgotten the first time she'd seen David, standing alone at the ship's rail, and the feeling she'd had, nebulous but strong, that there was a dark cloud hanging over him, and if she was honest, she felt it still.

It was as though his life before they'd met him was a closed book. They knew nothing, really, about him. Or she didn't. Perhaps he'd confided something of his past to Josh, and Josh had chosen to keep that confidence, as if he were a priest in a confessional.

But she was just being silly, she told herself. If Josh knew some dark secret from David's past, or if he suspected there were unsavoury elements in his present, he wouldn't be such close friends with him, and would certainly never contemplate having him around the children.

Yes, to all intents and purposes, David would be the perfect tenant and neighbour, and she must put any fantastic notions out of her head.

Almost before she knew it, their offer for Hillview Farm – or simply Hillview, as they intended to call it – was made and accepted, and with a heavy heart Maggie put the home that Lawrence had left her on the market.

She sleepwalked through viewings, half hoping the prospective purchasers would not be interested. She'd wished they could rent it out again as they had whilst they were in America, but she knew they needed the money its sale would bring to be able to afford their new home and all the necessary renovations.

David, she was forced to agree, was working like a Trojan to help Josh make the house and stables habitable. They were there every spare moment doing the necessary repairs and even the basic cleaning – Josh had refused to allow her to do heavy work in her condition, almost as concerned as she was that no harm should come to their unborn child, and even more anxious about her well-being.

One Sunday in late April, he and David came back from their latest stint on the house, paint-splattered but smiling, and when they'd cleaned themselves up and eaten the roast dinner

Maggie had cooked, Josh suggested that she and the children should go back with them that afternoon and take a look at the progress they'd made.

Maggie washed the dishes and the children dried up while the men had a well-earned sit-down, and then they all set out.

It was a fine clear day, fluffy white clouds sitting like giant snowflakes in a pale blue sky, and already there was warmth in the sun.

'I think you'll be surprised at how different it looks,' Josh said.

Maggie was glad it wasn't too far to walk. She seemed to tire very easily these days, whereas she'd sailed through her earlier pregnancies. I'm getting too old for this, she thought, though she'd never say it out loud.

As they turned into the farmyard, the heaviness in her limbs and body seemed to creep into her stomach. The out-buildings looked just as they had the last time she'd seen them, dilapidated, depressing, even with the sun shining on them. Imagining having this outlook from her kitchen window instead of a bush where birds nested made her sad. Once she'd seen a blackbird feeding its young – three eager open beaks peeking up, for all the world like an illustration in a book of nursery rhymes.

But as they approached the farmhouse door, she saw that it was no longer faded and peeling; it glistened under a coat of new paint, a beautiful forest green. And when Josh threw it open, she stepped into a kitchen similarly transformed. The walls had been given a coat of whitewash, and the paintwork was also green – a pale leafy shade instead of the previous dirty brown. The stone sinks had been scrubbed of all the grime that had made them so disgusting, as had the flagged floor. The table was still there, but cleaned up – Maggie could see that Josh would be able to work his magic on it when he had time – and it now stood on a green and gold patterned rug.

'Where did that come from?' she asked, astonished.

'David got it in a house clearance sale,' Josh said.

'It's lovely, David! You must let us pay you for it.'

'Not a chance. It's a house-warming gift,' David said, and Maggie wondered why she still felt so uneasy about him when he was so kind and thoughtful.

It was the same upstairs. The boards still creaked and the ceiling on the landing was still too low, but everything looked clean and perfectly habitable.

'It all looks lovely. How in the world have you managed it?' Maggie asked.

'Elbow grease,' Josh said with a smile. 'So what do you think?'

'I'm amazed!'

The children were running from one bedroom to another arguing about which would be theirs. The view from the windows was spectacular, the valley bathed in sunshine, the hills on the far side clearly visible, a vista in shades of green.

Perhaps, Maggie thought, it was going to be all right after all.

A month later, their old home sold, they moved in.

When the last of their belongings had been loaded into the cart they had hired – it had taken three journeys to move everything – Maggie walked around the now empty rooms, pausing in each one to soak up the memories and store them away for ever. So much happiness, and grief too – all part of the rich pattern of life. So much a part of her.

Last of all she crossed to the workshop.

Strange to see it bare of all the tools, lead and paints. Even the kiln had gone – Josh was going to install it in its new home.

Yet she could still feel Lawrence's presence, and guilt washed over her.

'Forgive me, Lawrence,' she whispered. 'I'll never forget you, or stop being grateful to you, but it was time to move on.'

Tears were gathering in her throat; she pressed a hand over her mouth and moved quickly to the door.

'There's nothing to forgive.'

The words were as clear in her head as if they had been spoken aloud in Lawrence's gentle tones.

The tears filled her eyes now. She paused in the doorway; the sky sparkled like a million tiny diamonds as she stared up at it through wet lashes, and the sunlight slanting through the trees was like a blessing.

'Be happy, my dear.' Lawrence's voice again, soft, loving.

Maggie swallowed hard and wiped the tears from her lashes, but the sky still seemed to sparkle, and her lips curved up into a tremulous smile.

'Thank you, Lawrence,' she said softly. 'For everything.'

Then she pulled the door closed after her and walked towards her new life.

By the time the baby arrived at the beginning of August, they were settled happily in their new home. There was still a great deal to do before it was exactly as they wanted it, but they were getting there.

David had moved into the room above the stable. He took his meals with them, but refused to allow Maggie to do his laundry – she had enough on her plate, he said. Once a week he brought his dirty washing to the kitchen and did it in one of the big stone sinks, then put it through the mangle outside the back door and pegged it out on the washing line. Maggie had insisted she iron it, though, and after he'd scorched and very nearly ruined Josh's newly restored table, he had reluctantly agreed.

She was beginning to feel more comfortable about him, and really couldn't understand why she'd allowed her imagination to run away with her so. Just because he was a private person didn't mean he had anything to hide. And it was good that Josh had a pal to chat to – working for himself, he'd missed the company of other men, she knew.

It was the middle of the night when her labour pains started. She tried to lie still, so as not to disturb Josh, but as they intensified, she couldn't help wriggling about in an effort to get some relief. She was beginning to feel a little anxious, too, as she didn't want to be caught unawares – 'After the first few it's like shelling peas,' her mother had once said – so she was quite grateful when Josh grunted: 'Are you all right?'

'I think I've started,' she said, just as another pain gripped her, sharp enough to make her gasp.

Josh was up and out of bed in a moment, reaching for his trousers.

'I'll wake David.'

The plans had been carefully laid: when Maggie went into labour, David would go on his bike to fetch the midwife – not the horrible Mrs Harvey; they'd booked a woman who lived in Dunderwick and who seemed very nice as well as capable – while Josh remained with Maggie.

Now, though, Maggie couldn't help remembering that it had been David who had gone for help when she had lost Matthew, and she felt a stab of fear that history might repeat itself.

But this was quite different, she told herself. Matthew had been born too soon. She'd carried this baby full term. Everything would be all right. It had to be!

As Josh came hurrying back upstairs, Patrick was at his bedroom door, rubbing sleep from his eyes.

'Dad? What's going on?'

'It's all right, Patrick. Go back to bed. No – on second thoughts, go in with Nora.' The last thing he wanted was for her to burst in on a scene unfit for a child's eyes. 'Your mam is having the baby. Stay with Nora until it's all over. I don't suppose it will be too long.'

'I don't expect so either,' Maggie said as he came back into their bedroom. 'I hope David hurries.'

'He will.'

'And you'd better get some water on to boil . . .' Another pain gripped her like a vice. 'Can you hurry too?' she managed before her world contracted to a space that encompassed only her and her labouring body.

The water was on the boil, the clean linen piled on a chair. The midwife arrived, bustling and cheerful in spite of having been roused from her bed. And then, just as dawn was breaking, the baby was born.

For just a moment, after the first wash of relief as the little body slithered from hers, Maggie experienced a sharp stab of panic. But it was quickly dispelled as she heard the first lusty cry.

'You've got a beautiful baby boy,' the midwife announced. 'And my, hasn't he got a fine set of lungs on him!'

She wrapped the baby in a towel and placed him in Maggie's arms.

'I'll clean you up, and then I'll get your husband.'

Maggie couldn't wait. She so wanted Josh to share this moment, share the gratitude and love that was coursing through her. But she couldn't let him see her like this. She had to be patient for a little while longer.

When the midwife had done what was necessary, she fetched Josh. He stood for a moment in the doorway, Patrick hanging back shyly behind him, Nora trying to push past in her eagerness.

'Come and meet your son.' Maggie's voice was full of pride.

He crossed to the bed, bent over and kissed her damp forehead. She eased the towel clear of the baby's head, revealing the small wrinkled face and a shock of still slick dark hair. Nora, goggle-eyed, leaned on her elbows on the bed.

'Careful!' Josh cautioned her.

Patrick was still hanging back.

'Come on, Patrick,' Maggie urged. 'Your brother won't bite.'

Cautiously, Patrick approached.

'A brother. Good.'

'I wanted a sister!' Nora complained.

'And perhaps you'll have one next time,' Josh said, his eyes meeting Maggie's.

'Perhaps,' she said, while thinking: never again!

'So what are you going to call him?' the midwife asked, busying herself with rinsing washcloths.

Maggie and Josh looked at one another. They hadn't talked about a name. They'd been too afraid they would be tempting fate.

'Eli?' Josh suggested.

'I was wondering . . .' Maggie said tentatively, 'whether we could call him John. That was Jack's proper name, wasn't it?'

She'd been thinking about it for some time, but had been uncertain how Josh would take it. Would he be pleased to have the new baby called after his brother, or would it be tactless to suggest it since she had been engaged to Jack at the time of his death?

She knew at once though from his expression that Josh was delighted.

'I've been thinking that too,' he said, 'but I was a bit reluctant to suggest it in case it upset you.'

'It would be nice to think he isn't forgotten. And it's such a good strong name.'

'John it is then.'

It was, Maggie thought, a special moment.

The baby was here, safe and sound, and they were all together. A family. And naming their little son for Jack would be keeping his memory alive.

She looked from one to the other of them, and sent up a prayer of thanks that she had been so blessed.

# Chapter Sixteen

'Hello!'

At the cheery greeting, Rowan looked up from rearranging the books in her satchel, which lay beside her on the bench. There weren't usually many people on the station platform at this time of the morning, and even fewer that she knew to speak to.

'Patrick! What are you doing here?' Faint colour had risen in her cheeks, and her stomach did the funny flip that it always did on the rare occasions when she met him.

He grinned. 'Catching the train to Bath, of course. Same as you, I expect.'

'Well . . . yes,' she said, feeling a little foolish. 'But you don't usually . . .' Her voice tailed away.

'I shall be every day now,' he said.

He looked pleased, whether to see her or because he was going to Bath she didn't know.

'Why?' she asked.

'I'm starting an apprenticeship. At Stothert and Pitts. They're an engineering company,' he added when he saw her puzzled expression. 'I'm going to be a draughtsman.'

'Oh!' Rowan didn't know what a draughtsman was either, but it sounded impressive.

'I left school in the summer.'

'Oh, yes.' She'd have left in the summer too, she supposed, if she'd gone to the board school instead of getting her scholarship. But most boys who went to the board school ended up going down the pit, or working on a farm, while the girls either went into service or, if they were lucky, a job in a shop. They didn't end up as apprentices with an engineering firm in Bath. 'How did you . . . ?'

'The headmaster and my mom fixed it up.' He still called her 'Mom', though it was five years now since they'd come back from America.

A distant whistle. The train was coming, slowing as it approached the station. Rowan fastened the straps of her satchel and stood up, smoothing down the skirt of her uniform pinafore dress so that it sat neatly over her hips. No pudgy tummy to worry about now! In the last couple of years her puppy fat had melted away. She had a waist she was proud of when she looked at herself in the bedroom mirror and – something she was less pleased about – she'd developed breasts, small firm mounds. She tried to ignore them when she looked in the mirror; was, in truth, embarrassed by them.

She liked the way her face looked now, though. The double chin and chubby cheeks she'd hated had gone, so she could see her cheekbones and the heart shape of her jaw. It was an altogether differently shaped face to the one that had elicited so much teasing, and Rowan thought it was evidence that God did hear prayers, the ones she'd whispered like a mantra every night before going to sleep.

'Please, God, let me be pretty. And please, not fat.'

Automatically she now headed down the platform towards the end of the train and the third-class carriages, very aware that Patrick was following her. She went to open the door as she always did, but he reached past and opened it for her. She climbed up into the carriage and took a window seat, facing forwards. He sat down opposite her. The colour was mounting in her cheeks now and the tingle in her stomach getting stronger so that it felt as if it was turning over. She could scarcely breathe.

Was it going to be like this every day from now on? She and Patrick together for a whole half-hour?

She could hardly believe how much the idea pleased her.

All day when she should have been concentrating on her lessons, thoughts of Patrick occupied her mind. Usually she did concentrate, very hard, harder perhaps than any other girl in the class, but today the warm, excited feeling in her tummy refused to let her. She kept thinking about him – the way his eyes crinkled when he smiled, his thick, dark hair, his voice, which had a bit of a rasp in it as if it might be changing from a boy's treble to the deeper voice of a man. And most of all the way he'd leaned past her to open the carriage door. His arm had brushed hers, she'd smelled the clean, soapy smell of his hair and skin, felt his weight against her shoulder. It had made her feel cared for, the way she used to feel when Daddy lifted her into his arms or onto his shoulders, the way she still felt sometimes if he patted her arm or ruffled her hair as he passed her chair getting to his own place at mealtimes.

Thinking of Daddy momentarily punctured the bubble of happiness like a pin in a balloon. His chest was much, much worse these days and he'd begun coughing up that horrid black phlegm. She'd overheard him and Mammy talking about it one evening when they'd thought she was upstairs doing her homework but she'd come down to fetch a book she'd left on the living room table. She could tell from the tone of their voices that they were talking about something serious and she'd stopped on the stairs, behind the half-open door, and listened.

'I don't know how much longer I'll be able to keep on working,' Daddy was saying.

And Mammy had said: 'But what are we going to do? Sir Montague won't let us keep the house, will he? He's a stickler for turning folk out when they're no more use to him.'

'I've been thinking – perhaps our Earl and Vicky could move back with us. That is, as long as he's still got a job at the pit,' Daddy said.

Earl and Vicky still lived with Vicky's parents. No miner's cottage had become vacant in the four years they'd been married, or so they said, but Laurel had whispered that she thought it was because Vicky couldn't manage on her own. She still suffered periodically from the same symptoms she'd had before they were married, and there was a little one now – Reggie, eighteen months old and quite a handful.

'I don't know that I could cope with a baby at my age,' Mammy had said.

'Might be the only answer.' Daddy sounded stoic and accepting as he always did, but the rattle was there in his breath, the wheeze in his chest. 'And at least Earl would be able to give me a hand with the garden.'

It was one of his biggest regrets, Rowan knew, the weeds sprouting in the vegetable patch that had once contained neat rows of potato haulms – or hams, as Minty called them – cabbages, peas, parsnips and his prized runner beans, planted each year without fail in the last week of April on High Compton Fair day.

This year when he'd cleared the ground and dug the trench he'd come in saying he was done up, and sat in his chair doing nothing for the rest of the day. Seeing him like that had made Rowan wonder how he managed to hew coal for hours on end. When she'd mentioned it to Laurel, her sister had said she thought Earl was giving him a hand, but if the manager found out, that would put an end to it. It was only thanks to the complicity of his fellow miners that it had gone on this long.

Rowan worried about it, as she worried about everything, but today she was too happy to dwell on it for long. Her dreaming mind returned to Patrick before Miss Colville's strident voice snapped her out of it with a stern: 'Rowan Sykes! Are you listening?'

But still the happy feeling covered her like a warm blanket on a cold winter's day, and Rowan found herself looking forward to tomorrow morning and the likelihood that she would see him again.

He wasn't there.

Rowan looked up and down the platform, watched the station entrance like a hawk, but when the train arrived there was still no sign of him. Her heart sank. Where was he?

The train chugged along between embankments covered with undergrowth, charred in some places. In summer it was often set alight by a spark from a passing engine and would burn for days, spreading underground in the coal dust that had been used to shore up the banks when the line had been cut. Rowan stared out at them unseeingly, able to think of nothing but her disappointment.

But miracle of miracles, when they passed through the level-crossing gates in the centre of Hillsbridge and pulled up at the station, there he was, standing on the platform at the end where the third-class carriages would come to a halt and watching the windows as they slid past him.

Before she could stop herself, she put up her hand and waved, then, embarrassed by her forwardness, blushed scarlet.

He didn't wave back, but he did open the door to her carriage and climbed in, pulling it shut behind him.

'Hello again.'

'Hello.' She was overcome with shyness now, as if all her daydreams of yesterday were there, written on her face for him to see.

'Bet you thought I'd got the sack already,' he said, sitting down opposite her.

'Oh . . . no . . .'

'Hillsbridge is the closest station for me,' he said by way of explanation. 'I only got on at High Compton yesterday because the carter was at our house delivering a printing press for David, and he gave me a lift.'

'Oh.'

*Who is David?* she wanted to ask. *Why was he having a printing press delivered to your house?* But she didn't like to.

'It's all go since we moved into Hillview,' he went on chattily.

'You've moved?' This was all news to Rowan.

'Back in April. It used to be a farmhouse, so it's much bigger than our old house. And it has outbuildings that can be used as workshops. My dad does carpentry and joinery, and my mom does arty stuff.'

That Rowan did know. Cathy-next-door had told Laurel about the fledgling enterprise and asked her to spread the word to help drum up business.

'And then there's David and his printing.'

This time Rowan did ask.

'Who's David?'

'David? He came back to England on the same boat as us.

222

He and Dad are friends. And he does the most amazing printing. He used to make scraps and stuff – he gave some to me and Nora . . . well, we were a lot younger then,' he added, looking a bit self-conscious. He probably thought scraps were babyish now, Rowan thought. 'And he's going to do them again now he's got the proper equipment.'

'The delivery,' Rowan said.

'Yes, the delivery. It was really heavy. Dad had to help them get it out of the cart and into the barn.'

'That's amazing,' Rowan said.

'So where is it you go to school, then?' he asked.

Rowan told him.

'Why do you go all the way to Bath to school?'

Rowan coloured again. 'Because I got a scholarship.' She felt a bit awkward about it – she didn't want him to think she was showing off. But then he had got an apprenticeship at Stothert and Pitts, so that evened things up.

They chatted all the way to Bath, and the journey seemed to pass so quickly, Rowan could scarcely believe it when they pulled into Green Park station.

'See you tomorrow then,' he said as they parted company on the steps outside.

Rowan nodded. 'I expect so.'

Her heart felt as though it were bursting with joy. She couldn't wait to meet up with Mary.

'You'll never guess what!' she would say.

Or perhaps she wouldn't. For the moment, she wanted to hug everything about Patrick to herself. She didn't want to tempt fate.

David gathered together the invoices, receipts and scraps of paper on which he'd scribbled costings for quotations and piled them on top of the notebook he used for keeping his accounts. His printing business was going well, but the financial side of things was not his forte. In fact, he knew he'd be lost without Maggie. She'd agreed to do the necessary for him, just as she did for herself and Josh, but he felt guilty about landing her with such disorganised figures, and he knew she had less time to spare now that she had a baby to care for as well as the rest of her family. She often looked tired: broken nights and hectic days were taking their toll on her, and although she insisted she could manage, he was beginning to wonder if he could afford to employ an accountant or bookkeeper so that he was no longer dependent on her.

He'd suggest it, he decided. The last thing he wanted was to be a burden on the couple who had become not just business partners, but good friends.

Putting the whole lot into a big manila envelope, he ran down the stairs from his living quarters, through the workshop that now housed his printing press, and across what had once been the farmyard to the house.

He knocked on the door, opened it a crack and called round: 'Hello! Anyone at home?'

'Come in, David.'

Maggie was seated at the big kitchen table with a ledger open in front of her. Saturday was her day for making up the books. Baby John was in his perambulator beside her; she was rocking it gently with one hand. Nora sat opposite her mother, painting on a large sheet of paper. Of Patrick and Josh there was no sign.

'Come and see what I'm doing!' Nora greeted him.

'She's designing a stained-glass plate she'd like to hang in her bedroom window,' Maggie said.

David walked around the table, looking over Nora's shoulder at her work.

'That's really good, Nora,' he said, genuinely impressed.

Nora had divided a circle into segments, and he recognised a fretsaw and plane in one, a leaf in another, a miner's lamp in a third. The drawings were childish, of course, and would have to be redone more accurately in order to make templates, but the general idea was inspirational.

'It's all about where we live,' Nora explained. 'A leaf for lots of trees, the lamp for the pits, the tools for Daddy's work . . . I want to do a printing press for you, and Mommy's kiln, but they're really hard to draw. Mommy said she'd help me when she's got time, but she's always busy with something else.'

Guilt pricked David again.

'Perhaps you could design something for me,' he suggested. 'A greetings card. I'm doing some especially for Christmas. Or even some scraps.'

'Yes. Perhaps I could.' She considered, then, parroting what Maggie was prone to saying, added, 'When I've got time.'

David and Maggie exchanged amused glances.

'She's a chip off the old block, I'm afraid,' Maggie said with a smile.

'In more ways than one. She's obviously inherited your talent, Maggie.'

'Such as it is. I don't get much chance to use it these days.'

It was David's opportunity.

'I know, and it doesn't help me landing you with my accounts,' he said. 'I've been thinking maybe I should pay someone to do them for me. There must be accountants in town.'

'Who'd probably charge you an arm and a leg. Honestly, David, I'm quite happy to carry on as we are, at least for the time being. When we're all well established, then perhaps we can think again.'

Grateful as he was not to have to dip deeply into the profits he had begun to make, David still felt guilty.

'Well, at least let me take the children off your hands for a bit so you can concentrate,' he said. 'It's a nice afternoon – you'd like to take John out for a walk, wouldn't you, Nora?'

Nora was off her chair in a flash, running to fetch her coat, her designs forgotten. She liked David a lot: he was great fun, and always made a fuss of her. In fact, she'd decided she'd like to marry him when she was old enough, and hoped with all her ten-year-old heart that he would wait for her.

'I think you have your answer,' Maggie said, smiling.

When John had been wrapped up warmly with a bonnet and extra blankets, David manoeuvred the perambulator out of the door, then let Nora push it while he surreptitiously kept a helping hand on the handle.

Funny how things worked out, he thought. When he'd returned to England from America it had been for one reason and one reason only. That hadn't worked out the way he'd planned. But strangely enough, things now were even better than he'd ever imagined they could be.


With no interruptions to slow her down, Maggie worked hard for an hour or so, making good progress. At last she blotted the last entry in the ledger, closed it, and laid a large pebble that she used for a paperweight on top of the pile of invoices and bills. She'd file them away later. At the moment all she wanted was a nice cup of tea and five minutes to herself before David and the children returned. When they did, it would be time to feed John again, and get Nora something to eat – the fresh air would have made her hungry – and the endless round of daily tasks would have resumed.

She washed her inky fingers at the kitchen sink, set the kettle on the hob and sat down again at the table while she waited for it to boil, thinking for the first time about David's suggestion of employing someone to do his books. It would certainly make her life far easier if she didn't have extra paperwork to worry about, but as she'd said, that would be expensive, and would eat into his profits. She'd actually considered getting help with all the accounts, her own and Josh's included, and made enquiries of the firm of accountants who had their offices in Hillsbridge, but the fee they'd quoted had horrified her. No wonder they could afford their motors and big houses!

But there was another possibility. Cathy had once told her that Laurel Sykes, her next-door neighbour, was a bookkeeper at the hospital and also looked after the accounts for a number of local doctors. Of course, she might already have all the work she wanted, but if she was prepared to do a bit extra, perhaps her charges would be much more reasonable.

Maggie made up her mind. Next time she saw Cathy, she'd ask her if she'd sound this Laurel out. But she wouldn't say a word to David about it until she knew whether there was any chance it could work.

'Mommy! We're home!'

The back door opened and Nora came skipping in, her face rosy from the crisp, cold air. David followed, angling the perambulator through the doorway. So much for her five minutes to herself.

'Did you have a nice walk?' she asked.

'Yes! And we saw a squirrel! It ran across right in front of us! And some bunnies . . .'

'You were lucky.' A squirrel was quite a rare sight, and the rabbits didn't usually come out until later in the evening.

She lifted John out of the pram, nestling his firm little body against her, and his mouth opened and closed expectantly like a baby bird.

'He'll want feeding. I don't suppose you'd make a cup of tea when the kettle boils, would you, David? Nora can bring it in to me. I'm dying of thirst here.'

'I expect we can manage that, can't we, Nora?'

'I'm hungry too!' Nora announced.

'There are some rock cakes in the tin. Have one of those to tide you over.'

Maggie headed for the little sitting room, kissing the top of John's head and unbuttoning her blouse as she went. Constantly busy she might be, but she wouldn't have it any other way.

I must be the luckiest woman alive, she thought. But it would be nice if I could get some help with the books . . .

If it hadn't been for the fact that Ezra's failing health hung over the entire family like a threatening storm cloud, the weeks that followed would have been utterly magical. They *were* magical. As soon as she closed the door on the oppressive atmosphere at home, Rowan felt her spirits soaring like a wild bird freed from a cage. There was a spring in her step as she walked to the station, and excitement and anticipation fluttered in her tummy like a promise. And all the while she was wondering – does he like me too?

Oh, he must, surely! He wouldn't sit with her every day if he didn't, would he? But perhaps he felt duty-bound to since they knew one another. Perhaps he thought it would be rude not to, or it had become a habit he couldn't break.

If only he'd ask her out! Suggest they met somewhere other than just on the train. She'd know he liked her then.

But if he did – what then? Minty would never agree to her walking out with a boy, any boy, and especially not Patrick. Why she had such a down on the family, Rowan didn't know. She'd be furious if she knew they travelled to Bath together every day, innocent as that was – keeping it secret from her made Rowan feel a little guilty – and if there was anything more to it than that, she'd come down on Rowan like a ton of bricks. The very thought of it made Rowan tremble inwardly. No, perhaps it was best Patrick didn't ask her out. If he did, she'd have to refuse him, and that would be awful. He'd think she didn't like him, and he wouldn't sit with her any more, and she didn't think she could bear that.

Rowan was beginning to feel as if she were on a switchback ride. Ecstatic one minute, worried that things were going to go horribly wrong the next. Oh, why did falling in love have to be so confusing?

Had she but known it, Laurel was struggling with uncertainty that was not dissimilar.

She and Ralph were still meeting in secret, but nothing had really changed and she was beginning to doubt that he would ever leave his wife. Surely by now Bertie was old enough that his father should no longer feel obliged to remain in an unhappy marriage for his sake?

When he turned eighteen and went off to university – Oxford, no less – Laurel had been hopeful, but when she'd mentioned it, Ralph had argued that he wanted to be sure Bertie was settled in his new life before he did anything drastic.

'At the moment he's just finding his feet,' he said. 'If I rock the boat by leaving, the whole foundation of his life will fall apart. He's a sensitive boy, always has been. And a dutiful one. It wouldn't surprise me if he didn't feel he had to give up his place and come home to support his mother. That would be a tragedy. I'd never forgive myself if I was responsible for wrecking his whole future. When the time comes, we'll have the rest of our lives together. But to start out with something like that on our consciences would cast a shadow over every-thing.'

He'd kissed her then, and she'd melted as she always did. He was a good man, a loving father who was prepared to sacrifice his own happiness and exist in a loveless marriage for the sake of his son. They could never be happy together if they felt responsible for ruining Bertie's life; already she felt guilty about their clandestine relationship and breaking up a marriage, however unhappy it was. If waiting a little longer meant they could start with a fresh sheet, then she must be patient.

But as time went on it seemed as if there was always just one more hurdle to overcome. Nothing had changed, and Laurel was beginning to wonder if it ever would.

If only there were someone she could confide in, talk things over with, but the very nature of their relationship meant that there wasn't. There was only Ralph, and whenever she questioned the future, he had a way of allaying her doubts – for as long as she was with him, anyway. But when she was alone, they returned to plague her.

Was he just making excuses? It was starting to feel like that. In the beginning she'd been able to lose herself in their love-making, but even that no longer had the power to drive away the dark fear that Ralph was just using her. He still told her he loved her, that she meant the whole world to him, but she wasn't sure she believed him.

Perhaps she should end it, she thought. If she gave him an ultimatum, it might move him to action. But she was afraid to do it. She was thirty years old now – she knew the staff at the hospital already regarded her as an old maid, like Miss Perrett before her – and she'd invested too much hope and precious time in Ralph to risk losing him now.

It was a dilemma to which Laurel didn't know the answer.

# Chapter Seventeen

October came in wet and blustery, bringing down the leaves from the trees so that they lay in sodden clumps on the pavements and clogged the gutters.

'Can we have tea a bit early tonight?' Laurel asked Minty as she put on her coat ready to go to work and checked she had a couple of clean handkerchiefs in her bag. Her throat felt a bit raspy and her eyes prickled, and she thought she might be starting a cold – not surprising since she had got wet cycling to work several times in the last week.

'Why's that then?' Minty asked.

'The young man who works with Maggie and Josh Withers is coming over to see me to talk about the possibility of me doing their books for them,' Laurel explained.

Minty snorted. 'I wouldn't have thought you'd want anything to do with *them*.'

Laurel sighed. 'They run a perfectly respectable business, Mam, which is doing very well by all accounts. And if I can get a bit of extra work, the money will come in very useful.'

'Well, it's up to you, I suppose,' Minty said tightly.

'So if you could . . . ?'

'All right, all right. But just mind you don't do anything to jeopardise your proper job. You don't want to lose that.'

She'd expected opposition the moment Cathy had put the suggestion to her at Maggie's request, but she wasn't having any of it. Minty's opinion of Maggie and Josh Withers was, she thought, completely unjustified, and besides, as she'd said, she really could do with the extra money. Keeping up with all the things Rowan needed for school was a constant drain on her finances. Cathy had said she didn't think Josh, Maggie and David could afford to pay very much, but Laurel had said she was sure they could come to some arrangement that would suit them all, and thought that every little would help.

'It'll be fine, Mam,' she said, as she buttoned her coat and went out to fetch her bicycle.

To Laurel's relief, though her throat still felt a little dry, the cold didn't seem to be materialising. She really hadn't wanted to try to arrange a business deal with watery eyes and a streaming nose.

They were still washing up the tea things when David arrived; Minty hadn't put the meal on the table any earlier, a way of showing her disapproval, Laurel guessed.

'I think he's here,' she said as the narrow beam of a bicycle lamp pierced the darkness and a shadowy form appeared, passing the scullery window.

'You'd better go and see to him then,' Minty said. 'Take him in the living room. I'll finish off here.'

Laurel dried her hands on the kitchen towel and went to open the door.

'I'm looking for Miss Sykes. Do I have the right house?'

'You do. And it's Laurel. Come in.'

He was tall and slimly built, clean-shaven, with longish fair hair that had flopped down over his forehead. He brushed it aside as he came into the scullery, and for a moment Laurel thought he looked oddly familiar. But she must be mistaken.

To her knowledge she'd never met him before, and from his tentative enquiry as to whether he had come to the right place it seemed as if he wasn't familiar with Fairley Terrace.

'Good evening,' he said to Minty.

To Laurel's irritation, her mother merely nodded brusquely and turned back to immerse her hands in the hot soapy water.

'Come through.' She led the way into the living room.

Ezra was there, sitting in his chair with the day's newspaper open on his knee.

'Dad – this is Mr Mason.'

'Pleased to meet you,' Ezra said. He knew why David was here – they'd talked about it over tea. 'You'll excuse me if I don't get up?'

'Pleased to meet you too.'

'Is it all right if we go over a few things in here, Dad?' Laurel asked.

'Ah – don't mind me.'

Laurel pulled out one of the dining chairs for David and took another across the corner of the table.

'So – I understand you'd like me to take care of your books?' she said.

David nodded. 'Mine – and Maggie and Josh's too, if you could manage it.' He hefted a hessian bag onto his knee and took out Maggie's leather-bound ledger and his own scruffy notebook. 'I brought these with me so you can see roughly the amount of work it entails. I don't know whether the way Maggie does it is the proper way, but she seems to keep on top of things pretty well.'

Laurel opened the ledger, nodding approvingly at the neat columns of figures.

'It isn't quite how I was taught, but it all looks clear enough to me.'

233

They talked some more, David explaining that with a new baby Maggie really did not have the time to continue as she had been, but that they couldn't afford accountant's fees. Laurel had heard it all before from Cathy, but she nodded understandingly.

'I wouldn't expect to be paid what you would pay an accountant,' she said. 'I'm a bookkeeper, really, but I can't see that small businesses like yours need anyone more highly qualified. Except of course when it comes to auditing, but I'd arrange for someone to do that as part of the service.'

'So what would you charge?'

Laurel liked it that he'd come straight to the point. She named a figure that she hoped was within the range of what he and the Withers family could afford, and saw his brow clear.

'I think we could manage that.'

'Good. Do you think you could get the paperwork to me once a week? I wouldn't want to have to cycle all the way over to you, especially with winter on the way.'

'I can do that, no problem.'

'Then I think we're in business, Mr Mason.'

'David.' He stood up. 'Maggie is going to be very relieved.'

'I'm pleased to help. I'll expect you a week on Friday, and we'll take it from there.'

When he'd left, Laurel went back into the living room. She was jubilant at the thought of the extra money she was going to be earning, and also glowing with pride.

'What d'you think of that then, Dad?'

Ezra laid his newspaper down on his knee and smiled at her, that sweet, kind smile that still put a twinkle in his eyes.

'You're quite the businesswoman, our Laurel.'

'I am, aren't I?'

'I always knew you'd make good, m'dear.'

She knew what it was he was referring to, but being Ezra, he wouldn't say it out loud. He liked to keep to safe ground. Pleasant topics. He wanted everybody to be happy. 'As long as you're all right, I'm all right,' he'd say, and he meant it.

'And don't let your mam tell you any different,' he added.

'She's not best pleased about me working for Maggie Withers,' Laurel said.

'That David seems a nice chap, and it's him you'll be dealing with.'

'He does – but you know what Mam's like.'

'She's not always right, you know,' Ezra said. 'But when her mind's made up, it's the devil's own job to get her to change it.'

'Don't I know it.'

She knew they were singing from the same hymn sheet. For all the good it would do. Ezra gave her a wink and a sideways smile, coughed into his handkerchief and went back to his paper.

Every Friday evening, regular as clockwork, David arrived with the accounts for Laurel to make up. Sometimes there was hardly any work to do, sometimes there were untidy sheafs of paper-work, but at least Laurel had the whole weekend to attend to it.

She liked David. He was quiet, never talked about himself, and was unassuming, though it was clear he was making a great success of his printing business. Even Minty had quite taken to him: she would make him a cup of tea and give him a slice of cake before he set out for home on his bicycle.

Just one thing bothered Laurel a little. It had come to her where she'd seen him before – in Edgar Sawyer's office on the day she'd gone to Bath to collect her fountain pen. She remembered the unusual accent, too, a mixture of what she now knew was American and cockney. And how she'd wondered what he was doing there, since he wasn't typical of Edgar's clients, and hoped he and Edgar weren't doing some kind of shady deal.

Well, now that she knew him, she couldn't imagine it was that.

But all the same, and although she knew it was none of her business, she was still curious to know what he had been consulting Edgar about.

November came in with clammy fogs that trapped the smell of couch fires and rotting leaves. Summer seemed a lifetime away.

Rowan's birthday that year fell on a Wednesday. When he joined the train in Hillsbridge, Patrick climbed into her carriage as usual, but he was acting very strangely, avoiding her eyes and not at all his usual friendly self. Oh no! Rowan thought. If he did ever like me at all, he's gone off me . . .

'What's wrong?' she asked, steeling herself.

'Nothing.' Another long silence. Then, quite unexpectedly, he reached into his coat pocket and pulled out an envelope, thrusting it in her direction.

'Happy birthday.'

'Oh, thank you! But how did you know?'

'My aunt Cathy told me. I think your sister told her.'

For a moment, alarmed by this information, Rowan could think of nothing else.

'Do they know we see one another on the train every day, then?'

Patrick frowned. 'It's not a secret, is it?'

'If my mam found out . . .' She broke off. She couldn't tell him her mother's opinion of his family.

'What?' he asked, genuinely puzzled.

'Nothing.'

Her fingers trembled a little as she tore open the envelope, trying not to think about the conversation Laurel and Cathy might have had, a conversation that, if it reached Mam's ears, would almost certainly result in her being forbidden to sit with Patrick on the journey to Bath. Rowan was still the same obedient girl she'd always been. Defying Mam was something that never crossed her mind.

She eased the card out of the envelope, careful not to damage the paper lace edging. Such a pretty card! A bouquet of flowers tied with a bow of the same paper lace. She opened it. *May your birthday have all the fragrance of summer roses*. Beneath the greeting he had signed it simply *Patrick*. But he had added a single kiss.

'It's lovely. Thank you.'

She looked up at him; to her surprise he'd gone a little red. She'd never seen Patrick blush before. She thought it was something that only happened to girls.

'Glad you like it,' he said gruffly.

'I love it.' She'd melted inside.

She replaced the card in its envelope, then slipped it into her satchel between the books. She'd have to be careful not to let Mam see it. But she'd take it out and look at it often. Trace the name – and the kiss – with her fingertips. Treasure it for ever.

Just a pretty card. But it was the best birthday present she could have wished for.

That evening, the usual birthday traditions were observed, though tea was a bit later than it normally was because Earl and Vicky and baby Reggie were expected.

'We could open your presents while we're waiting for them,' Minty suggested, so they sat around the fire while Rowan unwrapped them. There was a scarf knitted in her school colours from Mam and Daddy – Rowan managed to act surprised, though it was no surprise at all: she'd seen Mam hastily thrust it behind a cushion one evening when she'd come downstairs from doing her homework and almost caught her in the act of making it – and a fountain pen from Laurel, just like the one she used herself.

'Did you get any cards from your friends at school?' Minty asked.

'A couple, yes.'

She fetched her satchel and got them out, careful not to pull out Patrick's by mistake. Minty sniffed contemptuously at the one from Mary – hand-made and drawn by a girl who was clearly never going to be an artist – then propped them up on the mantelpiece alongside the ones they'd given to Rowan this morning.

'No others?' Laurel asked. There was the hint of a smile in her eyes, and Rowan's stomach clenched. She knew. Rowan was certain of it.

'No,' she lied, terrified Laurel was going to say something that would let the cat out of the bag.

Fortunately at that moment the back door opened and Earl came in, stamping his feet and blowing on his hands.

'No Vicky?' Minty asked, surprised.

''Fraid not. She's not feeling too good. And it's a long way to walk.'

Minty huffed. 'I should have thought she could have made the effort seeing it's Rowan's birthday.'

Earl took his mother's criticism in his stride; he was well used to her.

'It's a bitter wind. It wouldn't do her or Reggie any good.'

'Take your coat off then. Now you're finally here, we can have our tea,' Minty said, still aggrieved.

'Good. I'm starving. And your cake looks as good as it always does.'

'I should hope so. I've had enough practice.' Minty was somewhat mollified.

The cake was delicious, moist and sweet and bursting with fruit. But for once Rowan was finding it hard to swallow. She was still on edge in case Laurel should mention Patrick. She'd have to say something to her the minute she got the chance. She'd wanted to talk to her sister about it for ages, but somehow she'd always chickened out, afraid that Laurel might tell her it was wrong to be seeing him behind Mam's back. She didn't *think* she would, but she was afraid to take the chance. Now she didn't think she had any choice.

It was almost bedtime before the opportunity arose. Earl had left, and Daddy had gone with him as far as the pub at the end of the road – 'We'll have a quick pint,' he'd said, and Earl had said: 'It will have to be a quick one. I've got to get back to Vicky.' At which Minty had snapped: 'That girl's got you on a tight leash and no mistake. I'd have thought she wouldn't begrudge you a drink with your dad,' even though she didn't like Ezra going to the pub, especially on a night like this, when the cold wind wouldn't do his chest any good.

'When I come back, I might have something for you in my pocket,' Ezra had said with a twinkle, and Rowan knew what that would be. Sometimes he brought Mam a little miniature of gin. She liked a drop of gin in the evening as a special treat.

Once they'd left, Rowan had gone upstairs to make a start on her homework – she'd have to get up early tomorrow morning to finish it – and after a bit she heard footsteps on the stairs. It was Laurel, coming up to her room for something.

'Laurel!' she called.

Her sister's head appeared round the door.

'Did you call me?'

Rowan nodded without speaking and beckoned to her, indicating that she should shut the door behind her. Then she extracted Patrick's card from between the books in her satchel.

'I did get another card,' she said in a conspiratorial whisper.

'Ah!' Laurel smiled, an amused sort of smile.

'I couldn't say in front of Mammy. It's from Patrick Withers.'

Laurel's smile broadened. 'I thought you might get one. Can I see, or is it private?'

Rowan handed her the card; Laurel looked at the flowers and the paper lace on the front, but didn't open it. Rowan was grateful for that. She didn't want anyone else to see the kiss, not even her beloved sister.

'You won't tell Mammy, will you?'

'Not if you don't want me to.'

'And will you tell Cathy not to say anything either? About him going to Bath on the same train as me?'

Laurel chuckled. 'I don't think Mam and her talk that much.'

'No, but . . . she is very chatty. And if she did say something, Mammy . . .' She hesitated, not wanting Laurel to think she was being deceitful, though of course she knew she was. 'Well . . . she's really got it in for Patrick's family, hasn't she? I don't know what she's got against them. Patrick is really nice.'

'I'm sure he is. Don't worry about it, my love. It's just Mam being Mam. And she can be wrong, you know. She's as fallible as the rest of us.'

Rowan was quite shocked. It was the first time she'd ever heard anyone suggest that Mam might not always be right. To Rowan she was all-knowing as well as all-powerful. Yet she supposed she *had* begun to question Mam's judgement, otherwise she wouldn't be sitting with Patrick every day on the train, chatting to him, dreaming dreams about him . . .

'Why is she like it?' she asked. 'Why does she have to always look on the black side of everything?'

A shadow crossed Laurel's face. Her smile had vanished, and she looked almost as if she might cry.

'I expect there are things in her life that haven't turned out the way she'd have wanted them to.' She turned towards the door. 'Birthday or not, you'd better get on with your homework, my love,' she said, her hand on the knob. 'Otherwise you'll be in trouble at school tomorrow.'

She still sounded sad, Rowan thought, a little puzzled by her sister's sudden change of mood.

But she didn't dwell on it. Alone once more, she looked again at Patrick's card, feeling the glow spreading inside her again. She touched a finger to her lips, and pressed it against the kiss beside his name.

If this was what growing up felt like, she was going to enjoy every moment of it.


Laurel went to her room, picked up the shawl she'd come upstairs to fetch, and went back down.

Oh, Rowan, she thought, her heart contracting with tenderness, and also anxiety as she remembered the bittersweet intensity of her own first love. She hoped desperately that Rowan's heart wouldn't be broken the way hers had been. That Patrick would not treat her the way she had been treated by Callum. That she would not make the same mistakes.

She was so young, so vulnerable. Laurel stood for a moment, her eyes tightly closed, her hands pressed together, and prayed that Rowan would not find out the hard way that life and love were sometimes far from kind.


When Laurel returned to the living room, her mother was sitting in the easy chair beside the fire, her feet propped up on a footstool.

'Do you think my ankles are swollen?' she asked, raising her skirt to expose them.

'I think they are a bit.' But it was hard to tell really – Minty's legs, like the rest of her, had always been on the plump side.

'I don't know why that should be,' Minty grumbled. 'In the summer, when there's a heatwave, you expect it. But not when it's weather like this.'

'You've been on your feet all day, what with baking for Rowan's party as well as getting your washing jobs done. That'll be it,' Laurel suggested.

*And you've put on even more weight lately*, she added silently.

Aloud, she said: 'Shall I make you a nice cup of tea?'

'I could drink one, certainly,' Minty said, rubbing her ankles.

Laurel went into the kitchen to fill the kettle.

As she turned away from the sink, she froze. Someone was outside the kitchen window, looking in.

'What . . . ?'

For a brief, startled moment she stood stock still, staring at the disembodied face, not even aware of the water that had sloshed from the spout of the kettle and onto her feet. Then it disappeared. She slammed the kettle down on the kitchen cupboard, hurried to the door and opened it.

'Who's there?'

She could see nothing in the darkness beyond the light spilling out from the window and the open door.

'Is there anybody there?' she called again.

No answer. Just the clang of a dustbin lid hitting the hard frosty ground, and a cat streaking across the track in front of her. She looked up and down the rank, but she could still see nothing, though her eyes were becoming used to the dark.

She drew a deep steadying breath. She must have imagined it. There was nobody there, and even if there had been, why would they have been looking in at the window?

She went back inside, still trying to tell herself it must have been a trick of the light. Her own reflection, perhaps. But the feeling of unease remained, and in her mind's eye she could see it still, that oval globe suspended on the other side of the glass. A young face, that was her impression. A girl's face. Not threatening, but decidedly spooky.

Before she put the kettle on to boil, Laurel did something the occupants of Fairley Terrace rarely did until they went to bed. She turned the key in the lock and shot the bolt. Daddy would just have to knock when he came back from the pub.

She made no mention to Minty of what she'd thought she'd seen. There was no point in alarming her unnecessarily. But Laurel felt decidedly unsettled, and there was no way she could rationalise the disturbing incident, no matter how hard she tried.

As the back door opened, the girl had slid hastily into the shadows, pressing her skinny frame tight against the wall of the house.

'Who's there?'

The voice was young and strong – the young woman she'd seen in the kitchen: Laurel Sykes, she presumed. And a stumbling block to her plans, even if she hadn't spotted her looking in.

The kitchen of the house next door was all in darkness. Kezia Smith inched further along the wall, away from the light spilling out of the door of number 5. In the darkness she didn't notice the dustbin and stumbled into it, dislodging the lid. It clattered to the ground, startling a cat that must have been outside the door waiting to be let in.

Kezia froze, holding the quick intake of breath deep in her lungs. Her heart was pounding in her chest, every nerve ending alive and tingling. For seemingly endless moments she remained motionless, her eyes fixed on the irregular patch of light, fearful of seeing a shadow fall across it. Then the patch of light was gone, and she heard the click of the door closing.

Kezia's breath came out on a sigh of relief and she moved swiftly away along the track. Things hadn't worked out tonight according to plan. With Laurel – if indeed it was her – in the house, there'd never been any chance that they would. But at least she hadn't been caught. And there would be other chances. Times when Mrs Bloody Sykes was alone.

Kezia's hand tightened over the flick knife in her pocket.

She'd waited this long to do what she was determined to do. She could wait a little longer.

# Chapter Eighteen

As a rule, Rowan looked forward to Christmas. This year, however, was different. Christmas meant a three-week holiday from school. Three whole weeks when she wouldn't see Patrick! She didn't know how she was going to bear it.

And then it happened, that thing she had been longing for and dreading in equal measures.

'I won't be on the train tomorrow,' she said. 'We break up for the holiday today.'

'Bet you're glad about that,' Patrick said.

'I suppose.' She didn't dare tell him what she was really feeling. That three whole weeks without seeing him would be torture. That she wouldn't enjoy a single moment of it. That she'd be willing it to be over so she could see him again.

But perhaps he felt the same way, because to her surprise he said: 'How about we meet up? I could come over to my gran's and we could go for a walk.'

Rowan began to tremble. Not outwardly, so as he'd notice – or at least she hoped not! – but the whole of her insides. Her tummy was flipping over, her arms turning to gooseflesh, every nerve tingling and jangling, her heart thudding. She didn't know what to say.

'Only if you want to,' he added. 'I just thought . . .'

Jennie Felton

Only if she wanted to! Of course she wanted to! With every fibre of her being. But . . .

'I don't know if I can.'

'Oh – right. Doesn't matter.'

But she could see the hurt of rejection written on his face.

'I'd really like to,' she said quickly. 'It's just that . . .'

'You've got better things to do.' He tried to make it sound casual, but the hurt was there in his voice too.

In that instant, Rowan made up her mind.

'No, I haven't. And I'd love to go for a walk with you.'

She was blazing now with rebellion and determination. Why shouldn't she go for a walk with Patrick? How she'd manage it she didn't know, and she didn't care.

His eyes met hers; he was flushed now with relief and pleasure.

'Really?'

'Yes, really. When?'

'Well . . . it will have to be in the evening or on a weekend. I don't get three weeks' holiday like you. Just Christmas Day and Boxing Day – oh, and the day after, because Christmas Day is on a Sunday.'

Her mind was working overtime now. She couldn't see how she could possibly get away on a dark winter's evening. But maybe she could make some excuse on a weekend . . .

'What about Saturday?' she suggested.

'Christmas Eve?'

'Yes.'

'All right. Shall I call for you?'

'No . . . no! I'll meet you at the end of the rank. By the main road. Say . . .' she thought quickly, picturing Minty busy with the preparations for Christmas Day, 'half past two?'

Patrick looked puzzled, but he nodded.

'All right,' he said again.

She wanted to ask him not to tell anyone, but didn't want to have to admit that she would be sneaking out without her mother knowing. If Laurel had kept her promise, she'd have told Cathy-next-door not to say anything, and she didn't suppose Mam would find out from Patrick's grandmother. Minty being so reluctant to talk to the neighbours had its advantages!

'See you on Saturday, then,' he said when they parted outside the station, and Rowan nodded.

'See you.'

She was still shaking inside, scared witless by her own daring. If Mam knew, she'd have forty fits! Somehow Rowan had to manage this without her finding out. It was the first time she'd ever really deceived her mother, and the first time she'd defied her.

But however guilty it made her feel, it would be worth it to see Patrick.

Rowan was not the only one who had not been looking forward to Christmas. Laurel, too, was dreading it. Every year now it was the same. While she was at home with her family, Ralph would be celebrating with his wife and son. She would have to pretend to be enjoying herself, while all the time she was aching to share the festivities with the man she loved. Smarting with envy, yet hating herself for her uncharitable thoughts. Surrounded by her family, yet lonely. Feeling more alone than at any other time of the year.

It was brought home sharply to her again on the Wednesday before Christmas. A hospital drinks party for all staff was to be held the following evening. Laurel usually saw Ralph on a Thursday, meeting him in his consulting rooms, and she'd intended that this week would be no different. But when she'd told Matron she wouldn't be attending, Matron had gone into officious mode.

'Mr Sinclair won't like it,' she said severely. 'He's made it quite clear that he expects everyone, including the auxiliary staff, to attend.'

Back in the summer, Mr Seabrook, who had been chairman of the board of trustees when Laurel had started her job at the hospital, had retired, and his place had been taken by Aubrey Sinclair.

He was a very different kettle of fish to the genial Mr Seabrook. Laurel had disliked him the first time she'd met him, and nothing had changed her opinion since. Aubrey Sinclair seemed to be determined to set his stamp on the running of the hospital, making all manner of unnecessary changes and enforcing them with a rod of iron.

The Christmas drinks party was his idea – to foster relations between management and staff, he said, but Laurel thought it was just another opportunity for him to lord it over everyone. She didn't want to attend, and didn't see why she should have to. Her secretarial work had nothing to do with nursing the sick, and she'd thought no one would miss her.

Now here was Matron more or less ordering her to attend or face the consequences, and little as she wanted to, Laurel knew it would be wise to comply. Matron was something of a martinet, and Mr Sinclair could make Laurel's position intolerable or even dismiss her if he chose to. Although with the two of them constantly looking over her shoulder the job was no longer enjoyable, she couldn't risk losing it.

As soon as Matron was out of the way, she telephoned Ralph, catching him between patients, and explained she wouldn't be able to come to Bath on Thursday as arranged.

'I could come on Friday instead,' she said. It meant she

wouldn't be there when David brought the accounts, but he could leave them with Minty.

But Ralph told her that wouldn't be possible. The Christmas tree he ordered each year was being delivered on Friday, and he had to oversee its erection and help with the trimming. It was a family tradition.

Laurel couldn't see why it was necessary for the tree to be put up at a particular time, or even why Ralph had to be there at all. The delivery men would put it up, surely, and Bertie, home from university, could help his mother trim it.

'I'll see you next Thursday as usual, then,' he said breezily. 'Have a happy Christmas, darling.'

'Happy Christmas,' she managed, but disappointment was a hollow place inside her, and as she put down the phone, despair washed over her.

How could he be so casual about it? Just where did she fit into his life? All these years, and still she had to take second place to his family, like a dog sitting patiently beside the dining table waiting for the scraps his master chose to throw him. All these *wasted* years.

Oh, why hadn't she stuck to her guns when she'd first discovered he was married? She'd been so determined to be strong, even going so far as to leave her job with Edgar Sawyer so that she could make a clean break with Ralph. Determined not to be 'the other woman' even though her heart was breaking. And then she'd gone to see him to ask him to treat Vicky and he'd sweet-talked her into resuming their affair, making promises that seemed as far from being fulfilled now as ever they had been. Would things ever change? Somehow she couldn't see that they would.

In all fairness, the drinks party was not as bad as she'd expected it to be. A festive air had prevailed all day in the hospital, with as many patients as possible being discharged to their homes for the holiday and no new ones being admitted. The wards, waiting room and offices had been decorated with holly, mistletoe and paper chains, and in the staffroom a trestle table groaned beneath the weight of plates of food prepared by the ladies of the Friends of the Hospital, and bottles of alcohol and soft drinks donated by the professional men of the town when Mr Sinclair had appealed to them to show their generosity. All the local doctors without exception had turned up, and were chatting to the nurses and even the orderlies while Sinclair strutted around for all the world as if he were the lord of the manor.

Halfway through the evening, a man with an accordion turned up to play carols and soon had the assembly singing along. Even Matron joined in with 'Silent Night', her rich contralto drowning out the feebler voices. But the jollity did nothing to cheer Laurel. She'd reached a crossroads in her life, she thought. She'd played second fiddle for too long, and if Ralph didn't deliver on his promises, she'd tell him it was over – and this time she wouldn't go back on her word. Even if it meant she had to spend the rest of her life alone and unloved.

Sometimes she thought that fate was deserved. Karma for all her past mistakes. Tonight, in the midst of all the festivities and merrymaking that she felt unable to truly share, was one of those times.

Christmas Eve dawned bright and clear, and Rowan didn't know whether she was relieved or not. She was looking forward to meeting Patrick – of course she was! – but her stomach was also tying itself in knots of anxiety at the thought of lying to Minty, and she was nervous about the new twist in her relationship with Patrick too. Suppose he tried to kiss her? What would she do? While she thought she'd like it, she was also scared. Nobody except Mam and Daddy, Laurel and her brothers had ever kissed her. How was it done? How did you manage not to bump noses? Would it be horribly awkward? And what then? How could she behave normally with a boy who had just kissed her? If she got it wrong, everything between them could be spoiled for ever. If it had been raining, the walk would have had to be called off and things would go back to the way they had been. But it wasn't raining. There was nothing for it but to put her plan into action.

She'd spent the last couple of days racking her brain for an excuse she could make for going out, and at last she'd come up with one. She'd told Minty that she was going into town to meet a friend who lived in Hillsbridge, a girl who went to her school, and whom she'd met on the train. It wasn't a complete lie, she'd told herself to ease her guilt. Patrick *was* a friend and he *did* live in Hillsbridge – well, more or less – and she *had* met him on the train. The only part that was untrue, although she had to admit it was probably the most important part, was that it was a girl she was going to meet.

'What's her name then?' Minty had asked.

Rowan's mind had gone blank.

'Mary.'

'I thought that was your friend in Bath?'

'Oh . . . yes . . . they're both called Mary.' Rowan had felt the hot colour rising in her cheeks – she just wasn't used to lying.

But luckily Minty was too preoccupied with her preparations for Christmas Day to notice.

'Well, mind you're back before it gets dark,' was all she said.

* * *

As she left the house, Rowan's stomach felt as if a whole flock of butterflies was fluttering in it. She was early, she knew – she didn't want to risk Patrick knocking on the door, even though she'd told him not to. But what if someone saw her waiting? She should have said she'd meet him in town, but he would have thought that very odd.

She'd walk up and down the lane, she decided. Then she could pretend she was on her way into Compton or going home for something, depending on which way she was headed. And similarly if anyone saw her with Patrick, she could always pretend she'd bumped into him by accident. But the thought made her more nervous than ever. She wasn't any more used to deception than she was to lying.

In the event, none of this was necessary. When she turned the corner, Patrick was already there, waiting, hands thrust into his coat pockets, stamping his feet against the cold.

'Hello,' he said. 'You came then.'

'Did you think I wouldn't?'

'Well, yes, I did wonder whether your mother would let you. She's pretty strict, isn't she?'

For a moment Rowan wondered what Cathy had been saying, then she remembered that Patrick had caught the rough edge of Minty's tongue more than once when he was younger. But at least the remark gave her the chance to confess.

'She doesn't know I'm with you. I told her I was meeting a friend.'

'I'm a friend, aren't I?'

'A girl. So . . . could we go somewhere we're not likely to bump into anyone that knows me?'

'If you like.' But he gave her a narrow look. He wasn't altogether comfortable with deception either, she guessed. 'It'll be muddy across the fields, though.'

'There's a track a bit further along the road. It goes all the way round the batch.' The batch was the mound of coal waste that in some parts of the country was known as a slag heap. High Compton and Hillsbridge were surrounded by them.

'All right.'

They headed along the road, but conversation was not flowing as easily as it did on the train – they were both a little self-conscious. It was, after all, the first time they had actually arranged to meet.

The track, when they reached it, looked a little muddy too, but there was a good covering of last year's dead leaves on each side, and though the sun had thawed the frost on the puddles sitting in hollows in the rough ground, it was possible to avoid them.

On one occasion Rowan's foot skidded a little, and though she managed to save herself, Patrick reached for her hand.

'Don't want you falling over.'

'I'm all right.'

But her hand in his felt good, and Rowan was glad the mud had given them just the excuse they needed.

The track curved round the batch, past a stile leading into a field. They were out of sight of the road now. Patrick stopped, leaning back against the stile and pulling Rowan towards him. Not a word was spoken, but she caught her breath as his arms went round her waist. Automatically she closed her eyes, and felt his chin brush her cheek. Then his mouth was on hers, just the gentlest fumbling pressure, and to her amazement she found herself responding. It was the most wonderful sensation she had ever experienced; she felt as if she was suspended in time, and there was no one in the world except her and Patrick, nothing but his lips on hers, his arms around her, her hands resting on his shoulders.

Then, abruptly, he pulled back.

'I'm sorry. I shouldn't have done that.'

'Don't be sorry!' she said, confused.

'It's just that I've been wanting to, every day on the train . . .'

Happiness burst in her heart like a Roman candle on bonfire night.

'Then let's do it again.' She couldn't believe she had said that!

'Sure?'

She nodded, tilting her face towards his, her eyes open this time so she could see the curve of his jaw, the dimple in his chin. She put her arms around him too, feeling the strong sinews in his back, and loving that they were so close. Kiss followed kiss; she wanted time to stand still so that they could remain here for ever. But of course they couldn't. Already an early dusk was beginning to fall and reluctantly Rowan remembered Minty's warning to be sure to be back before dark.

'I'm going to have to go,' she said.

Patrick grinned. 'We didn't get very far, did we?'

'No, we didn't.'

'Will you come out with me again?'

'Of course I will! But not until after Christmas . . . Say a week today?'

'How will you manage it next time?'

'I'll think of something.' She had to. She absolutely had to.

'Christmas is a time for families,' Rose Donovan, Maggie's mother, had used to say, and Maggie would tease her – 'I know, Mam, you've told us that before' – because she trotted it out every year without fail.

Now, to her own amusement, she heard herself saying the same thing.

'I get more like my mother every day!' she said, laughing. 'But it's true. It's so lovely being all together.'

'It's going to make a lot of work for you,' Josh warned.

'At least I don't have to worry about the accounts any more. Laurel Sykes is doing a marvellous job with them. And I don't care how much work it makes. It will be worth it.'

This year was going to be extra special, as her brother Walter and his family were coming down from Yorkshire to stay for a few days, and Ewart and Cathy and their children were also going to join them for Christmas dinner.

'We've got plenty of room for them all here,' she said. 'I'm really glad now that we decided to make the move.'

'Just as long as you don't wear yourself out.'

'They'll all muck in and help. And I'm well on with the preparations.'

It was true, she was. She'd made the puddings back in October and they now sat ready in a row on the top shelf in the walk-in larder, each covered with a cloth tied with string. She'd made the cake at the end of November; it just had to have a topping of almond paste and icing. The cockerel was ordered to be delivered on Christmas Eve, and she'd even wrapped some of the children's presents and hidden them in a corner of her bedroom between the wardrobe and the dressing table. There'd be a last-minute rush, of course, to make mince pies and a sherry trifle, and get mountains of vegetables prepared, but she felt sure Walter's wife, Connie, would give her a hand with peeling the potatoes and doing the sprouts – Walter had said he'd bring those with him, grown in his own garden. And Cathy had promised to make a bowl of stuffing, her mother's speciality – onion, sage and breadcrumbs with plenty of added lard, and cooked in the oven until it was crisp and crunchy.

The biggest problem was finding enough cotton sheets and

blankets to make up the beds, but Josh's mother had offered to lend her some, and Maggie had suggested she and Josh's father should join them on Christmas Day too.

Walter, Connie and their brood arrived early in the afternoon of Christmas Eve, having taken a pony and trap from the station, and Walter had got a lift back to High Compton as he was anxious to see his brother Ewart. Both busy with their families and living so far apart, it was years now since the two had met, and when they had, it was generally Ewart who had made the journey up to Yorkshire. Walter was curious, too, to see what they had done with what had been the old family home, where he had grown up. And he'd be seeing plenty of Maggie over the rest of the holiday.

The pony and trap dropped him at the end of the rank, and memories of long ago washed over him as he walked along the track. Hard now to imagine that he had been one of the varmints playing Knock Down Ginger, or putting a parcel with a string attached in the middle of the track, hiding behind a hedge, then jerking the parcel away when someone tried to pick it up. Or that he and a pal had scrumped apples, burying what they couldn't eat in his friend's vegetable plot. His father, coming across them, had remarked: 'Well, Mother, that's the first time I've planted taters and dug up apples!'

It all seemed so long ago now, and yet at the same time as clear in his mind as if it was yesterday.

As he approached number 5, a man emerged and crossed the track in front of Walter – on his way over to the privy, by the look of it. An old miner, for sure: taller than many, he had the slight stoop that came from crouching in low seams day after day, and as he pulled the kitchen door closed behind him, he coughed, the telltale wheeze and rattle of silicosis. Poor bugger, Walter thought. The man glanced in his direction and nodded, and Walter could see that he wasn't that old – in his fifties, perhaps. But it wasn't that that brought him up short. It was the feeling that he knew him, or at least had seen him somewhere before. A former neighbour, perhaps, grown old? But he remembered Mr Button who'd lived in number 5 when he was growing up, perfectly well, and he was certain it wasn't him.

Oh well, he was probably mistaken. Or else it would come to him when he wasn't thinking about it.

He rapped on the door of number 6, and opened it, just as he always had.

'Hello? Anybody at home?'

The unmistakable aroma of sage-and-onion stuffing wafted out, and then Ewart was there, clapping him on the back, delighted to see him.

Walter forgot all about the man who had come out of number 5, and who had looked so puzzlingly familiar.


'Christmas is a time for families to be together,' Minty said. 'Our Earl and Vicky should be here. And our Samuel too.'

She got the cockerel out of the oven and plonked it down on the table, prodding it with a fork to see if it was done.

'They're grown men, m'dear,' Ezra said wheezing a little from the smitch that had filled the kitchen when Minty opened the oven door. 'They've got wives, and their wives have got families too.'

'Yes, Mam, just be glad *we're* here,' Laurel said, a mite shortly.

She was feeling wretched and bad-tempered, not at all in the mood to humour her mother. She could think of nothing but that at this moment Ralph would be celebrating with his family. Having luncheon, as he called it, at the Francis Hotel, no doubt, or some other posh establishment that would save his wife from having to slave over a hot stove.

257

She couldn't believe how bitter it made her feel. And that just wasn't like her. She took after her father, accepting what couldn't be changed and getting on with it. But these last few weeks, all the frustration of the years of waiting for Ralph to leave his wife as he had promised had really got under her skin.

After Christmas she was going to have to tell him – the time had come for him to make a choice. Her or Amy. She couldn't go on like this. He couldn't be allowed to get away with having the best of two worlds. Maybe it would condemn her to being an old maid, but anything was better than this.

And she wouldn't be completely alone as long as she had Rowan.

She glanced across the room to where Rowan was leafing through a new book. She seemed so happy. Laurel had never seen her more alive, more glowing.

If Rowan's happy, I'm happy, she told herself.

Really, nothing else mattered.

The big farmhouse kitchen was perfect for a family gathering, just as Maggie had known it would be, and after a fine meal and a few drinks everyone was in high good humour. During a break to let the first course go down, Father Christmas distributed nuts and clementines to the children. It was Gilby Withers, dressed in a red suit and a flowing white beard that he had borrowed from the Buffs – the Royal Antediluvian Order of Buffalos – a sort of working man's Masonic Lodge, of which he was a member. The children were all awestruck, apart from Nora, who asked loudly, 'Where's Grandpa Withers?'

'He's gone to the lav,' Grandma Withers said, hushing her, and the awkward moment passed.

The pudding was brought in, flaming in a pool of brandy and with a sprig of holly stuck in the top, and they all sang

'We Wish You a Merry Christmas'.

Merry was certainly the word for it. Both Maggie and Cathy had drunk a little too much sherry, and Cathy was reverting to her old flirtatious self. She found a branch of mistletoe that Maggie had propped up in a vase, and plonked herself down on Walter's knee.

'I want a kiss from my brother-in-law!'

'Behave yourself,' Ewart said, but they were all laughing, and Walter gave her such a smacker that she almost fell off his knee onto the floor.

'Bet you wish your young lady was here, Patrick,' she said, waving the mistletoe under his nose. 'Then you could give her a kiss too.'

'You haven't got a young lady, surely, Patrick?' Grandma Withers said.

'Oh yes, didn't you know?' Cathy was in full flood now. 'Rowan Sykes from next door to us at number 5.'

'She's not my young lady,' Patrick protested, blushing scarlet, but of course they all joined in the teasing.

None of them noticed that Walter had gone very quiet.

'Did you say Sykes?' he said, when the merriment died down a little.

'Yes. Minty and Ezra. And their daughters Laurel and Rowan. Minty's a misery-guts, but the rest of them are nice.' Cathy waved a finger teasingly at her nephew. 'Aren't they, Patrick?'

'Oh, leave the poor boy alone!' Connie said. 'And I think that baby of yours wants changing, Maggie. It's whiffy round here, and I don't think it's your sage-and-onion stuffing, Cathy.'

They were off again, laughing and chatting as Maggie scooped up little John and took him off to change his nappy. But Walter sat quietly, drinking what was left of his brandy.

259

Ezra Sykes. So that was who it was. He thought he'd looked familiar. But by gum, he'd aged since he'd seen him last.

Ezra wouldn't have recognised Walter, of course – they'd never known one another well, as they'd worked in different gangs, and Walter had been just a young lad back then, fresh up in Yorkshire from the Somerset coalfield.

Fancy him living next door to our Ewart! he thought. It's a small world.

Maybe he'd mention it to Ewart when they were on their own. And then again, perhaps he wouldn't. If Walter remembered rightly, the Sykes family had left Yorkshire under something of a cloud. He couldn't be sure of the details; he'd never been one to listen to gossip. But if they'd come to Somerset to get away from something up there, he didn't think he should be the one to let the cat out of the bag. Especially if Patrick was keen on the daughter.

'Come on, let's have a game,' Maggie suggested.

'Pin the tail on the donkey?'

'Yes! And you can be the donkey first, Walter. That's your punishment for kissing Cathy.'

Walter grinned, and got up reluctantly. Ezra Sykes and the mystery surrounding his family was forgotten.

# Chapter Nineteen

Laurel was still set on the decision she'd made on Christmas Day. Things couldn't go on the way they were any longer. When she next saw Ralph she would give him an ultimatum. Either he left his wife and committed to her, or she'd tell him it was over. And this time she wouldn't go back on her word.

The very thought that it might come to this filled her with dread. He'd meant so much to her for so long. Yet at the same time a small part of her was wondering if a clean break might be for the best. If he ran true to form, there would be more empty promises, more torturous weeks of waiting and hoping, more frustration and disappointment, more guilt. She didn't think she could stand that. In fact, she wasn't even sure she really wanted him any more.

It was the *idea* of him that she was clinging to. The hopes and dreams of so many years. The reluctance to admit to herself that they had been wasted. That he had never had any intention of leaving Amy for her, and his declarations of love were nothing but weasel words, silken threads to bind her to him as surely as the gossamer of a spider's web held a fly. He had been portraying himself as a loving father sacrificing his own happiness for the sake of his son when it was no more than an excuse for having the best of both worlds. If his marriage was really as unhappy as he claimed it to be, if he truly loved Laurel, then surely the time to have made a move would have been when Bertie had left school and gone away to university.

If her suspicious were true, she told herself, then he wasn't worth shedding a single tear for. And yet she had, time and again. Oh, there was no denying he was a very attractive man and the first since Callum who had made her feel the way she did. But why, against all her finer instincts, had she allowed herself to be embroiled in an illicit affair for so long? Was it because as a result of things that had happened in the past she had been so desperate to be loved; to feel she was worthy of love? Because, unsatisfactory as the situation was, it had bolstered her self-esteem, the self-esteem that had taken such a battering all those years ago and never really recovered?

Laurel was not only taking a good hard look at Ralph and their situation, but at herself too, and she didn't like what she was seeing.

No, things couldn't go on the way they were. She wouldn't be taken for a fool any longer. It was up to him now. Either he delivered on his promises, or she would walk away.

All this was playing on her mind when, on her first day back at work after the Christmas holiday, Ralph telephoned her.

'Am I forgiven?'

'Forgiven for what?' Her voice was taut; she wasn't in the mood for playful banter.

'For not seeing you before Christmas and giving you your Christmas gift.'

A Christmas gift. But this year the prospect of receiving it gave her no pleasure. Expensive jewellery, no doubt, to keep her sweet. As if she were no more than a common prostitute.

'Your wife and son had to come first,' she said in the same taut tone.

'Oh, Laurel – I've upset you, and I am so, so sorry. But yes, you're right. This will be the last family Christmas for Bertie. One final happy memory. I couldn't deny him that. Next year you and I will be together, and we'll make up for all the time we've lost. It will be special, I promise you,' he wheedled.

'Really.' It came out as a curt comment, not a question.

'Yes, my sweet, really. We'll meet this Thursday as usual, won't we? Then I can give you the very special gift I have for you.'

'Ralph . . .'

She was about to tell him here and now what was on her mind. But at that very moment her office door opened. Matron was there, her hand on the knob, finishing a conversation with someone in the corridor before coming in.

'I have to go,' Laurel said.

'But you will . . . ?'

There was no time now for saying what she wanted to say, and in any case, perhaps she owed it to both of them to say it face to face.

'Yes.' She slammed the phone down just as Matron entered the office. She was shaking all over, the words she'd so nearly spoken echoing in her head.

'Is everything all right, Miss Sykes?' Matron was looking at her narrowly.

With an effort Laurel gathered herself together.

'Perfectly fine, Matron.'

'Good.' Matron placed a fat manila folder on Laurel's desk. 'Then perhaps you'll deal with these returns. If you can find the time between making telephone calls,' she added tersely, and bustled out, closing the door behind her.

Laurel pulled the folder towards her and opened it. But the figures on the sheet were blurring before her eyes as emotion overwhelmed her and the tears came to fill them.

They were tears of frustration and regret. Tears for lost years, lost dreams and lost innocence. Tears not only for Ralph but for another love, and what might have been. But what was done was done. All the tears in the world could not change that.

Laurel swallowed hard, brushed her eyes with the back of her hand and tried to drag her mind back to the job that was her lifeline.

When she arrived at Ralph's consulting rooms on Thursday evening, Laurel was as set as ever on forcing the issue once and for all, but she certainly wasn't looking forward to it. Like her father, she hated confrontation of any kind, and she knew this was going to be a very difficult conversation.

The outer door was on the latch, a sure sign that he was expecting her. But when she pushed it open and went inside, she was surprised to find someone else in the waiting room. Ralph's appointments with patients had usually been concluded long before she arrived.

'Oh! Are you waiting to see Mr Riley?' she asked.

The man who had been pacing the small room turned to face her. He was, she saw, middle-aged, mutton-chop whiskers framing a face that gave the appearance of one a little too fond of the bottle – red-veined cheeks and a bulbous purpling nose. But the creases between nose and mouth and the furrowed brow spoke of deep anxiety, and he was twirling a stubbed-out cigar between finger and thumb as if he was fighting the urge to light up again.

'Nah.' His accent was unmistakably cockney. 'I'm waiting

for my wife. She's with the doc now.' With his free hand he wrestled a fob watch into his line of vision. 'Shouldn't be long now. She's been in there a while.'

'I see.'

Laurel half turned, thinking she'd go back outside and walk around the square while waiting for Ralph's patient to leave, but the man's voice stopped her.

'Is he any good, do you know?'

'Mr Riley?'

'Yeah. A pal of mine recommended him, but I'm not sure what to think about all this jiggery-pokery.'

'You mean homeopathy?'

'Is that what they call it? I knew it was some long word. But what I want to know is – does it work?'

Laurel hesitated. To be truthful, she wasn't entirely convinced. It was true that Vicky seemed to have improved initially under his care, but recently all the symptoms had begun coming back – the tiredness, the chills, the hair loss, the flaky patches of dry skin. 'He certainly has a lot of patients who swear by him,' she said evasively.

'He'd better be damned good, the fee he's charging. That's all I can say . . .' He broke off as the door to the consulting room opened and a lady emerged.

Although no longer young, there was a timeless elegance about her that owed something to her astrakhan cape and a fawn felt hat trimmed above its turned-up brim with a sweep of ostrich feathers. But it wasn't just the fine clothes that drew the eye: there was something about her that was almost magnetic, though Laurel couldn't have said for the life of her what it was.

'Molly, my dear.' The man started towards her, then addressed Ralph, who stood behind her in the doorway. 'Is she going to be all right, Doc? Are you going to put my Molly right?'

The lady gave a small amused shake of her head and smiled at Laurel, a conspiratorial smile that seemed to say: 'Men! What are we to do with them?' but which, in spite of her pallor, seemed to light up the room. Then she laid a gloved hand on the man's arm.

'I'll tell you all about it on the way home, Daniel. We've taken up enough of Mr Riley's time.'

'Which I'm paying handsome for! Come on, Doc, I don't necessarily trust her to tell me the truth.'

Ralph threw a glance in Laurel's direction, and she wished now she'd managed to escape. Being forced to witness their conversation felt like an intrusion into these people's privacy, though the man, in his anxiety for his wife, seemed to have forgotten she was there.

'You can rest assured I shall do my very best for her, Mr Trotter,' Ralph said smoothly. 'I've prescribed some medication, and I'll see her again in a week or so to assess the situation. In the meantime, I have advised her not to take any more of the potion her regular GP has given her. I think it may well be doing more harm than good.'

'You think so? But this stuff of yours should do the trick?'

'I have high hopes that it will. If not, we must look for other answers.'

The man – Mr Trotter – nodded, looking somewhat relieved, and felt in his pocket for his wallet.

'What's the damage, Doc?'

Ralph raised a hand, stopping him.

'I'll send you my bill in due course. I prefer that to dealing in cash here in my consulting rooms.'

'As you wish.'

Ralph moved to hold the door open for his patient and her

husband. Laurel slipped out of the way to let them pass and Ralph followed them out, closing the outer door behind them, clicking the key and shooting the bolt.

'Well, well,' he said, coming back into the waiting room and reaching for Laurel's hand. 'Who'd have thought it?'

'Thought what?' She drew away, tucking her hand into her pocket.

Ralph raised an eyebrow, but made no comment on her clear gesture of rejection. He thought she was playing hard to get, no doubt, but was confident of winning her round in his own good time.

'That lady, my sweet, was a successful actress and singer in her time,' he said with a self-satisfied smile. 'She's plain Mrs Daniel Trotter these days – though her husband is the owner of the Lyric Theatre here in town – but she used to be known as Belle Dorne.'

'Belle Dorne?' Laurel repeated. 'I don't think I've heard of her.' Though it explained the woman's magnetism, she thought.

'Before your time. And mine, come to that. You'll have heard of her niece, though. Lucy Dorne? She's a great hit on the London halls. And she hails from High Compton.'

'Goodness, yes!'

Certainly she'd heard of Lucy Dorne, or Lucy Day as she used to be. Folk locally were very proud of the fact that the girl who'd started out singing at chapel anniversaries and with Stanley Bristow's concert parties had ended up as a star of the music hall. And her roots were even closer to home – she and her family had once lived at number 2 Fairley Terrace, though they'd moved away before the Sykes family arrived. Her father had been one of those killed in the terrible tragedy at Shepton Fields Colliery, and her mother had married again. Laurel even knew Lucy's sister by sight – she was the wife of the Reverend Callow, the Methodist minister.

'I'm sorry they were still here when you arrived,' Ralph said. 'As you know, I don't usually consult so late in the day. But Trotter was anxious to get his wife seen and I couldn't offer her a regular appointment until next week.'

'He did seem very worried,' Laurel said.

'With cause.'

'But you'll be able to help her?'

'I doubt it.' Ralph's tone was breezy, unconcerned.

Laurel frowned. 'But you said . . .'

'One has to take a positive attitude with patients. They really are not happy if you tell them the unvarnished truth. What point would there be in that?'

'But you've given her medication. You're going to see her again.'

'That's how I make my living, Laurel. The reason I can afford to take you to expensive restaurants and buy you nice things. Which brings me to your Christmas gift.' He moved towards his consulting room. 'Shall we go in and make ourselves more comfortable?'

Laurel followed, but at a distance. She was shocked by Ralph's attitude and the implication of what he had said.

'You don't think the medication you've given her will do any good, then?'

Ralph turned, smiling slightly and shaking his head.

'I'm afraid no one can help Mrs Trotter. Her general practitioner and a consultant at the Royal United Hospital have already told her that. Which is why she has turned to me.'

'But what . . . ?'

'A growth. In her womb, or ovaries, it seems. She's been told she has only a year or so to live, and even that may be an optimistic prognosis. But let's not talk any more about it. Come here, my darling. It's been too long since I tasted your sweet lips.'

Laurel made no move towards him. She was outraged by his callousness.

'How can you, Ralph?'

'How can I what?'

'Give those poor people false hope! Take their money when you know there's no hope of a cure!'

'If they have money to spend – and they do – who am I to refuse them the comfort of knowing they've left no stone unturned?'

'But it's cruel, Ralph! It's deceitful!'

He smiled slightly. 'It's business. But let's not waste any more time on such things.'

He crossed to his desk and took a box from one of the drawers, a small black leather box with the name of an upmarket Bath jeweller inscribed on it in gold lettering.

'For you, my darling. Happy Christmas – or rather, now, happy New Year!'

She made no move to take it, disgusted by the thought that it might have been bought with money earned from what was essentially a fraud perpetrated on the vulnerable.

'Don't you want to see what's in the box?' he asked, cajoling.

'No, I don't! Those people . . .'

'Oh, forget about them, for goodness' sake!'

Laurel said nothing, simply staring at the man she loved – or had thought she loved – and seeing a stranger.

'Look.' He opened the box, holding it out towards her. A necklace set with what looked like emeralds glinted enticingly in the light from the overhead gas lamp. 'Let me put it on for you.'

He moved towards her; angrily she dashed the box from his hand.

'I don't want it, Ralph.'

There was a steely glint in Ralph's eye now; his handsome face had become ugly. He bent down and picked up the box, the necklace lying askew now on its bed of dark blue velvet.

'What's got into you?'

'I can't take something bought with other people's misery. Every time I wore it I'd think of them.'

'You'd let something like this come between us? Ruin what we have, and all for nothing?'

'What do we have, Ralph?' she demanded. 'I came here tonight with the intention of telling you I've had enough of waiting for you to make up your mind. Of creeping about behind your wife's back. That if we couldn't be together properly—'

'We will be.'

'I doubt it. And in any case, I don't know that I want it any more.' Her voice was trembling, but hard. Any last remaining doubts had been dispelled by his callous behaviour.

For a moment he stared at her with something like disbelief. Then he put the jewellery box down on his desk, and shook his head, smiling.

'Come here, my darling.' His tone was silky again.

'No, Ralph. It's over.'

'I don't believe you. What we have is precious.'

He took a step towards her, pulled her into his arms. Before she could turn her head away, his mouth was on hers, soft at first, then, as she attempted to twist away, harder and more demanding.

Revulsion rose in her throat like bile. Could this really be the man she had thought she loved, wanted to spend her life with? He was nothing but a cheat and a charlatan and full of his own importance and sense of entitlement. Slimy, too. How could she have let herself be deceived by his cold, calculating charm? He raised his head a fraction, looking down into her face with a smile that she could see now was self-satisfied, confident.

Furious with both him and herself, she wriggled a hand free and slapped him hard across the cheek, then, still not satisfied, drew her hand back to slap him again. This time, however, he caught her wrist and held it fast.

'You little bitch!' His face was ugly again, an almost feral glint in his eye.

'Let me go, Ralph! This minute!'

'You think you can do something like that and get away with it? I'll show you who's master here!'

He caught at the neck of her blouse, ripping it open to the waist, at the same time pushing her back against the wall. His mouth came down on hers again with such force that her head cracked sharply back against the plaster. Pain like a lick of fire ricocheted down her neck and her head spun so that for a moment she scarcely knew where she was, let alone what was happening. Then somehow she found her voice.

'Ralph! Stop this!'

He growled, a low, guttural sound deep in his throat.

'You're mine, Laurel, and don't you forget it!'

With one arm beneath her knees, the other pinioning her to him like a trapped butterfly, he swept her up, depositing her roughly on the consulting couch. As she attempted to fight him, he caught both her wrists, yanking them above her head. She cried out with the pain as her arms were almost wrenched out of their sockets, and kicked out wildly, but he was out of reach of her flailing feet. Holding her wrists with one hand, he began to unbutton his trousers with the other, and then his weight was on her, pinning her to the couch.

'Mine, you hear?' he growled again.

And raped her.

'I don't ever want to see you again. Ever!'

She was shaking, crying, trying to rearrange her clothing, bringing the torn edges of her blouse together to cover herself.

Ralph was leaning against the edge of his desk, arms folded, once again master of all he surveyed.

'What are you making such a fuss about? It's not as if we haven't done it a hundred times before.'

'Not like that. How could you!'

'Oh, don't be so melodramatic.' He was back to his suave persona. Superior, mocking. 'You know you enjoyed every minute.'

She couldn't find the words to reply. All she knew was that she wanted to get away from here, away from Ralph. She'd meant to end it between them – but not like this. Oh, not like this . . .

'You've learned your lesson; now let's forget about it.'

Nonchalantly Ralph reached for her again. She sidestepped him, snatching up the jeweller's box that lay on his desk and ramming it hard into his smirking mouth. The emerald necklace came out of its retaining clips and fell to the floor. Laurel stamped on it with a booted foot, then headed for the door.

*Give that to your next floozy*, she wanted to say, but she didn't trust herself.

Her hand was on the handle when he spoke.

'Get out, you ungrateful bitch. And don't bother coming back.'

She turned, her eyes sparkling with tears, her teeth gritted.

'Don't worry, I won't.'

\* \* \*

It was raining. The spattering of drops mingled with the tears on her cheeks but did nothing to wash away the degradation or her distress. Laurel wanted nothing more than to climb into a hot bath and wash away every trace of him. But she couldn't, even if she went home now, this minute. How could she explain a bath on a week night? And she couldn't go home yet for the same reason. Even if there was a train, and she wasn't sure there was, there'd be questions as to why she'd come back early.

She went to the station anyway, bought herself a mug of tea and sat on the platform holding it between shaking hands, willing its heat and its sweetness to bring some warmth back into her body.

Her shoulders still ached, and so did her head, a dull throb that echoed down her neck. In spite of the hot tea, she couldn't stop shivering. Shock ran over her in icy waves. How could he have *done* that? The question echoed round and round in her head like a mantra and her lips moved as she repeated it soundlessly. As yet she was too shocked to think clearly.

Laurel wrapped her arms around herself, bowed her head and huddled on the platform bench to wait for her train.

Daniel Trotter – or Spike as he was more generally known – helped his wife out of his motor and supported her up the path and into the drawing room of their house on the outskirts of Bath. There, he eased off her coat and plumped the cushions in her favourite chair. The trip into town to see the homeopathic doctor had exhausted her, he knew.

'You sit quietly for a bit,' he urged her. 'I'll just go and see to the motor and then I'll get you something to drink.'

'A glass of stout would be nice.' Molly's voice was weary, but still edged with humour and the huskiness that was the legacy of years of singing in smoky halls.

'You and your stout!' Spike teased.

'At least it's one thing I can still enjoy.'

Molly had always liked a glass of good beer, much preferring it to wine or spirits. And even now, when food had lost its flavour so that she was hard pressed to force down the barest mouthfuls, ale still tasted good to her.

'It's what keeps her going,' Spike had told his cousin Doris when he'd been in London on business and called in to her Bermondsey home to bring her up to date on the deterioration in Molly's health.

Doris had been shocked. 'But she's always been as strong as an ox!'

'Don't let her hear you say that,' Spike had replied, but it was true. He'd never known Molly to suffer much more than a common cold.

When she'd first begun losing weight, it had pleased her. In middle age her waist and hips had spread and she'd missed the hourglass figure that had once been the toast of the halls. But thin as her face, arms and shoulders had become, her stomach had remained bloated, and she was complaining of discomfort too, in her back and in her tummy. Now she'd been told there was nothing to be done, and in desperation they'd turned to Ralph Riley.

'Well, let's hope this new stuff the doc's given you does the trick,' Spike said, coming back into the drawing room with a glass of beer for her and a Scotch for himself. He set her drink down next to her and his on an occasional table beside his own chair. 'Why don't you take a dose straight away?'

Molly reached for her bag and took out the bottle. Truth to tell, she didn't have any great hopes for it: her own doctor had been blunt about her prospects, and she trusted him far more than she trusted Mr Riley. Smarmy, she'd thought him. But she didn't want to admit that to Spike, and in any case, she'd never been a very good judge of character.

'Ugh!' The potion tasted bitter, and for a moment she thought she was going to gag. She stoppered the bottle and took a quick pull of her stout. 'That's better! That stuff is vile!'

'Worth it, though, if it does you good.'

'Is it?' She eyed the bottle with distaste. 'I'm not so sure. But I'll take it if it pleases you.'

The potion, whatever it was, was still burning her throat. She took another sip of beer and stared reflectively into her glass, at the pure white head on the richly dark liquid.

'You can't say I haven't seen life, Daniel. It hasn't been without its ups and downs, but on the whole I've been lucky. Having you, for a start. I don't know what I'd have done without you. You know that, don't you?'

He gave a small harrumph. He loved her dearly, but there had been things he'd thought she'd never forgive him for.

'I've seen places most women never get to see,' she went on, 'and done things most women never get to do. If I could have it all over again I don't think there's anything I'd change, except . . .' She broke off.

'Don't talk like that, Mol. It ain't over yet.'

She looked up at him, licking at the beer foam on her lips, and some of the old determination was shining in her eyes.

'No, you're right. I'm not ready to go yet. There's still unfinished business. You know my dearest wish, that before I die . . .'

Spike knew exactly what she was going to say, and he didn't want to hear it. He leaned across and put a finger to her lips.

'I know, Mol. I know. But it ain't going to happen, m' love.'

But still the hope was there, burning in her eyes, and he knew that as long as there was breath in her body, it would never die.

'Drink your beer,' he said gruffly.

And took a long swig of his whisky.

# Chapter Twenty

'You're getting very friendly with this Mary,' Minty said, banging the flat iron back onto the hob and spreading a pillow-case out on the thick ironing blanket she had used to cover the table. 'You see her all week at school, and now it's Saturdays too.'

Rowan crossed her fingers in her coat pocket.

'We like going for walks.'

'This time of year?'

'It's a nice day.'

It was, the sun shining, the air crisp, much to Rowan's relief. Yes, she was now back at school, and travelling to Bath each day with Patrick, but it was no longer enough. On the train they sat on opposite sides of the carriage as they always had. There could be no touching, apart from the occasional brush of hands, and certainly no kissing. Rowan loved kissing. She loved it when his arms were around her and his lips on hers, loved the sweet, soapy smell of the skin on his neck and the feel of his cheek against hers. Loved the closeness and the little thrills of excitement that tickled in her stomach.

'I won't be late back,' she said.

'Four o'clock sharp,' Minty said. 'It'll be getting dark by then, and I don't want you walking home on your own.'

In the scullery, Laurel was at the sink washing some of her underwear.

'Going out?' she asked without looking round.

'Just for a bit. For a walk with my friend.'

Rowan hated deceiving Laurel. She'd never kept a secret from her before, except the bullying when she'd been at primary school, and she longed to tell her now about her meetings with Patrick. Laurel knew, of course, that she saw him every day on the train, but this was different. She couldn't be sure her sister wouldn't agree with Mammy that she was too young to be walking out with a boy, and certainly she wouldn't approve of Rowan lying to her. She just couldn't take the risk. If Laurel told her what she was doing was wrong, she couldn't bear it.

And besides . . .

Laurel seemed to have gone into herself the last few weeks. Rowan had asked her what the matter was, but she'd just replied 'Nothing' in a tone that said very clearly that she didn't want to talk about it. Rowan had wondered if perhaps she had problems at work. But she also wondered, as she sometimes had over the years, why Laurel didn't have a sweetheart, or any men friends except for the one who had come out from Bath to see her on his motorbike. But nothing seemed to have come of that, and it puzzled Rowan. Laurel was really pretty, she was kind and sweet-natured; she'd have thought that she would have fallen in love and married long ago.

Now, with her new-found awareness, she wondered if perhaps her sister had had a secret love, and it had all gone wrong. She hoped not.

'Have fun,' Laurel said now, but her voice was flat and lifeless, not at all like the old Laurel.

'I'll see you later,' Rowan said.

She set out into the bright, cold afternoon. Her heart was pounding with anticipation, as it always did.

But for some reason today it was overshadowed by a feeling of foreboding.

Through the scullery window, Laurel watched her sister go, a lump rising in her throat. Dear Rowan. The light of her life. She hoped with all her heart that life would be kinder to Rowan than it had been to her.

And yet who could she blame but herself? No one. She'd been a fool twice over. There were good men out there. Her father for one. Always there, unassuming, but a rock in all their lives. Her brothers, too. Samuel, taking good care of his family in Yorkshire. Earl, who had been such a tearaway in his youth, and probably broken more than one heart, but who was now a wonderful husband and caring father. Why hadn't she fallen for someone like them? Instead she had been drawn to the dark and dangerous. Bewitched by Callum's romantic background and wild streak – she should have known it would end in disaster. Besotted by Ralph's charm and fooled into thinking he loved her because that was what she wanted to believe.

The blinkers were well and truly off now, though, and she could see him for what he was. A practised liar. A cheat. A man prepared to use anyone or anything if it was to his own advantage. A man who loved no one but himself. A man who'd cheated on his wife for years and made her complicit in his adultery whilst also deceiving her.

And a bad loser. One who had to assert his mastery. A rapist. Her stomach churned now as she thought of that last night in his consulting rooms.

She was worried out of her mind too, and couldn't shake off a really bad feeling. They'd made love before – at least, that was how she'd thought of it at the time – but he'd always been careful. That night, that awful night, taking care had been the last thing on his mind, and Laurel was terrified of the possible consequences.

'I'm going to have to go,' Rowan said.

The sun was sinking towards the horizon in a ball of ruby-red fire and the light was dimming under the canopy of trees.

As always, they'd walked, scuffing through last year's dead leaves, talking as though there would never be enough time to say all they wanted, stopping to watch a squirrel skittering up a tree, pausing for the kisses and cuddles Rowan enjoyed so much. And yet still that ominous feeling remained in the pit of her stomach, made worse by the fact that they'd had the bad luck to bump into the two Donovan boys, Patrick's cousins, towing a set of trucks that they'd been using to slide down the lower reaches of the batch.

The boys had nudged one another and jeered.

'What you up to, Patrick?'

'And with Rowan Sykes, too! Does your mam know, Rowan?'

'Ignore them,' Patrick said, but Rowan's face was flaming with guilt at having been caught out.

'You don't think they'll say anything to Mam, do you?' she said anxiously.

'Why would they? They're scared to death of her. But I don't know why you don't just tell her yourself. It's not right, sneaking about behind her back. I don't like it.'

'I can't tell her,' Rowan said. 'If I did, she'd stop me seeing you.'

'But why?'

'Oh . . . you don't know my mam. She just would.'

'Well I still think you should tell her,' Patrick said stubbornly. 'If she did find out you've been lying to her, it would be all the worse for you.'

Rowan bit her lip. It was the first time they'd ever had a disagreement. He was right, of course. If Mam found out, there'd be hell to pay. Perhaps if she plucked up the courage to confide in Laurel, she'd intercede on her behalf. But she shrank inside all the same at the prospect of what Mam would say, the awful mood she'd be in for days . . .

Patrick said no more about it, but Rowan was still feeling edgy as they made their way back along the path.

A sudden beating of wings broke the stillness in the wooded area to their left and a big black crow flew out of the trees immediately in front of them, so close its wingtip almost brushed Rowan's face. She squealed in fright, jumping back.

'It's only a bird.' Patrick reached for her hand again. 'It's gone now.'

The crow was gaining height over the fields on the other side of the track, disappearing into the fast-fading light. But Rowan's bad feeling was escalating into one of dread. It was an omen. Something terrible was going to happen.

They stopped for one last kiss, then emerged from the track hand in hand.

And there, at the side of the road, arms crossed over her ample bosom, an unmistakable figure was waiting for them.

'Oh no!' Rowan whispered. 'It's Mam!'

She didn't come towards them, just stood there waiting for them to reach her. Her jaw was set, her eyes blazing, chins wobbling as if all her pent-up fury was trying to burst out of her.

She'd known something wasn't right. Known Rowan wasn't telling the truth about where she was going. The minute she was out of the door, Minty had fetched her coat and hurried out into the scullery, determined to follow her. But an argument with Laurel had held her up.

'Where are you going, Mam?' her elder daughter had asked.

'To see what our Rowan is up to. There's something funny going on, and I'm going to find out what it is.'

'Mam – you can't follow her!' Laurel was horrified.

'I can, and I will.'

'No!' Laurel managed to get between her and the door, dripping soap suds on to the tiles. 'You've got to let her have some freedom. She's growing up, Mam.'

Minty snorted. 'That's what I'm afraid of.'

'You can't keep her a child for ever. Watching her every movement, it's not going to do any good. I don't know why you do it.'

'I would have thought you know very well,' Minty snapped. 'But I'm not going to go through all that again. Now, are you going to get out of my way, or do I have to move you myself?'

Laurel shook her head, sighing. There was no way she was going to win this argument. They'd had it, or something like it, many times before.

'I just want to make it clear I don't agree with it,' she said firmly.

'And what right do you have to question the way I'm bringing up Rowan?' Minty demanded furiously.

The answer to that hovered on Laurel's lips, but she said nothing. What right *did* she have when it came down to it?

She moved aside and Minty flounced out. But by now Rowan had turned the corner and was out of sight, and by the time Minty reached the end of the track leading to the main road, there was no sign of her.

Having no idea which way she'd gone, Minty stood there,

looking up and down the road, and fuming. This was all Laurel's fault. How dare she interfere? And how dare Rowan deceive her? She was more certain than ever that that was the case.

As she hesitated, wondering what to do, she spotted the two Donovan boys racing along the side of the road, taking turns at giving one another a ride on their trucks.

As soon as they came within earshot, she called out to them.

'Hey, you two, have you seen our Rowan?'

'Course we've seen her.' That was Ollie, the elder of the two. 'She d'a live next door to us, don't she?'

Both boys laughed.

'Don't you be so cheeky,' Minty snapped. 'You know very well what I mean. Have you seen her this afternoon?'

'Oh yes, we saw her.' They were giggling and nudging one another as Percy took his place in the trucks.

'Well?'

Charging off up the road again, Ollie called over his shoulder, 'She were up by the batch with our Patrick.'

She'd known it! Known something was going on! But that Patrick Withers . . . Oh, the stupid, deceitful girl! Without another word, Minty started up the road, turning into the track on the other side. But in her haste, she hadn't changed out of her house shoes; she'd ruin them in two minutes flat. Besides, she didn't know which route they'd taken around the base of the batch. If she went the wrong way, she might miss them. She stopped at the stile leading into the field and leaned against it. She'd wait here and hope to goodness they weren't up to something they shouldn't be. It wasn't really the weather for it, but one could never be sure . . .

Wrapping her arms around herself to try to keep warm, she stood and waited.

Her eyes fixed on the track leading around the batch, Minty

had no inkling that someone had followed her down the road, hidden behind the hedge that bordered it, and was still there, peeping between the twigs, bare now for winter, but thick enough to offer concealment.

The minutes ticked by. Minty was cold and her bunions were hurting her. The Donovan boys were still charging up and down the road, coming as close to her as they dared – on purpose to annoy, she knew – sniggering and pointing.

'Haven't you two got a home to go to?' she called once, but of course they took no notice.

But still she was determined to stick it out. And at last she was rewarded. The pair of them appeared on the track – holding hands, if you please! As she saw her mother standing there, Rowan let go of Patrick's hand, putting a little distance between them – as if that could make it all right! She was scared stiff, Minty could see that. Well, good!

'Mam . . .' It sounded as if she was close to tears. But Minty had no pity.

'And where do you think you've been?' she demanded. Her voice, like her chins, was wobbling with suppressed rage.

'Just for a walk . . .'

Minty snorted. 'I can see that. With this *boy*!' She spat the word out as if it was an insult.

'We're not doing any harm,' Patrick protested. Although he too was shaken by the sudden appearance of this human equivalent of an avenging angel, he felt obliged to defend Rowan.

Minty turned on him furiously.

'I hope not! But don't you dare make excuses to me, my lad. And stay away from her in future. Do I make myself clear?'

She grabbed Rowan by the arm, pulling her away from him, then gave her a sharp push in the centre of her back.

'Home, my lady!'

Another push, propelling her along the road.

Rowan's cheeks were burning with the humiliation of it, and also with resentment and fear, and tears pricked her eyes.

A stunned and chastened Patrick could do nothing but watch them go.

Unseen by him, in the deep shadow behind the hedge, the watcher followed.

Minty marched Rowan home in tight-lipped silence, but as soon as the back door closed behind them, she turned on her once more, giving vent to the anger that had been stoked up by waiting for so long in the cold.

'You wicked, wicked girl! I'm ashamed of you! Get in there!' She gave Rowan another shove, into the living room.

'Whatever is going on?' Ezra, who had been dozing in front of the fire, came to with a start.

'You may well ask! She told me she was meeting some girl in town. A pack of lies. She was with that boy.'

'What boy?' Ezra asked, genuinely puzzled.

'That Patrick . . . Maggie Donovan's son.'

'Oh, you d'a mean Maggie Withers. He seems a nice enough lad . . .'

'She's been creeping out to meet him. Goodness only knows what they've been up to.'

'I don't suppose there's any harm done,' Ezra said mildly, and Minty turned to vent her fury on him.

'No harm! Hah! You know where these things lead. Step up to the mark for once, Ezra, and don't leave it all to me. Maybe she'll take notice of you.'

'Well . . . you know it's wrong to tell lies, Rowan,' he said uneasily.

'And going out with boys – at her age.'

'Best to wait till you're older, m'dear.'

Laurel appeared in the doorway at the foot of the stairs, looking anxious.

'Did you know about this?' Minty demanded. 'Is that why you tried to stop me going after her? I should have thought you, of all people . . .'

Suddenly Rowan could bear it no longer. Tears streaming down her face, she bolted across the room, pushed past Laurel and ran up the stairs.

'Come back here, my girl! I haven't finished with you!' Minty shouted after her, but she took no notice. She ran into her room, slamming the door behind her, and threw herself down on the bed. But even with the door closed, she could still hear the angry voices from downstairs, and she buried her head beneath the pillow, sobbing as if her heart would break.

She was still sobbing, though dry sobs now, for she had no tears left, when the door of her room opened.

'Rowan?' Laurel's voice was soft, almost as if she thought Rowan might be asleep and didn't want to wake her.

Rowan hiccuped, but didn't reply.

Laurel came into the room, closed the door behind her and dropped to the floor beside the bed, her legs curled up beneath her.

'Rowan, darling . . .' She reached out and stroked her sister's tangled hair. 'Sweetheart, don't cry.'

Rowan spluttered again. 'I hate her!'

'No you don't, my love. Not really. Oh, she can be difficult, I know, but her heart is in the right place. She only does what she thinks is for the best. For your own good.'

Rowan rolled over. Her face was puffy and tear-stained, her eyes red and swollen.

'It's not fair!'

'Life often isn't fair,' Laurel said gently. 'But believe me, Mam only has your best interests at heart. She's afraid of what might happen.'

'What are you talking about?'

'Well . . . sometimes things can get out of hand between boys and girls . . .'

'You mean . . .' Rowan's eyes had gone wide now with shock and horror. 'You mean . . .' she couldn't bring herself to say the words, 'what married people do?'

'You don't necessarily have to be married,' Laurel said carefully, all too aware of the irony of the situation.

Rowan twisted herself upright.

'That's disgusting! How could you think for even a minute that we'd do something like that?'

'It's not disgusting,' Laurel said. 'It's natural. But it's also dangerous. And you might not see it coming. It's all too easy to get carried away.'

'We wouldn't! Patrick wouldn't! Not in a million years!'

Her naivety touched Laurel to the quick.

She had been thinking this might be an opportunity for a heart-to-heart. Rowan was fifteen, not a child any more. Now she realised this was not the time to say what she had been thinking of saying. That would have to wait for another day.

'It's not as if you won't see him again,' she said consolingly. 'He'll still be on the train every day, won't he?'

Rowan nodded, and an expression of consternation crossed her face.

'You won't tell Mam about the train?'

'It's our secret. And when you're older, if you still like each other, you'll be able to go out with him again.'

Rowan nodded. If any good had come out of this at all, it was that she felt closer to Laurel than ever.

The angry voice carried clearly across the track to where Kezia Smith stood deep in the shadow of the outhouses. The same angry voice that had frightened her so all those years ago when she'd followed Callum here and seen him attacked. B'Jesus, how she hated her, the woman she was convinced had murdered her beloved brother.

She'd sworn her revenge all those years ago. She was a gypsy, and gypsies never forgot. Hatred and cold determination had hardened in her heart and spread through her body like a cancer eating away at all reason. Somehow she would get the truth out of the woman. And then she would avenge Callum.

There would be no chance today. She'd had high hopes earlier, when the woman had been all alone, at the entrance to the track that led around the batch. But those boys had been there, racing up and down the road with their stupid trucks. She'd willed them to go away, but it hadn't worked. And then the girl and boy had appeared on the scene and her chance was gone.

But it would come again. If only she was patient. Now that the fair had taken to overwintering in Somerset, there were far more opportunities than there had once been, and one day luck would be on her side. She'd never give up. Not if it took her a lifetime. One day, somehow, she would make sure there was justice for Callum.

# Chapter Twenty-One

Kezia Smith was thirteen years old in the spring of 1901 when the brother she adored disappeared.

At twenty-one, Callum was tall and good-looking, of wiry build but with the rippling muscles that came from working on the travelling fair since he was old enough to help erect and dismantle the rides in whatever town they visited. He was as swarthy as the rest of his family, with eyes the colour of the sea swirling into sunlit caves and a tangle of coal-black curls framing his strong-boned face .

Though he had a devil-may-care attitude to most things, and got into at least as many fights as his father had at his age, with Kezia he was always patient, kind, tender even, and she was as devoted to him as he was to her. He was her hero and also her protector, far more than her father had ever been. It was Callum who spirited her away when the drink was in Will Smith, as it so often was, Callum who bought her baubles and ribbons for her hair, Callum who saved her from many a beating. When he was working on the switchback, Callum would let her ride in a gondola if one was empty as a special treat. She'd loved that; loved the music of the barrel organ, the smell of the traction engine that drove the ride; loved the delighted shrieks of the riders as they were whirled around and around, up and down, in undulating circles. That all changed after Callum disappeared. The memory of happier times was too painful. She could see him still, swinging easily between the gondolas on the moving platform, lithe as a monkey, and the pain inside seemed to be crushing her heart, leaving only darkness.

Home, for as long as she could remember, had been a brightly painted caravan; her best friend, Bobby the piebald that pulled it. They travelled the length and breadth of the country, Kezia sitting on a box behind Bobby with Callum beside her, urging the horse on with a flick of the reins. If he was not sleeping off the skinful he'd had the night before, Will, her father, would be looking after the traction engine that pulled the switchback ride, whilst Clodagh, her mother, worked on the corn dollies and clothes pegs she would sell at their next stopping place. When her husband was incapacitated, she took his place beside the traction engine.

The family's roots were in Ireland, but they had always been nomadic. Folk called them gyppos, didicois, tinkers, pikeys, but Clodagh insisted they were Romani. Her parents had not been best pleased when she had married Will, a member of another gypsy family. He'd served time in prison for drunken affray, which he was proud of, and petty theft and burglary, which he was not, though most of his regret was that he'd not committed it on a much bigger scale, one that would be worth getting caught for.

Clodagh had had plenty of time to regret her choice of husband, yet she remained fiercely loyal to him. Kezia had learned from the moment she could talk that you uttered a word against Da at your peril. Ma always took his part, even when he and Callum got into fights, a not infrequent occurrence. Kezia remembered only too well one occasion when things had got particularly violent and she'd thought they were going to kill one another. It had started over some girl Callum was seeing – Laurel, her name was – and ended with both of them battered and bloody. But even though Callum's face had looked like a piece of raw steak and his nose was broken, Ma had still defended Da. He was the head of the family, and Callum shouldn't go against him, she had said. Kezia, who had been about six at the time, had of course been on the side of her brother, and she was distraught when the next day he had taken off without a word to anyone.

'So he's shinned it,' Will had said. 'But he'll be back with his tail between his legs before long, worse luck.'

In fact it was long months before she saw Callum again, months when she was lonelier than she'd ever been in her life and when she often cried herself to sleep. Da was even more short-tempered than usual because he had to do Callum's work as well as his own. It was a miserable time.

They'd been in Yorkshire at the time of the fight. The fair had overwintered there, then, with the advent of the better weather, set up in various towns and villages in the vicinity. But they'd moved further afield by the time Callum caught up with them again, in the industrial heartlands of the Midlands.

He'd been to London, he told Kezia, but he hadn't liked the smoke and the heat and if he hadn't come back he'd have been reduced to begging on the streets – 'maundering', he called it.

'I had to come back for you anyway, didn't I, Shaver?' he'd said. Her heart had swelled with love and pride, the lonely times forgotten.

Life had returned to normal. The endless travelling from April to November. The winters parked up near some town or other, with the rides open on Saturdays for the benefit of the locals. The schools she was forced to attend when they were in one place for long enough – hateful, hateful schools where she was ostracised by the other children, who looked down on her and called her names, and scorned by the teachers because she was so far behind in her lessons. She helped Ma pick heather, both purple and white, which they tied into small bunches to sell in the towns, and learned to read palms as Ma did. She never saw anything remotely prescient in those hands, some soft and white, some with dirt ingrained into the deep criss-cross of lines, but she knew what to say.

'You've had a hard time, but things are going to get better soon.'

'There's money coming your way.'

'I see a tall, dark stranger from across the seas.'

And, of course, before she prophesied anything at all: 'You've got a lucky face, missus. Cross my palm with silver and I'll tell you more . . .'

At Christmas she went with Callum to gather mistletoe; he could shin up a tree, his knife between his teeth, as agile as a monkey. And then they'd take that into town to sell, along with holly. She could help with cutting that; she was tall for her age, and some of it, at least, was within her reach, though by the time they finished, her hands and wrists, bare and bony beneath the too-short sleeves of her coat, were covered in pinpricks and scratches that stung horribly. But she didn't care. She was helping Callum. That was all that mattered.

At last spring would come, and they'd be off again, the whole glorious summer before them.

They were back in Yorkshire the winter before Callum disappeared – Kezia thought of it as an accursed place. It had been here that he'd had that terrible fight with Da, and now he was in a strange, dark mood, snapping at her and quite unlike his usual happy-go-lucky self. She asked him what was wrong, but he just told her to leave him alone and walked off, scowling.

She hoped when they moved on he'd get over it and go back to normal; with him behaving like this it was almost as bad as those long months when he'd shinned it to try his luck in London.

When the furry white pussy willow was in flower and yellow lambs' tails dangled from the hazels, they set out for the West Country, where they invariably spent the summer.

Kezia was soon bored with the long journey, sitting beside the plodding Bobby day after day.

'Why do we have to go so far?' she complained to Clodagh.

'Because spring comes earlier down south. And there's plenty of good mops and fair days. You know you like it once we get there.'

It was true, she did. She preferred it when they overwintered there too, in Dorset, or Devon, or Somerset. The schools there might be just as horrid, but at least it didn't seem as bitingly cold, and now that she was thirteen, nobody was going to force her to go to school anyway.

'So why don't we just stay there?' was her next question.

'Because, my girl, we go where the drum takes us,' Clodagh said, using the Romani word for road.

Kezia knew before long that the drum would take them to High Compton. The street fair there was always held at the end of April, and it was a long-standing arrangement that their outfit should provide the entertainment. Along the way they stopped, set up and dismantled several times, but eventually it was April and time for them to head to High Compton for the annual street fair.

The change of scene hadn't done anything to change Callum's mood. If anything he seemed to be edgier by the day, forever getting into rows with Da. The weather wasn't helping, either – on the Saturday morning they woke to the sound of heavy rain pattering on the roof of the caravan.

'We won't be doing much business if this keeps up,' he said glumly.

Clodagh was looking at the sky.

'It'll clear later.'

As usual, she was right. By midday it was brightening up. Undeterred, Will went off for a drink – the pubs had now opened – and Callum and Kezia went to get the switchback ride ready for business. There was still no sign of Will by the time the customers began arriving, though it was closing time at two, and they guessed he had gone to the caravan to sleep it off. It scarcely mattered, though: they could manage between them without him. It wouldn't be the first time, and probably not the last.

It was Kezia's job to help Callum collect the money and make sure all the punters were safely in their seats before he set the gondolas in motion. When he did, she would step off onto the boarded platform that surrounded the ride and lean against the rail until it came to a halt. Then the whole routine would begin again.

Sometimes, though, if she was bored, she would use the time to pop over to see her friend Liza, who was manning the roll-the-penny stall on the corner of the square where the switchback had been set up. All Liza had to do really was to give change to anyone who wanted it, pennies for threepenny bits, sixpences or even sometimes a shilling or a florin, so there was plenty of time for them to chat, and Kezia could easily see when the ride was stopping and go back to do her bit.

That was where she was now when she saw the gondolas slowing.

'Gotta go.'

With Callum in his present mood, she knew she'd catch the edge of his tongue if she wasn't at her post watching the riders as they disembarked, and making sure they got down the step safely. Sometimes the ride made someone dizzy, and there were a lot of people with small children this afternoon. They couldn't afford an accident.

Callum was swinging his way easily between the gondolas. There were two pretty girls in one of them. Kezia grinned: she guessed he was on his way to give them a hand himself. He really was a terrible one for the ladies, and the ladies seemed to like him. There was a romantic aura about the fairground workers, she supposed. And of course, he was so good-looking.

But to her surprise he stopped suddenly, holding onto one of the supports. He wasn't looking at the girls at all, but out over the square and the people milling about as they waited their turn, his face frozen into an expression of shock or surprise. He didn't seem to even notice as the girls glanced expectantly at him, then shrugged and linked arms as they climbed down the step. Then, to Kezia's amazement, he darted between the gondolas and down the step himself, into the milling crowd.

'Callum!' she called. 'Callum!'

Though he passed her by almost close enough to touch, he didn't hear her, or at least gave no indication that he had. She tried to push her way after him, but the crowd had swallowed him up.

There was chaos on the steps now, people trying to board and grab a seat barging their way past those trying to get off. Kezia didn't know what to do. She couldn't operate the ride; though she knew more or less how, Callum had never actually allowed her to do it, and in any case she wasn't sure she'd be strong enough. There was only one thing for it – fetch Da. And he wouldn't be best pleased about that.

She pushed her way through the crowds, making for the caravan, which was parked in a cul-de-sac at the top of the square.

As she'd expected, Will was stretched out on a bunk, snoring. The caravan reeked of beer fumes.

'Da! Da!' She shook him and he came to, bleary-eyed. 'Da – you've got to come! There's nobody to start the ride!'

'Don't be daft. Callum's there.'

'No, he's not. He's gone running off, and they're all waiting.'

'What d'you mean? Where's he gone?'

'I don't know. Please, Da!'

Swearing, Will roused himself and followed her out of the caravan, stumbling a bit. Alarmed, Kezia wondered if he was in any fit state to operate machinery.

The people who had secured seats in the gondolas were becoming restless, looking around, puzzled as to why the ride seemed to have been left unattended. Will blundered his way to the traction engine in the centre, leaving Kezia to collect the money and starting the ride before she was halfway round. A bit frightened, she hung onto the curved roof of one of the gondolas, then, gaining confidence, managed to take a few more fares before it gathered too much speed, slipping the coins into the leather money bag she wore across her body, then hanging on again for dear life.

Kezia was never sure how many more times she and Da ran the ride between them before Callum appeared, jumping on while it was still moving. He was out of breath, and beads of sweat were trickling down his face and neck.

'Where in feckin' buggery have you been?' Will roared.

'Something I had to do.'

'What, for Chrissakes? What you had to do was run this fecking ride!'

'Aw, feck off back to your sleep, Da. I'm here now, aren't I?'

Kezia was afraid they were going to come to blows again, right here on the switchback. Mercifully that did not happen. To

296

her enormous relief, Da went back to the caravan, still swearing and yelling that Callum had not heard the last of this.

'I had to fetch him. The punters were getting restless,' Kezia said. 'Where did you get to?'

'Mind your business, Shaver.'

He went back to work and so did she. But she was still wondering what had made him take off like that. He seemed different, too, purposeful, taut, like a coiled spring. Something had happened. She didn't know what, but she was sure that it was something momentous.

'I'm shutting up early tonight, so you can get off when you like,' Callum said.

'Why?' Kezia asked, suspicious.

It was only eleven o'clock; usually he kept the ride going as long as there were punters about, and there were still plenty of those milling around in the light thrown by the carbide lamps and gas flares. Things were getting rowdy, and a few scuffles had broken out, but Callum didn't usually let that worry him. As long as there was money to be made, he kept the gondolas turning.

'Mind your business.'

He still had that air about him, as if he were bursting with tightly controlled energy. Kezia couldn't remember ever seeing him like this before. She knew that asking him what was going on would be useless. But there were more ways than one of killing a cat . . .

'I'll leave you to it then,' she said.

In case he was watching, she walked away in the direction of the caravan, then doubled back, keeping in the shadows along the wall of shops and behind the attractions. She watched him pack up the ride for the night and turn off the lamps, then, as he made for the road, she followed at a distance. He was heading out of town by the look of it.

Away from the gaslit street, it was very dark, the moon and stars hidden in a thick blanket of cloud. Kezia shortened the distance between them so as to keep him in sight. A cow lowed suddenly and loudly just the other side of the hedge, making her jump, and she was terrified she had given herself away, but Callum didn't seem to have heard anything. He was still striding on, so fast that she had to almost run to keep up with him.

Her eyes had become used to the dark now, and when he crossed the road and turned into a track, she followed. After thirty yards or so it dog-legged so that for the moment she lost sight of him. Then, as she reached the junction, she realised that it ran along the back of a row of cottages. On the opposite side were outhouses and what she imagined must be gardens.

About halfway along the track Callum stopped and looked around. Kezia shrank back, fearful that he had seen her. But no, he was fumbling for something in his pocket and she breathed again. A moment later a match flared and he held it up to the door in cupped hands. What was he doing? Checking the number of the house, perhaps? The pinprick of light died as he dropped the match. Then he knocked loudly on the door.

Kezia crossed the track swiftly and soundlessly and, melting into the shadow of the outhouses, inched closer. The door opened, light from inside pooled out and she ducked back into a garden gateway. She almost tripped over a pile of bean sticks beside an open trench, but saved herself and, avoiding the trench, crept still closer under cover of a prickly hedge of loganberry bushes.

Callum spoke, then a man, but she couldn't make out what they were saying. Callum again. She inched nearer. Then the man's voice, raised now, loud enough for her to hear.

'She's not here, I tell you. And if she was, she wouldn't want to see you. Not after what you did.'

A woman appeared in the doorway, a stocky shape silhouetted against the light. She was shouting too.

'You! You! How dare you come here, bothering us!'

More shouting. Kezia was frightened now, wishing she hadn't followed Callum. Whatever was going on, she no longer wanted to know. Starting to inch back the way she had come, she clapped her hands over her ears, but in any case the thunder of her blood pounding in her veins was so loud the words were lost to her.

A little further, a little further, and she could make a run for it . . .

A yell and a sudden thud made her turn back, and she froze. Callum had careered back against the wall of the outhouse and the woman was hitting him with something, something that gleamed dully in the reflected light – fire irons, perhaps?

What was she *doing*? What . . .

For a moment that seemed to last an eternity, Kezia hesitated, torn between running away as fast as she could and going back to help Callum. But Callum was well able to look after himself. If he could fight Da, hold his own in scraps with gangs of thugs, he could certainly get the better of an old woman. And if he knew she'd followed him, he'd be furious with her.

Letting discretion be the better part of valour, Kezia took to her heels and ran. She didn't stop until the dark countryside gave way again to the lights of the town. She was breathless, trembling.

There were still revellers in the town square. One of a group of lads recognised her.

'Hey – that's the girl off the switchback! Why've you shut up, darlin'? Can't you start up again and give us a ride?'

'Leave me alone.'

At the foot of the steps into the caravan, she stopped. She didn't want Ma or Da asking her where Callum was. Or why she was hot, out of breath and close to tears.

She continued on up to the end of the cul-de-sac. There was a big house there with stables where Bobby was lodged. She crept into the grounds, found Bobby's stall, called his name softly. A big head appeared over the half-door; a nose nuzzled her. Kezia buried her face in the coarse hair of his neck and sobbed as if her heart would break.

Next morning there was no sign of Callum.

'He didn't come home last night,' Ma said.

Kezia's blood turned to water, but she said nothing.

'Where the fecking hell is he?' Will demanded when it was time to dismantle the ride. 'Lazy, fecking good-for-nothing.'

Still she said nothing.

'If he's shinned it again . . .'

'He'll turn up,' Ma said.

Kezia wasn't so sure. Perhaps he was holed up somewhere nursing two black eyes, or worse. But her trembling heart was telling her different.

They'd killed him. Those people had killed him. Buried him, most likely, in the freshly dug trench for the runner beans. And she'd run away and left him there at their mercy. Shame added yet another dimension to her awful secret.

She should tell Ma and Da what she'd seen. They should get the police on that evil man and woman . . . especially the woman. But what good would that do? If they had killed him, there was no bringing him back. And if they hadn't, then Callum would be furious with her for drawing attention to whatever it was they'd been quarrelling about.

If he came back, that would be an end to it. She'd never tell him what she'd seen and heard.

And if he didn't, she'd know that that woman had murdered him with whatever it was that had been gleaming in her hand as she hit him and hit him.

She didn't trust the police to get justice for Callum. Her family were gyppos, didicois, pikeys. The police had no time at all for them. Far better that she extract revenge herself. And she would. Oh, she would.

Kezia went to the drawer where she kept her most precious possessions and pulled out the knife. Callum had given it to her. Ma had said she was too young to own a knife, but Callum had slipped it to her on the sly. 'You never know when you might need it,' he'd whispered in her ear.

Now she hitched up her skirt and drew the blade sharply across the fleshy part of her thigh. As the blood spurted, she caught it on her index finger and rubbed it on her chest close to her heart. More droplets, anointing her forehead on the spot that she knew as the third eye. Yet more, and she licked her fingers, relishing the salty taste. It was her own special ritual.

As she performed it, she made a solemn vow to Callum. If he didn't come back, she would make sure that woman paid. She'd have to wait until she was older, had more freedom. Then, when the fair was within striking distance of High Compton, she'd slip away, spy on the old witch, stalk her. She'd discover the truth, and when the opportunity arose, she'd take her revenge. If it took her the rest of her life, she'd find a way.

Callum did not come back.

# Chapter Twenty-Two

> Darling, I am growing old
> Silver threads among the gold
> Shine upon my brow today
> Life is fading fast away . . .

The sweet soprano voice filled the Lyric, as pure and clear to the patrons on the hard benches in the gallery as it was to those in the well of the theatre, and the buzz of chatter, clink of beer glasses and the occasional jeer that had accompanied the previous artiste – an inebriated comic whose jokes had fallen horribly flat – gave way to appreciative silence.

Lucy Dorne had always commanded the full attention of her audience, from the very start of her career. The reputedly raucous crowds who frequented the London halls listened to her enthralled, just as folk back home in High Compton had done whenever she was on stage. Nowadays she was a star, as Spike Trotter had always known she could be.

His chest swelled with pride as he watched her from a box at the side of the stage. He'd discovered her, promoted her, made her what she was today. And now she was back here, on the stage where she'd made her first professional appearance, for one night only. One special night, slotted in on a Sunday evening when the cast of the pantomime that was still running from Monday till Saturday took a well-earned rest.

The announcement that she would be performing had pulled in the crowds; the house was full, and the old Spike would have been rubbing his hands together at the prospect of the extra takings. A provincial theatre didn't always make as much money as the proprietor would like. But tonight Spike wasn't thinking of profits.

He cast a glance at his beloved wife, Molly, sitting beside him on one of the crimson-velvet-upholstered chairs with their gilt spindle legs. She was watching the stage intently, one hand pressed hard against her mouth, but he knew that it hid a smile of pure joy and the same pride that he was feeling. Lucy was her dearly loved niece. She'd encouraged her, tutored her, and never felt a moment's resentment that Lucy's career had reached greater heights than she had ever achieved. She could have made it too, of course, if she hadn't fallen for that tyke Anthony Thorpe-Bleasedale. The disastrous outcome had destroyed her reputation and wrecked her career. But there was no changing history, and Molly had taken pleasure in reliving her glory days through Lucy's success, with never a moment's jealousy.

It was because of her that Lucy was here now, performing at the Lyric.

'I'd so love to see Lucy on stage once more,' she'd said.

But she wasn't fit to travel all the way to London. The only way she'd see Lucy perform was if it was here, in Bath. When she'd first fallen ill, she'd been adamant that she didn't want her niece worried, but later she'd agreed that Spike should contact her, a sure sign, he thought wretchedly, that her condition was worsening and she was losing hope of a cure.

Lucy had been shocked when he'd told her that Molly was

seriously ill, and she'd agreed to cancel an engagement so as to come down to Somerset to visit her aunt and make a special appearance at the Lyric, the palace of varieties that Spike owned and managed.

A date had been fixed and Spike had hastily cobbled together a programme with the available performers. They were not ones he'd necessarily have chosen, but many of the best acts were tied up in pantomime all over the country. Still, the tumblers from his own pantomime had willingly sacrificed their day off, and Richard Rawlings, a fine baritone who knew Molly from the old days, and whose voice was miraculously almost as good as it had ever been, had agreed to appear. Spike had to trust that they, along with Lucy, would save the day.

Lucy and her husband Joe had travelled down from London yesterday, and there had been an emotional reunion. Then, later, when Molly was resting and the maid had brought a fresh pot of tea and a plate of shortbread, Spike had gone into more detail about Molly's illness than he had been able to do on the telephone.

'Surely there must be something that can be done?' Lucy had said, visibly shocked and upset by the seriousness of what he had to say.

'Her regular doctor says there ain't,' Spike told her grimly. 'But rest assured, I ain't giving up that easy. We've been seeing a chap in town wot specialises in natural remedies. He's given her some stuff to take, though I can't say as I've seen much improvement so far.'

'What is it?' Joe sat forward in his chair. As a practising pharmacist, he had a professional interest in such things.

Spike shook his head. 'You've got me there. I couldn't say.'

'Can I see it?'

'If you want.'

Spike fetched the bottle. Joe unstoppered it, sniffed it, studied the label, then sniffed again.

'What is it, Joe?' Lucy asked.

For a moment he didn't reply. He took the teaspoon from his saucer, poured a little of the raspberry-coloured liquid into it and tasted, screwing up his face as he did so.

'Ugh!'

'Yeah, Moll says it tastes evil,' Spike said. 'But if it's going to do her any good, I reckon it's worth it.'

Joe re-stoppered the bottle and put it down on the occasional table at his elbow.

'I'm sorry to say this, but I doubt it will.'

High spots of colour rose in Spike's cheeks.

'I'm paying good money for that!' he spluttered.

'I'm sorry,' Joe repeated, hating what he had to say. 'I don't think it's anything but coloured water and quinine. There may be some herb extract or other thrown in. But in my opinion the man's a charlatan.'

Spike bowed his head, resting it in his hands. It wasn't so much that he was surprised; he'd had his doubts from the start. But he had refused to give up hope. Now Joe's words were taking that away from him.

'I can't lose her,' he muttered brokenly.

'Isn't there anything we can do, Joe?' Lucy asked. Her blue eyes were sparkling with tears. 'Don't you know anyone who might be able to help? Harley Street is full of eminent consultants.'

'I can make some enquiries,' Joe said lamely. 'But I'm sure there are good people here too. If they say . . .' His voice tailed away.

Spike raised his head. 'I'll do anything, Joe. Money no object. Moll's not fit to travel to London, but I'd willingly pay for a top man to come down here.'

'Don't waste your money, Daniel.'

None of them had noticed Molly standing in the door-way. Too excited by Lucy's visit to be able to sleep, she'd come back downstairs and overheard the last part of the conversation.

'Moll!' Spike was up in a second, helping her to a chair. 'Don't you talk so silly now. If we can find somebody to get you better . . .'

She shook her head wearily.

'You know there's nothing anybody can do. We have to accept it. Please, let's not spoil Lucy's visit by talking about it.' She smiled at her niece, stretching out a hand across the arm of her chair in Lucy's direction.

'I'm so happy you're here, my dear. And so happy I'm going to hear you sing again. My, it seems like only yesterday I came to that chapel anniversary when you and Kitty were duetting. Do you remember?'

Lucy got up and dropped to the floor at her aunt's feet, taking her hand.

'Of course I remember!'

She could see her now, a vision in mauve and purple silk, standing at the very back of the chapel, and smell the scent of the rosewater Molly always dabbed at her throat and wrists and which had lingered after she left. 'We were so excited that you came.'

Molly smiled slightly. 'Perhaps you were. I'm not so sure about Kitty. But I knew then that you had the makings of a star, though you were only a little girl. And I was right.'

'And then you came to the town hall when I was with Stanley Bristow's concert party.'

'And now you've come here, to me. It's all I wanted, Lucy – to see you . . . hear you one last time . . .'

'Don't say such things, Moll,' Spike chided, but his words went over their heads.

'*All* you wanted?' Lucy said softly. Her eyes met Molly's, direct, questioning.

The rapport between them was such that Molly knew exactly what Lucy meant, and the sadness that never quite left her was there, casting a long, dark shadow over her heart.

Yes, there was something else she wanted, so very much, but it was never going to happen now. She had to accept that.

'That, my dear, was an impossible dream,' she said. 'I have Daniel, and I have you. And for that I am so, so grateful. Sing for me tonight, my love. It's all I ask.'

Now, in the darkened theatre, her heart swelled as she looked down at Lucy, centre stage, in a gown as blue as her eyes, her hair shining like spun gold in the glare of the lights. She heard her sweet voice soaring. Silently mouthed the words of the song.

Spike was mouthing them too. His hand closed over hers. She glanced at him and momentarily their eyes met. Sharing their pride. Sharing their enduring love. Sharing the words of the song. Meaning every word.

> . . . Silver threads among the gold
> Shine upon my brow today
> Life is fading fast away . . .
>
> But my darling you will be, will be
> Always young and fair to me
>
> But my darling you will be, will be
> Always young and fair to me.

\* \* \*

307

Rowan's pen flew across the page of the exercise book in a headlong attempt to keep pace with the words that were spilling out from her imagination.

> Charles clasped Elizabeth to his broad, manly chest. His arms were about her slender waist, his lips in her soft golden hair.
> 'My dearest love,' he whispered, and kissed her.
> Elizabeth's heart fluttered wildly and her lips trembled beneath his as she drank him in . . .

She paused, a tear trickling down the side of her nose; she brushed it away with her finger.

Describing a kiss on paper was the closest she could get to such a thing since Mam had put a stop to her walks with Patrick, and would be for years and years. Writing about a pair of star-crossed lovers felt right somehow.

Rowan had always enjoyed giving free rein to her imagination, and had never given up her dream of becoming a writer, like her heroine Jo, in *Little Women*. (And Jo's romance with Laurie, she remembered, hadn't worked out the way she'd wanted it to. Rowan had cried when she'd married that funny old professor.)

Lately, though, what had been a hobby had become almost an obsession. As soon as her homework was finished, she'd get out the exercise book she'd bought in the post office especially for the purpose and lose herself in her latest story. It was really the only pleasure left to her, the only thing that gave her satisfaction, even if it did sometimes make her maudlin.

It wasn't just that she couldn't meet Patrick any more, hard though that was. If it had only been that, she wouldn't have been quite so upset. It was that everything was different; *he* was different. Ever since that awful afternoon when Mam had caught them together, it was as if a curtain had come down between them, not a heavy velvet curtain like the ones across the stage in the town hall, or the winter-weight ones that hung at the living room window from October to April, but a filmy gauze. Through it she could still see him, but the image was hazy and distorted. They still sat together on the train, but the distance yawned between them, an abyss she couldn't find a way to cross. Mam had put him off, she thought. He wasn't comfortable with her any more.

And perhaps it wasn't just him that was different. Perhaps she was too. Guilty, nervous, ashamed. She couldn't forget what Laurel had said, intimating that Mam was afraid of what she and Patrick might have done, might do. It had made her aware of him in a way she hadn't been before. Made her look at him in a different light.

*Did* he want to do those things? She remembered one time when they'd been kissing and cuddling and he'd pushed her away quite abruptly, said it was time to go home. Had he been on the point of doing something . . . horrible? Did he think she was teasing him, leading him on? Her stomach curled in on itself at the thought. It made everything feel grubby somehow. Nothing was the same as it had been, and it never could be again.

But it wasn't like that in her stories. When she lost herself in writing about Charles and Elizabeth, or any of the handsome, adoring couples who lived in her imagination, the love they shared was pure and noble as well as passionate, the way she'd felt about Patrick before Mam and Laurel had spoiled it all. She could throw obstacles in their path, tear them apart so their hearts were broken, then put things right again. It was in her power to make things turn out the way she wanted them to.

309

For Rowan, it was the one thing that could, for a little while, make her feel happy again.

David had come to look forward to his weekly visits to Fairley Terrace. Much as he was enjoying building his business, content though he was with his accommodation over the workshop, much as he valued the friendship of Maggie and Josh, and fond as he was of their children, there had been something missing in his life. He'd barely given it pause for thought, had come to think of himself as a lone wolf, dependent on no one but himself.

That was how it had been for most of his life. He'd made a few good friends along the way, but he'd also learned that friends could not always be relied upon. That when the chips were down it was every man – or boy – for himself. He'd half fallen in love once or twice, but never given himself completely. He'd always been too aware that the rug could be pulled from under his feet at any moment. To be let down by someone you'd loved and trusted was worse than not loving and trusting in the first place. In the last resort it was less painful to depend only upon oneself.

Then there was the quest he'd set himself. For years it had consumed him so there was no room for anything else. Every move he'd made had been driven by it, and it had cost him the one girl he'd been closest to. Emma.

He still thought about her sometimes, remembered the feelings he'd had for her, and wondered what might have been had he not been so obsessed with his search.

She was small, dark, pretty, a shop assistant in a grocery store not far from the printing works where he'd served his apprenticeship. When he finished work for the day he would go and meet her, waiting under the striped awning, watching her through the window as she served the last late customers, weighing out pounds of sugar or flour or biscuits and quarters of tea. When the grocer eventually let her go, she'd emerge smiling to see him there, a smile that seemed to light up the street even on a grey winter evening.

They'd go to a tea stall, buy mugs of soup and crusty rolls, and eat them on a nearby bench or, if it was wet, sheltering beneath the railway arches. There, in the shadows, he'd kiss her, his senses stirred by the taste of her mouth, the scent of her hair. Rose water. A sweet, clean perfume that evoked in him a strange haunting emotion he didn't recognise but that called to him all the same.

Sometimes they'd simply walk, and then he would see her home. Sometimes they went to a show: not the grand halls – there was no way he could afford their prices on his meagre wage – but the small, smoky ale houses where the rising stars earned their spurs and the faded and falling has-beens eked out an existence. They fascinated him, those places, and Emma loved the music and the jollity.

When he got to know her better, he was sometimes invited to her home for tea, and envied her the warmth and security of a close family. But he never opened up to her, never spoke of his own family, or lack of it. Never shared his deepest hopes, the ones that drove him on relentlessly. Not even when his apprenticeship was finished and he booked his passage to America.

He had asked her to go with him, though, and been disappointed by her reaction.

'America!' Her eyes had widened in shock. 'Oh, I couldn't. My parents would never agree.'

'If we were married . . . ?' he'd said, shocking himself.

'No! Never! I'd love to marry you, David, but I couldn't leave London – all my family and friends – and go to America!

Why on earth would you want to go there?'

He couldn't tell her. If she'd agreed, that would have been different. But she hadn't. She'd dismissed the idea out of hand. If she couldn't commit to him unconditionally, he wasn't about to try to persuade her or explain. Better he'd found out where he stood sooner rather than later.

'I have to go,' was all he said.

'But why?'

'It doesn't matter if you're not going to come with me.'

'David – don't be like this, please!' Her eyes had filled with tears. 'Don't go away and leave me!'

He'd hardened his heart. 'I'm sorry, but there it is. Maybe when – if – I come back, we'll meet up again.'

It hadn't happened, of course. When he'd returned to London he had looked her up, only to be told she was married with two children. He was glad for her, sad for himself, though he'd known that it was unlikely she'd have waited for him. And it was probably for the best. He thought he'd be leaving London again soon and there would only have been more questions that he didn't want to answer. It would always be that way unless or until he could satisfy the demons driving him.

But these last years in Somerset he had become more at peace with himself. In part he'd achieved what he'd set out to do, and after much soul-searching he'd reached a decision. Enough was enough. It was time now to lay those demons to rest and build a new life for himself. No good could come from pursuing them any further.

And now there was Laurel.

He'd liked her the very first time he'd met her, liked her directness and her warm smile. Liked the way she looked, attractive but in no way showy, with the most beautiful eyes he had ever seen; liked the way she treated Rowan, never impatient with her as older siblings could sometimes be, always including her in the conversation.

As the weeks passed, he found himself thinking about her more and more, and wondering what she'd say if he asked her to walk out with him. She had no rings on her fingers and there didn't seem to be a sweetheart on the scene, but he couldn't be sure about that. Perhaps she did have a beau; she just didn't see him on Friday evenings. But if that was the case, he was surprised they hadn't married by now; Laurel was, like him, in her late twenties, he guessed.

He asked Maggie if she knew Laurel's situation.

'Fancy her, do you?' Maggie teased, and he was horrified to feel the heat rising under the collar of his shirt.

'I just wondered, that's all.'

She straightened her face. 'Well, I can't answer your question, but I'll ask Cathy when I see her,' Maggie said, and smiled to herself. It was about time David found himself a nice girl, in her opinion.

A few days later she told David that Cathy didn't think Laurel was courting. 'I think there was somebody, but he was married. I don't think he's on the scene any more,' Cathy had said, but Maggie kept that part to herself.

David wasn't at all sure the best way to go about asking Laurel out. It was so long since he'd done anything of the sort, he was very out of practice. He was anxious too in case she turned him down. Not just because he knew he'd be disappointed, but also because he was afraid of souring the easy relationship they shared.

And then the idea had presented itself, so simple he couldn't understand why he hadn't thought of it before.

Back in January, the Buffs had come to him with what they called a rush job. They were holding a Valentine's Day dance at the town hall and had been let down by the firm that usually printed their advertising material. Time was running short, and if they didn't get it out quick sharp, they wouldn't sell enough tickets to pay for the band and the hire of the hall, never mind making a profit for their funds.

Pleased to have attracted a new client and with an eye on getting more work from them in the future, David had given the job top priority, and within a couple of days had delivered the posters, flyers and tickets to a very relieved secretary. As he always did, he had kept a few back for a book of samples he was collating.

Now it occurred to him that this was just the opportunity he'd been waiting for. A social occasion – much more inviting than a walk at this time of year – and right on Laurel's doorstep. What was more, he wouldn't need to find a way to broach the subject. She invariably looked through the paperwork while he was still there, to check on any queries that might arise. If he slipped one of the flyers in amongst his invoices, the chances were she'd find it and comment on it.

That Friday evening he cycled over to Fairley Terrace as usual, the paperwork in a leather document case he'd bought especially for the purpose after one disastrous occasion when heavy rain had soaked the envelopes it was sorted into, rendering it almost illegible.

Today, it seemed, fate was on his side. The rain that had been coming down hard all day had stopped, and though thick mist hung in clouds round the gas lamps in town, it was not so bad that he couldn't see where he was going. Better still, Minty and Ezra were out, gone to a male-voice choir concert, Laurel told him, and Rowan was as usual upstairs doing her homework.

'Mam told me to be sure to give you a rock cake, though,'

Laurel said with a smile. 'I think she bakes on a Friday specially for you.'

'Oh, surely not . . .'

'I don't know how you've managed it, but she seems to have taken quite a shine to you.' Laurel moved the kettle from the trivet onto the hob to bring it back to the boil. 'All I can say is, you're highly honoured. Now, why don't you sit by the fire and get warm? It's a filthy night out there.'

David sat in Ezra's chair, spreading his hands out to the warmth. Laurel fetched a rock cake on a small tea plate and set it down on the hearth beside him. She made the tea, poured a cup for him and one for herself, and sat in the chair opposite him to drink it.

'We had a bit of excitement at the hospital today. One of the patients knocked over his water jug, and Nurse Sobey slipped in it, fell down and broke her wrist. At least, we think it's broken. Dr Mackay took her to Bath, to St Martin's, to get it set . . .'

She was in a chatty mood, much more so than when Minty and Ezra were present, and normally David would have enjoyed that. A fairly quiet chap himself, he nevertheless liked hearing her talk. Today, however, he was too much on edge, waiting for her to go through the paperwork and find the flyer.

He was actually beginning to wonder if she wasn't going to bother tonight, which would scupper his plans, when she sighed and got up.

'Right. I'd better have a look at your stuff, I suppose. Make sure I can read Josh's scrawl. Honestly, I thought doctors' writing was bad enough, but Josh . . .'

She crossed to the table and extracted the three envelopes from the document case, leafing through them one by one. David reached for Ezra's *News Chronicle*, which he'd left beside his chair, and opened it on his knee, pretending nonchalance.

'MAN IMPRISONED FOR BIGAMY CLAIM' read the headline. He scanned the story – apparently one Edward Mylius had libelled King George by asserting he had committed bigamy.

'I see that chap in London has been sent to prison for talking a load of tommyrot about the King,' he said conversationally.

Laurel didn't answer. She was too engrossed in what she was doing. He went back to scanning the headlines, not really taking any of them in. Then:

'What's this?'

He looked up, his heart hammering. 'What?'

She was holding up the flyer.

'Oh – sorry – that shouldn't be there. I must have picked it up with something else . . .' He got up, crossed to the table. 'It's for a dance next Saturday night. The Buffs . . .' He took it from her. 'You don't fancy going, I suppose?'

'Oh.' Laurel looked taken aback. He could almost see her mind working, wondering if he was just trying to sell tickets, or asking her out. 'I'm not much of a dancer. And I wouldn't want to go on my own . . .'

'I could take you,' he said. 'We could go together. I'd like to support them.'

She hesitated, frowning and chewing her lip.

'It should be a good do,' he said.

Quite suddenly, it seemed, she made up her mind.

'Why not?' She sounded almost defiant. 'When is it, did you say?'

'Next Saturday.' Although it was mentioned on the flyer, he didn't want to draw attention to the fact that it was supposed to be for Valentine's Day, which would be the following Tuesday. It sounded a bit presumptuous.

'And it's in the town hall?'

'Yes.'

'All right.'

There was still something like defiance in her tone, which puzzled him. But never mind. He'd done it, asked her out, and she hadn't turned him down flat. That was the main thing.

She went back to sorting through the invoices; he went back to the newspaper. But he still wasn't reading it. He was feeling too jubilant.

# Chapter Twenty-Three

Many times before the day of the dance Laurel wondered what she could have been thinking of to accept David's invitation. She really didn't want to go. But then there wasn't anything she wanted to do these days. Everything was a dreadful effort and had been ever since that last awful night when she'd ended it with Ralph and he had raped her.

At least she wasn't pregnant. Her period had come just when she'd been despairing it ever would, and for that she was relieved and grateful. But not even that was enough to jolt her out of the slough of despond into which she had fallen. She'd wasted the best years of her life on a man who wasn't worth a fig. And she was just as bad. She hated herself for being a fool, but also for the part she'd played in deceiving Ralph's wife. Perhaps Amy wasn't the scheming gold-digger Ralph had said she was. Perhaps she was a nice woman who'd had the misfortune to marry a lying philanderer. Laurel could scarcely believe that she could have been so stupid as to be taken in for so long, so ready to trust and believe, and the whole sorry affair had left her empty, drained of all emotion, with no faith in anything or anyone, least of all herself. There was a darkness encompassing the whole of her world, like an impending eclipse of the sun.

Life held nothing for her now; the future stretched ahead

bleak and empty. She couldn't connect with Rowan, who seemed to be avoiding her. She wasn't even enjoying her job any more. Of the doctors whose accounts she kept, the only one who made work a pleasure was Dr Mackay. Dr Hicks was a stickler, constantly questioning her figures and complaining about the way things had been done, and Dr Clarkson was grumpy and monosyllabic. She liked Dr Blackmore, but he was becoming more and more doddery and disorganised; sorting out his books, sending out the appropriate bills and making sure they were paid was enough to make her tear her hair out. At the hospital, Matron was a martinet who ruled with a rod of iron, interfered in matters that didn't concern her and delighted in picking fault. Worst of all was Aubrey Sinclair. Since he had taken over as chairman of the board, Laurel had discovered he was every bit as unpleasant as she'd feared he would be: pompous, overbearing, full of his own importance. But worse still, he was making her very uncomfortable.

Whereas it had been quite unusual for Mr Seabrook to come into the office without good reason, Aubrey Sinclair was making a habit of it. Scarcely a week went by but he'd call in unannounced, sweeping in without knocking. He'd lean over her shoulder, pretending to be looking at whatever she was working on, his pale, pudgy hand resting on the desk, his bewhiskered chin inches from her face. His breath smelled of whisky and cigars, even at ten in the morning, and his coat of mothballs. If she was at the filing cabinet, he would stand so close behind her it was almost as bad. Once he'd actually placed a hand on her bottom. She'd wanted very badly to slap his nasty, superior face, but she hadn't dared. She'd simply moved away with a sharp 'Excuse me!' but he'd been unabashed. His narrowed eyes followed her every move, and Laurel felt trapped and helpless. He was, in effect, her employer; there was no one she could

complain to, and even if there had been, she doubted she would
be believed. The great and good Aubrey Sinclair a lecher?
Impossible!

Since Ralph had raped her, Laurel was more uncomfortable
in Mr Sinclair's presence than ever. It was as if she'd shed a
layer of skin, leaving her so exposed that the revulsion she felt at
his proximity made her feel physically sick.

She wondered if she should look for another job, make a
totally fresh start. Perhaps that was what was needed to make
her snap out of her bleak despondency. But she didn't know
where to begin looking, and wasn't sure she had the energy to
try.

Only occasionally did a spark of her old resilience show itself
– such as when she'd accepted David's invitation. The hell with
everything! she'd thought.

Now she was regretting it. She didn't want to go to a dance,
didn't want to have to get all dressed up, or make the effort to be
sociable. When he came with the accounts on Friday, she'd tell
him she'd changed her mind.

But somehow when the moment came, she couldn't bring
herself to do it.

'I'll call for you tomorrow evening about seven,' he said.

'Oh – there's no need for that.'

'If I leave my bike here, I'll be able to see you home safely.'

He was just so *nice*. He'd got it all planned. He'd be hurt if
she let him down. And perhaps a night out was what she
needed . . .

The next evening, after she'd helped Minty wash up the tea
things, she went up to her room and changed from her workaday
dress into a clean white blouse and the dark blue skirt she kept
for best. She brushed her hair and fastened it up with tortoiseshell
combs, and put in a pair of ear bobs Ralph had given her. After

that awful last night, she'd almost thrown them away in disgust; now she was glad she hadn't. The tiny stones dangling on their delicate silver filigree chains were the exact same colour as her eyes. They might be sapphires or they might be coloured glass, she didn't know, hadn't asked and didn't care. They were very pretty and she liked them, even if she now loathed the man who had given them to her.

'You look nice,' Minty said when she went downstairs.

High praise indeed! But then Minty wholeheartedly approved of David. 'About time you went out with somebody decent,' she'd said when Laurel had told her about the arrangement.

Rowan, too, was looking at her admiringly – committing every detail to memory to use in her next story, most likely – and Ezra smiled and gave her a wink.

'That's my girl.'

Just as the Westminster chime clock began whirring in preparation to strike the hour, there was a knock at the back door.

'He's here,' Minty said, and then: 'Aren't you going to go and let him in?'

'Give me a chance!' Laurel got her coat and went through into the scullery. For some reason she was shaking a little, and there was a lump of nervousness in her throat.

She opened the door, wondering why she should feel so awkward about greeting somebody she'd spent time with every week for months now. But that was work. This was something quite different.

At just a glance it was clear David had made an effort too. Under his coat he was wearing a shirt with a stiffened stand-up collar and a grey tie with a gold tie pin. His hair, which was usually blown about from the cycle ride and flopping over his forehead, was fixed in place by Macassar oil; it gleamed in the light spilling out from the scullery.

'Ready?' he said.

'Aren't you coming in?' Minty had followed Laurel.

'I won't, if you don't mind, Mrs Sykes. We don't want to be late or we won't get a seat.'

'I thought it was a dance,' Minty said tartly.

'Well, yes, but we want to have somewhere to sit when we're not dancing. Is it all right if I leave my bike outside the back door?'

'You can put it in the outhouse – it's unlocked,' Minty said. 'I wouldn't trust those varmints next door not to take it for a ride if you leave it out there all night.'

'Okay. Thanks.'

David wheeled his bicycle across the track and stowed it in the outhouse, leaning it against Laurel's. Then they set off, Minty watching them go until they were out of sight, hopeful, perhaps, of seeing him take her arm, or something equally promising. If so, she was to be disappointed.

'At least it's a fine night,' Laurel said to break the slightly awkward silence between them.

'A bit nippy, though.'

'Yes, but we'll get warm walking. And it's nice to see the stars after all the fog we've been having.'

'Reckon there might be a frost later.'

Suddenly, for no reason except perhaps as an escape for pent-up nervousness, Laurel giggled. David gave her a sidelong glance.

'What?'

'What are we like? Talking about the weather as if we were a couple of old sailormen.'

'Oh ah – heave ho, my hearties,' David rejoined in an exaggerated West Country drawl.

Laurel giggled again, and the giggle turned into a laugh.

'Shiver me timbers.'

'Hoist the mains'l . . .'

'Haul for the shore, boys, haul for the shore . . .'

They were both laughing now, the tension between them disappearing like a light covering of snow in sunshine. Still giggling, Laurel linked her arm through David's.

A couple were approaching them along the pavement. Hester Dallimore and her downtrodden husband Sid.

'Oh no!' Laurel groaned. 'Just our luck!'

As they drew level, Hester slowed to a near stop.

'Good evening, Laurel!' She sounded triumphant, scenting something she could gossip about.

'Good evening, Mrs Dallimore.'

Laurel squeezed David's arm, making sure he kept walking.

'That woman!' she whispered when they were out of earshot. 'She's a real nosy parker. Before tomorrow evening all the neighbours will know we were out together.'

'Are you worried about that?'

'No,' Laurel said. 'Not in the slightest.'

And she was surprised to find she meant it.

It was almost too warm in the town hall, which was already crowded. A trio was playing, piano, drums and a red-faced man with a squeeze box, and couples were dancing in a big circle, changing partners every so often – a progressive barn dance.

They found seats on the chairs lined up around the dance floor and David went to the hatch in the wall that was serving as a bar and bought drinks – a beer for himself and a cider for Laurel.

The dance had come to an end and another was beginning – Laurel recognised it as a St Bernard's waltz, which she'd learned long ago, in the days before Ralph, when she and some of her friends had attended dances and socials. One, two and three – stamp, stamp . . . The jaunty rhythm made her feel young again, and she was eager to join in.

'Come on!' She put her cider underneath her chair and caught at David's hand.

'I don't know it,' he protested.

'It's easy! I'll show you.'

'Well, I'll try if you like . . .'

As the evening progressed, Laurel found she was enjoying herself, all her woes temporarily forgotten. She was surprised at how the steps of the dances had come back to her so easily after so long; it was a bit like riding a bike, she supposed. Once learned, never forgotten. And if David did frequently tread on her toes, she didn't mind.

'I'm sorry,' he said every time it happened, and she just laughed.

'Stop apologising! You'll soon get the hang of it.'

There was a break for refreshments – sandwiches curling at the edges because they'd been made too long beforehand, and slices of slab cake – and a conjuror performed a few tricks. He wasn't actually very good – 'You can see the coloured handkerchiefs up his sleeve!' Laurel whispered, and David raised his eyebrows and pursed his lips, shushing her, which made her giggle again.

At a quarter to midnight, the MC announced the last waltz, and quite suddenly Laurel was sober again. From what she remembered of last waltzes, they were slow affairs when the boys she'd danced them with had tried to hold her tightly. In the old days she hadn't minded too much, but since that awful last night with Ralph, the thought of being too close to any man made her feel quite panicky.

'Shall we go?' she whispered urgently.

'You've had your toes stepped on enough for one night?'

'No, silly. But we could get out before the crush.'

'If you want to.' He stood up, then held out his hand to her. 'Come on, risk it! I'll never improve if I don't get any practice.'

She hesitated, still reluctant, then relented and let him lead her onto the floor.

It wasn't nearly as bad as she'd expected. He didn't try to hold her too close. His hands weren't hot and sweaty: the one holding hers was firm and cool, the one in the small of her back made her feel safe somehow. His shirt front smelled fresh and soapy, his breath just faintly of beer, which was also comforting because it reminded her of Daddy. Ralph's breath had invariably smelled of whisky and cigar smoke. In fact she was almost sorry when it was over. The band played 'God Save the King', and they remained standing. David had dropped her hand but his arm was still around her waist.

Outside the hall the crisp night air felt arctic on her hot cheeks, and she took David's arm again as they began the long walk home, chatting easily.

Most of the houses in Fairley Terrace were in darkness except for a light burning in the bedroom window of number 2.

'She always keeps it on,' Laurel said, referring to Queenie Rogers. 'Has done ever since she lost her son in the pit disaster back in '95. Apparently she can't sleep in the dark, and she wants a light burning in case he comes home. Losing him sent her a bit funny,' she added.

'Terrible thing, that accident,' David said. 'Maggie's father and her fiancé, Jack, were both killed that day, and her brother . . .' He broke off, not wanting to go into details about Billy Donovan's part in the tragedy. 'Have you met her?' he asked instead.

'Not really, though I've seen her when she's been here visiting.'

'You'd like her,' David said. 'She's quite a woman.'

'I'm sure she is.' Laurel was equally as unwilling to repeat what her mother thought of Maggie Withers.

They reached the door of number 5.

'Would you like to come in for a hot drink?' Laurel asked. It seemed only polite, and besides, she was oddly reluctant for the evening to end.

'I wouldn't say no.'

Minty had left a lamp burning for Laurel in the scullery.

'Hot chocolate?' she asked David.

'Sounds good to me.'

She put milk into a pan and carried it into the living room, David leading the way with the lamp. The fire had been banked up; she poked it to bring it to life and set the pan on the trivet.

As she straightened up, she caught sight of the flyer for the dance propped up behind the china shepherdess on the mantel shelf where she had left it. She pulled it out.

'How on earth do you do this?' she asked, sitting down on the coal box beside the hearth, from where she could keep an eye on the progress of the milk.

'It's simple really . . .' He began to describe the process.

After a while, she shook her head. 'You've lost me.'

'The easiest way to explain would be to show you. Why don't you come over to my workshop one day? And while you're there, you could see how Maggie makes her stained glass. That's far more interesting.'

'I'd like that.'

'What about tomorrow afternoon? You don't want to have to ride all that way in the dark.'

'All right,' Laurel agreed.

The milk was simmering; she mixed cocoa powder to a paste with a little cold milk in each of the cups, then added sugar and stirred in the hot milk.

'Time I was going then,' David said when he'd finished his drink. 'Thanks for keeping me company.'

'No – thank *you*. I really enjoyed it.'

They carried their empty cups out into the scullery. At the door, he paused, his hand on the handle.

'See you tomorrow then?'

'Yes.'

He reached for her and she felt a moment's sharp panic. But he only kissed her lightly on the cheek, then drew away, opened the door and crossed to the outhouse to retrieve his bicycle.

Laurel stood in the doorway, watching as he rode along the track. As if he knew she was still there, he raised a hand in farewell as he turned the corner of the rank and disappeared from sight. Somewhere out over the fields an owl hooted mournfully, otherwise all was still and silent.

She went back indoors, put the used cups into the sink for washing tomorrow, and banked up the fire. Then she crept up the stairs to bed.

And all the while she could still feel the warm, light pressure of his lips on her cheek. Little as she'd wanted to go to the dance, Laurel was glad she had. And she was looking forward to seeing him again tomorrow.

David was waiting for her in Hillsbridge on the high pavement outside the church. When he saw her, he crossed the road to her side.

'I thought I'd come and show you the way,' he said, riding alongside her.

'I'm sure I'd have found it.'

327

'Maybe, but it's a long drag up the hill if you're on your own.'

It was. After struggling up the start of the incline, they dismounted, chatting as they pushed their bicycles up the steepest part.

'Not too tired after a late night?' David asked.

'No, it was lovely,' Laurel said, and she meant it.

'Maggie's looking forward to meeting you properly.'

'And I'm looking forward to meeting her.'

'You already know Patrick, I gather.' He cast her a quick meaningful grin.

'Not really.'

'Oh – I thought he was a friend of Rowan's. Didn't he . . . ?'

'Mam put a stop to that,' she said with a sigh.

'Oh dear. I didn't know. Anyway, he and Josh are out this afternoon. They've gone out collecting wood.'

'For Josh's carpentry?'

'It'll probably be too rotten for that, but dried out it will still burn.'

At the top of the hill they remounted, riding past a row of miners' cottages and into the countryside beyond. When they turned into what had once been the farmyard, Laurel was impressed by the big open space, the house itself and the barns and stables, all gleaming with fresh paint. A tabby cat lay in a pool of pale February sunshine, and a young girl was pushing a perambulator back and forth.

'John won't go to sleep,' she said as they approached. 'And Mom is trying to work.'

Sure enough, as soon as the pram stopped moving, the baby inside it began to wail lustily.

Maggie appeared in the doorway of one of the outhouses, wiping her hands on a big leather apron.

'Is he *still* awake? Just keep going, Nora. He'll go off in a bit – I hope!' She sounded frazzled, but when she turned to Laurel, her smile was welcoming.

'Sorry about that. I'm Maggie, and you must be Laurel. I can't tell you how grateful I am to you for taking all the book work off my hands. I never seem to have time to do everything I have to, even without the accounts.'

'I'm glad to be able to help.'

'Let me just finish what I was doing here and I'll make us all a cup of tea.'

'I can do that when I've shown Laurel round my workshop,' David said. 'And I think she's hoping you'll show her yours too.'

'Oh . . . yes . . .' But Maggie was sounding frazzled again.

'She's under a lot of pressure,' David said as they went into his workshop. 'There's been a great demand for doors with a stained-glass panel set in, and she's been working all hours to get her part done.'

'That explains why some of their accounts lately have been joint.'

'Exactly. And now one of the local gentry has approached Josh with what would be a really good order – windows for the passage that runs all the way along the front of the house and fitted with . . . well, you've guessed it. From the drawings I've seen, they would be mostly clear glass with just a coloured motif in the centre, but Maggie's worried about having to get it all done in a set time. And Josh is worried about losing the order, or worse still, taking the job and then being late finishing.'

'That's a shame.'

'One of the problems of trying to juggle a business and a family. Now, did you want to see my printing press?'

For the next half-hour he gave Laurel a guided tour,

explaining how things worked and showing her samples of some of his greetings cards and the sheets of scraps that were already finding a ready market.

'That one's based on a picture Nora drew,' he said pointing it out. 'But most of the designs are Maggie's. She's very talented.'

'They're beautiful,' Laurel said, but for some reason she was feeling a bit miffed. David seemed never to stop singing Maggie's praises. She couldn't imagine that there was anything untoward going on here right under Josh's nose and with two children and a baby in the house, but did he carry a candle for her? And if he did, why should she, Laurel, feel so put out?

When they eventually emerged from the workshop, there was no sign of Nora but no crying either coming from the perambulator, which was now parked outside the farmhouse door. The cat was busily cleaning itself, and Maggie was clearly still in her own workshop.

'What happened to that tea then?' David asked teasingly, poking his head round the door.

'I'm coming now.' Maggie was taking off the leather apron and running a hand over her striking red-gold hair.

'It's all right – I'll make it. You show Laurel what it is you do. She's dying to see.'

'I don't want to be a nuisance,' Laurel said.

'You're not. It's nice to have some female company. And . . .' she threw David a teasing glance, 'someone to make the tea for me.'

If Laurel had been fascinated by the tools of David's trade, she was totally mesmerised by Maggie's. The kiln, the brushes laid out on the workbench, the lengths of lead hanging from hooks on the wall, and a small panel of jewel-coloured flowers that Maggie had clearly been working on today.

'David tells me you have the chance of a really big order for a stately home,' she said, dying to run her fingers over the raised lead shapes with their bright glowing insets, but knowing she must not touch.

Maggie sighed. 'It's a bone of contention between us at the moment, I'm afraid. Josh wants us to do it, of course – it would be a feather in our caps as well as bringing in a good return. But I just don't see that I can commit to it. I simply haven't got the time to spare. The only answer would be if we took on some help – someone to do the everyday chores and cook meals and look after John while I was working. You don't know of anyone likely, I suppose? A nurse at the hospital, perhaps, who's looking for something a bit different?'

'I don't offhand, but I can ask around,' Laurel said.

'Tea's ready!' David popped his head around the door. 'Come and get it before it goes cold.'

'We don't need telling twice.' Maggie smiled at Laurel. 'I expect you've seen quite enough of our dusty workshops for one afternoon.'

'It's absolutely fascinating,' Laurel said. 'You are all so clever! I'm impressed.'

'You're clever too. It's each to their own.'

In the kitchen David had laid out the tea things and cut slabs of lardy cake.

'Did you make this?' Laurel asked, and Maggie laughed.

''Fraid not. I don't have time for baking any more. This comes from the shop in Dunderwick. A lady in the village keeps them supplied.'

They tucked in, and drank their tea sitting around the big kitchen table while Nora, seated at one corner, was occupied with painting a picture, her box of paints beside her and a jam jar filled with water to wash out her brush positioned in front of her. The whole atmosphere was warm and cosy, the heat from the large range warming every corner of the big room, the over-riding feeling one of people totally at ease with one another. Laurel couldn't help comparing it with the frosty silences that all too often chilled the air in her own living room. Busy and a bit fraught Maggie might be, but there was no doubt that this was a happy home, and it was she who had made it so.

The peace was broken by a wail from outside the back door.

'John is awake,' Maggie said, getting up. 'He's had a good sleep, though.'

She went out and came back with the baby in her arms. He'd stopped crying the moment she had picked him up. Fist stuffed into his mouth, he regarded Laurel with a wide blue gaze, fine wisps of dark hair covering a well-shaped head.

'He's beautiful!' Laurel said.

'Yes – when he's not crying.' But Maggie's face was full of love as she looked down at her baby son.

'I suppose I ought to be going,' Laurel said at last, regretfully.

'I'll ride home with you,' David offered, but she shook her head.

'Stay here and give Maggie a hand.'

He went with her out into the yard.

'Will I see you again?'

She almost laughed. 'I expect so!'

'No – I mean . . . will you come out with me? There's a concert on Wednesday in the church hall, a bring-and-buy in the chapel rooms on Thursday, or a whist drive on Friday . . .'

She did laugh then. 'I suppose in your line of work you get to know all about these local events.'

'I do indeed.'

'Well, I'm not sure I fancy a bring-and-buy sale . . .'

'And I'm not much of a whist player . . .'

'So that leaves the concert.'

'I'll see you there, then.'

She was still smiling as she wheeled her bicycle out of the farmyard and rode off along the lane into the fast-failing light. She wasn't sure what had happened to her, but she was happier than she had been for a very long time.

The idea came to her quite suddenly, a bolt from the blue. She'd promised to ask around to see if anyone was interested in going to work for Maggie, but really there was no need for that. She'd wanted a change of direction in her life – perhaps this was the answer. She thought of the warmth in the farmhouse kitchen, such a different feel to the cold, clinical office at the hospital. Of Maggie herself, as different in temperament to Matron as was possible. She thought of the little girl, Nora, who reminded her in some ways of Rowan when she was that age, so immersed in her favourite pastime, and of the beautiful baby who would be in her care. And she thought of David, how nice it would be to be around him instead of having to ward off the revolting Aubrey Sinclair.

Mam would have forty fits, no doubt, but Laurel wasn't going to give her the chance to try to talk her out of it.

She stopped, turned around and began to push her bike back up the hill. It would be dark before she got home, but she'd cycled in the dark before. This was something that would not wait.

As she made her way back to the farm, full of determination and enthusiasm, she felt she was embarking on a new life.

# Chapter Twenty-Four

Just as Laurel had expected, Minty was far from pleased at the news that she was going to give in her notice at the hospital and go to work for Maggie and Josh.

'Whatever are you thinking of?' she demanded incredulously. 'Giving up a good job to go and be a kitchen maid, and for *her* of all people!'

'I'm not going to be a kitchen maid. And I won't be giving up my private bookkeeping. I'm going to build up a business of my own alongside theirs.'

'Who with, I'd like to know?'

'I'm hoping Dr Mackay will still use me, and David's going to print some business cards for me that I can distribute around town.'

'You're *hoping*. What if it doesn't work out? All those years studying and you're throwing it all away.'

'Why do you always look on the black side, Mam?'

'Perhaps I've had cause to,' Minty said tartly. 'It seems to me you've taken leave of your senses.'

'I've been thinking for a while I wanted a change.' Laurel was trying very hard to keep hold of her patience.

'That's you all over. Forever chopping and changing. And you'll have to go all that way every day, in all winds and weathers. Have you thought of that?'

'No, Mam, I won't. I'm going to live in.'

It had all been arranged when she'd gone back and offered Maggie her services. 'I don't suppose we'll be able to pay you as much as you get now, for the moment anyway,' Maggie had said. 'But we can offer you board and lodging. We have a spare bedroom and you can take your meals with us.'

Minty's frown lines and the dissatisfied creases that ran from her nose to her chin deepened still further.

'I suppose that means I shall have to manage somehow without the bit of housekeeping you give me. There might be one less mouth to feed, but there's still Rowan.'

'I'll give you something for Rowan's keep, just as I always have. And pay her school expenses.'

Minty snorted dismissively. 'You'll be seeing too much of David, too.'

Laurel sighed. 'I thought you liked him.'

'I do, but it's not wise, being under the same roof.'

'We won't be. He has his own room over his workshop.'

'Hmm. Well, that's something, I suppose. I have to say, I had high hopes of you and him hitting it off. But more or less living under the same roof . . . you don't want to be too keen. You'll put him off, and that'll be the end of that.'

Laurel had finally had enough.

'We're just friends, Mam. Me working there isn't going to change that. I'm sorry if you don't like it, but it's all arranged, so you might as well save your breath.'

When she gave in her notice the next day, Matron was almost as sniffy as Minty, though less argumentative, and Aubrey Sinclair did his best to persuade her to stay, which only made her more determined. How glad she would be to see the last of the obnoxious man!

335

The doctors were regretful, and Dr Blackmore wished her all the best.

'I'm sorry to see you go, my dear, but I'll be retiring myself soon.'

And not before time, Laurel thought. It wasn't just his inability to keep his records in order; she didn't think he was really capable of looking after his patients any more either. She'd been trying for some time to get Earl and Vicky to put their loyalty to one side and change practices. Dr Blackmore had more or less given up on Vicky, and now that Laurel was no longer acting as go-between for her and Ralph, there was no one to take an interest in the illness that still plagued her. Not that Laurel had much faith in Ralph, especially after he'd admitted misleading the patients she had met that last night. His potions did seem to pick Vicky up a bit, but the symptoms still persisted, and Laurel couldn't help worrying about her.

She'd mention it to Dr Mackay when she saw him to tell him she was quitting the hospital, she decided. If Dr Blackmore was going to be retiring, Earl and Vicky would have to register elsewhere, and Laurel couldn't think of anyone better than Dr Mackay to take on her care.

She also had hopes that perhaps she could continue to work for him. It would be a bit towards making up the difference between her present salary and what Maggie was paying her until she found new clients. But she had no idea how he'd feel about that, or even if it would be possible, as she didn't know whether the arrangement with the hospital was a binding contract.

When she spoke to Dr Mackay, however, he quickly set her mind at rest.

'It's an informal arrangement, always has been,' he said in the soft Scottish burr that Laurel found so soothing. 'I'm not sure the hospital board will be best pleased' – Laurel couldn't care less what the hospital board, in the shape of Aubrey Sinclair, thought or didn't think – 'but I'll be very happy if you'll continue to keep me in order. And of course, I'll pay you the same as I've been paying them, so you'll receive the whole amount without them deducting their cut.'

'Thank you, Doctor,' Laurel said, relieved.

'My pleasure. And isn't it about time you started calling me Alistair?'

She smiled. 'I suppose it is. But you'll have to forgive me if I forget. Old habits die hard. And you'll also have to forgive me if I have to bring a baby with me sometimes – I'm going to be a nanny as well as all my other jobs – but I promise I'll make sure he doesn't disturb you or your patients.'

Dr Mackay laughed.

'A crying baby would hardly be unusual in my surgery.'

'But they come and go. This one will be there all the time I am.'

He smiled and shrugged his shoulders, as if to say 'so be it'.

'There is one other thing I wanted to talk to you about,' she said, changing the subject. 'My sister-in-law . . .'

She went on to explain the ill health that had dogged Vicky and he listened intently, stroking his chin with a finger and thumb.

'If I could persuade her to come to you, would you be prepared to take her on to your list?'

He nodded slowly. 'I wouldn't want to tread on Horace's toes,' he said. 'I know how hurtful it can be when a patient decides to go elsewhere. It happened to me a few times when I first started out. But if Horace is retiring, then yes, of course I'd be happy to see your sister-in-law.'

'Thank you, Doctor . . . Alistair . . .'

All in all the interview had turned out very well, and it was with a light heart that Laurel opened the ledger, pulled the pile of paperwork towards her and uncapped her pen.

'Do I get the impression you're rather smitten by Miss Laurel Sykes?' Maggie said, raising a questioning eyebrow at David.

'She's a nice girl,' David said non-committally, but from the very deliberate casualness of his tone, she knew she had hit the nail on the head. She wouldn't embarrass him by pressing the point, but she couldn't help hoping Laurel felt the same way. She'd never known him to show any interest in a young lady before.

Any doubts she'd had about David were now long gone. During the long evenings when Josh was still hard at work with his carpentry they'd become close, and at last David had put aside his reserve and opened up to her, talking of his life before he'd gone to America, and the obsession that had taken him there and eventually brought him back again to England, and to Somerset in particular.

She knew now why it was she'd been aware of that dark aura around him the first time she'd seen him on the deck of the ocean liner, and she knew of the decision he'd reached to put the past behind him and begin building a new life.

If anyone deserved to find happiness it was David.

Maggie hoped very much he might find it with Laurel Sykes.

Once she had worked her two-week notice, Laurel left the hospital for the last time without so much as a single regret, but rather filled with enthusiasm for the new life that lay ahead of her.

Packing her things in preparation to move to Hillview was a different matter entirely.

'I don't want you to go.' Rowan was sitting on the bed in her room, and was almost tearful as she watched Laurel sort the clothes she would need into neat piles and transfer them to a battered suitcase.

'I'll only be a couple of miles away,' Laurel said. 'I shall come home often, and you'll be able to come and visit me.'

'If Mam lets me.' Rowan was chewing the side of her thumbnail as she'd used to, a habit she'd managed to break recently.

'Ah. You mean because of Patrick.' Laurel slipped a pile of handkerchiefs into a corner of the suitcase and looked up at her sister. 'You still see him on the train, do you?'

Patrick's name had not been mentioned between them since they'd had their chat about Minty's reasons for objecting to Rowan seeing him.

'Yes, but nothing's the same. I think Mam put him off,' Rowan said wretchedly.

'You still like him?'

Rowan nodded, the colour rising in her cheeks. She couldn't tell anyone, even Laurel, of her deepest fear – that Patrick had found someone else, someone who was allowed to spend time with him, who didn't have to lie about where she was going. Or that if he hadn't yet found someone else, he soon would.

'I'm sure it will all work out in the end,' Laurel said, though she wasn't sure at all.

They were so young, and sweet as first love was, it almost always ended in heartbreak. All she could hope was that Rowan didn't make the same mistakes she had made. Then, in time, there would be other, more lasting loves.

But telling her that would do no good at all. Laurel remembered all too well her desperate obsession with Callum. The sweet stolen kisses. The yearning. The certainty that there would never be anyone for her but him. And then the pain and desperation as her world came crashing down around her . . .

Please God Rowan wouldn't go through what she had gone through. Much as she wanted to, there was no way she could protect her from heartbreak. But please God let it stop at that.

'I'll talk to Mam,' she said now. 'Don't worry, my love. We'll work something out.'

Rowan nodded, mute with misery. She was so afraid she'd lost Patrick, and now she was losing Laurel too.

She didn't think she could bear it.

On the Sunday, David came to help Laurel with her things – there was no way she could manage a suitcase and a holdall and her bicycle as well.

'I want to call in on Earl and Vicky,' she said as they set off with the holdall stuffed into her bicycle basket and David balancing the suitcase on his handlebars 'We pass right by their house.'

'Anyone would think you were leaving for the moon!' David teased her.

'Don't!' She knew he was referring to the effusive send-off. Rowan had been crying, Minty had admonished him brusquely to take good care of her, and even Dad had tears in his eyes. 'There's just something I want to say to them.'

'Well, don't be too long. We want to get back before that rain comes.'

It had been dry so far today, but now the light was fading fast as the clouds that had hidden the sun thickened threateningly.

David waited at the gate of the little semi-detached house while Laurel knocked at the door. It was Vicky who answered it, little Reggie clinging to her skirts.

'Laurel! What a surprise! Do come in.'

'I can't really stay long.' She stepped into the hall anyway. 'I just wanted to have a word with you about changing doctors.'

She went on to explain that she'd spoken to Dr Mackay and that he would be happy to take Vicky, Earl and Reggie on to his list.

'Oh, I couldn't leave Dr Blackmore,' Vicky said immediately. 'He'd be terribly hurt, and he's been so kind . . .'

'He told me that he's retiring soon. And in any case, your health must come first, Vicky.'

'She's right.' Earl had appeared in the passage behind his wife. 'We've got to try to find out what the matter is. It's been going on too long. And now there's your neck as well.' He looked at Laurel. 'Have you noticed how swollen her neck is?'

In the dim light in the hallway, Laurel hadn't seen it, but now that Earl had drawn her attention to it, she could make out a small mound in the region where the Adam's apple would be.

'Just make sure she goes to see Dr Mackay,' Laurel said to Earl. 'He's a lot younger and more on the ball. I'm sorry, I must go now – David's waiting.'

'I'll see she does,' Earl said. 'And do pop in when you're passing.'

'I will.' But Laurel didn't really like calling on Earl and Vicky; it was Vicky's parents' house, and she always felt as if she were intruding.

She and David pushed their bikes up the long hill, then rode along the flat stretch and out into the countryside.

Josh and Patrick emerged from Josh's workshop as they turned into the yard; Maggie, who had seen them arrive from the kitchen window, opened the door. The warmth generated by the range swirled out to meet them. Nora was at the table,

341

engrossed once again in her painting; baby John was fast asleep in his pram.

'Welcome to Hillview, Laurel,' Maggie said, smiling and taking the holdall from her. 'I hope you're going to be very happy here.'

The cosy family atmosphere was already drawing Laurel in. She returned Maggie's smile.

'I'm sure I am,' she said, and she felt confident she had made the right decision.

Without Laurel there, the house felt empty and Rowan was bereft. She could scarcely remember a time when she had ever been lonelier. The days when Laurel had worked and lived in Bath seemed a very long time ago. The years between had become the norm, and the bond between the two of them, always strong, had grown stronger still. Rowan realised she had come to depend on Laurel for companionship and support much more than on Mam.

She thought of how Laurel had rescued her from the bullies when she'd been at primary school, how Laurel had persuaded Mam to let her sit the scholarship, had bought her satchel, paid for her uniform and travel expenses. She thought about the fact that Laurel had colluded with her to keep the secret that she still saw Patrick every day. She wasn't the one who had followed her and made such a show of her in front of Patrick that he'd gone off her. Laurel would never do such a thing. She understood . . .

'For goodness' sake, Rowan, pull yourself together!' Minty snapped. 'Anybody would think somebody had died.'

'Oh . . . leave me alone.'

'Don't you speak to me like that! I think you'd better go up to your room until you can keep a civil tongue in your head.'

'Don't worry, I'm going,' Rowan muttered.

'And don't answer back!'

I hate you! Rowan thought as she stumped up the stairs. You spoil everything! It's probably your fault Laurel's gone too. She's had enough of living here. And so have I. I'll run away, that's what I'll do. If I go to Hillview, perhaps Laurel will let me stay . . . and I'd be with Patrick, too . . .

But tempting though the idea was, she knew it would never work. She couldn't get out of the house without Mam or Daddy seeing her; she couldn't walk all that way in the dark and wet – the rain that had threatened all day was now lashing the windows – and even if she did, Laurel would only bring her home again.

The door of Laurel's room was ajar; Rowan pushed it open and went in. Laurel might have gone, but a lot of her things were still here. It was all she had left of her sister, Rowan thought, almost enjoying wallowing in the sheer tragic drama of it. She sat on the bed for a little while, crying, then began pulling out drawers and crying again to see them half empty, with only odds and ends that Laurel didn't want to take with her left in them, and all her winter clothes gone from the wardrobe.

As she closed the wardrobe door, she noticed a small attaché case on the top of it. Rowan wondered why Laurel hadn't used it for some of her stuff. She had to pull the bedside chair across and climb on it to reach the case. It was covered in dust, which made Rowan sneeze as she lifted it down, and she noticed the stitching was coming loose around the handle and the locks were rusty. But from the weight of it, she could tell there was something inside.

Really she shouldn't be so nosy. But Laurel wouldn't mind. They had no secrets, did they? And there was something comforting in the thought of looking at Laurel's treasures. In some way it seemed to bring her close again.

The rusty locks were stiff; at first Rowan thought she wasn't going to be able to open them. Then, with a snap, first one gave, and then the other. The hinges creaked as she lifted the lid, very carefully, for the old leather felt brittle, and she found herself staring at a motley collection of items. A pile of letters with a Yorkshire postmark, and one addressed in a different hand and tied with a faded blue ribbon – curious as she was, Rowan knew that reading them would be a step too far. A photograph in a cardboard frame: dark eyes stared back at her from a good-looking face with a cheeky smile and framed with dark curls. Who was he? Rowan wondered. An old sweetheart, presumably. Perhaps the one who had written the letter tied with blue ribbon that Laurel clearly cherished. The writing on that envelope was childish and unformed, and this boy didn't look like one who had had much schooling.

She laid the photograph on top of the letters and turned her attention to the other items, deposited haphazardly in the other half of the attaché case. A knitted elephant stuffed with rags that seemed vaguely familiar to her. A well-chewed comforter. A little white bonnet. An envelope containing a soft curl no bigger than her thumbnail; a tiny milk tooth in a twist of tissue paper . . .

These were baby things! But why would Laurel have secreted away mementos of a baby? Unless . . .

Was it hers? Had her sister had a baby and given it up for adoption? Rowan could think of no other reason for her find, even though it didn't make any sense. And yet in another way it explained certain things. The reason Mam was so adamant she shouldn't be alone with a boy. What Laurel had meant when they'd had that excruciatingly embarrassing conversation about things getting out of control.

Laurel had had a baby and given it away. During the time

she was living in Bath, perhaps. Somewhere out there Rowan had a little niece or nephew she had never met and never would . . . It was so sad, and yet so wonderful, both at the same time.

There was something else at the bottom of the case, a piece of parchment folded several times into a small oblong shape. A birth certificate? Rowan took it out and began to unfold it . . .

'What in the world do you think you're doing?' Minty's voice, even sharper than usual. Rowan hadn't heard her on the stairs, and she jumped guiltily.

Minty strode into the room and snatched the parchment from Rowan's hand.

'Mam . . .' The colour was hot in her cheeks.

Her mother pulled the attaché case out of her reach across the bed, and as she did so, her eye fell on the photograph. Her face worked for a moment, eyes narrowed, cheeks bulging, jaw trembling, then she snatched it up, tearing it again and again so that some fragments fell onto the bedside rug. Rowan could only watch in shaken silence.

'Go to your room, Rowan.'

Rowan rose to her feet and fled.

It was some time before she heard the door of Laurel's room slam and her mother's footsteps descending the stairs. Silently she crept out onto the landing. She could hear Minty's raised voice in the living room below, but couldn't make out what she was saying. Telling Daddy she'd been prying where she had no business to, no doubt.

Half afraid, half defiant, she crossed the landing, carefully turned the handle of Laurel's door and eased it open. In the dim light she could see that the torn fragments of the photograph were no longer on the rug and the attaché case had been returned to the top of the wardrobe. She wished with all her heart that she dared get it down again, but she couldn't risk that.

She went back to her own room, wrapped herself in a blanket and sat on the edge of the bed thinking furiously. She'd thought she and Laurel had no secrets; it seemed she'd been wrong. But what did it all mean? And would she ever pluck up the courage to ask her? Once again, it seemed, Rowan's world had tilted on its axis. She felt shocked and shaky, but also curiously excited, though for the life of her she didn't know why that should be.

The door opened a crack; she tensed. But it was Daddy.

'Come on, my dear, come downstairs. It's cold enough to freeze a brass monkey up here.'

'Mam said . . .'

'I know what she said, but she didn't mean it. You're upset about Laurel going; she knows that.'

Could she ask Daddy? But no, of course she couldn't bring herself to. And it would do no good. Daddy hated talking about anything upsetting, and she thought he would be upset if she was right, and Laurel really had had a baby.

'Come on, m'dear. Come on down in the warm,' he said again.

And though the questions were spinning round inside her head, Rowan did as he said.

# Chapter Twenty-Five

As a wet, cold February became an equally changeable March, Laurel settled in at Hillview. Although her duties were new to her, she found no difficulty in adapting to them. She'd learned to cook from helping Minty, and she enjoyed the spaciousness of the kitchen and the efficiency of the range – so much easier to work with than the trivets and fireside oven at home. Looking after baby John was a pleasure; the first time he gurgled, smiled and held out his arms to her, the rush of joy she felt brought happy tears to her eyes. The only chore she really didn't like was the laundry. Her hands were soon chapped and sore, and long, painful cuts appeared at the side of her fingernails from doing an almost daily wash in the big stone sink and hanging it out to dry in the bitter wind on days when it wasn't raining. But it was a small price to pay for her new-found freedom.

When her day's work was done, she could do as she pleased until it was time to make tea. Sometimes she went for a walk with John in his perambulator; sometimes she took him to Maggie's workshop where she could watch both him and the fascinating process of the making of stained glass at the same time.

She and Maggie were getting along famously, though she knew better than to chat and divert Maggie's attention when she was hard at work. The order for the windows for the stately home had been placed, and even with Laurel taking care of the housekeeping, Maggie was struggling to keep up with Josh – the wooden frames were child's play to him, whilst the jewel-coloured inserts, each of a different design, was an intricate, time-consuming job.

Laurel's friendship with David was growing and deepening, too, helped by the fact that she saw him every day without any social pressures. David seemed to intuitively understand that he needed to take things slowly and that any move to take their relationship to the next level would frighten her off. For her part she was enjoying his company. When she was with him she felt more like her old self than she had done for years. He was warm but unthreatening; they shared the same sense of humour and he made her laugh. Maggie watched the easy way they were together and felt hopeful that love might blossom, though it was a painfully slow process.

Laurel had been hurt deeply, she guessed, remembering what Cathy had told her. But she knew better than to pry. Perhaps the other woman would tell her in her own good time, just as David eventually had. Really, they were very well suited – two intensely private people, each hugging their secrets to themselves. And until they were ready to share, they would respect one another's privacy.

Things were looking up for Vicky, too. As Laurel had suggested, she had been to see Dr Mackay and he had almost immediately spotted the cause of her long-term illness.

'I think you have a problem with your thyroid gland,' he said.

'Can it be treated?' Earl asked anxiously.

'It can, yes. Though whether it can be cured is another matter. I take it this has been going on for some time?'

'Years,' Earl said. 'And what I'd like to know is why Dr Blackmore didn't spot it long ago.'

'It's not easy to diagnose.' Dr Mackay was anxious not to be seen as criticising the older man. 'Symptoms can vary from patient to patient, and can just as easily apply to other conditions. It's the fact that Vicky's throat is swollen that confirms it for me. That's something recent, I'm guessing?'

Vicky nodded. 'I only noticed it a few weeks ago, when I couldn't fasten my choker.'

'And you have been receiving treatment from a homeopathic doctor, you say?'

'I was, yes. Not any longer.'

'Do you know what medication he was giving you?'

'Not really, but I think there might have been iodine in it.'

'And it helped you?'

'A bit.'

'So we'll keep on with the iodine, and I'll also give you desiccated porcine.' He smiled. 'Don't look so worried, it's not nearly as bad as it sounds. But I shall need to see you regularly, Vicky, to keep an eye on what's going on. The wrong doses of these things can make things worse instead of better.'

Vicky looked worried, but Earl was adamant.

'Doesn't matter what it costs, Doctor. We've got to get it sorted.'

They'd left the surgery optimistic, and Laurel was very glad she'd pressed for them to get a second opinion. She also felt angry with Ralph, that he had continued to issue prescriptions without insisting on seeing Vicky again. It wouldn't have been financially expedient, she guessed, remembering the Trotters once more. They were well off, and as long as they paid his not inconsiderable bills he was prepared to continue seeing Mrs Trotter despite the fact that he more or less knew he could do nothing for her. Vicky he'd seen free of charge just the once; there was no way she would have been able to afford his exorbitant fees and he hadn't wanted to waste his time on her.

Back in Fairley Terrace, Rowan was less than happy. Another boy of about her age had started attending a school in Bath, and more often than not he and Patrick got on the train together. They talked boy talk between themselves, quite often things Rowan didn't understand or have any interest in – steam locomotives, motor engines – and she felt horribly left out. What was worse was that Patrick was quite offhand with her, even more than he had been after Minty had caught them together. When she confided in Laurel, Laurel said he was probably embarrassed and didn't want his new friend to know he had a sweetheart.

'But I'm not his sweetheart any more,' Rowan said miserably. 'That's just the trouble.'

Laurel didn't argue with that. 'You're a girl,' she said. 'Sometimes boys can be shy about being friends with a girl.' What else could she say? She was sad for Rowan, but these things happened. She'd get over it in time.

But it was a shame. She liked Patrick. Since moving to Hillview and getting to know him, she had found him a thoroughly decent lad, reliable and trustworthy, who knew right from wrong. She only hoped that Rowan wouldn't go off the rails and fall for someone totally unsuitable as she herself had done. Then Minty's uncompromising attitude would backfire on her in the most disastrous way.

For the moment, though, it seemed that everything was proceeding on quite an even keel, and Laurel was more than satisfied with her lot.

\* \* \*

The first of the new windows was finished by the end of March, and Josh had ordered Fred Carson's pony and trap to take it to Hillsbridge House, since it was too heavy – and too fragile – to transport any other way. Fortunately it was a dry day, and Maggie and Josh set off sitting in the trap with the window propped up between them, leaving Laurel in charge at Hillview.

John was sleeping much less in the day now. He had learned to crawl and was so eager to practise his new-found skill that he objected to being restrained in any way, so the everyday tasks Laurel had been able to work through quickly in the past now took much longer, since she had to keep an eye on what he was up to.

That morning she managed to keep him occupied with a bag of oddments she'd put together for him to turn out – clothes pegs, a wooden spoon, his brightly coloured teething rings and a few other things – while she washed nappies. But it wasn't long before he'd lost interest in that game and started scooting around the kitchen. Twice she had to rescue him from going too close to the range; then, to her relief, he went under the table. Making his way between the network of table and chair legs should keep him quiet for long enough for her to get the nappies rinsed out, and then, whether he liked it or not, he was going to have to go into his high chair while she pegged them out to dry.

A gurgling sound quite unlike any of the noises he usually made in an effort to communicate made her turn sharply. He was still sitting under the table, but Laurel knew at a glance that something was very wrong. His ribs and chest appeared to be pulled in, and with each laboured breath she heard a high-pitched whining sound.

He was choking! Panic turned her blood to ice. What in the world had happened?

Her hands still dripping water, she rushed across the kitchen and scooped him up, opening his mouth with her fingers. She could see nothing. But the high-pitched whining continued, and to her horror, Laurel fancied that he was beginning to turn blue.

She rushed to the door with him in her arms, throwing it open and running into the yard.

'David! David!'

Mercifully the door to his workshop was open, and for once the printing press was not clanking and whirring to drown out her cries. David appeared in the doorway.

'What is it?'

'It's John! He's choking! He must have swallowed something.' She was shaking from head to toe.

David took one look at the distressed baby.

'Give him to me!'

He practically snatched John from her arms and ran past her into the kitchen, where he pulled out one of the dining chairs and sat, laying the baby face down across his arm and supporting his jaw with his fingers. With John's head now lower than his body, David struck him with his free hand between the shoulder blades, four or five forceful blows that made Laurel gasp in horror. But to her intense relief the baby spluttered, something dropped out of his mouth onto the flagged floor, and the awful high-pitched whining noise stopped.

'Have you cleared it? Is he all right?' Laurel asked, breathless with anxiety.

David tipped the baby upright, balancing him on his knee, and John began to cry lustily.

'I think you have your answer.' David looked up at her, his face betraying his own relief.

'Oh, thank God! Thank God! I thought . . .'

She was still shaking violently and tears were filling her eyes.

'He's fine,' David said.

She took John from him, cradling him in her arms while still examining him anxiously.

'Do you think we should get the doctor?'

'No need, I'd say. Just give him a minute or two.'

John's anguished cries were quietening. The colour had returned to his face. David bent over, retrieving something from the floor and holding it out in the palm of his hand for Laurel to see.

'That's what it was. A button.'

'But how . . . ?' Then realisation dawned. Nora had been doing some craft work at the kitchen table last evening; the button, round and shiny, was one of her collection that she threaded on to cotton to make necklaces and bracelets. It must have fallen onto the floor; somehow, when she had swept the kitchen this morning, Laurel had missed it, and John had found it.

'Oh, I should have been more careful!' Laurel castigated herself. 'At the moment, anything and everything goes into his mouth.'

'Don't blame yourself,' David said. 'It could have happened to anybody.'

'But I'm responsible for him! If anything had happened to him . . .' She closed her eyes briefly against the terrible thought, the tears threatening again. 'If you hadn't been here . . . How did you know what to do?'

He smiled. 'You won't believe this, but not so long ago I had to print some pamphlets on first-aid nursing. It's surprising what you learn typesetting and proofreading.'

'But you were so calm! I was in a complete panic.'

John was beginning to wriggle in her arms.

'I think he wants to get down again,' David said.

Jennie Felton

'I can't. I can't put him down! What if he finds something else?'

'You can't keep hold of him all day,' David said reasonably. 'Look, I'll check there's nothing else he can get hold of.'

He dropped down onto all fours, examining every inch of the floor.

'Nothing. He's quite safe.'

Still reluctant to let him go, Laurel set the baby down, and immediately he scuttled back under the table, undeterred by his experience and eager to find more treasure.

'I shan't take my eyes off him,' she said. 'Oh, David, I just don't know how to thank you.' Still watching John's every move, she reached out a hand to David, squeezing it tight.

'You're in a terrible state, aren't you? Come here.'

He pulled her towards him, wrapping his arms around her waist so that her head rested against his shoulder, and she let it stay there, taking comfort from his strength and the protective way he held her. For long minutes they stood there, not moving, watching the baby until he began to grizzle again in frustration at not finding anything else of interest within his reach.

'I think he might be tired,' Laurel said. 'Do you think it's safe to put him down for a nap?'

'I'd say he's made a complete recovery. And you could do with a cup of tea.'

Laurel turned, looking into David's face.

'Will you stay? Just in case?'

'If you want me to.'

'I do.'

'Then in that case I'll put the kettle on while you settle John.'

Laurel scooped the baby up, carried him to his perambulator and set him down, pulling a light shawl up to cover him. Certainly he seemed none the worse for his experience. His eyes

354

closed almost at once, but still she sat beside the pram, rocking it gently until she was sure he was asleep and breathing evenly.

David had made the tea; he brought her a cup, hot and sweet, handed it to her and pulled up a chair beside hers.

'Better?' he asked.

She nodded, sipping her tea. She was still unwilling to leave the baby's side. But she was remembering too the wonderful feeling of safety and comfort she had experienced in David's arms.

She reached out a hand to him, laid it on his knee, turned to look into his eyes. For all the closeness that had grown between them, still she had held back; now, for the first time, she found herself longing for physical contact, yet, beyond that small gesture, unable to bring herself to initiate it.

And David seemed to read her mind. He covered her hand with his own, his fingers cool and firm, his eyes meeting hers with an intensity of feeling that brought a dart of desire and almost took her breath away.

Without a word he took the cup from her other hand and set it down on the floor beside him, then pulled her to her feet and led her to the sofa. His arm went around her, pulling her towards him, and she raised her face to his. His features had gone out of focus now, but she could feel his breath warm on her cheek, smell the printer's ink on his hands, hear the beating of her own heart. His mouth, when it touched hers, was gentle at first, then, as she responded, his kiss became deeper and more demanding. She wound her arms around his back, loving the feel of the long, hard muscles and sinew, lost in the moment.

At last he pulled back, leaving her bereft and wanting more, but the expression in his eyes warmed her heart.

'Oh, Laurel,' he said, 'you have no idea how long I've been wanting to do that.'

A tiny smile quirked her mouth, and an imp of flirtatiousness made her cock her head to one side.

'So why didn't you?'

'That's what I'm asking myself.'

He kissed her again, and again, and a part of her wanted it to go on for ever and ever. But her anxiety for little John was niggling at her once more. He was in her care and she had almost lost him. The awful fright she'd had had reminded her how easily life could be snuffed out. She had to check on him; had to be sure he was safe and well.

'I'm sorry, I have to . . .'

She prised herself free, stood up and crossed to the pram, leaning over with her ear close to John's face to listen for the soft, even breathing, and saying a prayer of thanks as she heard it.

David came up behind her, put his arms around her as he had before.

'I'll see you later,' he whispered in her ear.

She nodded. 'Yes.'

There was a warmth in her, and a wonder. Not just that he had saved John's life by his prompt and cool-headed action, but for something else. Something that had begun in that shared moment and was far from finished yet.

Maggie might well dismiss her when she told her what had happened, and who could blame her? But whatever came to pass, she had the feeling that David would be there for her. For the first time in her life, she really felt that here was a man she could depend upon.

Inspector Turner of Bath Police was heading for retirement. It was now late April, and in just a few more weeks he would be able to hand in his warrant card, forget about killers, rapists, the crooked and the downright evil, and concentrate on his garden. There was nothing more relaxing than pottering about, pulling weeds and planting out seedlings, and nothing more satisfying than seeing it come to fruition, he thought. Once, as a keen young policeman, he'd been eager to trump that satisfaction with the solving of cases and the bringing of criminals to justice, but along the way he'd grown tired and disillusioned. Occasionally the long hours he put in had brought pleasing results in high-profile cases, but for the most part he'd found himself bogged down in a morass of petty crime, time-consuming fraud investigations and suspicious deaths that had turned out to be suicides or accidents. He'd become jaded, he knew, and he couldn't wait to hand over the baton of responsibility to his sergeant. Harry Choke, who had transferred from Bristol a couple of years earlier, had been earmarked for the promotion, and already Inspector Turner was letting him take the lead in new investigations. Choke was young and enthusiastic, as ambitious as he himself had once been and more than capable of handling things without his supervision. Giving him free rein allowed Turner to sink seamlessly towards his much-anticipated retirement.

One of the tasks he'd set himself was clearing his office in preparation for his retirement, sorting and filing away the paperwork that had been left to gather dust on the shelves over the years. It should have been archived long ago, but he'd liked to keep open cases handy just in case new evidence came to light, rather than stashing it away in the dank and dreary basement with all the other long-forgotten material.

One of those still stacked on the shelf in his office was the case of the murder of the private investigator Edgar Sawyer.

Though it was five years now since he'd so much as glanced at the statements and records of interviews he'd conducted at the time, Inspector Turner remembered the case as clearly as if it had been just yesterday. A brutal stabbing in the entrance hall of the house in Queen Square where the investigator had his office. He had been hopeful at first that he would be able to bring the perpetrator to justice. Apart from the man who had seen the girl in the square, there had been no credible witnesses to what had happened, but neither had there been any evidence of a robbery, and Turner had been convinced Edgar Sawyer had known his assailant. He'd find him, he'd thought, amongst either the private investigator's clients or someone associated with his dodgy dealings.

Yet every line of enquiry had run into a brick wall, and other more pressing cases had forced Turner to put the investigation on the back burner, where it had remained ever since.

Now, however, he found himself wondering. Had he missed something? Failed to press his interviewees hard enough? Was it worth putting in one last effort to solve the case? It would be nice to go out in a cloud of glory, and if he failed, he would have lost nothing.

He sat down in the chair that would soon no longer be his, pulled the file towards him, and began to read through every statement with a fresh eye in the hope of stumbling upon something that would give him the lead he needed.

'What's that then, guv?' Harry Choke asked.

Inspector Turner glanced up, irrationally irritated by the cocky attitude of the young man who was to take his place.

'Oh, before your time,' he said non-committally.

'One that got away?'

Turner didn't answer. He was looking at the notes he'd made about the girl who had been Edgar Sawyer's secretary in the years leading up to his murder.

She'd left his employ not long before the attack. She'd attended the funeral. And the answers she'd given to the questions he'd asked her in interview had been less than helpful. But if anyone knew about Edgar's clients, enemies and associates, it was her.

Inspector Turner gathered the relevant documents and put them in a new folder, pocketed his notebook and pen and stood up.

'I'm going out, Choke. I'm sure I can leave everything in your capable hands.'

Harry Choke smiled smugly. 'Too right, guv.'

'And I'm taking the motor.'

That wiped the smile off Choke's face. There was only one motor assigned to the CID, and he liked it to be at his disposal. But never mind. Soon he'd be the one to have the say about how and when it was used.

Inspector Turner went out to the police station yard, got the motor going and headed out on the road to High Compton.

Laurel was singing to herself as she went about her daily chores. 'Oh, I do like to be beside the seaside, I do like to be beside the sea . . .' She'd only been to the seaside once or twice, on day trips to Weston-super-Mare, but she liked the jolly tune; it fitted her mood perfectly. In fact, these few weeks she had felt happier than she had done in years. Partly, of course, because she loved her new life – Maggie hadn't sacked her over the incident of John and the button, thank goodness, and in fact had been very understanding – but mostly because of David.

Since that awful day, their relationship had gone on to an entirely new footing. They spent as much time as they could together and friendship had blossomed into something Laurel thought was love, though it felt completely different to the all-

consuming passion she'd had for Callum and for Ralph. This
was gentler, deeper, warm and safe. There were none of the
torments of the forbidden, nor the desperation that came from
uncertainty about where things were leading. Nothing to feel
guilty about. She and David were two adults who took pleasure
in one another's company, cared deeply for one another, and
there was not a single reason why they shouldn't. Laurel felt
free, like a caged bird spreading its wings in the fresh air and
sunshine.

She was in the kitchen making a stew for the evening meal,
Maggie, Josh and David were all out in their respective
workshops, and John was playing happily with some wooden
bricks Josh had made him, when she heard a motor turning into
the farmyard. Surprised, she glanced out of the window to see a
black Austin pulling up outside. For a moment she didn't
recognise the man getting out and approaching the door, then
she remembered – the police inspector who had interviewed her
about her connections with Edgar Sawyer. What in the world
could he want? Was Josh or Maggie in some sort of trouble? Or
David? It never occurred to her that it was her he wanted to see
after all this time.

Surprised that none of the others had come out to investigate,
but assuming they must be immersed in their work, she scooped
John up and went to open the door.

'Ah! Miss Sykes, isn't it?' She nodded, surprised he
remembered her. 'I wondered if we could have a chat.'

'A chat?' she repeated, puzzled. 'Have you arrested someone
for Edgar's murder?'

'Perhaps we could go inside?' From his tone, Laurel gathered
it was more an order than a suggestion.

She stood aside and he went into the kitchen, looking all
around, missing nothing.

'To answer your question – not as yet. But I'd like to run over with you what you told me before.'

Laurel couldn't remember telling him anything – or at least, not anything remotely useful.

'Shall we sit down?' Without waiting for her agreement, he seated himself on one of the dining chairs, laid a file on the table in front of him and indicated that she should sit opposite him, for all the world as if they were in an interview room at the police station.

'How did you find me?' Laurel perched uncomfortably on the edge of the chair, John on her knee.

'We have our ways.' In fact, he had gone to the only address he'd had for her and been redirected by a sharp-tongued woman he'd established was her mother. 'You've changed jobs yet again, Miss Sykes. You do seem to move around rather a lot. Why would that be?'

If he was trying to unsettle her, he was succeeding. But Laurel was determined not to be intimidated. She had nothing to hide.

'I'm sorry?' she said coolly, her voice rising into a question.

'I don't believe you ever told me why you left Mr Sawyer's employ.'

Laurel felt colour rising in her cheeks. She wanted to tell him it was no business of his, but didn't dare.

'For personal reasons.'

'Which were?'

'My reasons had nothing to do with Mr Sawyer or his murder.'

'I'll be the judge of that.'

Clearly he wasn't going to let it go.

'If you must know, it was to escape the unwelcome attentions of someone else who worked in the building.'

'Not Mr Sawyer himself?'

'Certainly not.'

'Then who?'

Laurel hesitated. But she owed Ralph nothing.

'The homeopathic doctor downstairs.'

'That would be Mr Riley, I presume?' He was making a note on a fresh sheet of paper.

'Yes, but I'm sure he didn't have anything to do with what happened to Mr Sawyer.'

The inspector was less sure. Recently there had been a complaint about Riley. Choke was dealing with it, but when he got back to Bath, Turner would follow it up himself.

John was beginning to get restless, wriggling to be put down.

'Look, Inspector, I told you everything I could when you interviewed me before,' Laurel said. 'There's nothing I can add.'

'If we could just recap . . . It won't take long.'

'Let me get something to keep the baby quiet.' She stood up and fetched a Farley's rusk. Hopefully that would keep John occupied for a bit longer.

'Why did you attend the funeral?' the inspector asked unexpectedly as she sat down again.

'He was my employer. I'd been with him a long time.'

'So you knew him well?'

'I wouldn't say that.' Laurel was feeling increasingly uncomfortable.

'Oh, come on, Miss Sykes. I'm sure you were familiar with his acquaintances. They must have visited the office from time to time. Did anything ever lead you to believe there might be something untoward going on?'

Laurel shook her head, as determined as she had been the last time he had spoken to her not to say anything detrimental about Edgar. If she'd believed any of his dodgy friends might have been responsible for what had happened, that would have been a different matter. But she didn't. Not really. In her heart of hearts she still wondered if Ralph had been the intended victim. Given what she now knew about him, that wouldn't surprise her.

'Let's look at his clients, then.'

'Inspector, I told you everything I could when I spoke to you last,' Laurel protested. 'And we're going back over five years now. I can scarcely remember who they were, never mind anything else.'

'Then let me refresh your memory.' He pushed a sheet of paper across the table towards her. 'These are the names of those who were seeking his assistance for one reason or another in the weeks and months leading up to his death. Some I've been able to trace and speak to; some appear not to want to be found. Perhaps you'd cast your eye over them and tell me if you had the slightest suspicion that any of them might be a threat to Mr Sawyer.'

John was chewing on the rusk; dribbles ran down his chin. Laurel wiped them away with a handkerchief as she glanced at the list. Yes, even after all this time the first of the names were familiar, but they triggered no warning signals. Perfectly ordinary cases, all of them. A couple she didn't recognise – they had presumably consulted Edgar after she had left. And then . . .

Laurel's heart missed a beat as one name jumped out at her.

David Mason.

Not exactly the most unusual of names. There must be others. But once again she was remembering the first time she'd met David, when he'd come to ask if she would take on the books, and how she had had the feeling she'd seen him somewhere before.

In a rush of memory, she was back in her old office on the day she had gone to Bath to fetch her fountain pen, listening to the hum of voices coming from behind the closed door to Edgar's sanctum, waiting for whoever was with him to leave. And then the door opening, Edgar looking surprised to see her there, showing out a young man. 'I'll be in touch.'

'I'll wait to hear from you.'

So clear was it in her mind now, she couldn't understand why it hadn't come back to her before.

'Miss Sykes?' Turner must have seen the change in her expression; he was looking at her closely, his eyes narrowed. 'You've recalled something of interest?'

Somehow Laurel gathered herself together. She knew instinctively that David must be one of the clients who had never been traced. She should tell the inspector that he was here, at Hillview, give him the opportunity to interview him. But she knew she wasn't going to do that. She couldn't imagine why David would have called on Edgar's services, but she was certain he couldn't have had anything to do with the murder. And obviously, whatever it was would be an intensely private matter.

She could feel the inspector's gaze on her, sense his eager anticipation.

'No,' she said abruptly. 'I don't know anything about any of them, and a good few are after my time anyway. And now I'd be grateful if you'd let me get on. I have a baby to attend to.'

She could tell he didn't believe her. She'd given herself away in that first startled moment. But he nodded slowly, gathered his papers together and stood.

'We'll leave it there for now. But I must warn you, I might well need to speak to you again.'

As he left, Laurel prayed that David wouldn't choose this

moment to emerge from his workshop. The policeman wouldn't recognise him, of course. But she didn't want anything said that might let the cat out of the bag until she had had a chance to speak to David herself.

Turner started the car and drove away. Laurel was horribly sure she had not seen the last of him. But somehow, just at the moment, that was the least of her worries.

# Chapter Twenty-Six

Laurel's head was spinning. Just why she should have been so upset to see David's name on the list of Edgar's clients she wasn't sure. As she'd quite truthfully told the policeman, she had no reason to suspect any of them of having had a hand in his murder, and although that day when she'd seen him leaving Edgar's office she'd been worried that it might have something to do with one of his shady deals, she couldn't honestly imagine David being mixed up in something like that.

Yet she *was* upset, dreadfully so. Perhaps it was because she had been so confident she knew all there was to know about him. Oh, not all the details of his past, of course – he never talked about that – but everything that mattered. To suddenly discover that in quite recent years he had felt the need to call on Edgar's services had jolted her considerably, and made her question whether she knew him as well as she had thought.

So many of Edgar's clients had been men with marital troubles of one sort or another. Had David been married – or perhaps still was, but separated from his wife because of infidelity? Had he engaged Edgar to confirm his suspicions that she was carrying on an affair with another man, or was he himself the subject of an investigation and had come to try and persuade Edgar not to reveal his secrets? Unsuccessfully, if that were the case, since he was now living the life of a single man.

If it was that, and he was hiding some important fact about his status, then she'd make sure to end things here and now. She had no intention of going through all that again. Laurel walked the kitchen distractedly, hoping desperately that it was no such thing. But her confidence in herself, so badly damaged not once, but twice, had dropped to rock bottom again. She didn't have a good track record in the men she fell in love with. Had she once again been taken in? If so, then it could only be her fault for making disastrous choices.

She honestly didn't know what to think, and it was driving her crazy. There was nothing for it: she'd have to talk to David when she got the chance. It was the only way she could set her mind at rest.

Somehow she finished preparing the stew and made lunch. When the others came over to the house to eat it, Maggie asked who the visitor had been – she'd heard the motor, but hadn't wanted to stop in the middle of what she was doing, thinking that if it was someone to see her, Laurel would have called her.

Laurel explained without mentioning the list of Edgar's clients the inspector had shown her. She wanted to be able to spring that on David when she spoke to him. She did watch his face closely, though, trying to gauge his reaction to the mention of the murder, and saw none.

When the meal was finished, Josh and David both returned to work; Maggie fed John and put him down for his nap, then she too went back to her workshop. This, Laurel decided, was her chance. She took off her apron and crossed the yard.

The printing press was rolling in David's workshop, and she had to call his name twice before he realised she was there.

The quiet as the thunderous noise stopped felt laden, and Laurel's courage almost failed her. But she couldn't stand for the uncertainty to continue a moment longer.

'I'm sorry to interrupt you, but I really need to talk to you. Could you come over to the house for a few minutes? I can't leave John unattended.'

Looking puzzled, David wiped his hands on a rag.

'What's the matter?'

'Just come to the house and I'll explain.'

David followed her back across the yard.

'Has this got something to do with the policeman who was here?' he asked.

'Well . . . yes. There's something bothering me.' She took a deep breath. 'Did you ever use Edgar Sawyer's services?'

She saw his face change and her heart sank.

'You did, didn't you?' she forged on. 'It was in the summer of 1905, just after I left Edgar's employ. I'd left my pen in my desk, and when I went back to collect it one Saturday, I saw you leaving his office. I'm right, aren't I?'

'It's possible,' David said evasively. 'But you've never mentioned it before.'

'I've only just realised it was you. Look, I don't like prying, but I really need to know what your business was with him.'

'Surely you're not suggesting I had anything to do with his murder?' He sounded shocked and disbelieving.

'No – no, of course I don't think that,' she said quickly. 'But a lot of his clients were married men. Were you one of them? Because I have to tell you here and now that if you have a wife, anything between us is well and truly over. I've been there once, and I've no intention of going there again.'

David shook his head, a half-smile lifting the corner of his mouth.

'Oh, Laurel. No, I'm not married and never have been.'

'Then . . . ?'

'It's a long story. The story of my life, really, and very few people know it. But yes, if you want to hear it, I'll tell you.'

Relief had made her knees go weak. And yes, she very much wanted to find out everything she could about this man that she knew now she had fallen in love with.

'Yes please,' she said quietly.

They sat down at the kitchen table.

'Your family is important to you, isn't it, Laurel?' he said by way of beginning. 'Well, I've never had a family.'

'Oh!' She was shocked, but David scarcely heard her. The years had been rolled back; he was no longer a successful, ambitious young man, but a boy in ragged hand-me-downs, struggling to survive in a hostile and uncaring world.

The orphanage. It was the first home he remembered. A bleak red-brick building on a mean London street, with bars on the windows and a wrought-iron fence running the length of it. He could see it now in his mind's eye, though back in the day he'd only ever seen the frontage once a week, when he and the other boys were taken to church. They'd march in a crocodile, faces and knees scrubbed clean, shivering in winter, sweating in summer, in the same coat that served as Sunday best, and people would cross the street to avoid them, as if they might be infected with some contagious disease.

The dormitories were lined with hard, narrow beds, which they were expected to make up neatly each morning when they were woken at the crack of dawn. They ate sitting in long rows on trestles in front of scrubbed board tables. Every meal tasted exactly like the one before – of nothing. It might as well have been soggy cardboard, but they devoured it because they were

Jennie Felton

hungry and because the punishment for not clearing their plates might be a thrashing.

There were plenty of those. Mr Gilliam, who ruled the place with a rod of iron, needed scant excuse to get out his cane. Lesser misdemeanours were punished with three strokes across the boy's open palm; more serious offences and it would be ten strokes across a bare bottom. For the most part David had managed to avoid that, but he'd suffered for it amongst the other boys, especially the ones whose backsides were too sore for them to sit down for days. They called him a creep, and worse, played mean tricks on him like mussing up his bed after he'd made it and putting unpleasant things between the thin sheets. Once it had been a dead sparrow that one of them had found in the exercise yard. Another time a turd. But David had kept quiet about it. To tell tales was the worst crime of all in the eyes of the orphan boys, and his life afterwards would have only been more miserable than ever.

The only bright spots were when Aggie came to visit him. She brought cheese and slabs of home-made fruit cake that tasted like the food of the gods. He seldom got to eat everything she left for him; the other boys made sure of that. But those few mouthfuls he managed while she was there, talking to him, made life worthwhile.

Aggie. The other boys thought she was his mother, no matter how many times he told them she was not. He was ashamed to admit it, they said; who would want someone who looked like her to be their mother? Fat, ugly, with greasy hair and a chinful of whiskers. 'Who is she then?' they'd ask – few of them ever had a visitor – and in the early years David had to admit he didn't know.

When he was old enough to understand, though, she told him. In another life she had been his wet nurse.

David's mother was a singer on the halls, his father a married gentleman who had washed his hands of her the moment he learned she was pregnant. There was no way she could keep and raise a child; she lived out of a suitcase in rented rooms, and with her reputation in tatters her engagements would soon dry up and she would be penniless. Her manager had arranged for her to go into hiding, putting about the story that she was ill, and found a couple who would adopt the baby as soon as it was born. The husband was a well-to-do businessman with a grand house in Essex, the wife desperate for a child. Aggie had been taken on as both wet nurse and nanny. If things had worked out as intended, David should have grown up wanting for nothing. But everything had gone horribly wrong.

The husband, it seemed, had never wanted children, and had only agreed to the adoption to appease his wife. At first she was over the moon, doting on the baby she had wanted for so long. But then, quite suddenly, she'd fallen into a deep depression, fretting that he wasn't really hers. 'Funny woman, she was,' Aggie told David. 'You never did know what was going on in that head of hers.'

Whereas previously she'd scarcely left David's side, now she wouldn't go near him, wouldn't touch him, wouldn't even look at him. It was left to Aggie to do everything for him, while his adoptive mother sank ever further into herself. He was just seven weeks old when she killed herself, using her husband's dressing gown cord to hang herself from a beam in the attic.

'Well, there was no place for you there after that,' Aggie told David. 'He was a miserable bugger, that man, never wanted you in the first place, and on top of that, he blamed you for driving the mistress to do what she did. He couldn't get rid of you fast enough. Had you sent to a baby farm. You know what I'm talking about?'

David looked at her blankly. A baby farm?

'Terrible places.' Aggie shook her head, her chins wobbling. 'Wicked women take in babies nobody wants and so-called look after 'em. Look after 'em my eye! They don't feed 'em proper, and leave 'em in a row of filthy cots all day long, dosed up so they don't cause any trouble. Fair broke my heart it did. But what could I do? I didn't have a say in the matter.'

'I don't understand,' David said. 'Why would they do that?'

Aggie snorted. 'For the money, of course. And when that dried up, they'd get rid of the poor little mites. You were lucky; at least that bugger who was supposed to be your father kept up the payments, though I dare say it riled him to do it. If he hadn't, you'd have ended up in the river in a sack with stones to weigh it down. That's what happened to some of the poor little souls.'

David gazed at her in horror and disbelief. 'The baby farmer drowned the babies?'

'She did that. Got caught for it in the end, and finished up with a rope round her neck and a trapdoor under her feet. And good riddance. Though I'd have had her chucked in the river with a brick tied to her ankles if I could have had my way. Given her a taste of her own medicine.'

David shuddered. 'So what happened to me then?'

'Well, they brought you here, didn't they? You and the others lucky enough to still be alive. His lordship didn't have to pay out good money for you any more, and at least I can come and see you sometimes, see how you're getting on.'

'Why do you?' David asked.

'Looked after you till you were nearly two months old, didn't I? Fed you at my breast. It's only natural I want to make sure you're all right.'

'What about my real mother?' David felt he had permission

now to ask the question he'd always wanted to. 'Did you ever meet her?'

Aggie shook her head.

'Never met her, no, but I did see her at the window. They sent me to collect you when you were just a few days old, and as we were leaving I looked up, and there she was. Watching. It broke her heart, I reckon, when she had to part with you.'

Hope flared in David's chest.

'What did she look like? Can you tell me?'

'I can do better than that.' Aggie fumbled in her bag and pulled out what looked like a clipping from a playbill. 'That's her. Belle Dorne.'

David gazed in awe and disbelief at the beautiful, glamorous woman in the picture, with feathers in her glossy dark hair; at the full lips curved into a provocative smile, the voluptuous figure in the daringly low-cut gown.

And this was his mother!

'Can I keep it?' he asked.

'Course you can, my cocker.'

It was the first indication he had ever had as to who he really was. Here he had nothing, not even a real name. All the boys had been given surnames taken from different London districts. Fulham was David's, David Fulham. Now he had a link to his heritage, a past that might have become his future.

In that moment, David knew. When he was old enough, when he got out of this place, he was going to look for his mother. And he wouldn't give up the search until he found her.

'It must have been awful for you, David,' Laurel said. 'But I understand now why you engaged Edgar. To help you find your mother.'

She was staggered by the story he had just told her – it was too awful to contemplate – and she was feeling guilty, too, that she had ever doubted him.

David nodded. 'Yes, but not before I'd travelled the world looking for her. That's the reason I went to America. That was where she'd last been heard of, working in vaudeville. I'd done an apprenticeship in printing and reckoned I could get a job without any trouble, which I did. But I couldn't find hide or hair of her. I might have had more luck if I'd still had the picture Aggie gave me all those years ago, but I lost it while I was still in the orphanage. One of the other boys took it for spite, I expect. But at least I knew her stage name – Belle Dorne – and eventually, by talking to other vaudeville acts, I found out she'd come back to England – Somerset, they thought. Trouble is, the average American's knowledge of England doesn't extend much beyond knowing that the King lives in London, and Somerset's a big place. I didn't know where to start looking for my mother. Or even what her real name was. I decided to go back to London, where I had friends, and get a private enquiry agent down here on to the case. That's when you must have seen me – the day I came down to give him what details I had.'

'And did he find her?' Laurel asked.

'I never heard another word from him. I know the reason for that now, of course. He was dead. But I was getting impatient and made up my mind to come to Somerset and do some investigation of my own. I'd met Josh and Maggie on the boat coming over, and they'd invited me to visit. When I told them I was anxious to move down here, they helped me out with a job and lodgings, and I started making enquiries.'

John was beginning to stir in his perambulator. She'd have to pick him up in a minute, Laurel knew, but she was anxious to hear the rest of the story.

'I presume you didn't have any luck?' she asked.

'On the contrary, I struck lucky in Bath. The doorman at the variety theatre there knew straight away who I meant. And believe it or not, she's now married to the theatre owner.'

'So you've met her!'

David shook his head. 'I haven't, no. After all that effort, all those years of searching, I got cold feet. I suppose I'm older and wiser now than I was when I first set out to find her, and I realised she might not appreciate me turning up on her doorstep. Her husband might not even know I exist; she's probably got other children, a whole new life that could be turned upside down. I couldn't have that on my conscience. But at least I know now where she is, and that things turned out all right for her in the end.'

John had begun yelling in earnest now.

'I have to see to him,' Laurel said, getting up. 'Look – I'm so sorry if I forced you to tell me something you'd rather not talk about, but—'

'Don't worry about it,' David said. 'I'm glad we don't have any secrets now.'

Bending over John's pram, Laurel felt hot colour rushing to her cheeks. David wasn't the only one with secrets. She'd felt for some time there were things she ought to tell him, but somehow she hadn't been able to bring herself to. The habit of pretence was too strong to break, and on top of that, she had been afraid of what his reaction might be.

'In any case, Josh and Maggie know,' he went on, 'so it's only right you should too. And should I ever change my mind, I know exactly where to find her. But I doubt I will. I've satisfied my curiosity; now I think it's time to let sleeping dogs lie. And it's also time I got back to work. I've a job to get finished by tonight.' He dropped a kiss on her forehead. 'I'll see you later.'

'Yes. And thank you again for telling me.'

He smiled at her, raising a hand as he went out the door, and Laurel was left alone with her racing thoughts.

# Chapter Twenty-Seven

As she fed John with the bottle of breast milk Maggie had left ready on the cold slab in the larder, Laurel thought about the terrible story David had related to her. The hardships he'd endured were beyond belief; just thinking about the little lost boy he'd once been brought tears to her eyes. How had he survived and somehow grown into the man he was now? It would have been all too easy for him to be dragged down into the morass, the London underclass of vagrants and thieves. Instead he'd made the most of the opportunities that had presented themselves, learned a trade, built a successful business. He could have been bitter and vengeful; instead he was kind, caring, dependable. And although he had finally achieved what he'd set out to do and found his mother, he was selfless enough to consider how his sudden appearance might impact upon her and any family she might have.

Laurel thought he was wrong. It was more than likely she had spent her life pining for her lost child. She couldn't imagine how terrible it must be to never know what had become of him, but then she was looking at it through her own eyes. Perhaps his mother's career had been the most important thing to her. Perhaps what she had wanted most had been the bright lights and the cheers of an audience . . .

Laurel tensed, small shock waves leaping in her veins. She'd been so numbed by the awfulness of his description of his childhood, she hadn't really taken in the rest of what he'd said. Now suddenly it leapt out at her.

His mother – a one-time music-hall singer. Now the wife of the owner of the variety theatre in Bath. Dorne – Belle Dorne. She'd heard that name before – Ralph had told her it had been the stage name of the lady whose husband she had talked to in his waiting room that awful night when she had last visited him in Bath. The lady he had callously dismissed as incurable, yet he was taking her husband's money for treatment he knew would do no good.

Mrs Daniel Trotter!

In her arms, John wriggled and protested, and Laurel realised that, preoccupied as she had been, the teat of the bottle had slipped out of his mouth. Automatically she pushed it back in, but her thoughts were racing. Mrs Daniel Trotter was David's mother. Laurel had met her, spoken to her, something he'd never done himself. And knew she was dying. Months, probably, Ralph had said – that was all the time she had left.

She must tell him. He might have made up his mind now not to rock his mother's life by turning up on her doorstep out of the blue, but one day he might feel differently. One day he might wish he'd at least tried to get to know her, and it would be too late. And what of Belle? Suppose she had spent her whole life longing to find her lost child, or for him to find her? It would be tragic that he had been so close and she never knew.

All her instincts were to rush across the yard to his workshop without delay, but really it wasn't the right time. She had John to look after, and this wasn't something she could talk to David about with a squirming baby in her arms. It would have to wait for a quiet moment when they were alone.

She finished feeding John, changed his bib and buttoned him into a jacket she'd knitted for him. She'd take him for a walk. Perhaps that would clear her head a little. But she had the feeling it would take more than exercise and fresh air to do that.

The evening meal was over. Maggie was upstairs putting John to bed and Patrick had gone out to meet some friends, but Nora was at the table, working on yet another drawing, and Josh was leafing through the weekly local newspaper while David checked some leaflets he'd printed for the Women's Temperance Society for any mistakes.

'Shall we go for a walk?' Laurel suggested.

David glanced up.

'I thought you went for a walk with John this afternoon.'

'I did. But it's a nice evening . . .'

'All right. Just let me finish this . . .'

Laurel waited, nervous at what lay ahead of her, but anxious to get it over with. The more she'd thought about it, the more sure she was that she had to tell David what she knew.

At last he was done, shuffling the leaflets together into a pile and packing them into a box.

'Ready then? I'll just put these in the workshop and then we'll go.'

She followed him across the yard and into the workshop.

'Actually, can we stay here?'

'Ah, just angling to get me alone, were you?' He reached for her hand, heading for the steep wooden staircase that led up to his room. 'Go on, you go first, then if you fall I can catch you.'

She didn't reply, the enormity of what she had to say a heavy weight in her chest, and for once she was almost oblivious to his hands on her hips, steadying her. But when they reached the upper room and he pulled her towards him, she stopped him by putting a hand on each forearm.

'No, David, that's not why I wanted to come up here. There's something I have to tell you.'

His hands dropped from her waist; his smile faded.

'You don't want me any more.'

'No, it's not that . . .'

'I should have known.' He went on as if she hadn't spoken. 'And I can't say I blame you. A boy who grew up in an orphanage . . .'

'Oh, don't be so silly!' she said impatiently. 'As if that would make any difference to the way I feel about you.'

His face softened a little but he still looked wary.

'What then?'

'It is about what you told me . . . Can we sit down?'

The little room was sparsely furnished: a bed, a washstand, a tallboy, a single upright chair. They sat on the bed, side by side, just far enough apart that she could turn to look at him.

'It's about your mother.'

He frowned, puzzled now.

'My mother?' he repeated.

'I didn't realise when we were talking before, but then I remembered.' Laurel drew a deep steadying breath. 'I've met her.'

His eyes widened. 'You've *met* her? How? When?'

She told him. He listened in silence, his expression giving nothing away, so she could only imagine what he was thinking, feeling.

'I'm so sorry to be the bearer of bad news, but I thought you should know,' she finished. 'I thought it might make a difference to your decision about not going to see her. If you don't do it soon it'll be too late and you might come to regret it.'

David was silent, deep in thought. Then he shook his head.

'It's very sad, but to be honest I don't think it changes anything. If she's so ill, the shock of me turning up out of the blue might be too much for her. I wouldn't want to do anything to upset her or worsen her condition. But thank you for telling me, and I will think about it.'

'You could always write her a letter,' Laurel suggested.

'That might be just as much of a shock.'

She reached out, covering his hand with hers.

'I'm so sorry, David.'

He smiled wanly. 'Not everything can have a happy ending, and for myself, I've come to terms with it.'

Laurel bit her lip. She still thought he was wrong, but the decision was his and his alone.

But she couldn't forget the lady she now knew had given birth to the man she had come to love. Elegant and somehow magnetic had been her first impression, a woman who must once have been very beautiful. But there was also a warmth about her, and a sense of humour – the way she'd smiled conspiratorially at Laurel when her husband was fussing over her showed that. A smile that had lit up not only her face but the whole room. And courageous too, facing what lay ahead with admirable stoicism. But who was to say what sadness lay hidden beneath that smile? Laurel felt that to know she was dying without ever getting to find out what had become of her lost baby must be unbearable, and she realised that it was more for his mother's sake than David's that she wished he would reconsider.

David had the choice; his mother did not.

She made up her mind that she would talk to him again, try to persuade him to change his mind. But not tonight. He needed time to absorb what she had told him.

'So – are we going for that walk or staying here?' David asked.

She moved towards him, offering her lips for a kiss.

'Let's stay here,' she said.

'Laurel, are you awake?'

She had been drowsing, halfway to falling asleep. A few moments ago she'd thought she heard knocking but had dismissed it as part of a dream. Now, however, there was no mistaking that this was real. She opened her eyes, saw Maggie silhouetted in the doorway.

'What . . . ?'

'Can you come? It's your brother. He wants to speak to you urgently.'

'Earl?' A sharp shard of alarm pierced the fuzziness in her brain. What on earth was he doing here at this time of night? It had already been past eleven o'clock when she'd come to bed, leaving Maggie in the kitchen giving John a last feed. Something must be terribly wrong.

She threw back the covers and got out of bed, reaching for her dressing gown. Still fastening the girdle around her waist, she hurried downstairs.

Earl was standing just inside the kitchen door. His face was flushed and his hair blown about from pedalling fast all the way from High Compton, and his expression was grim.

'Oh – you were in bed. I should have come earlier,' he said as she appeared in the doorway.

'Never mind that. What's wrong?' she asked. 'Is it Vicky?'

'No, it's Dad. He's taken bad. I called over earlier on like I usually do once a week and I could see he was proper poorly, but he just got worse all the time I was there. It started as a cold a couple of days ago, Mam said; now it's gone on his chest, and you know how bad that is at the best of times. He's having a job to breathe.'

'Oh dear, no! You want me to come? I'll get dressed . . .'

'There's no need for you to come now,' Earl said. 'I'm going back and I'll stay the night. But I shall have to go to work first thing in the morning and I don't think Mam ought to be left alone with him like this. I know Rowan's there, but she's just a kid.'

'Have you called the doctor?' Laurel asked.

'Not yet. Mam wants to leave it till the morning. Night-time call-outs are expensive.'

'Hang the expense!' Laurel snapped. 'If he's having trouble breathing . . .'

'You know what Mam's like. If her mind's made up, there's no telling her different. And she's in hopes he'll be better by the morning. These things are always worse at night, she says.'

'Well, I think he should be called now.'

'She won't have it, Laurel. But you can see to it tomorrow, can't you?'

'If he makes it till then . . .'

Once Earl had pedalled off into the night, Laurel turned to Maggie, who had been standing by anxiously, listening to the conversation, John in her arms.

'Are you sure it's all right if I get off first thing in the morning?' she asked.

'Of course. You must. And stay as long as you need to. We'll manage here.' Maggie was adamant.

They talked for a while longer, Laurel telling Maggie about the silicosis her father suffered, and how it had been getting worse for some time.

'Blooming coal mines!' she finished bitterly.

'Now you get off to bed and try to get some sleep,' Maggie said. 'And let's hope the doctor can help him tomorrow if he's no better.'

Laurel went back to bed, but sleep refused to come. She lay fretting and worrying until at last exhaustion overcame her and she dropped off into a restless slumber.

When she arrived in Fairley Terrace early next morning, Laurel knew the moment she opened the back door that things were no better. The painful rasp of Ezra's struggle for breath was carrying down the stairs, audible throughout the house.

Rowan was at the living room table, a slab of bread and jam uneaten in front of her.

'Oh, Laurel, thank goodness you're here!' she said as Laurel entered from the scullery. 'It's awful! Daddy's been making that noise all night.'

'Has Mam sent for the doctor?' Laurel asked. Rowan shook her head. 'Well, try not to worry, love. Everything's going to be all right.'

She went up the stairs and into the bedroom. Ezra was propped up on a pile of pillows, his hands clenched on top of the coverlet as he struggled to take air into his tortured lungs. Minty was sitting beside the bed, sponging his forehead with a face cloth moistened with cold water from the jug on the washstand. She was fully dressed; Laurel guessed she hadn't gone to bed at all last night.

She looked up at Laurel with eyes that had almost disappeared into the fleshy folds of her face.

'Well, this is a pickle, and no mistake. I told him to take better care of that cold, but would he listen? And this is the result.'

'M'dear . . .' Ezra managed between gasps.

'Daddy.' Laurel leaned over the bed, shocked at the state of him though it was really no more than she had expected. She put her hand on his forehead. It was burning hot, though his whole body was shaking as if he was cold.

'Oh, Daddy, what are we to do with you?' She pulled down the coverlet, exposing his chest. Instantly Ezra pulled it up again.

'You've got a fever, Daddy. We need to get your temperature down.'

They tussled for a few moments for control of the coverlet until Ezra, too weak to struggle any more, gave in.

Laurel straightened up. 'I'm going for the doctor, Mam. You should have called him last night.'

'I've been giving him his cough mixture.' Minty indicated a medicine bottle half full of cherry-coloured liquid on the table beside the bed. 'I don't know what more the doctor can do.'

'Well, he can't go on like this,' Laurel said firmly. 'I'm fetching the doctor now. And if it's the bill you're worried about—'

'It is. If your dad can't work . . .' Minty interrupted.

'Things will be tough, I know. But I'll see to the bill when the time comes, and I expect our Earl will chip in too.'

She touched her father's shaking hand.

'Hang in there, Daddy. I'll be as quick as I can.'

She ran down the stairs. Rowan looked up fearfully.

'I'm going for the doctor, love. Try and eat that bread and jam. You'll be ill too if you don't get something inside you.'

Just as she was about to mount her bicycle, the door of number 6 opened and Cathy and her children emerged – she was seeing them off to school, Laurel guessed.

'Laurel! Whatever are you doing home, and so early!' she exclaimed.

'It's Dad. He's in a bad way, Cathy. I would have thought you'd have heard him wheezing through the wall.'

'Oh – come to think of it, I did wonder . . . His chest, is it?'

'Yes.' A sudden thought struck Laurel. 'I don't suppose one

385

of your boys would like to earn a sixpence? Go and call the doctor for me?'

'Yeah!'

'Too true!'

Two pairs of eyes fixed on her eagerly.

'Oh, I don't know – it'll make them late for school . . .'

'They can take my bike. I won't need it before they get home this afternoon.'

Cathy still looked doubtful, torn between anxiety about a black mark from the schoolmaster and wanting to help. Neighbourliness won the day.

'All right then. Ollie can do it.' A groan from Percy. 'His legs are longer,' she told the younger boy. 'You can take Freda to school, Percy.'

'Just a minute . . .' Laurel fumbled in her purse, found a sixpence for Ollie and a couple of threepenny bits which she gave to Percy and Freda by way of compensation. 'I'm trusting you, Ollie,' she said as he pocketed the sixpence, grinning triumphantly. 'You know where Dr Mackay lives?' He nodded. 'Tell him it's urgent. He must come straight away.'

'Mind you do, Ollie,' Cathy cautioned.

He rode away along the rank, standing on the pedals: although he was tall for his age, the seat was still a bit too high for him.

'Your mam ought to have got Mrs Oglethorpe in to help,' Cathy said. 'Why don't you knock the door and ask her to come round?'

Dolly Oglethorpe, at number 3, was the person called on for her skills as a midwife and nurse, and also for laying out the dead. She was a friendly soul, but Laurel knew her mother wouldn't want a neighbour in the house, nosing about, as she was sure to put it.

'You know what Mam's like . . .'

'Oh, for goodness' sake, Laurel. At a time like this, you need someone who knows what they're doing.'

She was right, Laurel thought. Mam would likely be furious, but she'd have to put up with it. And Daddy would be more likely to do as he was told by someone who wasn't a member of the family. He wouldn't tussle with Mrs Oglethorpe when she told him he needed the covers back for his own good.

'And let me know if there's anything I can do.'

'Thanks, Cathy.'

She hurried along the rank and hammered on the door of number 3. Dolly Oglethorpe, plump, rosy-faced and homely, looked surprised to see her – the Sykes family were ones for keeping themselves to themselves – but when Laurel explained, she agreed to come and do what she could.

'Just as long as your mam—'

'Never mind Mam,' Laurel said crisply. 'It's me who's asking. If Mam doesn't like it, she'll have to lump it.'

Sure enough, when Dolly entered the bedroom with Laurel, Minty bristled, but Dolly ignored her, going straight to the patient.

'Goodness me, you're running a temperature, Mr Sykes! Come on now, let's get those bedclothes off you.' Sure enough, Ezra had covered himself up again. 'Open the window, Laurel. And get me another flannel. Just sponging his face will do no good at all. We need to cool you down all over, Mr Sykes.'

To Laurel's surprise, Minty, though affronted, didn't argue. Perhaps she was too relieved at relinquishing responsibility to someone who clearly knew what they were doing.

'And while I'm doing that, Mrs Sykes, perhaps you could boil a kettle and find a towel. We'll get some steam into him and that ought to make his breathing easier,' Dolly instructed.

Jennie Felton

Grumbling a bit under her breath, Minty did as she was bid.

By the time Dr Mackay arrived, with creditable alacrity, Ezra was certainly a little improved.

'Well, I'll be going now you're here, Doctor,' Dolly said – clearly she wouldn't be sorry to get out of the house she hadn't set foot in since the Sykes family had arrived in Somerset fifteen years earlier. 'But let me know if you want me. I'll be in all morning.'

'Amazing woman, that,' Dr Mackay said, opening his medical bag and preparing to examine Ezra.

'She's worked wonders,' Laurel said. Minty remained silent.

Dr Mackay spent some time listening to Ezra's chest and back, then removed his stethoscope and packed it away.

'It's my opinion that you need to be in hospital, Mr Sykes,' he said gravely.

'Oh, Doctor, I don't know . . . Will it do any good?' Minty had an ingrained fear of hospitals.

'I won't lie to you, Mrs Sykes, once silicosis takes hold, there's no curing it. But hospital is the best chance your husband has of combating this infection. There will be someone to keep an eye on him day and night and do whatever is necessary. I'll take him now, in my motor. If you'd like to come along too, I can run you home again later.'

He turned back to Ezra. 'Now, do you think you can make it down the stairs, my friend, if Laurel and I help you?'

A quarter of an hour later, the feat was achieved, and Ezra and Minty were ensconced in the rear of Dr Mackay's motor.

'There's room for you in the front if you want to come too, Laurel,' he said, but Laurel shook her head.

'I would, but I think I should stay here with Rowan. I can always visit later.'

She leaned into the motor, squeezed her father's hand and dropped a kiss on his forehead.

'Just get well, Dad, d'you hear me?'

Rowan was standing in the doorway, dressed for school but clearly in no state to go. Laurel went back to her and put an arm around her shoulders, and together they watched the motor drive off along the track.

# Chapter Twenty-Eight

The fair, and the travellers who worked on it, was back in High Compton. The rides and caravans had arrived late on the Thursday evening and parked up; the following morning they would be setting up ready for business. There would be nothing for Kezia to do until late afternoon, when the first trickle of customers began arriving, and even then it wouldn't be busy until much later. Saturday would be the day when everything was in full swing. For the moment, her time was more or less her own, to do as she liked. Her chance to check out the place she'd last seen Callum alive. The place where that woman had attacked him. Perhaps she would find out what had happened after she'd run off in fear. And take her revenge.

It was an obsession with her. Though she sometimes despaired of ever getting the woman on her own, her resolve was as strong as ever it had been. She'd sworn an oath that she would avenge Callum, and sealed it with her own blood. She'd do whatever it took, and never give up. Never.

When Da went out to start setting up the ride, she followed.

'Where ya going?' he called out to her as she passed him.

'Just for a walk.'

'Watch yourself, then.'

She knew what he meant. Sometimes local louts would pick

fights with the travelling folk, and a girl alone would be fair game for whatever took their fancy. But most of them would be at work at this time of day, and in any case, she had her knife in her pocket. She'd used it before, and she'd use it again.

'Don't worry about me. I can take care of myself,' she called back, and set out at a brisk pace up the main road.

Just as she reached the intersection where the road leading to Fairley Terrace branched off, she saw a motor coming towards her. She stepped onto the grass verge as it passed. A smartly dressed man was driving, with two passengers in the rear. An old man, slumped against the seat, and . . .

*Her.* It was her – the old witch.

Disappointment and frustration rose in Kezia's throat like bile. She'd thought she might find her alone at this time of day, her husband at work, that kid of hers at school. Thwarted again. Where were they going – and in a motor? It slowed, almost to a stop, and turned left, pulling slowly away and chugging up the hill.

That wasn't the way into town, or the road to Bath. From the knowledge she'd gained over all the years of coming here, Kezia knew that it led only to open countryside and a string of isolated villages. But she also knew that at the top of the hill was the hospital. She'd been there once when she was much younger, and had slipped on the steps of the ride and broken her arm. Even from here the red-tiled roof was just visible above a bank of trees. Was that where they were headed? Certainly the man, whom she assumed was the old witch's husband, had looked pretty poorly.

Kezia hesitated for only a moment. No point continuing on to Fairley Terrace now; better to follow the car at least as far as the hospital and see if she was right. She started up the hill, her young legs making short work of the incline.

The hospital was on the left-hand side on the brow of the hill, a sprawling red-brick building set behind a yard. And yes! Pulled up outside the main door was the motor that had passed her, though there was no sign of the driver or passengers.

Kezia crossed the road to the other side, where open fields stretched out behind a hedge, thickening now with new shoots, and sat down on the grassy bank, still damp with dew. She could wait. She had nothing better to do.

A good half-hour passed before she saw the man who had been driving come out of the hospital and go to the motor. He was alone. Kezia hazarded a guess that he was a doctor. He didn't look like a cabbie, and she couldn't imagine the Sykes family would have friends with motors. A bicycle was the limit of transport for ordinary working folk. She waited until he had driven away, then crossed the road, walked boldly up to the main door, and went inside.

The entrance lobby was empty; no one to ask her business. She pushed open the swing doors beyond the reception desk, which she guessed must lead to the wards. All she wanted was to see if the man she had identified as Mr Sykes had been admitted, which would leave the coast clear for her later on.

'Can I help you?' a voice boomed from behind her.

Kezia swung round to be faced with an imposing figure in a uniform much grander than ordinary nurses wore. The matron. She'd been caught by the most influential person in the hospital. She thought quickly. She didn't want to mention Mr Sykes's name; who knew if it might be linked to her later?

'I'm lookin' for me friend. He got hurt last night.'

'And he is?'

'Jack Green.' She plucked it out of the blue.

'I'm not aware that anyone of that name has been admitted,' Matron said stiffly. 'And in any case, visiting hours are six to seven thirty this evening. If you still think your friend is here, I suggest you come back then.'

A door behind Matron's starched figure opened, a nurse wedging it open with her foot while she spoke over her shoulder to someone out of Kezia's line of vision. But she had a clear view of a row of beds, and a woman unloading a carpet bag into a bedside locker. It was her. The witch. Kezia would have recognised that ample backside anywhere, and as she stared over Matron's shoulder, the woman straightened up and she saw the hated face to confirm it.

'I expect I made a mistake,' she said, and turned to leave before the woman saw her. Not that she'd know her from Adam: all the times she'd watched her, Kezia had taken care not to be seen. But she had what she wanted now. The husband had definitely been admitted to hospital, and better yet, the matron had informed her of visiting times. The old witch would most likely come back this evening to see him, and by the time she got home again it would be getting dark. If she skipped her duties helping Da on the ride, Kezia could waylay her, unseen.

She left the hospital and set out to walk back to High Compton. A triumphant smile was playing on her lips, and in her pocket her fingers caressed her precious knife. The knife Callum had given her. The knife she would use if she had to to find out what had happened to him and take her revenge.

The mantel clock was striking eleven as Laurel heard the back door open and Minty come in, flushed from the walk back from the hospital.

'Oh, Mam! There you are! I was getting worried. I thought Dr Mackay was going to run you home.'

Minty plonked herself down in a chair, fanning herself with her handkerchief.

'I wanted to see your dad settled in, and Dr Mackay had his surgery to get to, so I told him I'd walk.'

'How is Dad?'

'Still poorly, of course, and they won't tell us anything much. I suppose we have to trust they'll do their best for him, but you know how I feel about those places . . . And you should be at school, my girl,' she added as Rowan came running down from upstairs, anxious for the latest news.

'She wasn't up to going,' Laurel said. 'I don't suppose one day off will hurt.'

'When can we go and see Daddy?' Rowan asked.

'Visiting's six till seven thirty this evening,' Minty said. 'You two are welcome to go. I don't think I could face walking all the way there and back again, but I dare say he'd be glad to see the pair of you.'

'That's what we'll do then,' Laurel said. 'Now, Mam, you look as if you could do with a nice cup of tea. And then I think you ought to go and have a lie-down. I don't suppose you had any sleep last night.'

'You know, I think I will. You never know what the rest of the day will bring.'

Laurel smiled faintly as she went to make the tea. That was Mam all over, always waiting for the other shoe to drop. But really, it was no laughing matter. Her dear dad was very ill, anything might happen, and even if he got over this, the future was not bright. This setback had brought home to her all too clearly that the day was coming when he'd be reduced to the half-life of old Mark Lapham at number 8 – or in the graveyard.

The prospect was almost more than she could bear. But at least she and Rowan were going to visit him tonight, show him how much they cared. For the moment, she wouldn't think beyond that.

\* \* \*

The fair began opening up around six o'clock. Just some of the food stalls and sideshows, and the children's rides. Every so often Da gave the switchback a twirl, more to make sure it was working correctly and advertise its presence than anything else; the bulk of customers wouldn't come until later, and really, for the moment, there was nothing for Kezia to do.

'I'm going off for a bit, Da,' she said; it was easier to slip away now than it would be later.

'As long as you're back before we get busy.'

She wasn't sure she would be, but Da would commandeer help wherever he could find it, and she'd just have to take the flak when she did get back. Then she'd make sure she was a very visible presence on the ride, though she was confident none of the fair folk would give away the fact she'd been missing for a couple of hours. When it came to the rozzers asking questions, they always stuck together.

The day had become overcast; it would get dark earlier tonight, and that suited her purpose very well. Dusk was already falling when she set out for Fairley Terrace; by the time she reached the track leading off the main road, it was almost dark. She lingered for a minute or so, considering her options.

She could accost the woman here on the track, lined by hedges with open fields beyond, or she could wait until she reached her back door and follow her into the house. That would probably be the safest. There was always the chance someone would walk this way. It was the only route in and out of Fairley Terrace, and she didn't want to be seen loitering, or be interrupted when she had the witch where she wanted her. In fact, someone was coming now, turning in from the road.

As luck would have it, she was close by a gateway into the

field and was able to slip back into the deep shadow of the hedge. The boy – it was a boy, rather than a man, perhaps thirteen or fourteen years old – didn't even glance in her direction as he passed, whistling and kicking a stone in front of him as he went.

As soon as the coast was clear again, she made her way to where the track dog-legged along the rank of houses and peeped around the corner of the end one. The boy had disappeared and the track was deserted. Keeping close to the walls of the out-houses, she made her way along to number 5, planning to slip into the garden and watch for the woman from there.

To her surprise, however, lamplight was spilling out from the scullery window. Surely the old witch wouldn't go out for an hour or more and leave a lamp burning? Was there someone else in the house? Checking in both directions, she slipped across the track and peered through the window, just as she had that other time when she had so nearly been caught.

And there, in the scullery, was the woman. Her back was towards the window; she was putting crockery into a wall-hung cupboard. Kezia ducked back out of sight, her pulse racing. Had the old witch come back early, or not visited the hospital at all? Was she alone in the house, or was the daughter there too? Or the husband, already discharged? Well, whatever, this was the best chance she'd ever had. She'd already thought about the possibility of the daughter being there, but she was only a kid: Kezia thought she could be dealt with easily enough, or even used as a hostage. And even if the husband had been sent home again, he'd most likely be upstairs in bed, and too weak and ill to be any threat.

She made up her mind. Time to act. She'd try the door first; if it was unlocked, that would be the best option. If it wasn't, she'd knock and then be ready to push her way inside when it was opened. She waited until the woman left the scullery and disappeared back into the living room, then tried the handle. To her relief, it turned. She opened the door carefully, anxious not to do anything to announce her presence, and slipped inside, closing it behind her. Then, her fingers curled around the knife she always carried in her pocket, and, her heart beating hard against her ribs, she crossed the scullery and went into the living room.

The woman was beside the range, bending over to settle a kettle on the hob. Kezia took a few quick steps towards her; the woman, sensing someone there, turned sharply, overturning the kettle, which clattered onto the tiled surround, water spitting and fizzling on the open coals.

'Who . . . ?' It was a startled gasp; alarm made her fleshy features ugly. 'What are you doing in my house? Get out!'

For answer, Kezia flicked open her knife, pointing it at the woman's throat, where folds of flesh overlapped. With her free hand, she pushed her back to the easy chair beside the fire. As the back of the woman's knees connected with the edge of the seat, she stumbled, falling back into the chair.

'What are you doing?' Her voice was filled now with bewilderment and sheer panic.

Kezia bent over her, pricking her throat with the tip of her blade.

'You and me are going to have a talk.'

The woman's mouth opened and shut, for all the world like one of the goldfish in jam jars that they gave out as prizes at the fair.

'If it's money you want . . .'

Kezia's lip curled scornfully. 'I don't want your money. I want to know about my brother. What you did to him.'

'I don't know your brother! I don't know *you*.'

'Oh, I think you do. Callum Smith. A didicoi.' She spat the word contemptuously, the way people spat it at them. 'Not good enough for your precious daughter, was he?'

She saw the woman's face change as realisation dawned.

'Memory coming back, is it? Thought it would. So – where is he?'

Somehow the witch found her voice. 'How should I know?'

The point of the blade pressed harder against the soft skin of her throat; a single drop of blood oozed.

'Course you feckin' well know. You killed him, didn't you? Beat him to death with a fire iron. Don't deny it – I saw you with me own eyes. What did you do with his body? That's what I want to know. So feckin' well tell me!'

The woman was trembling from head to toe, her whole body turned to a mass of jelly. She was almost beyond words.

'He's in the garden, isn't he? In the feckin' garden?'

'No! He did come here once, looking for Laurel, but I sent him packing.'

'Is that what you call it? I call it murder. Where is he? Where? Tell me, you bitch, or I swear—'

The click of the back door opening. Kezia heard it, although the blood was roaring in her ears. She half turned as a girl – the daughter – came into the living room. She stopped, startled and frightened by the scene that met her eyes, and quick as a flash, Kezia seized her opportunity. Before the girl could move a muscle, she was on her, jerking her round into her grasp, pressing the knife against her throat and glaring at the woman.

'P'raps now you'll tell me, bitch!'

Laurel hadn't followed Rowan immediately into the house; she'd stopped for a minute to put her bicycle, which Ollie Donovan had left outside his back door, into the outhouse for the night. But the moment she stepped into the scullery, she heard the voice, completely unfamiliar to her, carrying out from the sitting room.

Puzzled, she hurried through, then stopped short, shock and horror turning her stomach to liquid. Mam was slumped in the easy chair, shaking and cringing; a girl she didn't know had Rowan in a bear-hug grip with a knife to her throat.

'What . . . ?'

For a fleeting second, the girl's startled expression mirrored her own, but she didn't relax her hold on Rowan, or her control of the situation.

'Get over there – now!' She jerked her head in Minty's direction.

Laurel's feet seemed anchored to the ground.

'Over there!' the girl repeated. 'Go on! Now! Or else she gets it . . .'

Unable to tear her eyes from the knife at Rowan's throat, Laurel took first one step, then another, while the girl, still holding Rowan fast, shuffled past her so that they changed places as if in some macabre dance. The girl backed into the doorway, facing into the room, while Laurel was beside Minty's chair.

'You're Laurel, aren't you?' she spat. 'You're the cause of all this.'

'What . . . ?' Laurel was totally bemused.

'Callum,' the girl grated. 'Callum Smith. Remember him?'

'Callum,' Laurel repeated, stunned. It was the first time in more than fifteen years that she'd spoken his name aloud.

'Yeah, Callum. My brother. He was crazy for you, more fool him. You're not our kind, but he couldn't let you go. Had to try to find you. And what did he get? Your ma killed him for his trouble. And I want to know where his body is. He should have a proper Romani funeral, not be left to rot under your beans.'

'You've got it all wrong. Let Rowan go!'

'I never did! I never killed anyone!'

Laurel and Minty both spoke together.

'So why did he never come back?'

'I don't know! I don't know!' Minty's head was rolling on her fleshy neck.

'If you don't come clean and tell me where he is . . .' the girl's arm was tight across Rowan's chest, the knife still hovering dangerously over her throat, 'I'll do for her, I swear. And don't think I wouldn't. I've stabbed a man before wot got in my way, and I'll do it again. A life for a life. That's fair, in't it?'

'For God's sake, have pity and let her go!' Laurel took a step towards the girl and the terrified Rowan.

'Get back!' The tip of the knife pierced Rowan's skin; a thin line of blood oozed and trickled. Laurel stopped, raising her arms in a gesture of surrender.

The girl's eyes fastened once more on Minty.

'You'd better tell me, or I'll slit her throat like a pig.'

'No you won't.' Though tremors were running through her body like sharp stinging barbs and her legs seemed not to belong to her, Laurel's voice was surprisingly deliberate and steady.

'Just feckin' watch me . . .'

Her eyes flicked to Laurel, the woman she believed had cost her beloved brother his life, and Laurel held the dark, blazing gaze.

'Would you really murder your own niece?'

'Wot you talkin' about?'

'That's my daughter you've got there,' Laurel said in the same steady tone. 'My daughter . . . and Callum's.'

Uncertainty flickered in those dark eyes. But:

'You're lying! She's her kid.' She jerked her head in Minty's direction. 'That's her ma.'

'Everybody thinks so, but they're wrong. I was just a child myself when I had her. Mam and Daddy brought her up as theirs. She's Callum's, I tell you. And that's God's truth.'

A shadow in the doorway behind Kezia and Rowan. Laurel froze, terrified that if startled, the gypsy girl's knife would slash Rowan's throat. Her eyes signalling caution to the person who had entered the house unnoticed through the open back door, she made one last desperate plea.

'She's your brother's child, your own flesh and blood, Miss Smith. And my mother never killed anyone. Callum isn't dead, or at least he certainly didn't die here. Let Rowan go, and I'll tell you what I know.'

Kezia wavered, relaxing her hold on Rowan a little, and with a quick, desperate movement Rowan twisted free. At the same moment, the shadow moved, swift as the blast from a shotgun, and Patrick made a grab for the knife. Its sharp blade slashed across the palm of his hand, but somehow he caught Kezia's wrist and it fell from her grasp.

For a long moment, her eyes, confused and wild, flickered from one of them to the other and back again. Then she shook off Patrick's restraining hand, darted for the door, and was gone.

# Chapter Twenty-Nine

Later, when Laurel looked back on that terrible evening, it seemed to her to resemble a hotchpotch of snapshots taken on a just-functioning Brownie box camera. Mam cowering in the chair, the knife at Rowan's throat, Patrick, his gashed palm spurting blood as he snatched the knife, Kezia fleeing, the commotion that followed.

Patrick had run next door to fetch his aunt and uncle. Ewart had come rushing round while Cathy bound up Patrick's injured hand – he'd had to go to the hospital later to have it stitched – and Ollie had been sent to the police station to fetch Sergeant Love. He'd arrived, hot and bothered, and seemingly unable to make head nor tail of what they had to tell him. A gypsy girl running amok with a knife, accusations of murder, and Mrs Sykes's almost hysterical denials that she had ever killed anyone – it was a rum do and no mistake, and he was anxious only to get back to the police station and hand the whole affair over to the detective inspector from Bath.

When he'd left again, Laurel had fetched the half-bottle of brandy that was kept for medicinal purposes and poured them all, even Rowan, a small glass, and for a wonder Minty had made no objection. Then she'd said she was off to bed, and Laurel and Rowan were alone.

Laurel glanced anxiously at the young girl, who sat on an upright dining chair, elbows on the table, head bent over them, knuckles stuffed into her mouth. Perhaps she should put her to bed too, but she couldn't imagine she'd sleep, not even with the brandy.

Whether in her terror she had taken on board what Laurel had screamed at Kezia in those last moments before Patrick intervened, Laurel wasn't sure. But what she did know was that the time for secrets was over, the pretence blown to smithereens with just a few words uttered in desperation to appeal to the crazy girl who was threatening Rowan's life. Words that once spoken could never be taken back. Perhaps they hadn't registered with Rowan yet, but as the mind-numbing shock and terror wore off, they would. And Laurel needed to talk to her, explain, and seek forgiveness from the girl whose world had been blown apart; the girl who meant more to her than life itself.

She had been fifteen years old and desperately, hopelessly in love. Her senses swam with the bittersweet magic of the new and exciting world she had discovered so that she felt as if she were standing on the edge of a peak, and if she spread her arms she would fly, soaring on the air currents like a kestrel over the moors. The air tasted sweet, with nothing of the metallic tang of coal dust; the biting winds barely seemed to touch her for her blood raced hot through her veins in time with the musical jangle of the fairground hurdy-gurdy and the clatter of the switchback ride.

The fair was overwintering on the outskirts of the Yorkshire town where they lived, and though much of the time the stalls and rides were shut and covered with tarpaulins, at weekends they would open up for the pleasure of the local folk. It was there that she had first set eyes on him, swinging confidently from gondola to gondola as the switchback slowed to a halt, coal-black curls gleaming in the light of the carbide lamps. He wore a dark donkey jacket with a scarlet neckerchief knotted around his throat. And as the ride slid slowly past where she was standing, he caught her eye and grinned. In that moment something happened to her heart, a thrill ticking through the deepest parts of her.

'You wanna ride?' he called.

Suky Taylforth, her best friend, with whom she'd gone to the fair, grabbed her arm.

'Come away!' she hissed. 'He's got his eye on you.'

Laurel shook herself free. Suky could be such a wet blanket.

The ride made one last slow revolution; as it came to a stop, the boy swung to the edge of the platform, holding out his hand.

'Come on! I won't charge you.'

The excitement twisted again in the pit of her stomach. Drunk on her own daring, she took his outstretched hand and climbed up onto the ride.

'Your carriage, ma'am.' He seated her in one of the gondolas, and when the ride started up again, he came and sat beside her, boldly draping an arm around her shoulders.

As the ride gained speed, dipping first down, then up again, she was thrown against him so that her cheek brushed the coarse wool of his jacket – it smelled of tractor oil and very faintly of tobacco smoke – and when she put a hand on his thigh to steady herself, she felt the taut, firm muscles beneath the coarse fabric of his trousers and quickly removed it.

'You can stay on,' he said when he got up to stop the ride.

'No, I've got to go . . .'

'Come back tomorrow then.'

Suky wasn't keen; Laurel persuaded her. She could have persuaded the birds off the trees.

That was how it had begun.

In those days Minty hadn't been the harridan she was today. She could be sharp, yes, and she laid down rules, but they weren't as strict. As long as Laurel was home by the time she stipulated, she didn't ask too many questions. Laurel and Suky had been friends for years; she was quite used to them going off together. What she didn't know, of course, was that when they were out of sight of the house, Suky would either go home or meet up with other friends, and Laurel would go to the fair alone.

At weekends, Callum would let her ride the switchback until she was dizzy; on week nights, when the fair was all shut up, she would meet him where the caravans were parked, and they would walk in the crisp, cold evenings under the stars to some secluded spot.

One night they'd almost bumped into Daddy, on his way to Buffs. When she'd seen him coming along the lane, Laurel had pushed Callum back into a nearby gateway and hidden her face in his jacket. 'What are you doing?' Callum had asked, and Laurel had hissed back: 'It's my Dad!'

'It's all right, he's gone now,' Callum said a few moments later. He was laughing. But Laurel was shaking from head to toe. It wasn't Daddy she was afraid of, but if he told Mammy there would be hell to pay!

She'd soon forgotten her fright, however. For her, there was magic in the air, and Callum had been touched by it. Everything about him seemed romantic and exciting. His thick coal-black curls and dark aquamarine eyes, the way he spoke, using words that were unfamiliar to her – 'cadger' for man, 'shavers' for children, 'dock' for a fortune teller, which was what his mother was, he told her. The brightly painted caravan that was his home, and the piebald horse that pulled it when they were on the road – 'the drum', he called it. His devil-may-care attitude. Even his name. Callum. She'd never met anyone called Callum before.

She loved his kisses, loved the feel of the rippling muscles in his back beneath her fingertips and the hard, lean length of his sixteen-year-old body pressed against hers. And when he wanted more, she lacked the will to tell him no. She thought he loved her as she loved him. Everything they did felt inevitable and right.

And then one night his father had caught them as they kissed goodnight outside the caravan. He was a big, rough-looking man and he roared at them in an Irish accent: 'What the feckin' hell're ya up to?'

'Shin it,' Callum muttered to her, and she didn't need telling twice. As she ran, the angry roar followed her.

There was no way Laurel was going to go near the caravan again: Callum had told her his father could be violent. He'd also said that the old man wouldn't be best pleased to know he was involved with a giorgio. She waited until the fair opened up again at the weekend, and headed for the switchback ride, her heart in her mouth, pulse racing in anticipation of seeing Callum again.

He wasn't there. It was his da operating the ride, with the help of a little girl of maybe six or seven. She had a head of curls as dark as Callum's, and skipped nimbly between the gondolas just as he did. Laurel guessed she must be Callum's sister, Kezia. He'd talked about her – 'Shaver', he called her. But where was Callum?

Laurel hung about near the ride until her fingers had turned numb from the cold inside her woollen gloves and she couldn't feel her toes, but there was no sign of him. In desperation she made her way to where the caravans were parked up; if his da was busy with the ride, he wouldn't be there. But the caravan was all in darkness. Puzzled, anxious, with an awful feeling of foreboding gathering in her chest like an undigested meal, she knew there was nothing for it but to go home, where she cried herself to sleep.

Laurel had never seen Callum again. He wasn't there the next week or the next. She couldn't eat, she couldn't sleep, simply couldn't understand where he was or what had happened. But the knot of foreboding had grown and hardened, hanging over her now like a thick mist over the moors. And just to make matters worse, her monthly courses were late. She tried to tell herself it was because she was upset about Callum's disappearance, yet all the time that same feeling of foreboding was whispering in her ear that it was more than that.

Eventually she summoned up the courage to ask another of the fair lads where he was. But the boy could tell her nothing. 'Dunno. He's gone. Been gone a coupla weeks and more.'

'Where? Why?' She was close to tears, but the boy merely shrugged.

'Got fed up with it here, I s'pose. Most of us get fed up in the end, hit the drum.'

Even now, all these years later, when she thought about that terrible time, Laurel could still feel the anguish, the terror, the sick dread that had consumed her. It was imprinted on her memory for ever, a malaise that would never quite disappear. How could Callum have left her, just like that, without a word? She'd truly believed they had something special, that he loved her as she loved him. Her heart was breaking. And added to that, the terrible anxiety was growing, the awful certainty that she had fallen pregnant and would have to face it alone. Despite the niggling pains in her stomach, her period had still not come. In the mornings she felt nauseous, her breasts were tender, and when she looked at herself in her bedroom mirror she saw that her nipples were swollen and darkening.

She couldn't tell anyone, not even Suky, and certainly not Mam. The very thought of it made her curl up inside with icy dread. She felt as if she was living in a nightmare from which there was no escape.

And then came the day when she could keep her secret no longer. She was in her bedroom, half dressed and washing herself at the jug and basin on the washstand, when Minty came into the room with a pile of freshly laundered handkerchiefs and underwear.

'Here's your clean stuff . . .' She broke off, gazing at Laurel, who had tried to hastily cover herself, but not fast enough.

'Laurel?' she said sharply, taking in the swollen breasts, the thickened waist. 'Laurel! Oh my God, you're not . . .'

Laurel's face was all the confirmation she needed.

'Oh, you stupid, stupid girl! I knew something was wrong! I knew it! Whatever is your dad going to say? Oh, my life! How could you be so silly?'

Laurel's face crumpled, tears streaming down her cheeks. She was beyond words, sick with shame.

Minty had put down the pile of laundry, sunk to the bed, where she sat regarding Laurel in shock and horror. One of her hands was clutching her throat, the other worked in the folds of her skirt.

'Who is he? Who's the lad?' Still Laurel said nothing. 'Does he know about this?'

Laurel shook her head.

'Well, he's going to know. And answer for it.' Minty was all ready to do battle. 'Why ever didn't you say something before? Oh my Lord, I never for a minute thought . . . Who is it? Who's got you in this pickle?'

Still sobbing, Laurel told her.

'What? A *gypsy*! Oh, whatever were you thinking of?'

'I love him, Mam!' she wailed.

'Well, we'll see about that.' Minty got to her feet. 'Where is it they're parked up? I'm going down there now.'

Laurel dashed the back of her hand across her nose and cheek.

'They've gone, Mam. They went last week.'

She'd paid one last despairing visit to the fair only to see them packing up, the first caravans already departing.

'Are you sure? Where've they gone?'

'I don't know. Down south somewhere. You know they always go when the weather starts getting better.'

'Oh, Laurel, Laurel, the shame of it. And a gypsy at that, not even a decent local boy.' Minty sighed. She looked old suddenly, the deep creases and frown lines that would become so deeply etched over the years truly noticeable for the first time.

Laurel was sobbing again. Minty squared her shoulders, suddenly resolute.

'For goodness' sake, pull yourself together. Tears won't do any good now. But we'll work something out. Just don't say anything to your dad or the boys before I've had time to think.'

Laurel nodded, feeling as if a burden had been lifted from her. In that moment, she was a child again. Mam would take care of things. She always did. She couldn't bring Callum back, but at least Laurel wasn't alone in this nightmare any longer.

'Oh, Mam, I'm so sorry . . .' she whispered.

Minty merely nodded. She was on fire with anger at the gypsy boy who had done this to Laurel, sick with shame. But her heart was heavy too for her beloved daughter, faced with becoming a mother when she was still no more than a child herself. Whose life would be blighted unless she did something about it.

Minty was determined that would not happen.

The first thing Minty did was go down to the caravan site to see for herself that the fair had moved on. At first she'd been furious to think that this boy, whoever he was, would be getting away with what he'd done; now she saw that it was for the best. The second was to talk to Ezra.

If anything, he was even more upset than she had been; he'd shaken his head in disbelief, his blue eyes filling with tears.

'Oh, not our Laurel! Just let me get my hands on the bastard who did this. I'll wring his neck with my bare hands.'

'He's gone, goodness knows where. But in any case, you'll do no such thing. This stays inside these four walls.'

'And how do you think we're going to manage that, m'dear?'

'We'll move away. As soon as the baby's born. Somewhere nobody knows us. And I'll make out it's mine. That way our Laurel keeps her good character, and nobody will be any the wiser.'

'Whatever are you talking about, m'dear? Move away? What about my job? And our Samuel's?'

'There's other coalfields besides Yorkshire.' Minty's face was set. Her mind was made up. 'And they'll have tied cottages, same as here. You just need to get something sorted out.'

'Folks round here will see our Laurel's in the family way, though. They're not daft.'

'You can leave that to me. But when we're somewhere fresh, nobody will be any the wiser.'

'I see you've got it all worked out.'

'Somebody's got to. I won't stand by and see our Laurel disgraced and her life ruined. And I don't want to see a grandchild of mine sent to the workhouse either. No, I've raised three children; I can raise another. Just as long as we get away from here.'

'What's Laurel got to say about it?' he asked.

'I haven't told her yet. But she'll see it's the right thing to do.'

Ezra shook his head sadly. He wasn't sure he agreed with Minty, but it was pointless to argue with her when her mind was made up. And she only had Laurel and the baby's best interests at heart. She might be a bit of a one for taking the decisions, but they usually turned out for the best. It was easier to just go along with her; Ezra had learned that long ago. And he didn't like the thought of Laurel's name being dragged through the mud either. Marked out as a scarlet woman before she'd grown out of being a child – his little girl.

'I'll make some enquiries,' he said.

Overnight, the whole atmosphere in the house had changed. Now they were all treading on eggshells. Minty snappy but immovable, Ezra aged ten years overnight, the two boys angry and mortified, Laurel a pale shadow of her old self. When Minty had put the plan to her, she had raised no argument. As yet she felt nothing for the new life growing inside her. She just wanted to be rid of it, get back to normal. Minty arranged for her to go to a cousin in York when she began to show; she was passed off as the daughter of old friends, but in the city nobody took much notice anyway. The only person outside the family she told of her plight was Suky. She knew she could trust Suky to keep her secret, and the letters the two girls exchanged were a lifeline to Laurel throughout the loneliest and most miserable time of her young life.

By the time Rowan was born, Ezra and the boys were working in Somerset, and had secured a house that had become vacant in Fairley Terrace. When Rowan was just a month old, Minty, Laurel and the baby joined them. As Minty had predicted, no one was any the wiser. But just to be on the safe side, she made sure she kept herself to herself. The secret weighed more heavily on her than she had ever imagined it would, and the bitterness and disappointment she felt, the anger that they'd been forced to move away from the old home she'd loved, the sense of injustice that this should have happened to them, to their family, to Laurel, ate away at her, corrosive as acid. Her sense of humour all but disappeared; ill-temper was her breastplate now against the outside world.

Yet through it all she could never find it in herself to blame Laurel. The girl had been young, taken advantage of. She wasn't the first, and she wouldn't be the last. And what was more, she could see how Laurel adored the child that she could never acknowledge was hers.

It had begun for Laurel the moment Rowan was placed in her arms. The love that had surged through her had almost taken her breath away. Young as she was, the maternal instinct would not be denied. As Rowan grew, it broke her heart that she couldn't tell her the truth – that she was her mother, not Minty, and she loved her more than life itself. But at the same time she believed that what they had done was for the best. Rowan would never be called a bastard. No one would point the finger and tell her that her mother was a slut. By the time she began to have doubts, it was too late. Minty was horrified when she suggested Rowan should be told the truth, and Laurel didn't feel she could go against her after all she had done. She shrank, too, from rocking Rowan's world to its very foundations. Best to let things go on as they were, be thought of as a loving sister whom Rowan could always rely on. It wasn't what she wanted, but it was the next best thing.

Now, however, the cat was well and truly out of the bag. And under the worst possible circumstances.

Rowan sat motionless at the table, paper white and shell-shocked, as well she might be with the startling revelation coming on top of the trauma of being held at knifepoint. Laurel reached across to draw her hands from her face, covering them with her own and looking into those dark green eyes, so like Callum's.

'I am so sorry, my love, that you had to find out like this,' she said. 'We should have told you long ago. But the time was never right.'

Rowan's lips moved but no sound came from them; it was as if she couldn't bring herself to articulate the words. Then, very softly, she whispered, 'Didn't you want me?'

'Oh, Rowan, of course I wanted you! I love you so much. I always have. But I was so young – younger than you are now – and I really didn't have any choice but to go along with what Mam decided. To move here from Yorkshire, where nobody knew us, and bring you up as her own . . .'

'So Earl and Samuel know too?' The pain was raw in Rowan's eyes. 'You all knew what I didn't . . .'

Laurel swallowed at the lump in her throat. This was no time to cry. She had to be strong, and goodness knows she'd cried enough tears over the years.

'They know, of course, but they've kept it to themselves. They may have told their wives, I don't know, but it's never been mentioned. Oh, please, darling, try to understand. I had to go along with it, little as I wanted to. At least I was able to watch you grow up, help look after you, be there for you. You were provided for as I could never have provided for you. And you didn't have the stigma of being illegitimate – you know how cruel people can be.'

413

A single tear squeezed from beneath Rowan's lowered lids and rolled down her cheek.

'Don't cry, my love – please don't cry. It's not so bad, is it?'

Rowan said nothing, and for all her efforts Laurel's eyes too were filling with tears.

'Darling Rowan, you know I wouldn't hurt you for the world, and it must be the most awful shock for you, but I had to say something to stop that terrible girl . . .' She broke off, shivering as she saw again in her mind's eye the knife at Rowan's throat.

'It's all right.' Rowan looked up, her eyes meeting Laurel's. 'You've been the best sister ever. But to think you're my mother . . . that's going to take a bit of getting used to.'

She smiled tremulously, then got up, came around the table and put her arms round Laurel. Laurel pulled her close, burying her face in Rowan's small, firm breasts, and for a long while neither of them moved or spoke.

Rowan was right, the change in circumstances was going to be hard for them all, but at least there were no more secrets within the family. Whether they'd still try to hide the truth from the outside world, she didn't know. That was something that had to be talked about. But not tonight. It had been the most dreadful, traumatic day, in so many ways.

'I think we both ought to try to get some rest,' Laurel said. 'We still don't know what tomorrow will bring with Daddy.'

'Can I sleep in with you?' Rowan asked. She knew that when she closed her eyes, the nightmares would come.

'Of course you can, darling.'

When they were both undressed and ready for bed, Rowan climbed in beside Laurel, and eventually they fell asleep in one another's arms.

# Chapter Thirty

When she woke next morning, Rowan was alone, and for a few moments, still heavy with sleep, she could almost believe the traumatic events of the previous day had been nothing but a bad dream. But she was in Laurel's bed, not her own, and when she touched her throat where the blade of Kezia's knife had pricked her skin, she could feel a lump where a little scab of dried blood had formed.

She shivered, remembering the blind terror that had consumed her. She'd barely taken in the confession Laurel had thrown at Kezia that she was Rowan's flesh and blood, nor even Patrick's timely intervention. It had all been an unreal blur; she'd been close to fainting, and her trembling legs had only carried her as far as the chair before giving way beneath her.

Now, though, she remembered him being there, and the blood. There'd been a lot of blood. She must find out if he was all right and thank him for saving her life.

For the moment, though, she couldn't think about that. Eclipsing everything else was the fact that her whole world had been turned upside down. All the things she'd taken for granted had crumbled; her whole life had been built on a lie. Laurel was not her sister but her mother. Mam and Daddy were not her parents but her grandparents. Samuel and Earl not her brothers but her uncles. And the thing she found hardest to stomach was that they had known, all of them, and kept it from her.

How could they have done that? She'd told Laurel it was all right, but it wasn't. They'd deceived her, and that hurt. Who was she? She wasn't sure she knew any more. Didn't know how she could ever get over this enormous deceit.

And yet, she thought, in a strange way it was almost as if she'd always known. It explained the closeness between her and Laurel, a bond far stronger than between her and Mam; explained why Laurel had always been there for her, fighting her corner. And it explained too why Mammy was the way she was.

It wasn't only Laurel's life that had been turned upside down when she had fallen pregnant at such a young age; it had been Mammy's too. It must have hit her dreadfully hard, the disappointment and shame unbearable for such a proud woman. She'd done what she thought was best, but it had meant the family had had to move away from all that was familiar to them and start a new life, and she'd been saddled with the burden of raising another child when she should have been able to take things a little more easy. On top of that, the secret must have weighed heavily on her, living with the fear that someone would discover the truth.

Rowan could see now too why she had been so strict. She'd been afraid the same fate would befall her as had befallen Laurel.

Oh, poor Laurel! she thought. She must have been so frightened. Heartbroken too. She must have felt about that boy the same way Rowan herself felt about Patrick or she'd never have let him do what he did. And then he'd abandoned her just when she needed him most.

And yet . . . if what that terrible girl had said was true, he had come looking for her. And Mammy . . .

Suddenly Rowan was trembling all over, her mind racing as

she found herself remembering that night all those years ago when she'd woken to the sound of angry voices, looked out of the window, seen Mammy hitting a man again and again with the fire irons. She hadn't thought of it in years now, and when she did, she'd assumed it must have been a nightmare. Now, however, some of the things the gypsy girl had said with the knife at her throat were coming back to her. At the time it had been just a jumble of words, half heard over the roaring of the blood in her ears. But some of it must have registered.

*He was crazy for you . . . Had to try to find you . . . Your ma killed him . . .*

Was that what she had witnessed? Mammy murdering Laurel's lover – Rowan's own father? It was too terrible to comprehend, yet still the gypsy girl's words were coming back to haunt her, as if the gates of her memory had suddenly been unlocked.

*. . . left to rot under your beans.*

The beans. Daddy had dug the trench for them so that he could plant them as he always did on High Compton Fair day, but it had been raining. He hadn't put them in until the next day. Was the girl right? Had they buried Callum's body in the garden and erected the bean sticks over his grave?

Bile was rising in her throat now and she found herself remembering other things. That afternoon when she and Daddy had gone to the fair, he'd been going to take her on the switchback ride as she'd kept begging him to do, then suddenly changed his mind. He'd acted so strangely, not like Daddy at all, dragging her away from the ride, jogging all the way home with her on his shoulders. He'd seen Callum, that must have been it. And Callum had seen him. Followed to find out where they lived. And come back that evening when the fair closed looking for Laurel.

But Laurel hadn't been here. Those were the days when she was working and living in Bath. Perhaps Mammy had never told her Callum had come looking for her. Certainly she wouldn't have told her what she had done. She was good at keeping secrets – the way she'd pretended for the whole of Rowan's life that she was her mother, not Laurel. But this was the most terrible secret of all.

The bile rose again in Rowan's throat, and this time her stomach was turning too. She leapt out of bed and rushed for the basin on the washstand, where she was violently sick.

'Rowan? Are you all right?' Laurel's voice from the doorway.

Rowan lifted her head, wiping her mouth with the back of her hand and reaching for the face flannel.

'Oh, Laurel!' she gasped. 'Laurel, Mammy killed him! And they buried him in the garden!'

'Whatever are you talking about?'

'My father! She said she didn't, but I saw her! I saw her hitting him over and over again! She told me I'd just had a bad dream. But it wasn't. It was real . . .' The words were tumbling out between her chattering teeth.

'Oh, Rowan, Rowan . . .' Laurel put her arm round the trembling body, led her back to the bed and sat down beside her. She didn't look shocked and horrified as Rowan would have expected, just dreadfully sad.

Rowan shrank away from her. Had Laurel known all along? Was she a party to it?

'You didn't . . .' The words refused to come.

'Rowan, darling, Callum isn't dead,' Laurel said gently. 'Mam didn't kill him or anyone. She gave him a good beating, perhaps, I wouldn't put that past her. She was furious with him for what he had done, and she didn't want him back in our lives. But she didn't *kill* him.'

418

'How do you know that?' Rowan desperately wanted to believe her, but she couldn't. She was five years old again, hiding beneath the bed, trying to escape what she had seen.

'Because he wrote to me after he'd been here,' Laurel said. 'He said Mam had attacked him, told him to leave me alone. He said he was sorry and that he'd been trying to find me . . .'

'I was five,' Rowan objected. 'He couldn't have been trying very hard if he hadn't come looking for you in all that time.'

'He didn't know about you. Had no idea. He'd had a terrible fight with his father – over me – and taken off for London for a while. By the time the fair came back for the winter, we'd gone. It was years later when he ran into my friend Suky and asked her what had happened to me. He was pretty shocked when she told him – I know because she wrote to me about it – and said that he'd try to see me when the fair was next in Somerset. To be honest, I didn't expect him to ever do that. But he did. How he found out where we lived, I don't know—'

'I do,' Rowan interrupted. 'Daddy took me to the fair. He must have seen him and followed us home.'

'Yes, that would make sense,' Laurel said. 'Mam never told me he'd been here, but I got a letter from him a few weeks later. It didn't say much – Callum wasn't a great letter writer – just that he was sorry, and that he had tried to see me but Mam had sent him packing. It was postmarked Ireland. He'd decided to take off again, it seems. And I can only think he went without a word to his family. He probably blamed his father for the fact that he wasn't there for me when I found out I was expecting you, and didn't want to set eyes on him again for fear of what he might do to him. Callum wasn't like us. He had very wild ways – part of his attraction.'

'Did you never talk to Mam about it?' Rowan asked.

'Of course I did. She just said to forget him, he wouldn't be bothering us any more. She'd sent him off with a flea in his ear and a sore head, more like than not. But she hadn't killed him, that's for certain. So you can put that idea right out of your head.'

Rowan drew a deep breath, relief washing over her like a warm bath.

'But that girl . . . his sister . . . she thought it too.'

'Yes, poor girl.'

'Laurel – how can you say that? After what she did?'

'I suppose she had to find someone to blame for him never going home again. She worshipped him, Rowan, and he abandoned her, just as he abandoned me. So I think I know how she must have felt.'

'But you would never . . .'

'She's wild, like him. It's in their blood.'

'What will happen to her?'

'If they catch her, I expect she'll go to prison for a very long time. But I can't be worrying about her any more. You're my priority. And Daddy. I'm going to ride over to the hospital and find out how he is. Will you be all right with Mammy while I'm gone?'

Rowan nodded. 'Yes, I'm fine now. You go, Laurel.'

Truth be told, she wanted to be alone for a while. She had a great deal to think about.

It hadn't taken long for the police to catch up with Kezia, and to his credit, it was Constable Knight, not the brightest of law enforcers, who found her. Slow and plodding he might be, but PC Knight was also dogged, and with an eight-hour night shift in front of him, he had decided to devote himself to the task.

He had accompanied Sergeant Love to the fair folk's campsite and stood stolidly by as the sergeant questioned the families, unsurprised by the negative responses: 'No, sir, no, sir, she ain't here, sir.' It was what they always said. Eventually Sergeant Love had given up and gone home to his bed, but Constable Knight was not so easily deterred. Having nothing better to do, he'd made a show of cycling away, then crept back and concealed himself and his bicycle in the bushes that surrounded the site.

He'd passed the time thinking about the breakfast his wife, Cissy, would have waiting for him when he came off duty in the morning – he never could sleep on an empty stomach – and he could already smell the delicious aroma of bacon and eggs that would greet him when he returned home to his police house. But he didn't have long to wait before the door of one of the caravans opened and a slip of a girl emerged.

For one so heavily built, Constable Knight could move fast when the occasion arose. Before she could cover the ground between the caravan where she'd been hiding and her own, he was upon her. She fought him like a little wildcat, and as other caravan doors opened and burly men emerged, he wondered for a moment if he was going to be assaulted. But a faint heart was not one of the constable's shortcomings. He stood his ground, snapping the handcuffs round her skinny wrists and banking on the fact that none of the fair folk would be anxious to end up in front of the magistrates. Just one man remained – her father most likely – bellowing threats as he dragged her away.

Constable Knight took her to the police station, Sergeant Love was roused, and Kezia Smith was locked in a cell for the night. The next morning she was taken to Bath, where she was charged, a seemingly broken girl who repeated over and over the mantra: 'She killed him. She killed him.' And: 'I'm so sorry, Callum. I tried my best. But it wasn't good enough.'

Inspector Turner shook his head at the senselessness of it all, glad that his retirement was not so far away. And as he authorised the release of the story and her photograph to the press, he little guessed that the unsolved case that had marred his career was about to be solved.

Laurel had not long returned from the hospital, with the welcome news that Ezra had had a good night and was much improved, when David appeared at the door of number 5, anxious to see how the family was after their ordeal. She was relieved to see that it was him and not one of the neighbours.

'Oh, David, come in quick and let me shut the door or Hester Dallimore will be down here before you can say Jack Robinson. She's having a field day, I expect.'

'Never mind her – what about you?' But he did as she asked, putting his arm around her the moment the door was closed. 'Are you all right?'

'I'm fine. She didn't hurt me at all. It's Rowan and Mam who had the worst of it. They're both pretty shaken up, as you can imagine. But thank God for Patrick! If it hadn't been for him, goodness only knows what would have happened. How is he? How's his hand?'

'He had to have stitches in it, and it's pretty painful, but he'll be okay.'

'I don't know how we can ever thank him, getting the knife away from her like that. It was like a miracle, him turning up when he did, and thinking so quickly.'

'It was lucky, yes. Cathy had asked him to pop in and ask how your father was doing, and he hadn't been keen. Your mam's given him the length of her tongue a few times, I understand.'

'Well, she won't do in the future. He deserves a medal.'

'He'd have done whatever it took when he saw Rowan in trouble. He thinks the world of her, you know.'

'And she does of him. I'm going to put my foot down. If they want to see one another, I'm going to make sure Mam raises no objection. Not that I think she will. She'll see him in a different light now. And in any case . . .' She glanced over her shoulder towards the living room, and lowered her voice.

'I have to talk to you. There's something I have to tell you. I don't know how much Patrick overheard, but it's all going to come out anyway. Perhaps we could go up to my room?'

'There's no need for that,' Minty said from the doorway – evidently Laurel hadn't spoken as quietly as she'd intended, or else Minty had been standing there listening. 'You can go in the living room. Rowan's upstairs, and I'm going to make a treacle tommy. I could do with something sweet.'

'Mam – are you sure you're up to it?'

'It'll do me good to keep busy. Oh, and by the way, I won't be stopping Rowan seeing Patrick any more if that's what she wants. He's not a bad lad, and in any case, I don't suppose I'll have a say in the matter now.'

So she had been listening.

'Mam . . .' Laurel felt guilty suddenly. After all Minty had done, it wasn't right that she should be pushed out now that Rowan knew the truth.

'Let's say no more about it. Go on, you'd better talk to David and explain yourself before he hears it from somebody else – if he hasn't already.'

Laurel glanced at David's puzzled expression and felt a wash of trepidation. He didn't know. If Patrick had overheard, he hadn't said anything. What would he think when she told him? He was such a straight chap. A private person, but straight as a ramrod. She was very afraid he wouldn't like the deceit one little bit, even if he didn't condemn her for landing herself in this situation in the first place.

But there was nothing for it. She had to do this, and hope that he would understand. If he ended it between them, she realised, it would leave a gaping hole in her life that she doubted would ever be filled.

He listened while she talked, not once interrupting.

'I'm sorry I haven't told you all this before,' she finished. 'But keeping it a secret for so long it's become ingrained in me some-how, and besides, it wasn't just mine to tell. Rowan didn't know, and Mam didn't want her to, though I thought it was wrong.'

'And how has she taken it?' he asked.

'She's shocked, of course. But I've always been there for her when she needed me – I made sure of that. So hopefully . . .'

'I should think anyone would be proud to have you as their mother,' David said, and his unexpected reaction brought tears to her eyes.

'That's a lovely thing to say. I'm not sure I've got very much to be proud of, though. Having a baby at fifteen is hardly a recommendation, and then there was Ralph . . .'

'Everybody makes mistakes. What is it they say? The person who never makes a mistake never makes anything.' He reached across and took her hand. 'Like you say, you've made sure you were always there for Rowan. It's thanks to you she's getting a good education that will set her up for life, for one thing. And I'm sure there are plenty of other instances too. Despite having such a bad start, you've really made something of yourself. How many girls have put themselves through accountancy and secretarial classes as you did? You're kind and you're warm. You're wonderful with children. Do I need to go on?'

'No, stop, please! You're embarrassing me!' But the warm glow inside her was mirroring the flush that had risen in her cheeks.

'As for secrets,' David went on, 'I was as guilty as you. I didn't tell you about my past until you forced it out of me.'

'But that isn't anything you need be ashamed of.'

'Well, I wasn't proud of it. And as for the obsession with finding my mother . . . I'm not sure what that says about me, either.'

'Just that you wanted to know who you really were. That is perfectly understandable.'

'I knew who she was. I even had a picture of her – until some rascal stole it from me. But I couldn't let it go. It ruled my life for far too long.'

'Yet now, when you know where to find her, you refuse to meet her. That makes no sense to me.'

'I thought I'd explained,' David said, obviously uncomfortable with the turn the conversation had taken.

'But you'd like to meet her, surely?'

'Perhaps. But suppose her husband knows nothing about me? The last thing I want is to turn her life upside down, especially now, when she's so ill. I'd never forgive myself if I caused her unnecessary distress in the last months of her life.'

'I think you're wrong, David,' Laurel said. 'I know that if it were me, I'd want nothing more than to find my lost child. If Mam hadn't kept Rowan for me, if she'd been adopted, or sent to an orphanage, it would have haunted me all my life. I was lucky. I saw her grow up, even if she didn't acknowledge me as her mother. It would break my heart not to know what had happened to her, if she was well and happy. I honestly think you should meet her while there's still time.'

'I'll think about it,' David said, but she thought it was more to bring the conversation to a close than anything else.

He'd pursued his mother doggedly; now he would stick just as stubbornly to his decision not to do anything that he thought would upset her. But Laurel could be just as single-minded. She was certain that nothing would make his mother happier than to see him again, hold him in her arms, after all the long years when she must have ached to do just that.

If Mohammed won't come to the mountain, the mountain must come to Mohammed, she thought.

Minty came bustling in, carrying a pastry plate pie filled with a mixture of golden syrup and flour.

'Right. That's the treacle tommy made,' she said, putting it into the oven.

The time for confidences was over.

# Chapter Thirty-One

Ezra was allowed home from hospital the following day – Dr Mackay ferried him back to Fairley Terrace himself, remarking to Matron that his recovery was little short of miraculous.

'These old miners are made of tough stuff,' he said, to which Matron replied tartly that he should try nursing them – the young nurses had their work cut out keeping them in bed where they belonged.

Though she did her best to hide it, Minty was happy and relieved when she saw the doctor helping him out of the motor.

'If I didn't know better, I'd think you being ill was a put-up job to keep out of the way of all the goings-on here,' she said as she settled him in his favourite chair.

'Well, there you are, m'dear, p'raps you're right,' Ezra returned equably, and as she tucked a blanket round his legs added: 'Now there's no need to fuss.'

'There's every need. I don't want you taking a turn for the worse again.'

She spoke briskly, but in her heart of hearts she knew it was only a matter of time before the sickness caught up with him once more.

Laurel was still at home. Maggie had told her to take as long as she needed, but she had promised to return in a few days, when everything had settled down.

'I suppose you'll be wanting to go with her when she goes back to Hillview,' Minty had sniffed, and to her surprise, Rowan had looked quite shocked.

'But my home's here!'

'Oh, well, that's all right then,' Minty said, gratified that not everything had changed.

It was Sunday morning. During breakfast Laurel had had one eye on the clock, and as they cleared away, she made a surprise announcement.

'I'm going to chapel.'

Astonished, Minty almost dropped the pile of plates she was carrying. As a family they'd never been regular worshippers.

'What brought that on?'

'I'd just like to go. I think we've got a lot to be thankful for, don't you?' Laurel said, and it was partly true. She wasn't going to say anything about the real reason she wanted to go to chapel today.

She'd been thinking a lot about David's stubborn decision not to contact his mother, and wondering what she could do to bring them together. She could ask Ralph where they lived and go and see her herself, but she didn't want to do that. For one thing she had no wish to set eyes on Ralph ever again; for another, she thought it might well be too much of a shock for Mrs Trotter given her state of health if she simply turned up on the doorstep to break the news.

Ralph had told her that Mrs Trotter was Lucy Day's aunt, and she knew that Kitty, the wife of the Methodist minister, was Lucy's sister. As delicate a subject as this would be best broached within the family, she thought. They would know how to break the news to her, or even if it would be better left well alone.

The Methodist chapel was on High Compton high street. Dressed in her Sunday-best blouse and skirt and with some change in her purse for the collection plate, Laurel hesitated on the pavement, a little daunted to see so many worshippers heading inside, some stopping to chat on the steps leading up to the main door. She hadn't realised how well attended the service would be, or that the majority of the ladies would be wearing hats. She didn't own a hat – hers had been ruined when she'd got caught in a rain storm, and she hadn't got around to replacing it – and the lack of one made her feel conspicuous. She wished she'd asked Mam if she could borrow her black straw. Too late now, though. She climbed the steps, weaving her way between the little knots of regular worshippers, and went into the chapel.

It was quite dim inside, the air heavy with the scent of spring flowers. To her left, a staircase led up to a gallery that ran around three sides of the main body of the chapel, and she decided to tuck herself away up there where it would be less obvious that she was unfamiliar with the service. The seats on the side that faced the altar were mostly occupied by what she correctly assumed to be the choir; she turned right and took a chair on the end of a row. From here she had a good view below and she could see a young woman she recognised as Kitty Day – or Kitty Callow as she now was – making her way to the front pew. She was painfully thin and fragile, but she smiled as she acknowledged people in the congregation, a nod here, a quiet word of greeting there. The perfect minister's wife, Laurel decided – and also the perfect person to approach about David's mother: serene, kind, and wise.

When the service began, to her surprise Laurel found herself enjoying it. The chapel was possessed of perfect acoustics; the swelling notes of the organ and the melodic voices of the choir seemed to surround her in a swirling cloak, and every word the

429

Reverend Callow spoke was clear and calming. She'd come again, Laurel decided.

At last it was over and people began filing out. Laurel hung back, waiting until the flow became a trickle, but keeping a sharp eye on Kitty, who was now at the rear of the chapel collecting hymn books and stacking them in a cupboard. Her husband would be outside having a word with each of the congregation as they left, Laurel guessed, and would come back inside when they had all gone, and really she wanted to catch Kitty on her own. Choosing her moment, she went down the stairs and stood waiting.

As Kitty finished her conversation with another lady, Laurel stepped forward.

'Oh, hello.' Kitty smiled. 'I don't think we've seen you here before, but you are most welcome.'

Laurel took her courage in both hands.

'No, I haven't been before, or at least not for a very long time. But actually the reason I'm here is that I wanted to speak to you.'

'To me?' Kitty looked surprised.

'Yes. I believe Mrs Trotter – Belle Dorne, as she used to be known – is your aunt.'

'She is,' Kitty said, a little wary now: surely this young woman wasn't old enough to remember the music-hall star in her heyday? 'And . . . ?'

The other woman who had been helping with the hymn books was returning.

'It's a bit private really . . .' Laurel said hesitantly.

'Then let's go where we won't be disturbed.' Kitty still looked puzzled, but she led the way to an empty pew about halfway down the chapel.

'I'm intrigued,' she said when they were both seated.

'And I hardly know where to begin.'

'Perhaps the beginning?' Kitty suggested.

'I'm not even sure where that is,' Laurel said. 'But here goes anyway.'

'Well,' Kitty said when Laurel had finished, 'I must say this is the last thing I expected when I came here this morning.'

She had listened intently to all Laurel had to say, only interjecting occasionally to ask a question or confirm a fact.

'I'm sorry to burden you with it,' Laurel said, 'but I thought it would be best to talk to one of the family rather than springing it on her – I understand she is rather ill.'

Kitty's face clouded. 'She is, I'm afraid. We pray for her every day and night, but . . .' She broke off. 'Are you quite certain this young man is telling the truth?'

'Absolutely.'

'Only we had a very distressing incident a couple of years ago when an imposter tried to pretend he was her son and worm his way in. He tricked my sister into believing him – he even had a picture of Aunt Molly when she was young – and almost murdered poor Lucy when she caught him out and threatened to tell Aunt Molly.'

'Oh my goodness!' Laurel said, shocked. 'But yes, I do believe every word of what he's told me. And after all, he has nothing to gain.'

'Aunt Molly has no other children. Like Jake Harper, he might think he stands to gain a considerable inheritance.'

'He doesn't even want to make himself known to her,' Laurel protested. 'He thinks he might be upsetting a lot of apple carts. And in any case, if I had any doubts at all – which I don't – you would just have allayed them. He told me he had a picture of his mother, cut from a playbill, that was given to him by the woman who had been his wet nurse. It was stolen from him by another boy in the children's home – that could have been your imposter. So yes, I'm absolutely convinced David is telling the truth. And I thought Mrs Trotter should have the chance to know him before it's too late.'

The Reverend Callow had finished seeing off the last of his congregation and clearing up in the vestry. Now he was standing in the aisle, a little way off, giving his wife and Laurel curious glances as he waited for them to finish their conversation.

'Look, let me think about this, and talk it over with Philip,' Kitty said. 'How can I get in touch with you?'

Thank goodness Maggie and Josh had had a telephone line put in as their business had grown! So few people had them. Laurel gave Kitty the number and she wrote it down in a little pocket book.

'I'll be back there by the middle of the week. But please, if David should answer, don't tell him what it's about. I don't want to scare him off.'

'Are you sure, then, that you're doing the right thing?'

Laurel nodded. 'David is the sort of person who thinks about others rather than himself. But I know deep down he would like nothing more than to meet his mother. After all, he did chase her over two continents.'

'Very well. Leave it to me,' Kitty said.

Laurel felt she was indeed leaving it in the best possible hands.

Rowan was staring out of her bedroom window watching the comings and goings in the rank. She should have been working – it would soon be time for the end-of-year exams – but since the traumatic events of Friday she had found it impossible to concentrate. She saw Mrs Withers, Patrick's grandma, on her way home from chapel, and a bit later Laurel too; saw the two Donovan boys go off with their trucks, and Freda playing with her doll's pram. Mrs Oglethorpe, wearing a big wraparound apron, came out of her house and went next-door-but-one to chat to Mrs Cooper, presumably. The one thing she didn't see was anyone hanging out their washing – that was taboo on a Sunday.

And then she caught sight of Patrick rounding the corner and making his way along the track. It was the first time she'd seen him since Friday, the first chance to thank him for what he had done. She'd never make it downstairs before he was past the house, so she pushed the window open and called down to him.

'Patrick! Wait!' He looked up, surprised to see her there. 'I'll be down!' she called, and scurried down the stairs and through the living room – where the delicious smell of roasting lamb was emanating from the oven – and the scullery where Minty was peeling potatoes.

'Where's the fire?' Minty asked, but she didn't stop to reply.

Patrick had come to a stop outside the back door, watching it expectantly. His hand, she saw, was heavily bandaged, and she was suddenly overcome by shyness.

'I just wanted to say thank you,' she mumbled.

He went a bit red and shuffled his feet, obviously feeling as awkward as she did.

'It was nothing. Anybody would have done the same.'

'You saved my life.' Her eyes went to his bandaged hand. 'How is it?'

He shrugged. 'It'll be okay. They said I was lucky she missed the tendons, though.'

'That would have been awful.' She didn't really understand the implications, but it sounded serious.

'Yeah.'

They looked at one another, looked away, neither quite knowing what to say, but both unwilling to move on.

The back door opened behind Rowan and Minty appeared. Rowan half expected to be dragged back inside; instead Minty spoke to Patrick.

'You did a good job the other night and I'm sorry you got hurt. I can see I got you wrong. And if you and Rowan want to be friends . . . well, I won't stop you.' With that, she went back in and closed the door behind her.

Patrick shifted awkwardly again, but his face had flushed with pleasure.

'And do you?' he asked Rowan tentatively.

'What?'

'Want to be friends?'

'Oh, Patrick, you know I do! I thought it was you who didn't.'

'Your mam was so against it, there wasn't any point. And I didn't want to get you into trouble, so I kept my distance.'

'But . . . you do still like me?'

'Course I do! A lot.' His flush deepened. 'Look – I'm having dinner with my gran, but p'raps we could see one another this afternoon?'

Rowan's heart skipped a beat, pure happiness bubbling in her chest.

'I'd like that.'

'Good. See you then – about three?'

'All right.'

They shared a shy smile.

'I've got to go now.'

Rowan went back indoors, threw her arms round Minty.

'Thank you, Mam! Thank you so much!'

Minty shrugged her off. 'Mind! Or I'll be cutting *my* hand on this potato knife. He's not a bad boy. But just you be careful what you get up to.'

'I will.'

Her heart was singing. The other night had been terrible. And yet some good had come of it. If she hadn't learned the truth, she would still feel bound to obey Mam's every word, and if Patrick hadn't come to the rescue, the chances were Mam would never have changed her mind about him.

Every cloud has a silver lining . . . It was one of Daddy's maxims, and surely not always true. But just at the moment it seemed to fit the situation perfectly.

Rowan went back upstairs but she knew she would still be unable to concentrate on her school books. Instead she sat on the edge of her bed, hardly able to contain her excitement. Patrick liked her. She was going to see him this afternoon. She'd have put up with Friday being a hundred times worse if it had meant this happy outcome.

'Molly, love, there's something I have to talk to you about.'

It was early evening, and Molly, a shawl around her shoulders and a light rug over her knees, sat in her favourite spot in the garden enjoying the sunset – pink streaks in a periwinkle sky, the swifts swooping in and out of the eaves of the house, the scent of lilies of the valley in a nearby bed and the pink blossom on the cherry tree.

She'd always loved this time of year with its promise of summer just around the corner and colour returning to the bleak greys of winter; this year it held a special poignancy. Perhaps she would never live to see another spring, but oh, she was making the most of this one. Strange how a sentence of death sharpened the senses, made everything brighter and clearer than ever before.

She lifted the glass of stout Spike had placed on the table at her elbow, sipping the strong dark liquor through the thick band of white foam, glad that she could still enjoy her favourite drink, though food tasted like nothing more than soggy cardboard.

'Must you?' They'd talked so much over the last months, serious conversations about her illness and the future, and from Spike's expression and the way he was downing his glass of whisky, she suspected that whatever he wanted to talk to her about now was just more of the same. She didn't want that. Didn't want to be reminded of the inevitable. Just wanted to enjoy the peace of the evening.

Spike twisted the whisky tumbler between his hands.

'Sorry, love, but yeah. It's important. I got a phone call this afternoon while you was having your nap.'

'I didn't hear it ring.'

'Well, you wouldn't, would you, seeing as 'ow you were fast asleep. It was Kitty.'

'Kitty?' Molly's eyes sharpened with alarm. Kitty suffered from a weak heart, the result of having a bad bout of rheumatic fever as a child. 'Is she all right?'

'Yeah, she's fine. She had something to tell me – well, to tell you, really, but she was leaving it up to me to decide whether to or not . . .'

'Daniel, you're making no sense at all. For goodness' sake get to the point!'

'All right then.'

He told her. She listened, still as a statue, the glass of stout clasped between her hands part of the tableau. Even when he fell silent she said nothing, her eyes fixed on a clump of purple crocuses in the middle of the lawn.

'Molly?' he said anxiously.

Her eyes flicked up to meet his.

'I'm not sure I can go through all that again.'

'That's what Kitty wondered. After that bastard Jake whatever his name was. But I thought it was only right to tell you. Give you the last word.'

'Does Kitty believe this is genuine? Not just another chancer?'

Spike nodded. 'She thinks so, yes. It would seem he's spent his adult life looking for you. But it's up to you, love. According to Kitty, he doesn't even know that this Laurel was going to speak to her.'

'What do you think?'

'I'm not saying anything one way or the other. It's got to be your decision, love.'

Molly slowly raised the glass to her lips and took another pull of stout. As she had said, she wasn't sure she had the strength to face the roller coaster of hope and disappointment again; she remembered all too clearly how the joy and delight had turned to dismay as she had realised she didn't actually like the young man who had professed to be her son, and the sheer horror of what had followed. But perhaps this time the claim was genuine and this was indeed the baby she had never thought to see again, grown now to manhood. Her heart had been broken when she had been forced to give him up and had never healed.

'Let me think about it,' she said.

But she already knew what her decision would be. If there was the slightest chance that she could meet her long-lost son before the illness claimed her, then she would take it.

Laurel returned to work at Hillview the following day, having satisfied herself that both Minty and her father were fit to be left. She arrived just before midday and Maggie was waiting to greet her.

'There was a telephone call for you,' she said when she had

enquired after the well-being of Laurel's family. 'It was Kitty Day as was – the minister's wife. She wouldn't leave a message but asked if you could call her back. The number's on the pad beside the phone.'

A prickle of anticipation tingled in Laurel's veins.

'Oh, thanks,' she said, striving to sound casual. Maggie was bound to be curious as to what the minister's wife wanted her for, but it wouldn't be right to tell her when David himself didn't know anything about this.

As soon as Maggie had left for her studio, she crossed to the dresser, found Kitty's number and lifted the heavy telephone receiver. She was shaking inwardly now, almost afraid of what Kitty was going to say, and as the lines clunked as the connection was made, she found herself hoping that the woman in whose cottage the Hillsbridge and High Compton telephone exchange was housed wouldn't be listening in. She had something of a reputation for doing just that if a call interested her. Hopefully she would think this was nothing more than business.

It seemed to Laurel that the bell at the other end of the line was ringing endlessly – perhaps both Kitty and her husband were out. Ministers usually took Mondays off after their busy day on Sunday. But just as she was about to give up and ring off, the phone was answered, and it was Kitty herself, sounding a little breathless.

'I'm sorry. We were out in the garden. I rang earlier, but you weren't there, and you did ask me only to speak to you.'

'Yes. But I didn't expect you to get back to me quite so quickly.'

'To be honest, I think time is of the essence. I spoke to Daniel yesterday – that's Aunt Molly's husband – and he called me back this morning. Aunt Molly would very much like to meet . . . David, is it?'

'David. Yes. Oh, that is good news!'

'I don't know what you were planning, but Daniel suggested bringing her out to you. Tomorrow, if the weather is fine and she's well enough.'

'Is she fit for that?' Laurel hadn't thought beyond contacting Molly.

'It seems she likes to go for a ride in the motor when she can,' Kitty said. 'Would the afternoon be suitable?'

'Yes . . . I should think so.' Laurel was becoming a little flustered.

'If you could give me directions, I'll pass them on.'

Laurel did so.

As she replaced the receiver, she realised she was shaking. She couldn't believe she'd actually achieved her objective and she was a little frightened now at the thought of what she'd done.

She'd have to confess to David; she couldn't have Molly turning up when he knew nothing about it.

Full of trepidation, she hoisted John onto her hip and crossed the yard to his workshop.

She'd astonished him, no doubt about that. But to her relief he wasn't angry with her. In fact he showed no emotion at all. But that was David all over. He'd learned long ago to keep his feelings under wraps, and really she had no idea what he was thinking.

'I'm sorry if I overstepped the mark,' she said, 'but I know how I would feel if I was Molly. And since you devoted so much of your life to searching for her, I reckon you must have wanted to find her very much once, even if you've had second thoughts since.'

He looked up at her, an almost unreadable expression in his eyes.

'I just hope she won't be disappointed in me,' he said.

'Oh, David . . . of course she won't be disappointed. She'll be proud of you,' she said, and added: 'Just as I am.'

His mouth twisted in a lopsided smile.

'Thank God for you, Laurel,' he said.


The story was front-page news in the *Evening Chronicle*. 'GYPSY GIRL IN KNIFE ATTACK ON HIGH COMPTON FAMILY', the headline shouted. Beneath it was a photograph of Kezia, glaring sullenly into the camera.

The *Chronicle* had a wide circulation locally, and next day the story was taken up in the nationals.

'Oh, the shame of it!' Minty wailed.

'Don't worry, m'dear, it'll be a nine-days wonder and soon forgotten,' Ezra said.

But the publicity was to have repercussions that none of them could have anticipated.

# Chapter Thirty-Two

Inspector Turner of Bath CID was cock-a-hoop. His career was certainly going to end on a high note, something to remember as he enjoyed his retirement. Not only had he apprehended the girl who had carried out the scurrilous attack on the High Compton family, he had also solved the murder that had defeated him all those years ago.

Following the newspaper coverage, the gentleman who had been the only credible witness in the case of the stabbing of Edgar Sawyer had come forward – he had recognised the scowling girl in the photograph as the one he had seen in Queen Square on the evening of the murder. The inspector had arranged for an identity parade, and the witness had picked her out without hesitation.

Now Turner sat in the small, dark interview room in the bowels of the police station with his sergeant on his right and the girl – Kezia Smith – facing him across the pockmarked table.

'You might as well come clean,' he told her. 'You've been identified as having been seen outside the victim's office, and the knife you threatened that family with fits the type of wounds inflicted. It was you, wasn't it?'

Today Kezia was a very different girl to the tearful one who had been arrested on the night of the attack on Minty and

Rowan. Now defiance shone in the dark green eyes, and the pointed jaw was set so tight the tendons in her neck stood out.

'So what if it was? He asked for it.'

'In what way?'

'I was looking for her – Laurel feckin' Sykes. She worked for him. But it was him came down the stairs, wanted to know my business, and when I told him, he grabbed hold of me. Said he was calling the rozzers.' A satisfied smirk twisted her mouth. 'Took him by surprise, I did. He never expected that from a girl. I'm only sorry it wasn't her. She has to pay, one way or another.'

'Pay for what?'

'I told you before. Her feckin' mother killed my brother and buried him in the garden under the feckin' beans. I saw her do it.'

'Bury him under the beans?'

'No – beat him to death. But the bean trench was there, already dug. That's where you'll find him.'

'Miss Smith, your brother is not dead. Miss Sykes received a letter from him postmarked after you claim her mother murdered him.'

'She's lying.'

'I've seen the letter for myself.'

'He's under the beans, I tell you.'

'Very well, I'll have my officers investigate the site.' He had no choice, really, he thought; though he was certain nothing would be found, he didn't want her defence bringing it up at her trial. 'But for now I have to tell you that you are charged that on the evening of . . .'

Yes, Inspector Turner thought as Kezia Smith was led away back to the cells, a very satisfactory outcome. And a fitting end to a long and successful career.

\* \* \*

The motor drew into the broad yard that fronted Hillview at just after three. Laurel, watching from the window, scooped John up on her hip and went out to greet them – David might not have heard the motor's approach if he had the presses running.

'You found it! I'm so glad! I'll tell David you're here.'

'Give her a minute to catch her breath.' Spike had turned off the engine and was making his way around to Molly's side of the motor. 'Are you all right, m'dear? Feeling up to this?' He was obviously all concern for her welfare.

'I'm fine.' Molly was folding the rug that had covered her knees. 'And I am so grateful to you,' she said to Laurel. 'You don't know what this means to me. If David really is my son . . .' She closed her eyes briefly, blinking back sudden tears.

Since Spike had told her of Kitty's phone call and she had agreed to meet David, her mood had swung from wild elation to trepidation that everything would go horribly wrong, as it had done when Lucy had introduced her to that charlatan Jake Harper. Now she was breathless with the same cocktail of anticipation and dread, so potent that it disguised for the time being at least that niggling pain deep inside that never left her, the pain that she knew could only grow worse until the last of her strength ebbed away and her tortured body at last found peace.

In her mind's eye she saw the baby who had been placed in her arms, perfect but for a scarlet birthmark on his foot – it had been the absence of this that had alerted Lucy to the fact that Jake was not who he said he was. The soft baby scent of him was in her nostrils, the peachy feel of his skin imprinted on her fingertips. And the agony when they had taken him away from her. They'd had to prise him from her arms, Daniel and that fat, greasy-looking woman who was to be his wet nurse. She had struggled up from her bed and felt that her heart was being wrenched from her body as she watched from the window. David, her darling son, in the arms of that awful woman, wrapped not in the shawl she had crocheted for him during the long months of her confinement, but in a blue blanket that must have been provided by the family who were adopting him. One last gut-wrenching glimpse of him and then the carriage door closing. Disappearing down the drive in a cloud of dust . . .

Was it really possible she was going to be with him again at last? Was it possible she would hold him in her arms again, a baby no longer but a grown man? It was incredible to her; she was afraid to believe it.

Spike opened the door of the motor, stepping close to help her down, his concern for her evident in every caring gesture, every anxious furrow in his face.

'All right, my love? Just lean on me and take it steady . . .'

It was clear to Laurel that Molly would not have the strength to remain standing for very long, and there was nothing to sit on in David's workshop.

'Come into the kitchen,' she said, holding the door open.

Leaning heavily on Spike, Molly did as she was told, and seated herself on one of the upright dining chairs.

'Can I get you a cup of tea?' Laurel asked, and Molly shook her head.

'No thank you. Just . . .'

David. Of course.

'I'll fetch him,' Laurel said.

Molly glanced just once at Spike, a quick, nervous movement. Then her eyes fixed firmly on the door. Her hands were clasped together tightly in her lap; it seemed to her she held the whole of her life encapsulated between her palms in this single moment.

The door opened. He stood there, silhouetted against the bright April sunlight, and she knew without a shadow of doubt.

This was David. He was physically so like Anthony, the lover who had betrayed her. The fair hair. The fine features. Yet she knew instinctively that in character he was nothing like Anthony at all. The eyes were kinder; the hesitance as he stood there in no way resembled Anthony's self-confident charm. But it was more than the fact that his physical appearance left no room for doubt. The rush of warmth she felt was pure maternal love, and the joy that lifted her heart left her momentarily speechless.

She levered herself up from her chair and took an unsteady step towards him. He came to her and she took him in her arms, burying her face in his chest, and in that moment all the years of longing became as nothing.

Her son had come back to her. As long as there was breath in her body she would never let him go again.

Kezia Smith stood in the dock at the magistrates' court, oblivious to her family and others from the travelling community who took up much of the public gallery, a small, still-defiant figure, listening as the charges against her were read out.

'Do you plead guilty or not guilty?'

She lifted her chin.

'Guilty – but not as guilty as that feckin' bitch Sykes!'

'Hold your tongue!' The chairman of the bench was glaring at her. But Kezia was not looking at him.

A movement at the back of the courtroom had caught her eye – a tall, dark figure entering the public gallery, standing on the steps. She clutched at the rail of the dock, her defiantly ugly expression transformed into one of astonishment and disbelief.

A single word left her lips, no more than a whisper.

'Callum!'

Then everything was becoming a blur, the voice of the magistrate lost in a roaring in her ears. As he started towards the dock, and the court usher rushed forward to restrain him, darkness seemed to close in from the edges of Kezia's consciousness. For the first and only time in her life, she slid almost gracefully to the floor in a dead faint.

Somehow Callum managed to shake himself free of the usher and push past him. He'd have socked the man on the jaw if he'd had to, but that wasn't necessary. He reached the dock just as Kezia was hoisted up onto the hard chair and her head pushed down between her knees by a burly uniformed policeman.

'Kezia?' His hands gripped the wooden rail; his sea-green eyes blazed.

The usher and another policeman reached him, taking an arm apiece and thrusting them behind his back.

'I'm here, Shaver.' His voice rang out above the hubbub that had broken out. 'I'm here for you!'

He wasn't sure whether or not she'd heard him, but she must have done; as he was bundled out, she called after him weakly: 'Callum! Don't leave me!'

He jerked his head round, straining against the arms that held him fast, and yelled back: 'Don't worry, Shaver, I won't. I'll never leave you again.'

It had taken a day or two for the Irish press to pick up the story of the attack on the Sykes family and carry it, but the Smiths had their roots in Ireland, so, in a quiet week, they had deemed it newsworthy.

Callum had seen it in a newspaper left behind by another customer in a greasy spoon where he and a couple of pals had stopped for breakfast, and it had shocked him to the core. Though she was no longer the child he'd left behind on the other side of the Irish Sea all those years ago, he recognised her at once from the photograph, and had he been in any doubt, the report below confirmed it. Armed with a knife, Kezia had broken into the Sykeses' home. Three people had been wounded – Mrs Sykes, her daughter Rowan, and a youth whose name Callum didn't recognise. Mrs Sykes's elder daughter, Laurel, had also been in the house, but according to the report had escaped injury. Kezia Smith had been arrested and was in custody at Bath police station.

The newsprint swam before Callum's eyes; his thoughts were racing. Why had she done such a thing? How had she even known where to find Laurel and her family? And the younger girl – Rowan. She might be reported as being Mrs Sykes's daughter, but Callum knew different, and his stomach clenched at the thought of what might have happened to her.

Rowan Sykes. Not Minty's child at all, but Laurel's – and his. The daughter he'd never known existed until she was five years old and it was too late for him to take responsibility for her.

He'd tried, b'Jesus, he'd tried. He'd been mortified when he'd run into Laurel's old friend back in Yorkshire and she'd told him what had happened. That when he'd run off after the fight with his father, he'd left Laurel pregnant; that the family had moved to Somerset, and Minty and Ezra were raising the child as their own. Though she couldn't remember the exact address off the top of her head, the friend was able to tell him that the town was High Compton, and that at least was something. Callum knew it – the fair went there for a couple of days every April – and he'd made up his mind that next time it did, he would find Laurel and his child, make amends as best he could.

He'd made no progress when, on the Saturday afternoon, he had spotted Ezra Sykes and a little girl in the crowd waiting to board the switchback. Though he'd only seen him the once before, Callum recognised him immediately. And the girl was just about the right age to be his own daughter. He could hardly believe his luck, but at virtually the same moment Ezra must have seen him too; he'd turned and hurried away, hoisting the child onto his shoulders. Callum had abandoned his post, leapt down from the ride and followed them. But once he'd seen they'd reached their destination, he'd decided against confronting them immediately. He didn't want to frighten Rowan. Better to go back later in the evening, when she would be in bed and asleep.

But nothing had worked out as he'd intended. When he'd knocked at the door of the house in Fairley Terrace that night, he'd met with an onslaught of aggression. Ezra had told him that Laurel wasn't there, and he'd better make himself scarce; Minty, in a fury, had yelled at him to stay away from them, and when he'd tried to argue, had attacked him with the fire irons, hitting him so hard and so unexpectedly that he lost his balance and fell. His head was badly cut and bruised, his pride was dented, but most of all he was sick at heart. He'd never stopped caring for Laurel; of all the girls he'd known before and since, no one had come close to the way he'd felt about her. She was etched in his memory and in his heart, a lovely laughing girl, his first love, forever sweet fifteen.

In the morass of churning love and loss Callum had known he had to get right away. The guilt that he'd abandoned Laurel when she had needed him most was a dark cloud that threatened to engulf him; the anguish that came from being denied the chance to see her, meet his child, wrenched his gut.

He'd fled in an effort to leave it all behind him; taken the ferry to Ireland, joined up with kinfolk there, with never so much as a goodbye to his parents or, more importantly, the little sister who adored him.

In the intervening years he'd thought about them often, but always pushed the memories and the feelings they evoked to one side, losing himself in his new life.

Now the regret and the guilt were there again, suffocating him. Horrified at the awful events his sudden departure had precipitated, he had taken the first boat he could get over to England.

This was all his fault. Once again he had failed those he should have protected. He couldn't understand why Kezia had done what she'd done, it made no sense, but it was clear she'd inherited his father's violent streak and perhaps the madness that he thought might run alongside it too. She'd been devastated when he'd disappeared without a word to any of them and for some reason she had blamed Laurel. She knew how much Laurel meant to him, and was dangerously jealous. Now she'd done this awful thing and was in desperate trouble, and he'd known he had to go to her.

The usher and policeman were dragging him out of the courtroom, his father was on his feet, yelling, and his mother looked as if, like Kezia, she might be about to faint. He'd have to deal with them later, try to explain why he'd taken off without a single goodbye, but for the moment he could think of nothing but his little sister. Burning with anger fuelled by guilt and a sense of utter helplessness, Callum glanced over his shoulder and shouted one last time:

'I'm here now, Shaver! I promise I won't leave you again!'

'Oh, David, I'm so happy for you!' Maggie said. 'It's wonderful that you've been reunited with your mother after all these years.'

'It's all thanks to Laurel.'

They were at supper; his eyes met Laurel's across the table, full of gratitude – and more. Warmth. Love.

449

Laurel's cheeks flushed pink, a reflection of the glow within.

'I'm just glad it worked out,' she said. 'If it hadn't, I'd have felt terrible for interfering.'

'You did the right thing,' Maggie said. 'Anyone could see how happy it's made her. You know what she said to me as they were leaving? "Now I can die content."'

'I only wish now that I'd had the courage to contact her when I found out who she was,' David said. 'I'll never forgive myself for all the wasted time.'

'It's no use thinking of the what-ifs now.' Maggie got up to get hot water to refresh the teapot. 'At least you have one another for however long she has left. You must go and see her often.'

'Actually . . .' David forked a pickled onion round his plate, 'she has suggested I should stay with her and Daniel for a while, to give us the chance to get to know one another properly.'

'Then you must go!' Maggie was pouring boiling water into the pot.

'I've got a couple of printing jobs to finish first . . .'

'Hang the printing jobs!' Maggie banged the lid back on the teapot so hard that it rattled on its trivet.

'I can't let customers down. There are programmes for the male-voice choir concert at the town hall next week, and tickets for the Women's Temperance League bazaar. But I can get them finished in a day or so – I'm going back to get on with it as soon as we've finished eating. Everything else will have to wait.'

'I should think so too!'

'Is there anything I can do to help?' Laurel asked.

'Well . . . yes, actually. It would save me time if you could box them up for me.'

'Of course I will.'

'And Patrick can deliver them on his bicycle,' Josh added.

'That's settled then,' Maggie said, pulling the tea cosy over the pot.

Laurel met David's eyes and smiled. She would miss him more than she could say, but she could not for a moment begrudge him this time spent with the mother he had only just found and would lose again far too soon.

He'd be back. She would be waiting. And they had the rest of their lives to build on their budding relationship. Laurel knew she could ask for nothing more.

# Chapter Thirty-Three

The magistrates had referred Kezia's case to the next assize in Bristol, and until then she was being held in custody. Callum had only been aware of the attack on the Sykes family – the report he'd read in the Irish newspaper had been published too early to include the charge of Edgar Sawyer's murder, and this new development had come as a shocking blow. Before he learned of it, he'd thought she might get off with a reasonably light sentence; he'd even planned to take her back to Ireland with him if she agreed. Now he realised she was in far more serious trouble than he'd thought.

She could hang for what she'd done, b'Jesus! Her only hope was a good lawyer to plead her case and a lenient judge who took into account her age when she'd stabbed the man. But he had no money to pay for good lawyers, and when was a judge ever lenient towards gyppos? At best she was going down for a very long time; maybe they'd even commit her to a lunatic asylum, and once there, she'd never get out again.

Just to make matters worse, if such a thing were possible, his family were blaming him for what had happened.

After being thrown out of the magistrates' court he'd waited for them in the street outside, and when they emerged, his mother had flown at him, beating at his chest with her fists.

'This is all your fault!' she'd screamed, her face so close to his that flecks of spittle had splattered his chin. 'Why did you go off like that without a word? She thought you were feckin' dead! That that woman had killed you!'

'I'm sorry, Ma.' What else could he say? This wasn't the time or the place to explain, and in any case, it was no excuse. She was right. It was his fault.

'Sorry? Sorry? Is that all you can feckin' say?' She turned away in disgust.

Beyond glaring at him, his lip curled into an ugly snarl, and shaking his head as a warning to stay clear, Da had ignored him as if he weren't there. He stood in a tight knot with the other travellers who'd attended the hearing, discussing what could be done next, which in fact was very little. The fair had been set up in the Victoria Park for the last few days; they should have left yesterday, and had already been told in no uncertain terms by the park officials to move on; in any case, they were due at a mop in Gloucestershire at the weekend.

Curly Farrell, who ran the boxing booth, approached Callum.

'You comin' with us?' He, at least, spoke civilly enough; he and Callum had been good friends once upon a time.

Callum shook his head. Clearly he would not be welcome in his parents' caravan, and in any case he wanted to stay as close to Kezia as he could. He'd promised he wouldn't leave her again, and he intended to keep his promise. Whether or not he'd be allowed to see her he didn't know, and what he could do to help her was even more of a conundrum. But he'd find a way somehow. He'd let her down once; he wasn't going to let that happen again.

'Naw – I'm gonna stay here,' he said.

'Come on, you lot, move along!' It was the burly policeman who, with the usher, had frogmarched him out of the court.

Grumbling, swearing, the fair folk started off along the street; Callum remained where he was.

'You too, Sonny Jim. We don't want any trouble here.'

'Sod you,' Callum said.

He took one last look at his departing family and set off in the opposite direction.

'Oh, David, I can't believe you're really here,' Molly said.

It was a warm evening, the sun low and rosy between the trees in her garden. Sitting in her favourite chair, a glass of stout on the table beside her and David in a matching chair nearby, she had never felt more contented. Her days might be numbered, but this wonderful thing that she'd doubted would ever come to pass was a reality.

As good as his word, when he had finished his urgent work, David had packed a bag and gone to Bath to spend a week with her. They'd talked for hours on end; there was so much to say and so little time to say it. Molly had explained the circumstances that had forced her to give him up. She'd told him of the lover who had abandoned her the moment he knew she was pregnant – 'He was a titled gentleman,' she'd said. 'Believe it or not, there's blue blood in your veins!' – and the adoption Spike had arranged.

'Giving you up was the hardest thing I've ever had to do,' she said, 'but I told myself Daniel was right. I was in no position to bring you up myself, and I thought at least with your adoptive parents you'd have a secure and happy home. That you'd want for nothing. Unfortunately, as you know to your cost, it didn't work out that way. Can you ever forgive me?'

'There's nothing to forgive,' David said. 'You did what you thought was best. You mustn't blame yourself for what happened afterwards.'

Molly closed her eyes briefly at the remembered agony, then turned to him, desperate to make her position clear even though he seemed to understand.

'If only I'd known your adoptive mother had turned against you . . . that your father had sent you to a baby farm . . . I'd have come for you. I'd have found a way to manage somehow. But I didn't know. Daniel only told me what had happened long afterwards. He'd done his best to trace you when he learned the truth, but it was no use. You were long gone . . .' She broke off, her eyes filling with tears. 'And I never knew that all that while *you* wanted to find *me*,' she went on after a moment. 'That you spent so many years searching . . . I am so, so sorry . . .'

'It doesn't matter. I'm here now. And I wish I'd made myself known to you as soon as I managed to discover your where-abouts. But I thought I might be throwing all kinds of spanners into the works. That you wouldn't want me turning up out of the blue.'

She reached for his hand. 'How could you think that? Never a day passed that I didn't think about you. And I never stopped loving you. Never, for a single moment. You must believe me.'

'I do.' It was no more than the truth. He believed her absolutely.

The conversations sometimes went on long into the night, and Daniel was concerned that they would over-tire Molly, but for the first few days she seemed reinvigorated, buoyed up by a happiness that had come just when she least expected it. This evening, though, both he and David could see it was taking its toll on her.

He was hovering beside her chair now.

'I reckon you ought to have an early night, Moll. David will still be here tomorrow, won't you, my son?'

'I certainly will. Daniel is right. You need to rest.'

'Soon, I promise.' She turned to David. 'But first there's something I want you to have.'

She began to struggle up out of her chair; instantly Spike was at her side.

'What is it, Moll? You stay there. I'll get it for you, whatever it is.'

She sank back and caught at his jacket, tugging on it until his ear was close to her lips. Spike nodded, smiling faintly, as she whispered to him.

'You know where it is?' she asked anxiously.

'Yeah, I know.'

He straightened, went off towards the house. A few minutes later he was back with a flat package wrapped in tissue paper, and laid it on Molly's lap. She turned to David, handing him the package.

'I made this for you. I know it's thirty-odd years too late for what it was intended, but I'd like you to have it.'

Puzzled, David carefully unfolded the tissue paper, brittle now with age, to reveal a fine lacy shawl, a little yellowed, but every stitch still holding the intricate pattern Molly had crocheted. Hours of work had gone into it in the weeks leading up to his birth. Distraught as she had been at the prospect of giving him up for adoption, she had desperately wanted him to have something of his own to take with him, something that would show him how much he had been loved by his birth mother. But when the wet nurse had taken him from her arms, she'd wrapped him in the blue blanket she had brought with her, and the shawl had lain rejected on the bed. Molly had been hurt, so hurt. The adoptive parents didn't want him to have anything from his previous life. From this moment on, he would be theirs and theirs alone.

When she'd left the house where she'd seen out the last

weeks of her confinement and given birth, she'd taken the shawl with her, the only reminder she had of her beloved baby. For years now, ever since she had moved in with Spike prior to marrying him, it had remained in a drawer in the room that housed all her old stage costumes. Lucy, her niece, had found it there when she was looking for something suitable to wear for her own stage debut, and at the time it had upset Molly dreadfully. Now, though, all the long years of pining for her lost son were over. And she wanted to give the shawl to David while she was still able.

'You made this, you say?' he asked now, almost afraid to touch the delicate weave in case he damaged it.

She nodded.

'It's beautiful,' he said.

Molly laughed, a small, brittle intake of breath.

'I know it's no good to you now, but maybe one day you'll have a son or daughter of your own. I'd like to think my grandchild might use it . . .'

'Thank you. So much.' A wave of emotion caught the words in his throat.

'My pleasure,' she said. Tears were sparkling in her eyes too.

'Right.' Spike moved towards her decisively. 'Now I'm having my way. It's time you went to bed.'

He helped her to her feet, supported her to the path.

In the doorway of the house she turned, looking over her shoulder. David was still holding the shawl, looking at it in wonder and awe.

She smiled at Spike.

'At last it's where it belongs,' she said.

The one-time parlour had been turned into a bedroom so she didn't have to use the stairs. Content, she allowed him to help her towards it.

\* \* \*

As the train to Bath pulled into Hillsbridge station, Rowan spotted Patrick on the platform and waved as he walked towards her carriage. He climbed in, stowed his briefcase on the rack and sat down beside her, reaching for her hand as soon as the train began to move. She smiled at him, loving the feel of his fingers intertwined with hers.

The very first time he'd held her hand, she'd been so afraid that if she moved, he would think she was rejecting him. Now, though, her confidence had grown. Not only did she not have to worry that someone would see, she was no longer tormented with doubts about whether he liked her. She knew he did, though she couldn't imagine it was as much as she liked him; couldn't imagine a boy could ever feel quite as she did. Her heart skipping a beat whenever she saw him – surely that didn't happen to a boy. Or the glow of happiness that suffused her whole body when he kissed her. Or the way she couldn't stop thinking about him. He was there in her thoughts all day; even if she was concentrating on a lesson he was still there, not a thought exactly, but a feeling of bubbling joy.

She loved too that they could talk about anything and everything.

'It must be really strange finding out your sister is your mother,' he'd said.

'It was, to begin with. But I'm getting used to it now. In a funny sort of way, nothing has really changed, except I can see now why she's always been there for me. I'm lucky if you think about it. It's like I have two mothers instead of just one.'

It was true. That was exactly how it felt to her. In many ways life had gone on just as it always had, but now she felt the special bond she and Laurel had always shared in a way she never had before.

The balance of power in the family had shifted subtly, too, and though still irascible, Minty seemed lighter somehow, as though a weight had been lifted from her shoulders.

It wasn't possible to keep the secret any longer; it would all come out in court. Hester Dallimore had had a field day, of course, gossiping to anyone who would listen and pretending outrage. But the other neighbours had been kind, Dolly Oglethorpe in particular.

'There's none of us fit to throw the first stone,' she'd said when Hester had buttonholed her, and Hester's lips had tightened.

'Speak for yourself.'

That would hit home, she knew. There was something very fishy going on with Dolly's son Charlie, who had suddenly arrived back home, supposedly married, with two children nobody knew he had. To her chagrin, Hester had not managed to get to the bottom of it yet. But at least *she* could hold her head up high. There were no skeletons rattling in *her* cupboard, thank the Lord.

Dolly had gone out of her way to nod and smile at Minty and offer her support.

'You've had a terrible time of it,' she'd said. 'You know where we are, don't you, if we can do anything to help.'

May Cooper, too, had tried to be friendly, though neither of them mentioned the family situation that was the talk of the rank.

Minty hadn't accepted their offers of help – it would have been too much to break the habits of a lifetime – and she'd shrunk inwardly to think she was the object of pity. But some-how, almost imperceptibly, she had softened, the hard shell she had erected around herself developing minute fissures, like the cracks in the ice on a frozen pond when the sun warmed it, so that something of the old Minty showed through. The Minty

Ezra had fallen in love with and married, the Minty Laurel remembered from when she was a child, before her world had caved in. Strict, yes, convinced that she and only she knew best, yes, but selfless too. Stoic, not bitter. A woman who would take up arms and fight to the death for her family.

That had been her motivation for doing what she had done. She'd preserved a veneer of respectability, but doing so had eaten away at her like corrosive acid. Resentment that she'd had to raise another child when she should have been able to take things a bit easier had come together with shame and disappointment to colour her outlook, and on top of all that, the fear that she had lived with for fifteen years that one day the truth would come out. Now that it had, now that the worst had happened, instead of being mortified she felt like a bird let out of a cage, and it showed.

Rowan didn't understand any of this. She only knew that something had changed for the better, and not only Minty's opinion of Patrick, forced upon her by his timely intervention when they had been threatened by Kezia Smith. She had even suggested he might like to come for his tea on Sunday!

Now, as the train slid between embankments of coal dust and wide green fields, Rowan turned to him and smiled.

'What?' he asked.

'Nothing.'

But the warmth around her heart was spreading, sending little jolts of happiness into her veins.

Really, it wasn't nothing at all.

The solicitor's office was at the top of a flight of steep stairs beyond a door with a brass plate screwed to the wall beside it. Callum took the stairs two at a time, his lithe, muscled legs working like pistons. At the top, a slightly built man with mutton-chop whiskers dominating a narrow face and receding chin stood barring his way. He looked anxious, as well he might. He'd hurried out when he'd heard the thunderous footsteps on the stairs, and he didn't like what he saw one little bit. Fotheringay and Nettles was a well-established and highly respected firm dealing mainly with will writing, probate and conveyancing, and when the occasional criminal case came their way it was generally embezzlement or fraud, committed by some hitherto respectable professional gentleman, or being caught for indecency, public or otherwise – and homosexuality was a crime Malcolm Carruthers, the firm's long-standing clerk, had every sympathy with.

This young man, however, was quite a different matter. If anything he looked like the type who would happily use his fists or his boots on any hapless pair of would-be offenders if he saw them disappearing into the bushes in the park.

Taking his courage in both hands, Carruthers confronted the newcomer.

'May I help you?'

'Are you the solicitor?' The brogue, which had grown stronger over the years he had lived in Ireland, was almost as intimidating as the man himself.

'No, sir, I am his clerk.'

'Well, I want to see the organ grinder, not the monkey.'

Malcolm Carruthers flushed, but stood his ground.

'And do you have an appointment, sir?'

'Naw, I feckin' well don't. But I want to see him anyway. Are you going to try to stop me?'

'What's going on here?'

Another man appeared in the doorway behind the hapless clerk, a big man with a gold watch chain straining across a rounded belly.

'This *gentleman* wants to see you, Mr Nettles. I am explaining that that is not possible without an appointment.'

'An' I'm asking who he is to stop me.'

'It's all right, Carruthers, you can leave this to me.'

'But, sir . . .'

'It's true I don't usually see clients without an appointment, but I have a few minutes free and in this case I am willing to make an exception.'

Unbeknown to either Callum or the clerk, Simon Nettles had recognised Callum. He had been in the magistrates' court on the day of Kezia's appearance, defending a client on a charge of buggery, and witnessed both Callum's entrance and his unceremonious eviction. The girl in the dock was charged with murder and unlawful wounding, along with other offences. And now the brother was here, in his office. If he could provide legal assistance, it would be by far the most interesting and high-profile case he'd handled in years.

The door to the inner sanctum was ajar; Simon Nettles pushed it wide and stood to one side, motioning Callum to enter. Then he crossed to the captain's chair behind the big leather-tooled desk and indicated that Callum should take the upright chair facing him.

Callum's eyes roved for a moment over the array of legal books on the shelves now facing him, and the stacks of cardboard folders tied with pink tape that towered on the floor beneath them. Then he fixed his startlingly green-eyed gaze on the solicitor.

'My sister's in serious trouble,' he said bluntly.

Although he was already aware of the building blocks of the charges Kezia Smith faced, Simon Nettles heard Callum out, asking the occasional question and making notes on a pad with an expensive-looking fountain pen. At last he steepled his fingers, resting his chin on them and looking Callum directly in the eye.

'A trial at assize or quarter sessions calls for representation by a barrister,' he said.

'You mean you can't feckin' do it?' Callum snarled.

'I would, of course, attend if you so wished. A barrister, however, is equipped to argue your sister's defence in a way I am not. But a good man doesn't come cheap – and, incidentally, neither do I. If you don't have the wherewithal to meet the fees, then I suggest—'

'I do,' Callum interrupted. He opened his coat, drew a wad of notes from an inside pocket and placed it on the desk between himself and the solicitor. 'If that's not enough, I can get more.'

Simon Nettles' eyes widened slightly, and Callum knew he was wondering how an Irish tinker had got together so much money. Well, let him wonder. Callum certainly wasn't going to enlighten him. He wasn't a thief by nature; most of his life he'd got by on what he'd earned honestly. But desperate situations called for desperate measures, and he'd spent the last few nights relieving some well-off townsfolk of their assets.

To his amazement, the solicitor pushed the wad of notes back towards him.

'I don't deal in cash, Mr Smith. You will receive my bill in due course. But perhaps a proportion on account would be acceptable? My clerk will take a down payment from you and issue you with a receipt.'

He drew a handkerchief, neatly pressed white cotton, from his pocket and wiped his hands carefully as if he feared contamination.

'My clerk will also make a further appointment for you to come back and see me,' he went on. 'In the meantime, I will make arrangements with someone qualified to argue the defence.

He will then want to talk to you, and most importantly, to your sister.'

'But she's in jug!' Callum objected.

'And her legal representative will be given leave to interview her there. I trust this is all to your satisfaction?'

Callum nodded and rose from the chair. He couldn't wait to get out of the solicitor's office. Everything about it was making him feel claustrophobic, as if the walls covered with dusty legal tomes were closing in to suffocate him. But he'd had to do this for Kezia.

How much worse must it be for her, locked up in a prison cell from which there was no escape, when, like him, she was used to fresh air and the freedom of the open road? He had to get her out of that place, and he would do whatever it took. Even without the crushing guilt that came from knowing this was all his fault, he would have done whatever was necessary. Kezia was, after all, his kid sister.

The city of Bath was abuzz with the gossip. Ralph Riley, the highly respected homeopathic doctor, had been caught in flagrante with a lady of the night. His wife had left him; it was whispered that she was to divorce him. The scandal would, of course, ruin him.

Spike was not a vengeful man, but when he heard of it, he felt nothing but quiet satisfaction. The man was a charlatan who'd finally got his comeuppance. Little did he know that a great many of Ralph's former patients shared his sentiments.

# Chapter Thirty-Four

The telephone call came late one night, six weeks later, while Maggie was giving John his last feed. Laurel was with her, the two women chatting over cups of hot chocolate and enjoying one another's company in the peace that followed the rigours of a busy day.

The insistent ring of the telephone bell in the quiet kitchen startled them both. In the normal course of events, no one called this late in the day.

John was still at Maggie's breast, sucking hungrily. He'd grown so much in the last months, he was now quite an armful, and heavy to juggle.

'Could you . . . ?' Maggie looked at Laurel.

'Course.'

She rose and crossed to the dresser. Already she had a bad feeling about this. The telephone was almost exclusively used for business; offices would be closed now, and no one would want to disturb them at this hour to talk about private commissions. She lifted the heavy receiver, taut with apprehension.

'Hello? Hillview Enterprises?'

'Who's that?'

She recognised the voice at the other end of the line at once, the cockney accent discernible even in those two little words.

'Mr Trotter?' she said. 'It's Laurel here. Did you want David?'

'I did. Yeah.'

She glanced out of the kitchen window. A lamp was burning in the workshop, light spilling out into the darkness of the courtyard. 'I think he's still working. I'll fetch him for you.'

These days David often worked long into the night so that he could take time off to visit Molly in Bath.

'It's all right. Just give him a message for me, will you? Moll's taken a turn for the worse and I don't want to leave her any longer than I can help. Tell David, and tell him I reckon he ought to come quick sharp if he wants to see her again.'

Laurel's heart dropped like a stone. She knew Molly's condition was worsening. She could no longer leave her bed, and in Laurel's opinion should be in hospital. But she hadn't wanted that and neither had Spike. He'd engaged the services of three nurses to care for her in shifts around the clock and scarcely left her bedside himself. But despite all evidence to the contrary, David had remained stubbornly optimistic that he might still have weeks, if not months, to spend with the mother he had only recently found.

Now Laurel dreaded having to tell him that Spike clearly thought the end was imminent.

'I'll let him know straight away,' she said.

Maggie, who had overheard Laurel's side of the conversation, raised a questioning eyebrow.

'Molly?'

Laurel nodded. 'It doesn't sound good. Mr Trotter wants David to know he doesn't think she's got long.'

She hurried across the yard and opened the door to David's workshop. The printing machine was whirring; she had to shout to make herself heard.

'David!' He glanced over his shoulder. 'Can you turn that thing off?'

She saw the first flash of alarm in his eyes.

'What's wrong?' he asked sharply into the ensuing silence.

She told him.

'I'm so sorry, David . . .'

He was already reaching for his coat.

'I'll go right away.'

'But there won't be a train at this time of night.'

'I'll go on my bike.'

'Are you sure that's a good idea?' It was easily nine or ten miles to Bath.

'I just hope I get there in time. I was planning on going tomorrow, when I'd finished this job. Why the hell didn't I go today?'

He found his bicycle clips and fastened them around the legs of his trousers just above the ankle, tucking in all the loose fabric.

'I'd offer to come with you,' Laurel said, 'but I have to go to court tomorrow.'

Kezia Smith was due to appear at the assize; the case against her with regard to Edgar's murder was to be heard first, and Laurel had been called as a witness for the prosecution. Later, when her attack on the Sykes family was brought into it, Minty and Rowan would have to give evidence too, but they were not needed tomorrow.

'It's all right,' David said. 'You'd only slow me down in any case.'

He pushed past her, heading towards the door. She followed, but he seemed unaware of her. He grabbed his bicycle, which was leaning against the wall outside, and mounted it at a run without so much as a word of goodbye.

Laurel could only watch him disappear into the night.

467

Jennie Felton

* * *

The Bristol courtroom was vast and impressive compared to the one where the Bath magistrates heard their cases. In the well of the court, robed and bewigged barristers, and solicitors mostly in morning suits set out files and legal tomes on the polished oak tables. A public gallery faced the podium where the judge or recorder sat in state; beneath it, a flight of steep steps led from the dock to the holding cells. The jury benches lined the third wall and on the opposite side were benches for the press, more seating for the public, and the witness box, which sat in a corner at right angles to the judge's podium.

Today there were no rowdy travelling folk in either of the public areas – the fair had moved on again and again, each time a little further from Somerset – but a good number of people had found the case interesting enough to warrant spending a day in court: a murder trial was always well attended and drew an audience, much like the peasants who had surrounded the tumbrils and the guillotine as heads rolled during the French Revolution.

By the time Callum arrived, the gallery was already full. He'd been sleeping rough now for weeks, and had taken himself to the public baths to make himself more presentable for the hearing, but it had taken longer than he had anticipated. He managed to find a seat at the end of one of the benches opposite the jury box.

For all his efforts to clean himself up, the blowsy woman next to him shifted uncomfortably and then moved away as if he was contagious, affording him more elbow room. Looking like a vagrant had its advantages, he thought grimly.

The bustle in the courtroom was increasing, and with it Callum's anxiety. His thoughts whirled dizzyingly as they had ever since he'd found out the gravity of what Kezia had done, chasing one another in undulating circles as if his brain was on his old switchback ride – despair, hope, despair again. For all his determination to help her, there was nothing more he could do now, and the sense of helplessness made him angry. The outcome was in the hands of the legal team he'd engaged. But what could *they* do, beyond plead her case? She'd admitted to serious crimes; there was no way back from that. The portly, strutting barrister sitting now in the well of the court with a stack of legal books in front of him had warned him to be prepared for the worst. No matter what he said in Kezia's defence, she would be going down for a very long time. The best they could hope for was that she would escape the hangman's noose. Callum's stomach clenched at the thought of it.

And if she was lucky and got away with a prison sentence, what was he going to do? Would he go back to Ireland? Or remain here in England so as to be able to visit her sometimes? But he knew that when it came down to it, there was really no decision to be made. He'd promised he'd never leave her again, and he would keep that promise, whatever it cost him.

A stir in the courtroom: Callum looked towards the steps leading up from the holding cells and saw Kezia emerging between two prison officers. Against their bulk she looked small and slight. Her hair was a dark tangled frame to her pale face, her mouth set in a defiant pout, hands clenched, shoulders rigid. At least they hadn't put her in handcuffs; he supposed they thought she was small enough to be easily controlled, not knowing what a wildcat she could be.

As the small procession reached the dock, Kezia's head swivelled, her gaze raking the courtroom, and he half rose and raised a hand, wanting her to know that he was there. Recognition flared in her eyes, her face contorted into an expression of agony and she mouthed his name, a silent scream.

And then everything seemed to happen at once. She and the first prison guard were already in the dock; the second was behind her at the top of the steps. So swiftly that she took him completely by surprise, she aimed a kick at his shins and simultaneously thrust her fingers into his face, aiming for his eyes and succeeding. As he staggered, the first guard lunged for her, but Kezia was too quick for him. Pushing the half-blinded man out of her way, she grabbed the banister and attempted to vault it. But nimble as she was, in her desperate haste her toe caught the edge and she catapulted forward, head first, into the well of the court. The crack as her chin connected with the wooden rail that divided it from the public benches was loud in the shocked hush, and she fell like a rag doll.

Callum was on his feet in an instant, pushing past officials who tried to bar his way. There was uproar now, a tide of voices rising like a tsunami out of the shocked silence of a moment before. He reached Kezia, who lay motionless where she had fallen, her head twisted at an unnatural angle, and dropped to his knees beside her.

'Shaver! For the love o' Jesus . . .'

Her eyes flickered open briefly.

'Callum . . .' It was no more than a whisper, like the breeze in a husk of dry corn.

'It's all right, Shaver. I'm here . . .'

But her eyes flickered again and closed.

'Move aside!' The voice was firm but cultured. 'I'm a doctor.'

He had been sitting in the area outside the courtrooms waiting to be called to give his evidence in a quite different case when he had been summoned by a panicked court official. Now he knelt beside Kezia, examining her gently, then looked up, his expression grave, and shook his head.

'No!' Callum yelled. 'No! Shaver . . .'

470

He reached for her again, cradling her in his arms, and this time no one tried to stop him.

'Help her, can't you?' he grated at the doctor. 'You must be able to help her!'

But even as he said it, he knew that his crazy but beloved sister was beyond help.

He held her close, rocking gently back and forth. He had not cried in years, but now the tears streamed down his cheeks.

'Oh, Shaver,' he groaned softly. 'Oh, Shaver.'

Really there was nothing else to say.

At last tortured, tormented Kezia had found peace.

Thankfully, David had arrived in time. He'd pedalled as hard as he could through the night, cursing the hills for their steep gradients, then freewheeling recklessly down the other side. He had arrived thirsty and exhausted, his muscles screaming in agony, a black void inside him warning him he might be too late.

Spike answered the door in response to his frantic knocking. He looked grey and drawn; in the last few months he'd aged years.

'Is she . . . ?' David hardly dared ask the question.

'Hanging on,' Spike replied. 'She's a fighter is Molly. Always was. Always will be.'

The irony of his last words went unnoticed. Fighter Molly might be, but this was a battle she could not win.

He preceded David into the parlour that was now equipped as a sickroom. A uniformed nurse sat beside the bed where Molly lay, her hands working convulsively at the drawn-up hem of the sheet, her head occasionally twisting first to one side, then the other. Her eyes were half closed, unseeing, and she seemed to have shrunk even in the few days since David had last seen her.

'She won't settle,' the nurse said, her eyes never leaving her patient.

Spike groaned. 'Oh, Moll, love . . .'

David approached the bed, sick at heart.

'May I?' he asked the nurse.

She vacated her chair and he took it, reaching for one of Molly's restless hands.

'Molly?' Since he'd found her, he'd always called her by her given name. It had seemed a little late in the day for anything else.

Now the sound of his voice seemed to penetrate the mists of whatever hell she was in. Her head turned towards him and did not roll back; her eyes opened a little wider; her previously restless fingers lay still within his gentle grasp. And her lips moved.

'David.'

He leaned closer and spoke the word that had so far eluded him.

'Mam.' The faintest smile lifted the corners of her cracked lips. 'I love you, Mam.' Each time he said it, it came more easily.

She nodded, almost imperceptibly, unable to voice what he knew was in her heart.

A whirring sound made him glance up, and to his surprise he saw that Spike was winding up a gramophone that had been placed on the table near the window, placing a record on the turntable. What on earth was he thinking of?

Then, as a sweet soprano voice filled the room, David understood. *'Darling, I am growing old . . . Silver threads among the gold . . .'* It was Lucy, Molly's niece. Molly herself had never made any recordings, but Lucy, darling of the music halls, had, and as she heard it, Molly smiled faintly again. Everyone who mattered to her was here with her now.

Spike went to the opposite side of the bed from David, taking her other hand in his. His eyes were full of tears; his voice was choked but steady.

'It's time to go now, my love. We don't want to lose you, but we don't want you suffering any more either.'

'It's time, Mam,' David echoed softly.

As if she'd been waiting for permission, Molly sank into the pillows. She was leaving them now, little by little, slipping back into semi-consciousness. Her breathing changed; the nurse stepped forward anxiously, then, thinking better of it, retreated to the end of the bed. Spike and David held her hands gently but firmly, their eyes never leaving her dearly loved face.

A last shuddering gasp cut through David's heart like a knife.

And then there was silence.

Two funerals. Two very different funerals.

Molly's took place in the chapel she and Spike had attended in the last weeks after it had become clear she was terminally ill and before she was confined to her bed. The service was taken by Kitty's husband, the Reverend Callow; the family were all there, and friends and acquaintances filled the remaining pews. When it was over, she was buried in the same cemetery as Edgar Sawyer, but unlike that day, when unrelenting rain had fallen, the sun shone for Molly. Afterwards the chief mourners returned to Spike's house and a cold buffet that the maid had prepared for them. They ate sandwiches and slices of veal pie and raised a glass to Molly's memory. There was sherry for the ladies and good single malt Scotch for the gentlemen, but also Molly's favourite tipple, stout.

The mood then was warm and reflective – all their tears had been shed in the chapel and at the graveside. It was time now to

473

celebrate Molly's life, share anecdotes and remember the incredible woman she had been.

Everything about Molly's funeral was genteel and understated, with any excess of emotion kept in check. A fitting tribute to a lady who had retained her dignity to the end.

She wouldn't want a lot of weeping and wailing, Spike said, though his red-veined eyes bore witness to his own grief. She'd died happy, and that was all thanks to finding David.

When at last they dispersed, David and Laurel took the train home to Hillsbridge – the Reverend Callow had offered them a lift in his motor, but it really wasn't built for passengers, and they declined. On the journey, David was silent, lost in thought, and Laurel was unsure how to comfort him, or whether she should even try. He was such a private person, and she knew that nothing she could say could ease his terrible sense of loss. Instead she reached out and covered his hand with hers, simply letting him know that she was there if he needed her.

Summer dusk was falling, the countryside through which the train was passing bathed in a haze of pinkish grey. In the fields the cows had gathered in groups, some lying down, some standing beside them as if to keep guard. A couple of horses cropped grass; an owl flew low over a stand of trees, then swooped down, a flash of white against the darkening landscape.

'Are you all right?' Laurel asked softly.

He looked up, nodded.

'At least I found her. And I was there with her at the end. It's all thanks to you, Laurel. If it hadn't been for you . . .' He broke off.

'I'm glad,' she said.

They sat in silence for the rest of the way home, two people who now had a complete understanding of one another that needed no words.

\* \* \*

In contrast, Kezia's funeral was conducted according to Romani tradition.

As soon as her body was released by the coroner, Da came with a wagon, with Bobby between the shafts. Their differences forgotten for the moment, he and Callum transported her to the rolling Dorset hills where the fair had made camp.

The Smiths' trailer had been thoroughly cleaned, hung with white sheets and decorated with fresh wild flowers. One of the fair folk who was a Giorgio, not a Romani, prepared her body, dressing her in her best skirt, blouse and heavily embroidered jacket. Candles were lit, and the family gathered round to ask her forgiveness for any wrongs they might have committed against her, something that was particularly painful for Callum, weighed down as he was by guilt as well as grief. Then, with the candles still burning, as they would continue to do until after the funeral, they took turns to keep vigil.

Clan members, friends and travelling folk, some of whom had never even met Kezia, came from far and wide to attend the burial, causing quite a stir in the small Dorset town. They followed Kezia's coffin, borne once again in the wagon drawn by Bobby – along the winding lanes to the cemetery on the outskirts of town in a long and mostly silent procession. Afterwards, many of them accompanied the family back to the campsite to witness the last rites.

Traditionally, the trailer of a deceased Romani would be burned as part of a solemn ceremony; today this was not possible, of course, since it was still Ma and Da's only home. But a bonfire was made of all Kezia's possessions except for some personal items that had been sealed with her in her coffin, and as darkness fell Da set light to it.

Callum watched, raw yet numb, as the flames devoured the

pitifully small mound of clothes, toiletries and keepsakes, and remembered the good in his sister before hatred and madness had possessed her. He saw a small girl running and skipping in dew-wet grass, felt the weight of her as she threw herself into his outstretched arms and heard her merry laugh as he spun her round and round, small booted feet describing circles in the air. He saw a young woman with wild flowers in her hair, the wicked twinkle in her sea-green eyes, the determined thrust of her chin when she wanted something she had been denied. Remembered her eagerness to help on the switchback ride, her delight when Da allowed her to count out the money she had taken and keep a few pennies for herself.

That Kezia had long gone, but it was her he mourned.

As the flames flickered and died, Ma turned to him.

'Will you be staying with us now?'

It was the first conciliatory thing she had said to him. Perhaps, with her daughter dead, she felt some urge to cling to her son. But Callum shook his head. With Kezia gone there was nothing now to keep him here.

'Nah – I'll be going back to Ireland.'

She didn't argue, and he thought he saw something that might have been relief flicker in her dark eyes.

The Irish mourners would be leaving for home the next day, and Callum could have gone with them. But first there was something he had to do.

'I'll follow you later,' he told them.

And set out for Somerset and High Compton.

From the kitchen window Laurel saw him crossing the yard. Shock and surprise made her stand stock still for a moment, as if she had been turned to stone. Then her heart began thudding in her throat, a host of butterflies took wing in her stomach and the blood tingled in her veins. Suddenly it was as if she was fifteen again. She had seen him briefly in the magistrates' court, but with all the commotion of Kezia passing out it hadn't really registered, and she hadn't seen him at the assize at all – she had been sequestered in the area reserved for witnesses. Now all her old feelings for him hit her with full force, as if the years between had never been. Oh, Callum . . . still the same tall, well-muscled young man she had fallen in love with, if a little thicker-set; the same swarthily handsome face, if a little older; the same dark green eyes meeting hers through the window pane.

What was he doing here? How had he found her? What did he want?

She scooped up John, who had been crawling around under the table, holding him tight against her thudding heart and trying to keep her hands from trembling as she opened the door.

'Callum.'

'Laurel.'

Into the awkward silence that followed he said, 'I had to see you. Is it all right?'

'I suppose.' But she didn't ask him in, simply stood there looking at him, at her past suddenly colliding with the present. The sun sparkled on the gold ring in one ear and the chain around his neck; everything felt unreal.

'Is he . . . ?' He jerked his chin in John's direction.

She shook her head. 'No. I look after him. I work here.'

'So they told me.' He'd asked around in High Compton until he'd found someone who could tell him her whereabouts; he'd known better than to go to Fairley Terrace. He hadn't supposed the welcome there would be any warmer than it had been the last time.

'Look, Laurel, I wanted to explain . . .'

She smiled slightly.

'There's no need. I think we worked it out from what your sister said when she attacked us.'

He shifted awkwardly. 'You've got to understand . . . she wasn't in her right mind. She thought—'

'I know what she thought. That Mam had killed you and buried you in the bean trench. I'm sorry she went for you that night. It must have taken courage for you to come here, and it means a lot to me. But I never knew until Kezia . . . They never told me.'

'I wanted to see you – and my daughter.'

'That was exactly what Mam didn't want.'

'She made that pretty clear.' He hesitated. 'How is she . . . Rowan, isn't it? Does she live here with you?'

'No, she's with Mam. She's fifteen now. Doing well at school.

'Can I meet her?'

John was becoming restless. Laurel shifted him onto her hip.

'I don't think that would be a very good idea. At least not at the moment. She's still coming to terms with everything. Perhaps sometime in the future . . .'

'I've been in Ireland, and I'm going back.'

'Oh. Right.' For some reason that hurt.

'At least, that's what I planned. Unless . . .'

'What?'

'Unless you want me to stay.'

Those sea-green eyes were boring into hers, playing tricks with her heart. For just a moment she envisioned what might be. She, Callum and Rowan, a family. The outcome she'd longed for once. But that had been when she was young and naive. She might still be susceptible to his charm, but she knew now that she and Callum lived in two different worlds. He would never be able to curb his wandering ways; she couldn't live a life without roots.

'It's too late, Callum,' she said. 'But if you're ever back in this part of the world, look me up. If Rowan wants to meet you when she's older . . . well, perhaps we could work something out.'

'Fair do's.'

She couldn't tell whether he was relieved or disappointed.

'And let me just say . . . I'm sorry for your loss.'

He nodded abruptly, and this time there was no disguising his feelings. She saw the raw pain in his eyes and felt her heart breaking for him. Whatever Kezia had become, whatever she had done, she was his sister.

'Right,' he said. 'I'll be going then.'

'Goodbye, Callum. Good luck.'

'You too.'

Laurel swallowed at the lump in her throat as she watched him walk away. The first man she had ever loved. The father of her daughter. But also her past.

The door of David's workshop opened and he emerged, wondering, perhaps, who the visitor had been.

Laurel gave him a wave and a smile. Yes, Callum might be her past. But she knew now that David was her future.

# *Postscript*

---

## December 1911

Laurel and David were married on a crisp day when the pale sun shone from a periwinkle-blue sky and the early-morning frost still lingered like delicate sugar icing on the evergreen bushes and the leaves of the flowering chrysanthemums in the flower beds at the top of the steps leading to the door of the chapel.

Inside, the organ played softly as the guests eagerly awaited the arrival of the bride. David, sitting in the front pew with Josh, who was acting as his best man, cast frequent looks over his shoulder, while Minty, on the opposite side of the aisle, crumpled a handkerchief between her fingers in readiness for the tears she knew would start to her eyes when Laurel walked up the aisle. She could scarcely believe the day had come at last when her daughter would become a respectable married woman – and the wife of a man she had come to love as if he had been her own son.

In the pew behind her, Samuel, who had travelled down from Yorkshire for his sister's wedding, chatted quietly to Earl. He, too, was casting anxious glances towards the back of the chapel. Little Reggie was to be a pageboy, and Vicky was waiting there to make sure he was still looking immaculate when he arrived with Rowan, who was of course bridesmaid. The door was open and he hoped she wasn't in a draught. Though she was so much better these days since her thyroid problem had been diagnosed, he still worried about her.

Behind David, Spike sat with Kitty. Though he had protested, David had insisted he should take a prominent place as his stepfather-in-law. 'It's where you would have been if Molly were still alive,' he'd said. Now Spike could think of nothing but her. If only she could have been spared to see her son married; just picturing her joy brought tears to his eyes, and he blew his nose hastily.

Maggie and the children were there too, of course, Patrick eagerly awaiting a glimpse of Rowan. He hadn't seen her in the days leading up to the wedding – she'd been too caught up in the preparations – and he'd missed her. But at least these days they didn't have to meet in secret. And tomorrow he'd been asked to tea at the Sykes house, where the family were going to have their own private celebration before Samuel went home to Yorkshire.

A sudden stir rippled through the chapel – 'She's here!' All necks craned round in anticipation, and Vicky, satisfied that Reggie was looking as he should, his face clean and his knickerbockers fluffed, hurried back up the aisle to her place beside Earl.

The Reverend Callow, Kitty's husband, was to perform the ceremony – neither Laurel nor David had any particular allegiances when it came to a place of worship, and it was because of Philip that they had chosen to be married in his chapel. He stood waiting at the door. In the porch, Laurel was straightening the hem of Rowan's dress, cerise velvet that Vicky had made for her and which suited her perfectly.

There'd been some disagreement about what Laurel herself should wear. In spite of the fact that the world now knew she was no virgin, Minty had wanted her to wear white, which Laurel felt was wholly inappropriate, given her age if nothing else. At last they had reached a compromise. Laurel had settled for a skirt and blouse in palest pink, with a cerise sash and cerise silk flowers in her hair. And she had agreed to carry flowers – a small, neat bouquet of Christmas roses. Now she held them firmly in one hand and tucked the other through her father's arm, saying a silent prayer of thanks that he had been fit enough to give her away. Since his pneumonia back in the summer, he had never quite regained his full health, and she knew it was unlikely he ever would. But at least at the moment he was still continuing to work – with Earl's crafty support – and at least he was beside her today. Worrying that he might not be had brought it home to her all too clearly how David must be feeling about his mother. But at least they'd found one another and been able to spend some time together before the end came.

'Ready?' Philip Callow asked with a smile.

She nodded, and Rowan took Reggie's hand and ushered him into place behind Laurel and Ezra as the organ struck up the Bridal March.

Holding tight to her father's arm, Laurel began the long walk up the aisle, smiling at the guests whose faces were turned towards her, but seeing only one – the one who waited for her at the altar steps.

True happiness had eluded her for so long, and she knew she had no one but herself to blame for her mistakes. Yet now she could no longer regret them. She loved Rowan with all her heart; couldn't imagine life without her. And if she hadn't wasted so many years over that rat Ralph, she might have met someone else and married them, though they would never be more than second best. As it was, there'd been nothing to stand in the way of her falling in love with David. The most wonderful man she'd ever known. And who was about to become her husband.

I must be the luckiest woman on this earth, Laurel thought.

They had reached the altar. As David smiled at her, the love shining in his eyes, Ezra went to move away, his part done. Laurel turned to him and squeezed his hand. Daddy had always been there for her; she only hoped he knew how grateful she was. But it was David who would be there for her in the future.

As the organ notes drifted away and Philip Callow spoke the first words of the marriage service whilst the winter sun slanted in through the chapel windows, Laurel lifted her eyes to the altar and whispered a silent prayer to a God she had been unsure she believed in, thanking him for all her blessings. And also a prayer for the future.

That Minty would continue to return to her old self, the woman she had been before the problems she faced had embittered her. That Daddy might be spared for many years to come. That Rowan would find the happiness she herself was feeling now. That she could make David as happy as he made her.

It was an ending and a beginning, all wrapped into one.

The marriage ceremony had begun.